Ernst Weiss

Georg Letham

Physician and Murderer

Translated from the German by Joel Rotenberg

archipelago books

First Archipelago Books Editions 2010

Library of Congress Cataloging-in-Publication Data
Weiss, Ernst, 1882–1940.
[Georg Letham. Arzt und Mörder. English]
Georg Letham: Physician and Murderer / by Ernst Weiss ;
translated from the German by Joel Rotenberg.
p. cm.
ISBN 978-0-9800330-3-8
I. Rotenberg, Joel. II. Title.
PT2647.E52G413 2009 833'.912–dc22
2008048790

Archipelago Books
232 Third St. #A111
Brooklyn, NY 11215
www.archipelagobooks.org

Distributed by Consortium Book Sales and Distribution
www.cbsd.com

Jacket art: Folkwang-Auriga-Verlag

This publication was made possible with support from Lannan Foundation,
The National Endowment for the Arts,
and the New York State Council on the Arts, a state agency.

Georg Letham

Physician and Murderer

FOREWORD

Whether we appear as defendant or as witness, we unfinished human beings are not spared the trials of this even more unfinished world. Cruelty and futility are what we meet with, and during our brief existence we see them ad nauseam. No one can avoid this first philosophy Constant hardship for the individual who battles in vain in the grim war of all against all; in this best-ordered of all possible worlds, pain, affliction of mind, inconceivable physical suffering, together with an idiotic waste of the energy and means given by nature. Who could make sense of it?

To make some sense of the world, to gain knowledge – this is what one tries to do every day of one's life, without success. So what is a thinking man with any strength of will going to strive for, if not fleeting pleasure? And what can this pleasure be, if not a delirium that, to be replicated, requires greater quantities of deliriant each time? But if increasingly violent efforts are needed simply in order to make life bearable, the moment will soon come when one will violate the law of the polity and of human solidarity and recklessly infringe upon the rights of others. And, very naturally, those others will try to protect themselves and stop the violator from doing what he is doing.

The profound, truly disastrous disorder and futility of nature and the world – what in the scientific realm we call the pathological, in the moral realm the criminal – these are constant, they will always be with us no matter what the future brings. Even after the most terrible catastrophes have happened, nature and society will still gaze at us with the same expression of mindless, animal earnestness. But it is only the thinking man who must watch all this with awareness and understanding, and that is why he is to be pitied. Find a place for yourself! But how? Nations are as mindless as individuals. Pitch in, contribute what you can! Help out! Try to change things! Change? But where to begin? If only it were possible to help. But in nine hundred ninety-nine cases out of a thousand, the individual will not be strong enough. If only one could at least believe in a transcendent order, find a big idea to hang on to, call it Jesus Christ or love of country or – science!

Beauty, peace, harmony – all this, too, is no more than a delirium. Only wealth and knowledge give the individual a bit of a foothold.

Too weak to be of help and lost to faith from childhood; given over to all the antisocial urges of his heart (the original sin?); never understood by his fellows and thus always profoundly alone; tugged this way and that by internal contradictions, like a malaria patient who sweats and shivers as he oscillates between subnormal and supranormal temperatures; with scientific ideas in his mind, but no hope in his heart, a heart that ages year by year yet never grows up; with a human life on his conscience, but no real conscience among his contradictory and self-canceling character traits – is all that my self? No, only part of it.

Yes, to give an account of such a life – not just some of it, but all of it – this might be a task for the modern novel.

That I have not only passed through my life but am also attempting to give an account of it – is this not already a great deal? Such an attempt requires strength and clarity of mind, more strength and clarity of mind, perhaps, than I can credit myself with. Already I feel the difficulties of a coherent confession and work of art that will move and enlighten. My greatest fear is that I will not be understood, and fail for that reason.

If only I can convey all I have gone through! That is everything. I will try. Let it be an experiment. My last, perhaps.

It will not be easy. I am the protagonist who both acts and is acted upon. Scientist and criminal. Physician and murderer. The two are difficult to reconcile. Inevitably I will stumble. But will I be able to record my errors faithfully? Or will I be content simply to record the events as I see them? The rules of art are foreign to me too, I have no art at all. As I write this, at the age of more than forty, I know little of aesthetic laws, notwithstanding the odd love I have for the beautiful and the perfected – for the perfect. My hand is not clumsy and is fairly steady when doing experiments, but it lacks such art.

I set to work without great faith, without optimism. But where there is no optimism, is realism possible, can there be a work at all? I will try nonetheless. I will hold up a mirror to myself. With a steady hand. With the exacting eye of a scientist. Without mercy toward myself, just as I showed none toward others. What is man, that he shows mercy toward his own kind?

This is the best I can do. Perhaps someone else will be able to create a realistic novel out of my report on these "experiments on living souls."

ONE

I

How could I, Georg Letham, a physician, a man of scientific training, of certain philosophical aspirations, let myself be so far carried away as to commit an offense of the gravest sort, the murder of my wife? And to commit this crime chiefly for financial reasons? Or so it would appear to the outsider. For money was in fact the one thing I could never get from that woman, who was doglike in her attachment to me. Am I reviling her with this word "doglike"? No. I am only attempting to explain, and so far I have not succeeded. There is a gaping internal contradiction here, and yet that is how it was.

There was astonishment in legal circles and among the general public, as represented by opinions in the metropolitan press, that during my trial, when it was a matter of life and death to me, I yawned. It was the third day of the trial, the heat was oppressive, the oral arguments were telling me nothing new, and yet – how could a person accused of such a crime be so blatantly uninterested in the outcome of his trial? But this contradiction is only apparent, unlike the many true contradictions in my character. It may have interested others what became of me. But it could not interest me what others thought of my crime or by what "punishment," under what section of the law, they exacted redress for the purpose of "retribution and deterrence." I could not have gone through all I had gone through and still acknowledged the logical connection between crime and punishment. What law would apply to me? Common law and traditional law do not do me justice. And natural law? Too often I had seen the innocent suffer, while the guilty – vile and despicable creatures – attained happiness. They could sentence me. But they could not force me to recognize this sentence, execution or exile to C., where yellow fever and other tropical scourges were at that moment raging, as punishment.

Or were these arguments supposed to be enlightening me about my antisocial nature, about my "morbid character," about my unfitness to live as a respectable citizen in a well-ordered state? My own experience of this "well-ordered state," as whose moral exponent the court presented itself, had shown me that it was anything but a healthy, moral organism of orderly character.

But I had done the deed. Indeed I had, and nothing else mattered. And if a human being has on his conscience a crime so irrefutable that it can never be denied or glossed over or excused – if I had actually been driven to extinguish a human life, what is the good of talk, of lengthy oratory and presentations of evidence? The one who committed the crime cannot save himself now. But then he never could, not even *before* his crime. Even if he had foreseen *everything*, would not the internal forces that drove him still have been stronger than the counsel of reason?

His outward fate may be decided now. There is hardly anything left to hope for. If my skin is thick, I will survive a good deal. If I am sensitive,

I will perish. What is, is. Everything has happened. Everything is over.

In my youth, after my father had carried out his educational experiments on me, I worshipped objective knowledge in the form of natural science and subjective enjoyment of life in the form of money. Money was more than a superficial pleasure – it seemed to me the only and therefore the best substitute for God in our otherwise faithless time. Money is the ground beneath one's feet. He who has money at least has something. He is standing on the securest foundation there is in the contemporary world order.

To know and to possess as much as possible – such a simple recipe, and yet so difficult to follow! How devotedly I toiled, in my heart always disinterested, cold, and isolated, in the service of these two gods, spending my nights in experimental bacteriological facilities and pathology laboratories or at the gaming table – and in both my endeavors I had luck. With the help of my winnings, I carried out the most extravagant experiments (chimpanzees and rhesus monkeys are incredibly expensive). I sought distraction in work when I was tired of gambling, and sought distraction in gambling when I no longer had the drive and concentration necessary for intellectual work. At the green baccarat table, I had new ideas for scientific experiments. My fortunes were happy, but I was seldom happy myself.

I lost my mother early. My siblings, one brother, one sister, were strangers to me. My father played a central but calamitous role in my life; we could not be friends.

Though I had long since become weary of my way of life, I refused a chair at a small university. I had no interest in teaching. I did publish the results of my bacteriological experiments, which threw light on an interesting rare disease, rat-bite fever, but for the time being I was not pursuing them. I had won a fairly large amount at gambling. I locked my door and traveled. I met my future wife. She was very well-to-do, unbeautiful, no longer young. Thoughts of financial gain were far from my mind at first. There was nothing about community of property in our marriage contract, which we drafted one heavenly morning beneath palms and fruit-laden orange trees. And there was (and still is) a daughter from my wife's first marriage; she was her legal heir and would soon be of marriageable age. Looking out over the azure sea, we discussed our future ménage. Far too many rooms, but only the one (shared) bedroom. A luxurious household, whose upkeep would come from my wife's interest earnings and my income as a physician, contributed on an equal basis.

I had completely forgotten that I was not only a researcher but also a credentialed, qualified physician. And I was a good diagnostician, even if I knew human diseases and physical abnormalities more from the lecture hall, from the dissection table, and from the microscope than from bedside clinical observation. Modern scientific analytical methods – X-ray examination, chemical analysis, biological-function testing – are so well developed now that these accurate tests are an ample substitute for bedside experience.

I also had adequate manual skills from my experiments. Vivisection experiments, experiments on living material, cannot be performed without a certain degree of surgical skill. The laws of asepsis, the secret of all surgical practice, are also applicable here.

More than anything else, I had a certain interest in surgery and gynecology, an interest that deepened when I spent some months working as a volunteer at a large clinic following my return. Thus I considered moving and eventually did move from theoretical science to practical surgery and gynecology.

I married and became a practicing physician. My wife was soon devoting all her energy and irrepressible vitality to making things easier for me. I opened a private clinic on a lovely quiet street in the city. Medical colleagues who had previously sought my advice as a pathologist sent me patients, and everything seemed to be going well. Illnesses interested me, the ill did not. This is the case and is necessarily the case with ninety percent of all surgeons. Of my own free will I had promised my wife (she was softhearted, much too much so) that I would end my experiments with animals and never again set foot in a casino. I led a well-ordered life.

What was it at bottom that I wished to do "of my own free will"? To become a human being, as millions are. Then came the war. I was inducted, but was not deployed as a field surgeon. Instead I was granted the special favor, so it was thought, of being assigned to a bacteriological laboratory. A mobile task force, sent to trouble spots when needed. It was a time not only of senseless waste of life – millions dead – but also of terrible epidemics. All manner of bacteria were being unleashed, and these were necessarily more dangerous when people were starving, careworn, weakened, and half dead from loss of blood than they would have been in peacetime. Under the wretched hygienic conditions prevailing among the people of Europe in the final years of the war, Spanish grippe took forms that recalled the plagues of the Middle Ages. People dropped like flies.

I was not lazy. I worked day and night. I did my utmost. I had superiors and subordinates. I had regulations to follow and orders to carry out. Serum supply, epidemic control, practical research. It made a difference.

I expressed no views about the whys and wherefores of the war and the strategic operations. Nor was anything said to me about them.

My wife wrote to me every day. I wrote back when I could. I was surrounded by people, but did not speak of personal matters for weeks on end. I was respected. I won no friends, but I did win commendations and decorations. After my crime many years later, I was sentenced not to the guillotine but only to exile, and I have these tokens of appreciation for my patriotic effort to thank for that. For the person who had had a hand in epidemic control during that critical period had rendered outstanding service to his country.

But about what that time destroyed in me – I will say nothing. How it brought to fruition what my father had begun – I will not describe it. He – my father – and my country too, in fact all the countries of the world, are hardly blameless for the development of my character. But is there any way to tell that to the judges, the jury? Better to cover mouth with hand and yawn discreetly.

II

Yes, my father had a determining influence on my youth. My life was the continuation of that of my parents by other means. My parents were in conflict with each other, and so I was in conflict with myself. My mother died comparatively young. From her I reaped the benefit only of a good physical looking after and the usual maternal warmth – she taught me how to talk. My father taught me how to think. Whatever I am as a thinking person, for better or worse, I owe to him. It took me a long time to escape from this childish thralldom. My wife, too, kept me in thrall – a thralldom of kindness, if I may put it that way.

I married her so that I would not be alone. The idea was that she would be around, give me the illusion of companionship, but not control me. Unfortunately she had other ideas about our relationship. She was ugly, as I said, a light brunette who wrongly thought herself blonde, narrow shoulders, broad hips, a clay-colored face as flat as a sheet of paper, with a snub nose, large nostrils into whose hairy interior it was possible to see. The usual depilatories were no help, only aggravated this ugly feature. Her teeth were few and unlovely, and so she did not like to show them when speaking or laughing. Later they were replaced with splendid dentures. For she was not without vanity and did more to conceal her ugliness than many women of acknowledged beauty do to maintain it. Her eyes were light brown to light gray – a rare tint, although it harmonized with her also light, fairly luxuriant eyebrows. From the beginning her ugliness had not repelled me but, in combination with her good social standing, her positive attitude toward life, and her unassuming nature, had actually attracted me, since I knew that this was not a lady who would ever lead me astray with her beauty and sensual appeal. Those gifts by which women generally influence men like me could in her case never have driven me to such an act as I have committed. But there are other complications, other conflicts.

My father had dominated me because he impressed me by his very existence. He would have existed without me, but not the reverse. He dominated me all the more strongly because of his formidable ability to take hold of people, to handle them. Taking hold implies letting go, and handling is never far from manhandling. He was older than I was. This was not yet a reason to look up to him. But he was also stronger and more beautiful (beauty, even in the oddest forms and guises, has always had an almost magical effect on me). But most of all he dominated me – banal, but true – because I loved him. He was aware of all this. For he was clever with people, perhaps because he was psychologically independent of anyone and everyone during the greater part of his life. Later, when he needed *me*, when, with graying but always dyed hair, with bitter creases appearing in his small, sharp-featured face, with deepening and ever more depressing perceptions of life, he was rapidly growing solitary, suddenly he was stranger to me than any stranger.

He was feared at work, and he was influential, more influential than the minister. He was polite, rich and tightfisted, pious and an anarchist, a misanthrope since his unsuccessful expedition, and always and in all things basically insincere – perhaps even against his will at times. He had wearied of lying, dissembling, playacting. They were no longer worth his while. He had attained everything they could attain for him. But he had to go on as he was. I no longer asked his advice, I had only myself to thank for my scientific career. The two of us reluctantly sorted out financial matters directly; in my youth, when they were important to me, they had been settled through his attorney and my legal guardian. The estate inherited from my mother was soon no longer worth talking about anyway.

In the postwar years he repeatedly came to me and guardedly stated his interest – but he never gained any insight into what was of critical concern to me. He suddenly took it into his head to drop his artificial mask of youth, which he had cherished for too long. Once I spent some time away, vacationing with my wife in a southern port. When I came back, he had snow-white hair. But, strange to say, his white, slightly curly, still thick hair looked like a wig in a theatrical hairdresser's window. Yes, it was like the journeyman's piece of a hairdresser's assistant, resting on a milliner's block. I smiled and held my tongue. I looked at him as though he were a wax doll in a carnival museum and gravely wished him all the best on his most recent promotion, which made him directly subordinate to the minister. He had risen that high already. The ministers changed and he remained.

He had awakened my compulsion to heedlessly, ruthlessly, look to the heart, had shown me as a defenseless child how to get to the bottom of things and ideas, how to control people and circumstances. He had told me of his experiences on his unsuccessful voyage to the North Pole. Not to amuse me. The impact he had on me was like that of a torpedo on a ship in passage. Over time I got to the heart of him too, of course, for finally what made him tick was no simpler and no more complex than what makes most people tick. He no longer needed to tell me anything. I looked at him steadily. I spoke of the events of the day as described in the most recent newspapers, we did not argue, we were in agreement about everything, asked nothing of each other, exemplary father, exemplary son, we both smiled, we shook each other's hands, offered each other a glass of wine or the like; I inquired, feigning an interest I did not have, as to the health of my siblings, he responded to my questions with a wave of his hand – they're immaterial to me too – but then he became more serious and asked how I had invested my money. As though he were unaware that everything belonged to my wife and nothing to me. But I ignored that, only smiled and said: "Wisely, of course!" Nothing more. And yet this point concerned me a great deal. My father and I were strangers to each other. More than that: he bored me. I understood him and he bored me. What did he have to say to me? I knew his ballad of the rats.

He bored me to tears with his love especially. Just the same as my wife. No, different in one way. Loving and not being loved did her heart good. Most women never entirely cast off masochism. If not in every respect the ideal man as imagined by a woman of her age, to her I was certainly like a child particularly cherished by its mother because of the pain and perils of bringing it into the world. If only she had kept her demonstrations of affection to herself! All too often she behaved toward me like a brooding hen, all warmth and filthy plumage, or like an imbecilic, sanctimonious, provincial wet nurse, or something. Unfortunately my father had picked up this manner from her, and it was often enough to drive a person to distraction. Had she given me hard cash (or a gun) instead of all the endearments and demonstrations of love, everything would have turned out differently. But no doubt her feelings were too soft for that. Both of them had considerable fortunes. But she kept hers from me, perhaps as a last way of binding me to her if it came to that. I could have understood that, certainly. But why shower a defenseless person – one internally at odds with himself – with demonstrations of a feeling that he will not and cannot reciprocate!

I was less a stranger to my wife than I was to my father. When *she* derived pleasure from suffering, *I* learned to find pleasure in making her suffer. We complemented each other splendidly. I experimented with great care to see how far I could go without losing her love. I went as far as I could imagine. Almost all the way – the thread still held, though stretched to the breaking point. But it snapped under the ultimate test. I had credited a human being with superhuman capacities for the "pleasures and sorrows of love," and I had to pay the price. For human nature is fragile, and the average character never transcends it. So I had bet too much, and the bet was too risky. It was a calculated risk, but I had miscalculated.

But was I sorry on that account? No. Even the death penalty held no terrors for me. I am thinking of the time of the trial. Any earthly court was too weak, too absurd, too petty to punish me. God or Satan himself would have had to reveal himself to me. I yawned. I would have repeated my infernal experiment under different test conditions if it had been in my power, but I still would have done away with that love-addicted old woman, that bottle blonde with shining, light gray eyes in her flat, enameled face and blue varicose veins on her legs, and if possible my good old hoary-headed father too. There are such people.

III

There is someone else I must mention, someone who may have been the most important person for me – perhaps. Who knows? Walter, a contemporary of mine in medical school. Once during a lecture we had a singular experience, whose details I thought I had forgotten. But while I was in custody, in the interval between crime and verdict – during those difficult hours of solitude when I was left to my own devices, brooding and analyzing in the extraordinary anguish to which isolation will drive anyone, particularly if he has led an intellectually vigorous life until then – this episode, insignificant in itself, came back to me.

It happened during a long lecture on the optical properties of the human eye. As the old physiology professor was speaking, a small door opened to one side of the large blackboard. Through this door the lecture hall communicated with the rest of the physiology department.

At first we paid no attention. We were focused on the difficult calculations and formulas that the professor was writing with squeaking chalk on the blackboard, now dazzlingly illuminated by the midday sun.

I can still see my comrade's hand, shapely, slender, yet masculine in its strength and sinewiness, copying down the formulas in a somewhat disorderly notebook; while the dark gray, shining eyes with their expression of total, I might even call it joyful, intelligence were fixed on the blackboard, the hand transcribed the figures almost autonomously, the lines wandering up and down.

There was a sudden stir. The students near the lectern began to laugh, to stamp, to get up out of their seats. Something not even knee-high, shaggy, outlandish, reddish white, was wriggling and squirming among them. What was it? A dirty-white poodle with a bushy, frantically waving tail, its head covered with blood down to the bare light brown nose, a large, square wound on one side of its head, its tongue, bruised at the edges, hanging out, its eyes rolling, was weaving silently past the feet of the horrified – no, not horrified! – only astonished professor. Gnawed-through narrow leather straps dragged from the hand some pasterns of the thin legs. No barking or whining was heard. Only raspy breathing.

My father had inured me, I will tell the tale later in great detail, to the ghastliness of life as it really is. Otherwise I would never have chosen to study medicine, I would have resisted the temptation to learn the secrets of physical life. Would have had to resist! So I thought I was impervious to even the most dreadful sights. I wanted to be. That was how I wanted to be. I actually seemed to be. I had dissected cadavers with total composure like every other first-semester medico, even smoking a cigarette as I worked. I had also been present at vivisection experiments, which are performed for third-semester students for purely pedagogical purposes. In the interest of scientific inquiry for the betterment of mankind, I had always been mentally prepared for this dark side of life and had endured it, if not easily. But I was unprepared now and was horrified when the animal scrambled higher and higher up the steps of the amphitheater, its tail swishing, and looked up at us with terrified madness in its eye. Now the beast breathed deeply and noisily through its tow-colored, somewhat bloody nostrils, to let out its anguish finally in a howl. My neighbor quickly got to his feet. The animal was running up in a quick zigzag, possibly toward a door to the outside that had been left open in the summer heat, and was already up to our bench at the very top of the amphitheater. From this distance the wound on its skull was clearly visible. The skin had been neatly removed, the milk white cerebral membrane was incised in the shape of a rhombus, and two very small, silvery instruments, I no longer remember exactly what kind, perhaps hypodermic syringe tips, still hung in the open wound, which was pulsating plainly.

The tumult around us was very loud. But it was merry. The students took the thing as a lark and the professor followed suit. He erased the figures on the board with a large sponge as though trying to wipe away this little episode of the puppy dog on the run from the embrace of science. The students, men and women, surrounded him; he fended them off, sweating and gesticulating. I especially remember the laughing face and fine teeth of a female student who wore her blonde hair in the madonna style of the time. Hitching up her long skirt, she skipped lightly after the animal. She followed it up to where the two of us were, cajoling it as young girls do their lapdogs when they have escaped the leash and trying to coax it back with blandishments such as "precious," "sweetie," "baby," "you bad boy," and so on and so forth. The upper part of its body was pressed against our feet, its wounded head turned toward the pretty young woman. It was ghastly the way the howl died in the unfortunate animal's throat at the sound of this deep, cooing, coaxing human voice, the way it suddenly deceived itself, eternally trusting in its god, man.

But it did not return to its tormentors. My friend crushed what was left of the animal's cranium from behind with the silver handle of his walking stick. He had raised his left hand, had aimed, had struck. A thud – and that was that. The animal went over without a sound and was no more.

The student stood up, descended to the lectern holding the walking stick by its other end, washed the bloody handle there, dried it on the towel next to the blackboard. And returned to his seat. The most peculiar thing was that no one, neither the professor nor the female student, found anything remarkable in what he did. The professor rang for the lab attendant to remove the carcass, the female student, after fruitlessly fluttering her blue eyes in the direction of my neighbor, sat back down in her front-row seat, which, thanks to her punctuality, she had occupied from the first lecture on, my neighbor turned back to his disorderly notebook, instantly a jumble of writing, and that was the end of it. I found out later that the experimenter who was working with the dog had been called to the telephone. Then the lab attendant had slipped out of the hot experiment area for a cigarette, and the unusually strong, intelligent, unanesthetized animal had freed itself – no one knew how – and in its misery had trotted toward the lecture hall, for which it was not yet entirely ready. It should not have been brought out until some weeks later, when the paralytic effects of the partial lobotomy had developed properly.

In the strangest way, for which there are no words, I felt attracted toward this student Walter. As the patient beyond saving is to the doctor, perhaps. But what does one have to do with the other? Nothing. Beyond saving . . . doctor. God couldn't make sense of it.

Walter passed his exams at about the same time as I did. He was hearty, strong, the picture of blooming health. Originally he had been bound for the service; his father was a high-ranking military officer. But he had preferred the university. And he had taken up experimental pathology and bacteriology – the same fields as mine. He was left-handed, and, like many left-handed people, unusually clumsy. Everything went wrong for him sometimes. But he persevered.

I made many attempts to get closer to him. They never succeeded. He was a constitutionally cheerful, athletic person. He seemed to me to be tough inside and out, in a way that was not without humor – to be a "man without nerves." He appeared to be fairly free of excessive humane sentiments or compassion. Rightly interpreted, his *coup de grâce* had been administered not out of compassion for the animal's suffering, but because, once it had broken loose and come into contact with the students, infectious matter must in all likelihood have entered the artificial opening in its cranium; he, Walter, had therefore been forced to regard the dog as doomed and in any event useless for the purposes of the experiment.

I avoided the beautiful student, who was often around us later and who in all innocence exhibited a provocative nature. I paid no further attention to her. My wife was physically and mentally her exact opposite, if there are different types among females.

I saw Walter often. The very look of him was a source of joy. I found his captivating, boyish laugh contagious. I liked to laugh, I even imitated other people's laughs. But he always avoided personal conversation. I apparently did not interest him – and in this he was unlike many women, upon whom I made an impression without wishing to, who became a burden on me in one way or another, and who usually took me much more seriously than I did them.

IV

One might have thought that an experience such as this, the poodle fleeing in the middle of a scientific experiment, would have made me give up medical school in general and animal experiments in particular. What could have been more natural? I had an innate sense of the aesthetically interesting. As an art historian or the like, I would always have been able to hold my own. But I was driven to experiments (perhaps as a consequence of childhood experiences that I have yet to recount). I wanted to pit myself against a Walter, against this classical type of the excessively practical man who, for example, could see the animal in question as simply a piece of material, the way a carpenter does a piece of dense, nicely dry, knot-free wood.

But so long as it was animals that were the subjects of my experiments, all was well. The civilized world gladly shuts its eyes to this practice, as it does to war and so on. It was not until a human being met her maker that society got up in arms and had nasty things to say about my character. The fact is that if one day I decided to send my wife to her grave, and made this decision as coolly as I might have selected a laboratory animal for an experiment, that does not mean I undertook these two actions with total composure, with a completely clear conscience. There was thus consistency in that I never made these decisions *without scruples*.

But this scrupulousness was not a religious fear of sin. I did not believe in God. I was unable to countenance a world that included supernatural explanation. I would have liked to. It was not possible.

We are too young for godless anarchism. Thousands of generations before us have lived under the shadow of faith and, if they really had to suffer, at least suffered believing in a higher order and suffered for its sake. Perhaps a future generation will be equal to a life without faith. Will be able to look life in the eye, to see it for what it is. Will not lurch one way, then another, in benighted uncertainty. But I was not so fortunate. I was benighted from childhood on. Only from the outside did my career seem to run in a purposeful straight line – in reality it did not. Would I have lived only in and by experiments otherwise? When not performing an experiment, I felt no pleasure, indeed no connection with life at all. But *in* the experiment? Did I obtain satisfaction here at least? I must answer no.

The experimenter is like God, but on a small scale. He is as immeasurably small as God is great.

So it was with the animals. So it was with my wife. The animals were mine to do with as I pleased. I had paid cash for them, on one occasion four hundred rhesus monkeys for a transmission experiment that required that species. No one could stop me from doing what I did – there are so few moral impediments to the investigator anywhere in today's world.

The animal has no inkling of its fate. The investigator does, of course, the experimenter knows what is coming. He alone knows what must come. He has long since weighed his basic interest in the matter against the animal's interest in being alive and staying healthy and untormented, and found the weight of the suffering creature to be wanting. Perhaps he deigns to take the condemned animal, a dog, say, out of its cage himself. It barks merrily, lifts its head high, looks around with curiosity. It tries to run, stiff from lying down so long. It is cheerful. It needs him, too. Did I make the world the way it is? It sniffs the air with its moist, dark nostrils and supposes that the man in the white lab coat is going to lead it outside on the grimy cord about its neck, or to a feeding dish. The man now lifts the animal up by the scruff of the neck and lays it out. On the table. On the plank, which has been well sluiced down. He grasps the rib cage. He feels the little creature's heart thumping excitedly against its ribs. A monkey is another matter. A monkey is a caricature of a man. Or is a man a caricature of a monkey? But in the way they react to great pain, man and monkey are much alike. An older, well-nourished rhesus monkey – especially the male, whose system is more finely tuned than the female's . . . I will not go on with this here. Perhaps later I will get around to describing what happens in a scientific experiment in which hundreds and thousands of animals are sacrificed one after another *ad majorem hominis gloriam*. Many experiments have had a positive outcome; thousands of times as many have yielded nothing positive whatever. And for the subjects of the experiments, the animals destined to suffer, the service they were objectively rendering for science was a matter of indifference.

Perhaps we mean no more and no less to the higher power above us (I cannot believe in it and yet it is in my thoughts sometimes) than our cats and dogs, rats, guinea pigs, monkeys, horses – even bedbugs and lice do to us. I have experimented on bedbugs and lice, too. Science has long known that body lice transmit a very dangerous infectious disease, which, during wartime especially, has caused tremendous loss of life, namely, epidemic typhus, typhus exanthematicus. I believed I had found the pathogen of this disease in a certain bacillus. (Unfortunately this was not an error.) In 1917 I carried out experiments with body lice in the military epidemiology laboratory at the Russian-Polish front. This insect is so minute that the technical difficulties will be appreciated. What is the task? One must infect the insect with typhous blood, so that it becomes infectious. Is this clear? It is not easy. Nevertheless I was able to give the animal a stab with an exquisitely fine needle. But another researcher, a Pole, was even more resourceful. He was able to employ a very beautiful method to fill the gut of the millimeter-small insect with infectious material from behind. This procedure is not child's play either, of course. It needs to be mastered in the same way as other bacteriological research methods. The result in any case is that a body louse fed with a certain pathogen becomes ill and dies. If its mortal remains are now smeared onto the skin of an ape and the ape licks the spot, it too becomes ill and dies quickly. And so it goes, first here, then there, from warm-blooded creature to cold-blooded creature. Lice, monkeys, lice, monkeys. It sounds grotesque, comical, but it is not.

At least momentarily, a positive result from a scientific experiment affords the investigator terrific satisfaction. I use the word "terrific" advisedly.

All the nightly vigils, all the diligent, exhaustive study, all the gnawing doubts and anxieties, all the time and expense, everything the investigator loses by giving up a social life, giving up reading, going to the theater and to concerts, above all by giving up a truly vigorous, conscious family life – it is all (for the moment) richly repaid by the feeling of knowledge gained, of having solved a puzzle, of having increased man's power over things.

The renowned French physiologist Claude Bernard once called the scientific laboratory the "battlefield" of the experimenter. Certainly blood is shed. But there is a victory, too. And when he describes the task of the experimenter as to *prévoir et diriger les phénomènes*, who will dare to disparage the scientific investigator as a "cold mechanic of medicine"? No, he is much more like an experimenter-demigod probing the depths of the cosmos. And if he really is what he should be as an experimenter, he rises above the vulgar interests of men. He becomes a tragic figure. Or – and here the conflict begins – is he only a tragicomic figure? Was his "scientific result," which in the best case is hauled for decades or a century through medical journals and scientific periodicals and books under his byline, really worth the trouble? Was it in many instances not even worth the electrical current that flowed through the lamps in his laboratory while he worked? Does it give meaning to meaninglessness? Does it take the horrifying out of the horror? Does it help? Can it be gratifying? Does the investigator's interest not turn immediately to other problems, precisely like the hand of a cold mechanic? Is his thirst for happiness and inner peace ever appeased? Did the suffering of the sacrificed animals bring the investigator great things? If so, did it bring the nation great things too? Humanity? Did it transform the terrible disorder of nature into order and meaningful structure?

V

After the war I returned to my wife and immediately reopened the private surgical and gynecological clinic. But human disease could not hold me now. In my earlier zeal, I had made do with trained nurses. Now I brought in an assistant physician.

Success or failure, recovery with adverse effect or without it: I had seen the cheapness of an individual life too close at hand in combat and in military epidemic hospitals. Previously I had sacrificed animal lives on a vast scale in order to find something that might be of use in restoring even one human being to health. Now it was the opposite. Animal experiments became the main point.

With great caution, so as not to arouse the suspicions of my wife, I resumed my bacteriological experiments alongside my work as a physician, and as ill luck would have it, two of my patients at the time perished within a short period "following successful surgery." There are such strings of bad luck everywhere, in accordance with the law of large numbers, but here there was a connection, as follows. I was concerned at that time with the etiology of scarlet fever. Notoriously, the bacterial cause of this exanthem (like that of numerous other infectious diseases, I mention only lethargic encephalitis and yellow fever among many) is still wrapped in complete mystery. Every known method has been tried without success despite the greatest experimental ingenuity and the keenest determination. No one on earth has seen the "virus" of scarlatina, scarlet fever, in the flesh! And yet it exists. It must be possible to find it. But how?

Now the matter of scarlet fever is particularly curious. Other pathogenic microorganisms are found as fellow travelers of this disease, identified streptococci readily seen on suitable specimens under the microscope; spherical bacteria arranged in chains can be cultured without difficulty on synthetic growth media. They cause ulcerations, they excrete extremely virulent toxins, they produce, when injected or circulating "naturally" in the bloodstream of the scarlet-fever victim, dangerous effects, beginning with high fever and ending in death.

The following line of thinking seemed plausible to me. The true pathogen of scarlet fever and yellow fever and so forth must, as has been gathered, be so small that it can traverse even the tiniest pores of the clay filter through which the bacillus cultures have been drawn. But the streptococci involved in scarlet fever, while not as big as potatoes, are of measurable size, even measurable volume and weight – and they never pass through such a small-pored filter, they remain in the old culture fluid, while the scarlet-fever toxin and pathogen slip through.

Would it then be conceivable that the unknown scarlet-fever pathogens are tiny freeloaders or parasites living on the much larger bodies of the streptococci, and that they are both being separated by the filter? Some such thing is imaginable, maybe even worth an experiment. Good! I devoted myself to this question, setting up experiments that would answer it one way or the other.

In my office I discharged my tasks as one discharges a duty. I neglected none of the imperatives of antisepsis when I performed the two operations mentioned above. And yet! And yet!

The first was an appendectomy in the "cold" or nonacute stage, generally an entirely safe intervention. Nevertheless a septic fever resembling streptococcal fever had already developed on the evening following the operation. What was inexplicable to my assistant was the appearance of virulent streptococci in the blood of the patient. I will keep it short. We lost the patient. Had I unwittingly transmitted dangerous microorganisms? My wife tried to console me. She took an interest in my successes and failures as a physician. I could not be silent, the thing touched her. I forced myself to stay away from the laboratory for a few weeks. Everything went splendidly in the interval. Even technically difficult operations were successful, and my patients marveled at my "gentle, blessed touch"!

But the day came when it was necessary to transfer the costly and painstakingly prepared scarlet-fever streptococcus cultures to fresh medium. Otherwise these organisms, which were living in the old culture fluid and continuously excreting toxins in the incubator, maintained at a uniform thirty-seven degrees, would eventually have poisoned, sterilized, exterminated themselves. They had to be settled on virgin soil. This job too I performed with extreme care. I used rubber gloves to handle the glass rods tipped with flame-sterilized platinum loops when I transferred tiny drops of the old culture into vessels containing fresh nutrient. My clandestine visit to the laboratory might have taken six or eight minutes at most. The cab was waiting by the side entrance of the Pathology Institute with its meter running, which is why I am able to estimate the time.

Moreover I was firmly resolved not to perform any operations during the next few days. I had, of course, washed my hands, my body, with the greatest possible fastidiousness following this visit to the laboratory, had even had my hair cut. Out of pure self-interest alone, I had done everything I could in order not to be infectious. As ill luck would have it, I must now repeat those ominous words, my wife welcomed me home with the news that there had been a call about a friend of my brother and sister, a woman. There was severe pelvic bleeding. My name came to mind for many reasons.

This was the second calamity. This time I could not be said to have done anything unwittingly. I would have liked to say no. But my wife pressed me; my siblings, who otherwise lived their own lives just as they let me live mine, besieged me with entreaties, particularly my sister. I wanted to have my assistant do the operation. Objections all around. He had so little experience, he was heavy-handed, etc., and most of all: no one wanted an outsider to know too much about the operation. I gave in and performed it. Again a minor, ten-minute procedure, assisted only by the clinical nurse, as, in view of its nature, we wished to prevent the assistant from finding out about it. For the law is not for such things. I knew the patient, a pretty, Rubenesque, golden blonde individual.

She was a widow, prominent in society – she wished to avoid a scandal, had to avoid one. I did not understand it entirely, but I complied with her fervent request. Misplaced compassion! The man involved did not show himself.

This time I was not as calm as I had been after the appendectomy. I went out again to the clinic late in the evening or at night.

My wife was waiting down at the gate in her car. She had on her lap a small, long-haired, wheat-colored dog, a kind of Pekingese, the pet of her daughter, who was traveling. As I stood beside the bed of my patient, still asleep after the anesthesia, I looked down at the street. My wife seemed to be getting along well with the little dog. Her long, beautiful fingers played in the silkily gleaming, slightly wavy coat of the large-eyed little creature, sprightly unlike most of its breed. Suddenly it barked and snapped at my wife's gloved fingers, which she had held out to it. It was summer, the car was open, the trees in front of the clinic swayed in the breeze. A fine day, very fine. Meanwhile the nurse had taken the patient's temperature. It was 37.1. This is actually a fairly normal temperature, but I could not shake an uneasy feeling. And at the same time a sensation, an intuition (how shall I put it?) that only an experimenter will recognize. Could there be something amiss? Something that was not as it should be? Not from the experimental subject's standpoint, perhaps – but surely everything was fine . . . I will not go on with this. I will merely state the patient's course. The patient contracted an exanthem resembling scarlet fever. But the blood was persistently free of streptococci. Had I transferred not the streptococcus but the invisible scarlet-fever virus this time? My theory – was it correct? Had the unknown virus still clung loyally to the streptococcus cultures?

Difficult to describe my state of mind during the period that followed.

The animal experiments secretly resumed at full tilt, the microscopy and culturing throughout the day whenever I was not by the bed of the poor delirious patient, and at night, since I was unable to sleep and could not bear the presence of my all-too-tender wife, the visits to gambling clubs, where I was now dogged by misfortune, by bad luck.

In addition the acquaintance made of a beautiful, very young, light blonde gambler, with whom I took up intending at first only to satisfy a momentary craving and whom I then installed in a first-class hotel and attempted to surround with great luxury.

Finally the death of my patient, the "almost" airtight result of my final experiments, the tearfulness of my wife, who did not understand my elevated mood despite these events. Suddenly the reversal. I noticed a suspicious redness on my underarm. Had I myself been infected in my experiments? I almost confided in my wife. For until then I had remained silent. But everything passed off well. I remained healthy. A big question mark still hung over the experiments, but on the other hand I was fortunate elsewhere. The young person loved me. She proved this by demanding a lot from me: money, time, love.

I did what I could. I was short of time most of all. Love can sometimes be a substitute for money. Money can sometimes substitute for love. There is no substitute for time.

VI

As a result of my large expenditures on my work and on M. (the girl) as well as my gambling losses, I now ran into certain financial difficulties, which were not particularly pressing at first. The household cost money too, my income was not significant, my savings practically zero. But I was able to borrow money, the gentlemen at the gambling club knew quite a number of fairly respectable moneylenders, and for a time I paid my short-term debts to one lender with loans I obtained from a second or third.

If I had at least had some peace! I needed every minute of my time. I pressed my wife to do some traveling. She resisted. Her tenderness began to take on a more desperate character from one day to the next; only seldom did her naturally happy, sunny nature come through. My stepdaughter insinuated herself into the foreground after a period of haughtily avoiding us. She would not leave her mother and persistently tried to alienate my wife from me. But that aging, love-addicted woman only became more attached to me, gazed at me with her shining, light gray eyes, did her best to be near me all day long.

In the course of my scientific investigations I had neglected my practice almost entirely. I had forgotten important appointments – had, to give only one example of this kind, scheduled an elderly patient for surgery but was not at the clinic by his side when the time came. How difficult it was for me to persuade him later that I had his best interests at heart, that intensive radium treatment would stand him in much better stead than a surgical procedure. He believed it all in the end and died peacefully in his bed, instead of on the operating table. But who knows, perhaps my "gentle, blessed touch" could have gained him a few more years of life after all. And this same old man had a liking for me. He remembered me in his will, if not with a proper bequest, then at least with encomia, and lauded in particular my "loving heart." Well, peace to his ashes. In my "loving heart" there was little peace. And no love.

My waiting room became emptier and emptier every day, the telephone calls were increasingly ones of a personal nature, that is to say, they were from my expensive golden blonde mistress and her sister, to whom I was lately held by "bonds of love," and further I was being hounded by creditors, who had abruptly begun to be troublesome. It was a natural idea to attempt to stop the gaps in my budget with winnings from gambling, given that luck had favored me early on. But regrettably this was not the case now. Perhaps I was too worn out when I came to the club, for at that time my experiments were of the greatest importance to me, requiring the closest attention and the greatest care. Nothing is more humiliating for an experimenter than to present his results to his audience of physicians, to lay himself open to the criticism of shrewd, skeptical reviewers, and then see his results unable to withstand the sharpest scrutiny. It was imperative to avoid this. Unfortunately things were very far from what they should have been.

I had cages of animals set up, initially in the basement rooms, then in other spots in my now-deserted private clinic. The clinic belonged to my wife. But, of course, she could know nothing. For her benefit I simulated a brisk business at the clinic, I sent myself fake doctor's fees, I had my mistress and her sister (they got along very well) telephone me when I wished to get away from my wife, pretending to be patients needing my assistance. And even if this deception and many similar ones were easy to practice upon my credulous wife, I was uneasy. A nervous disquiet, a presentiment of disaster, never left me. My irritability increased day by day, I never really slept, was never really awake, and more than once vented my rage upon my innocent wife.

But when she, enlightened by her daughter and perhaps by my father too (he had hated me since I once jokingly dubbed him a "loving heart"), saw "evil" in me, she did not oppose this evil. Faithful, more than faithful, to the words of Scripture (she was religious, and a thousand times

I envied her this mindless faith), she turned the other cheek when I struck her on the right. I can still see her rapidly aging face. Nature had botched the job, but an animated play of expressions had at one time lent it some life and appealing mobility nevertheless; out of vanity, she had had it elaborately enameled, hoping to still have an effect on me by some means at least. Now it was as smooth as the head of a statue made of butter that has been in the sun a while, a bleak, grotesque spectacle. On one occasion she was pressing her face close to me in her love madness. I tried to push her away, unsuccessfully. I repeated my attempt to fend her off, the ball of my left hand wedged into one of her eye sockets, from which copious tears were flowing. Through the wetness of her tears I suddenly felt something slightly bristly tickling the inside of my hand. Startled, I turned on the light (all of this was happening at night in our shared bedroom), and what did I have in my hand? False eyelashes, the latest product of the big-city beauticians' art, miniature brushes of curving little hairs cunningly designed to adhere supraorbitally. And this in a woman of over fifty, the mother of a grown daughter! Her wrinkled neck (the neck cannot be enameled and its furrows cannot be filled) was shiny, like creased, crumpled parchment, on the sides especially. There were reasons for this too. It was slight burn scarring. Once she had poured a load of strong perfume on her neck and then imprudently exposed herself to a sunlamp, which had practically seared the stuff into her skin.

If only she had stayed as she was! I might have been able to see the mother in her. But that was abhorrent to her.

She did not understand that she was played out as a woman, and that a ruined castle with electric lights and central heating is an absurdity. One evening, when I returned home after further large gambling losses, she received me with distinct coolness. For me a moment of calm. I only wish it had gone on longer. But she pressed herself to me, her face pouty as ever (to the extent that her enameled mask was still capable of a pout). She wanted me to ask why she was angry. But I had many things on my mind that day, not just her. My experiments were refusing to yield a positive result. And also: my financial difficulties were mounting. But the longer I was silent, the more she was driven to speak; the cooler I was, the more vehement she became. As finally emerged, she had found out that I had completely neglected my practice, that the once clean rooms of our clinic were now polluted with animal material of an infectious nature. How had she happened on it? Only through her accursed love for me! I had dismissed my assistant in order to save money. She knew this and had thought to lighten my load with the help of a young doctor, a friend of her daughter, and the three of them had toured the premises, which she had a legal right to do as owner.

Her surprise was understandably great. She had never thought me capable of a lie. She loved me so much and knew me *so well*! And now? She became upset, she opened her mouth wide and showed her blindingly white, gold-rimmed false teeth, her sumptuous dressing gown hung open, she stamped on the floor, and one of the thin elastic stockings that she wore underneath the flesh-colored silk ones, stretched around the varicose veins, tore with a sizzling sound.

She was in the right, I was in the wrong. And yet she angered me, I had had enough of her, I vented my desperation upon her, the miscarriage of my experimental plans, my poisoned youth, all the disappointments of my life. I hurled myself upon her, I at last gave voice to the cruelest, most hurtful words, I balled my fists, I did to her both mentally and physically everything that one person can do to another without causing lasting damage – brutal, but within the law.

She doubled over in pain, her enameled mask twitched like a fish, but suddenly a sentimental, sensual smile came to her lips, she threw herself at my feet, and when I pushed her away, disliking such theatrical scenes, she crawled after me, she began to giggle coyly, and the more brutally I kicked her, the more blissful she became.

And the ghastliest thing of all was that her arousal was transmitted to me, that she overpowered me sexually. Ugly, aging, with gold-rimmed porcelain teeth, enameled face, wrinkled, perfume-scorched skin – what is the point of enumerating all her physical imperfections, down to the singed smell of her body – she was stronger than I. I, who had wanted finally to break with her, was possessed by her in the midst of my cruelties. Never before, neither with my beautiful young mistress nor with her still more beautiful virgin sister, had I felt what now thrilled me, what shook me to the marrow.

My father had taught me how to do away with a living creature and do it coldly. It came back to me now, the thing he had stirred up in me when I was young, perhaps thirteen. Pleasurable sensations, disgusting animals, and death had parts to play. This is not the time to go into it. But why was I thinking of him now, now of all times? Was I not "making love" to my wife? Or was it that I hated her, was I clinging, still, more than ever, to him? My wife – but why speak of it?

Her little dog was howling.

VII

This little dog, as innocent as it was, became the source of new conflict. The howling of which I spoke just now must have been an expression of its terror of me. And the terror experienced by this thinking, feeling animal (albeit one with thoughts and feelings quite different from those of a person) was not entirely without foundation. For that little dog, which had mysteriously vanished some weeks earlier, had been found unexpectedly by my wife and the young doctor in the basement rooms of the clinic, shut in an animal cage made of heavy iron wire. They had released it, and the caretaker at the clinic had enthusiastically lent a hand. It was just his job to lend a hand and he would have strapped the Pekingese to the dissection table with the same friendly smile. But how did it get there? Pekingese dogs – expensive purebreds are surely accustomed to a better life! I do not wish to make myself out to be better than I am. I had lured it there one day, and the only reason it had managed to cling to its miserable life in the dark cellar as long as it had was that dogs were poorly suited to my experiments of the time.

My stepdaughter was fond of the little beast. Why did she not keep an eye on it? She was happy to leave the inconvenience of its care and feeding to others such as her mother, who gladly sacrificed herself here too. What consternation when Lilly had suddenly disappeared. My slender, (natural) blonde stepdaughter's cute little mug puffy from crying, such a to-do, ad after ad inserted in the papers, the neighborhood scoured the minute anyone caught sight of a canine resembling the missing Lilly-poo crossing the street! And the solution to the puzzle known all the time! I will not drag it out. It was just a joke. I had to pay for it. For from that day on the cute young thing's hatred toward me became so fanatical that she was able to act intelligently, that is to say, quite intuitively and shrewdly and with feminine guile, and in the end it was due to my stepdaughter and her future husband, the young doctor, that the district attorney's office came after me immediately following my wife's demise. Admittedly that called for no special "feminine guile." It was all just too obvious.

There was no outward change after this episode. Except that I got tired of both the M. sisters. Not the reverse, unfortunately. They did not wish to lose their income or my masculine affection, and they stayed on at the fancy hotel at my expense. The registered or courier-delivered letters containing unpaid bills came thick and fast, there was nowhere to hide from the two shrews. Finally they tried to cozen me with love and desperation. But I knew what this meant and withdrew in time into my immediate family. In time?

My wife, who had always been quite thrifty, now became mistrustful and something beyond miserly as the result of her daughter's constant malicious innuendos. She barely even shouldered her contractually stipulated fifty-percent share of the expenses of our luxurious three-servant household. She always miscalculated in her favor. Contributions from the privy purse could not be squeezed out of her by any technique. Yet she was munificent in outfitting her daughter, who had wasted no time getting engaged to the young doctor, in a style that was more than up to standard. It made her touchingly happy to put the couple in possession of a fine eight-room country house, with the most expensive furniture throughout. The young man, who got the well-appointed clinic in addition to the cute blonde and then the villa in the stylish garden suburb to boot, was to be envied.

He was successful. All my life I have respected success wherever I saw it. My liking for the young doctor, for this publicly recognized "loving heart," was not reciprocated. When the four of us sat together, he and his wife, I and my wife, there was chilly silence after a few exchanges. He shrugged his shoulders at my experiments. I had not "cracked" the typhus pathogen, as he put it, or the scarlet-fever pathogen either.

My wife, with her doglike affection, tried to see me through everything that had been going wrong for me lately. But I never even managed to be frank with her. Everything about her love was a misunderstanding – and, as grotesque as it may sound, here too she always miscalculated in her favor. *She* loved openly and honestly, but I had to be dishonest all the time, because she forced me to be. And this soon sickened me. I am not a liar. I had my fill of it.

Lie after lie to do with the phone calls and with personal visits I had begun to receive from the impatient, extortionate moneylenders. But nothing about the failure of my experiments, which became all the more anguishing when I learned that my medical school classmate, the aforementioned Walter, had been dealing with the same topic as I and, at least in secondary experiments, had had far better luck. Was he beating me to it?

The urge toward stupefaction, toward intoxication in any form, grew day by day. My mental breakdown *must* have been noticeable, but nobody wanted to know anything about my true torments – neither my father, who had been making a pest of himself lately with his tedious visits, nor my wife, who was annoying me with her insipid, driveling, grandmotherly love.

Neither one of them could give me what I yearned for in the depths of my soul, but there was one medicine that they could have given me to ease my suffering: the original medicine, money.

My father condescended to give me a birthday present of a couple of thousand cash, a drop in the bucket. My wife was even more cunning (she thought): she showed me the duplicate of her will, which she had made on the eve of my stepdaughter's wedding and in which I was named sole heir. Her daughter was thus given a statutory portion, and it was I upon whom she doted. More than ever. Well, I knew that. But our relationship was shaping up as more and more repugnant just the same.

I cannot even say whether it would have been more natural if we, that is, I, a man plagued by morbid urges and living without hope or belief, with no ground beneath my feet at all, and she, an aging, coquettish woman who felt alive only in suffering – I do not know, I say, whether there might have been another natural solution to these problems. Ultimately, perhaps, I might have found a way out if I had had a *friend*, another human soul who was intelligent yet had not succumbed to despair, who trusted me and was truly intimate with me, a man I could have looked up to – Walter, perhaps. But Walter, with all his brilliant accomplishments and outstanding qualities, was having his own difficulties at the Institute now and would be lucky even to finish his most recent work. Space at the Institute is always very limited, and, under orders from the Ministry, his seat, his workbench, were being assigned to a military physician, Major Carolus, a queer specimen about whom I will have much more to say.

I was working at the Institute again, or rather still, and my dear spouse ventured no further objection. I was permitted to go on working there (and work was the only solace I had left) not because of anything to do with myself or my own achievements but only because of my father's influence, which grew year by year, the clergy constantly by his side in a supporting role, as he by its. Not the first or the last anarchist and atheist to live in perfect harmony with the Church, at least outwardly.

How then could I expect him to stand by me inwardly, whole-heartedly, when I, with a presentiment of what was coming, for the first time considered a divorce? I do not remember how this idea entered our formal and excessively polite conversation. But I had the feeling when I expressed it that this might be a way for me to save myself and my wife. Yet he stared at me, dumbfounded. He did not even hear me out – for him the matter was settled before it was discussed. Divorce, remarriage were impossible. Catholic marriage permits separation only; canonical law does not recognize divorce.

He even warned me not to mention the possibility of divorce to my wife. But the idea must already have taken root without my realizing it, for I did it just the same. More tears from the old lady, more despondent scenes, and, most appalling of all, more ecstatic debauches with this woman who found the ultimate satisfaction only in doglike suffering and could never be kicked enough. And I? I was part of it.

We took a trip to the south and were no different when we came back. What did she care about my happiness? Did she ever understand me at all? That is, was such an abnormal individual as I ever able to really make myself understood to such an abnormal individual as she?

I was preoccupied with an attempt to isolate the two different poisons from the scarlet-fever streptococcus cultures. Now just *one* poisonous substance or toxin is already extraordinarily difficult to isolate perfectly in crystalline form. It has been done properly in relatively few cases. So imagine the difficulties of separating the toxins into one component ascribable to the known streptococci and another component ascribable to the unknown scarlet-fever pathogen. A project like this requires superhuman diligence, great sacrifices of time and money. I lacked time, especially. I wanted to live at the workbench, but my wife wanted something else. She would hear no talk of my money worries. She herself had more than enough money, after all. The marriage, as fragile as it was, ate up a lot of time. The less I loved my wife, the more she craved my attention. And pinched pennies drastically. Who does not understand that? She loved me and feared me. A state of affairs intolerable in the long run.

VIII

I have never in my life been entirely free of stirrings of compassion. "Conscience doth make cowards of us all." Hamlet, archetype of recent Europeans. True, I never had so much of a conscience that it exerted a compelling effect on my life. I always felt compassion in the wrong places, all the more when I resisted it. In my youth my father had wanted to tear this evil (and it is never anything but an evil) out by the roots. But who can get hold of the roots of a personal trait? I knew what I was doing when I put an animal, a living creature that feels pain and has a certain degree of consciousness, on the torture rack. Other people did not know. Other people did not require intoxication, mental anesthesia, forcible calming after their horrific bloody experiments, other people did not suffer from a constant craving for excitement. But why speak of animals when we are talking about a person so close to me that . . .

Just the facts. As the intolerability of the overall circumstances of my life emerged, becoming clearer every day (if it would not have taken us too far afield, I would have liked to give a full account of a day during this period, in all the hellish endlessness of its twenty-four hours) – when I had recognized the intolerability of my circumstances clearly enough, I made a final attempt to free myself from my spouse in an amicable manner. We had been married in church like everyone we knew. But the bond generally expected to hold a marriage together, conjugal love, existed on her side only. I did not love her. To this day I really do not know whether I was still capable of this much-discussed feeling at all, indeed, whether I was *ever* capable of love. Who does know?

The cornerstone of marriage is supposed to be the partnership of the sexes, a partnership craved for the purpose of satisfying natural urges and entered into in the hope of mutual succor. So says the Church, citing the procreation of offspring as the primary purpose of marriage. I wanted a child very much. But at the same time I was afraid to have one. I feared the responsibility of bringing one more life into this most terrible of all worlds – and this was one reason for marrying my wife, for in view of her age alone it was extremely unlikely that she would be granted another child. She herself did not believe she would be. Nevertheless she was unswerving in her conviction that any marriage between Catholics was an indestructible, objectively existing bond that could not be broken even if love turned to hatred and revulsion.

She stood firm in her belief (it was possible for her to believe, only I had to be constantly doubting) that my fondness for her would return one day, because after all it had been there once, namely, when I had asked for her hand. One error compounded by another. Why should I explain to her my true motivations in marrying her? I had taken this desperate step only because I could not face living with myself on a permanent basis. For the same reason that so many individuals, and not the most worthless ones in many cases, resort to alcohol, morphine, or cocaine, or take pointless trips, amass idiotic collections. It was only to escape myself that I had courted her.

I had expected her to provide her share of the "mutual succor." *That* I could tell her. But she did not wish "base motives" to shackle me to her.

Like so many rich people, she did not understand what money means to one who does not have it. She spoke to me as to a good but unreasonable child. She even went beyond the will that I have mentioned. On her own initiative, she began lengthy negotiations with an insurance agent. One evening she showed me the result. She had just paid the first premium on a mutual insurance contract: upon the demise of one party, the surviving party was to receive a large amount of money. I, if she died before me, and vice versa. What was she trying to do? Did she understand me after all? She was certainly rich enough already. What would she do with even more money after my death? But *I* needed money, she knew that. I would get it only after her death, but then without fail. Was she trying to test me? Had she caught the morbid desire for experiments from me, like an infection?

I could only shrug. But she misinterpreted that as proof that her love and her life were more valuable to me than any earthly possessions. And yet even a fraction of that insurance money would have let me leave the city, go to America, break with everything I had done until then, and begin something new and different. For what was my life now? Just whatever the current experiment was, a positive or negative result. And then? When that experiment was over, when it got a thumbs up or a thumbs down, a new hypothesis was next in line, to be confirmed or disconfirmed, the result in turn forming the basis for further work. As idiotic as it sounds, as much as this kind of work seems to resemble the monotonous play of infants, or something even sillier, that really is how it is. This is what countless people do all their lives. The only joy is a flutter of the nerves, a sensation, an artificially evoked and just as artificially gratified arousal. But the "craving for excitement" is never satisfied, only thwarted, and so it goes to the last breath. Let anyone who does not believe this read, for example, the reports of the scholars, let him cast his eye upon the numerous scientific journals and weigh the immense, truly colossal *volume* of this work against its meager *content*; let him set the work and the energy expended on it against its useful effect, whether in respect of the advances in what is actually known about reality or in respect of the instrumental capabilities by which needy humanity has been enriched through this activity.

My wife was so little able to follow me here that she regarded me with compassionate eyes as though I were an incurable mental patient and often did not even take my words seriously. She was serious only about the sensual aspect of our relationship, and this angered me a great deal. Yet I was compliant, if I may use the word, despite my antipathy; I was her slave despite my alienation, dependent upon this woman who made me accede to her voluptuous compulsion to suffer, which afforded me a kind of satisfaction too. And all the while becoming I cannot begin to say *how* strong, *how much* more uncontrollable every day, the wish for freedom, for complete disentanglement from her! (From myself.) That was the ultimate sensation I sought.

Even my wife did not find complete serenity in her false bliss. How would that even have been possible?

She was declining visibly. She placed herself in the care of her son-in-law, who administered an arsenic treatment to fire up her animal spirits, already inordinately overheated in my view, to a still greater pitch. She now often gave off a garlicky odor due to transpiration of arsenic through the skin, her eyes glowed still more brightly and ardently than before, sudden flush alternated with sudden pallor behind her enameled mask; one day she collapsed with symptoms resembling those of stroke. I hastened to her bed, shed tears, nursed her devotedly, and thought, with a feeling of deliverance in my heart of hearts, that this was the end. I gave her an injection of morphine from a small Pravaz syringe. This did her good. I wanted to make it as easy as possible for her. Unfortunately we were all fooled, my father, her daughter, my son-in-law, and I. We had not recognized her superhuman toughness. She was one of those people who are still hiking long distances at eighty and outdoing the fifty-year-olds at ninety. She recovered. She became healthier than she had been before. She traveled with her daughter to a spa, and I entertained the absurd hope that some happenstance would save me from our reunion.

And yet I did not hate her.

IX

My wife had been looking forward to a romantic spring and was very reproachful toward me for not going along on this trip. But how could I have gone? I longed for nothing so much as to be relieved of the burden of her presence for as long as possible.

But it was not a good time for me nevertheless. My creditors did not leave my heels, they constantly forced me to dodge them, to pretend to be someone else on the telephone, to rearrange my whole life, to do everything I could to fend off their all-too-legitimate demands. Some of them professed to be agreeable to a refund without interest, others to an out-of-court settlement, but I could not think about it. And yet I had no prospect of ever being entirely rid of them. Some of them were highly impertinent and threatened me with all sorts of things. But that got them nowhere.

I was no longer so welcome at the club. Ugly rumors about me were circulating. It was said that I was unreliable and greedy as a physician, had tortured animals for no reason, had sprayed eau de cologne in their eyes, had secretly borrowed (stolen) dogs from my acquaintances, had destroyed their vocal cords before the experiments to stop them from howling, and so forth. It was said that I had squeezed the last remnants (!) of my wife's fortune out of her by abusing her sadistically, having first hypnotized her and deprived her of the faculty of volition. It was said that my scientific work was done by other, more talented persons in exchange for payment. It was said that I had subjected people as well as animals to pointless and excruciating experiments in my clinic and had extricated myself from criminal action brought by the surviving dependents of my victims only at great financial sacrifice (allegedly the cause of my money problems). I was never able to pin down the source of these defamatory rumors. It must have been someone close to me, in all likelihood my stepdaughter's husband. My letters to my wife were never taken seriously, that is to say, never properly answered. I wrote every day, yet received plaintive letters in which she reproached me for never thinking of her. What was I to do?

Wrenched from my usual occupation (I had had to stop my experiments because my funds were totally depleted, and just when I had nearly isolated Toxin Y, a whitish hygroscopic crystal), I wandered about the city in search of novelty. I had shaken off the sisters. The older one had abandoned me because of my lack of money. The younger one still liked me, but I had absolutely no use for her and brutally told her so to her face. She cried openly on the street, but then she got the point and retreated. I never heard from her again.

By chance I ran into an acquaintance, a former classmate. At one time he had been among the least talented people in the class, but he had been the quickest to make a career for himself, was codirector of a chemical plant that produced medicines. Hair restorers, calcium supplements, rejuvenation tonics. He ran an experimental laboratory in a distant city. He made me an offer.

That evening I wrote to my wife again. I suggested to her that we put an amicable end to the marriage, inasmuch as it was wearing the two of us down both physically and mentally. Instead of replying, she came herself. She had received this letter "by accident," she said, the earlier ones having been kept from her by her daughter. She was agitated, fearful. Clear signs of physical decline could no longer be ignored. Occasionally she clutched her heart with her heavily beringed, wizened hand (no one yet knows how to enamel hands). It flashed through my mind how happy both of us would be if she met with a painless death that day or next. Her varicose veins were giving her trouble. A small venous blood clot had once come loose and made its way from the lower leg to the brain. She doubted whether she would ever be quite well again. She was afraid to have an operation, perhaps because my example had proven to her that doctors are not infallible gods. Yes, nothing less than that. Through a curious association of ideas, there came into my mind the peculiar action that I had observed as the effect of Toxin Y, the toxic substance in crystalline form that I had obtained from scarlet-fever cultures: similar abnormal clotting phenomena, producing sudden death – a pulmonary embolism, a heart attack, a stroke – in experimental animals. It was a possibility. They had not suffered. I believe.

On some pretext, it was late afternoon, I disengaged myself from my wife, who was exhausted from her journey and from being overwrought. She tried to stop me. She wanted to tell me all about how her daughter and her husband had threatened to have her declared legally incompetent and her property confiscated if she did not leave me. She tried to throw her pale arms around me. I escaped with some effort.

The domestics had not been paid and the landlord had not received the rent. I had to get away from these disagreeable confrontations with my wife. My clinic was almost entirely empty. I had no patients and the son-in-law who had been sharing the costs had made excuses and put his patients in another private clinic. For an instant I considered seeking out my father. His signature on a check was worth just as much as that of a physician on my wife's death certificate putting me in possession of the money. But I did not dare to go see my father.

I betook myself to the laboratory. Some letters of a professional nature lay on my desk. I took from the locked cabinet a small test tube containing about four centigrams of Toxin Y. Whether I had already conceived a definite plan of my crime or was only testing myself, asking, "What if . . ." – this I am no longer able to say today, any more than I can say what drew me to the vicinity of the house in which I was born and spent my youth with my parents and siblings, the "Rat Palace" as it was called, a rambling and rodent-plagued old villa on a river. To toughen me, my father once made me spend three nights in a room with rats (which he hated). The house had now been free of rats for a long time. It had been broken up into apartments for laborers and office workers. Rats hardly cared to live there anymore. Instead there were a great many children, the place was teeming with them. Bratty, undernourished, but full of glee and noise. I envied them their youth.

The garden no longer existed. On the same plot of ground rose a tenement, its walls covered with damp spots. I was flooded with memories of my childhood as I passed by. Bitternesses, inconclusive broodings.

Feelings of hatred toward my father, feelings of envy toward my brother and sister. Pity for my wife and for myself.

I returned late. I had had dinner in town and assumed that my wife, exhausted from her journey, would have long since gone to bed. In such cases I sometimes spent the night on a comfortable leather sofa-bed in my study, so as not to disturb her light sleep. I too was extraordinarily tired. The barometer was unusually low for this time of year, mid-August, the air suffocatingly close. Humid, but with no tendency toward rain. Before going to bed, I took the little glass vial containing the toxin out of my pocket and put it aside, on the mirrored top of a cabinet. But I could not sleep. Suddenly I heard my wife walking back and forth in her room directly above my study. She was awake now, or had not yet gone to bed. She was talking in a loud voice. To herself?

No sleep. I had gone quietly into the bathroom, where there were always pajamas in a closet. But the closet was locked, and I had given the key to my wife. So I did not undress. The footsteps in my wife's room had stopped now, as had the sound of her voice. I was just about to settle down when she appeared on the landing, wrapped in a sumptuous salmon-colored nightgown heavily embroidered with glass beads. In her eyes was an expression that in the most unfathomable fashion always both attracted and repelled me, a doglike tenderness, a lust to be beaten. I drew my shoulders together, I bowed my head. Rage against this woman, who could still *smile*, even now, welled up in me. I let her know that all I wanted was to be left alone. She turned on the lights in the study and saw the glint of the glass vial that held the toxin. She thought it was morphine. First she started reproaching me for a thousand petty things, then she cried, and without so much as a pause, smiling foolishly, she asked me to give her the same injection that I had given her before her trip.

I felt the deadly irony of fate so strongly that I could not help smiling too. Or was I just imitating her awkward, glassy grimace? No matter, it put her in a better mood immediately. She embraced me with her short, rosily powdered little arms. Conquered once more by her voluptuous urges, she dragged me upstairs to our bedroom, drew the curtains, and enfolded me. I pushed her away firmly, and that was the beginning. She wanted what she had always gotten. I could not fight her off. The more terrible the things I did, the more obstinately happy she looked! I was in a state of dreadful agitation. In her masochistic rapture, would she forget what she had asked me for? The injection? I wanted her to, and I didn't want her to. Never had one part of me been so much at war with another. For, as of a short time ago, a violent solution was no longer so urgently needed. I could accept the position in the distant city and begin a new, respectable life without her.

The telephone rang. I thought – why now? – of my father. It rang again. In a particularly shrill, maddening manner, it seemed to me. But neither I nor my wife went to the phone. The ringing must have soon stopped.

X

Immediately following my wife's death, which I ascertained conclusively, I opened the two windows and woke the housemaid. I told her to telephone a physician who lived nearby: my wife had taken ill, she was having fainting symptoms. The girl, in short cotton pajamas, her black hair disheveled, half asleep, her face pale and pasty, carried out my instructions. The physician apparently did not come to the phone immediately. Then he had every word repeated three or four times, the girl had to spell everything out. Had he become hard of hearing overnight? Finally I lost patience and took the receiver myself. Did I have so little control of myself? Apparently so. The physician immediately understood what I had to say extremely well. I don't know why, but this entirely insignificant circumstance, that the telephone connection between us two physicians now functioned perfectly, gave me a feeling of happiness, put me in a kind of high spirits.

The physician recalled my name immediately as that of his colleague. But he seemed to have little desire to come now, at night, asked if I would not see to the patient again myself, take her pulse, check her breathing. The maid was looking strangely at the bed and the figure lying motionless on it. I gave no sign of noticing. I pretended to perform the examination as advised by the physician, then pulled the coverlet up over my wife's open mouth and continued my conversation with him. He said with satisfaction that this was the normal course (of what?), that he would counsel me as a colleague, that I should quickly administer an injection of caffeine and let him know what happened. Of course he would be available if it was absolutely necessary (he carefully stressed the word "absolutely"). I gave my assent, hung up, turned out all the lights but one, and sent the maid out of the room with a feeling of relief. I walked through the adjoining rooms four or five times, sat down for a moment in the armchair, then tiptoed into my wife's bathroom and dressing room and put the poison there for the time being. Then I called the physician again and informed him that my wife's pulse had stopped while I was giving her the injection. The physician did not respond immediately. Then he took a deep breath – or he yawned – and finally, in a changed voice, meant to sound moved, asked me to try an injection of camphor, so that everything conceivable would have been done. Directly into the heart?! Of course he meant the cardiac musculature. I said nothing. Then he asked whether I still insisted on an immediate visit. He himself had given up administering camphor injections to the dying, he said. They never saved anyone. Again I found no suitable response. Otherwise, he continued, he would appear the next morning at seven thirty in order to comply with the legal formalities and fill out the death certificate. I surely had blank forms in the house. And he did not need to tell me that he had the deepest sympathy for me in my loss. I thanked him briefly and hung up.

The telephone then rang once more. I answered it. No one there. Wrong number? Ten minutes later the same thing. Yet a third time – now I felt I ought to call the operator and complain. I waited. My heart pounded. But there was silence. Good.

I believed I had taken care of the aftermath of my actions in the most straightforward manner. I would have told my father everything only too gladly. But the absurdity of this notion became clear to me at once and I laughed out loud.

I was happy. But not at ease. In the bedroom I turned on the light once more and got a clean hand towel from my wife's small bathroom, which was charmingly done in almond green and pale pink. I spread it out over the still uncovered upper part of my dead wife's face. Then I turned back the coverlet and spread the towel over her throat and chest as well. The window was still open; the hot, moist breeze caught in the dry, bright linen, lifting it where it swelled over the curves of the chest. Rhythmic rising and falling. But I knew what was what. I turned out the light. The wood in a built-in wardrobe suddenly contracted with a sharp crack.

I returned to the bed once again. The towel felt warmish and soft as silk. I touched the sides of the neck underneath. Warmth and silky softness here too. But there was no trace of a pulse at the carotid artery. The blood vessels were all clearly palpable, like thick knitting needles. Evidently there were masses of coagulated blood here as in the other blood vessels. Thus the old miracle test would fail. Come who might to the bed of the deceased, the coagulated blood would never liquefy.

Toxin Y, whose composition was known to no one but me, could not have been identified by a forensic chemist. Besides, it would have broken down into entirely innocuous constituents within the body in less than four hours, as I knew from animal experiments. Solid proof of organic toxins is in any case one of the most problematic chapters of forensic chemistry, though science has made great strides in this area in the past thirty years. It has been possible to determine toxicity limits by experimenting on living organisms, human or animal. But only when known toxins are involved. Mine was unknown. Once four hours had elapsed, there could be no result incriminating me, no matter what methods were used to examine the blood. And who would come here in the next four hours?

I locked the door and put the key on the small corner table in the hall. From the hall I went back into the bathroom, reluctantly and with great unease; the adorable pale pink and almond green walls, the white tile, the effete mirrors, the gleaming nickel-plated taps nauseated me. Hurrying to be finished there, I hastily dumped the vial of Toxin Y into the toilet bowl and switched off the light.

I seemed to have a hunger. I had, much more even than that afternoon, a need to see someone and to talk. I left the building. I went out onto the street. In front of the building, I met a young couple who lived on our (my) floor. I said hello first. They gave me a friendly glance in the strong glow of the street lamps and both returned my greeting politely. Evidently they were on their way home from a party. I walked to a post office that was open at night in order to wire my stepdaughter, who I assumed was still at the spa with her husband. I handed in the message marked urgent but then noticed that I had no cash on me. In view of the content of the message, the clerk was kind enough to send the telegram for me on credit. I wanted to leave my watch with him as a deposit, but he refused this with a smile. Perhaps, too, my father's name was not unknown to him.

It occurred to me that I might tell my father what had happened before doing anything else, or rather it did not "occur" to me, I was simply unable to resist the mad urge. I had to do it. I called a cab and went to his house. His servant of many years opened the door. He reluctantly agreed to wake the old man. I followed him into my father's bedroom.

Once again I heard him, as I had in my childhood, grinding his teeth fiercely in his sleep. The room, crowded with elegant furniture and antiquities, was dark and gloomy. He had become a collector in his latter days.

I had difficulty waking him. He fell asleep with difficulty, he awoke with difficulty. He threw himself furiously about, croaked and beat with both fists on the blue silk quilt. At last he opened his eyes. Why did he resist awakening so much? He stared at the light of the lamp I had turned on, like a hen at the butcher knife. From below came the honking of the cabdriver, whom I had asked to wait without paying him. I stared too, gazing at my father, at this white-haired, blue-eyed old man. He was the one I hated, not my wife. I asked my father for money. A lot of money. He should have asked why, but he did not give me that. He did not ask, Why do you come in the middle of the night, wake me up, and demand money? He bit his lip, turned his face to the wall, and did not reply. The servant, who had retreated as far as the door, was silent too. He yawned discreetly. My father yawned openly.

At last he was sufficiently lucid. He turned to me, eyeing me as though I were an adolescent son asking him for money to meet paltry obligations. With his scrawny hand he fumbled on the night table, where loose change lay next to an old pocket watch. Finally I lost patience. I ordered the servant to run down and pay the cabdriver, thus leaving me alone with my father. I sat on the edge of his bed. My father ran his fingers through his snow-white, still thick hair, then wrapped his long, gaunt body more tightly in the bedclothes, rolled over again, a little closer to the wall, as though avoiding contact with my coat. And yet he knew nothing! Had he always been so observant, such a good judge of character? I took a carafe of water from the night table, poured out a glass. I put it in front of me without drinking from it. My father looked surprised, but still said nothing. Was he half asleep even now? How was it that an old man slept as soundly as a child? But he had to wake up eventually. I gave him the full glass. I made him drink it, and only now did he come to full awareness and take fright.

I will never forget what happened then.

But just the fact of it. My motive, what drove me to do it, that had become inexplicable to me even five minutes later, and five minutes earlier I had had no premonition.

It arrived like a shot from a pistol, or, to use a more topical expression, from a Pravaz syringe, or like a torpedo from a submarine, or like a poison gas bomb out of a clear sky. I torpedoed the old man with a brief report of the incident. This "torpedo," the response to another that had been launched fifteen years earlier, had an incredible effect. As an experimental dog, unprepared by anesthesia, howls when its peritoneum is opened with a neat incision, so my father began to howl. Only not so loudly. But so horribly that I immediately held his lips shut. At first he bit into the ball of my thumb, but then he understood the necessity of his silence and frantically held my hand more tightly against his flaccid lips and his silky, warm mustache.

And if what I had done made no sense, what he did was no better. Without giving me any counsel (at that point there were still many expedients that might have saved me), he sprang shakily out of bed, dressed in frenzied haste, rushed behind my back (I stood trembling at the window, looking out) to the door, then through the hall and down the stairs. It all happened in no time. Despite his age, he moved so fast that he was able to overtake the cabdriver. For the latter, drowsy as drivers often are at such a late hour, had trundled off at a crawl after carefully counting the fare he had taken from the old servant and placed in the breast pocket of his leather jacket. My father leaped into the old crate, and away they went. I did not hear what he shouted to the cabdriver, I only saw him wave to the old servant, who had run after him and was still standing there despondently; then he had the cab roar off at high speed.

XI

I will now be extremely brief, despite the fact that what follows, what I wish to get out of the way in this section, the eleventh, is the bread and butter of that literary genre considered the most enthralling in our era, namely, the detective novel. What concerns me here is facts, such as those of the original "torpedo" episode, which dates back at least fifteen years now and in which my father plays a starring role, and then facts that did not come to light until after my sentencing, and also those later facts surrounding the figure of that friend (as I have actually only been able to call him since he ceased to be one) of my youth, Walter.

First, however, comes my return home (I went on foot, made detours, and it took me almost an hour), my surprise upon finding two burly uniformed policemen waiting for me on the dark landing. They brutally but adroitly seized me the moment I came through the entryway and turned on the stair light. And as, between them, I climbed our staircase with its clean, soft, dark blue velour carpet, half unconscious yet still composed, heart pounding madly, with teeth clenched and thus silent, their hands on my shoulders, I heard from above, through the open door of my apartment, the choked cries, the howling sobs of my stepdaughter, alternating with the soothing, solemnly drawling, oleaginous voice of my son-in-law, whose bromides, whose sonorous gentleness, kindness and manly compassion aroused in me the desire to throw up.

But, speaking of such things, I was now thrown upon the mercies of official justice. From that point on, I was never free again.

If only my father had listened sensibly that night, instead of cravenly running off! In comical disarray, the ends of his tie hanging down around his scrawny old man's neck, one of his suspenders dragging on the ground from under his coat, so that he tripped over it, he had valiantly fled from me, his son, because I had made him an unwelcome confession, one for which the grand old connoisseur of human nature had not been prepared. Yes, if only my father had consummated his life as an anarchist by showing at that moment that he was still equal to existence as it was, is, and will remain, yes, truly, if, in the expected war of all against one, he had bravely fought on the side of his best student, on the side of his sole *blood* relative, namely, my humble self, if he had at least *tried* to understand me at the point when I was involved with experiments quite different from his own, then everything would have turned out differently.

Far weaker, more morally mediocre, more banal spirits, such as my brother, whom he had always ridiculed by comparing him with me, have done far better. But now is not the time for that, when I am marching upstairs between the two police officers to be confronted with my son-in-law and my stepdaughter – and my victim. Poor old lady, who might have done me the favor of *voluntarily* departing this life if there had been some particular pleasure in it for her and some particular advantage for me! She loved me, after all. She was just made that way. The good dowager, over fifty, had endured all sorts of experiments (her loveless first marriage, for example) and had needed all that in order to arrive at a proper understanding of herself. Death at the moment of the greatest pain and pleasure was doubtless in her mind – here we had always understood one another. But her relatives had no grasp of the thing whatever, any more than did, later on, the superficial official justice that was not even at the level of a serving girl, and least of all popular morality as represented by the press. To the papers it was just a vulgar slaying, a kind of insurance murder by poison, I was a Landru with Toxin Y, and they simply let the facts speak for themselves (and against me) as brutally and nakedly as possible.

But how was this disaster possible? It all happened as quickly as a test-tube reaction.

Nothing could have been simpler. My wife, the only person who knew me, at least to some degree, the only person who saw me as I really was, at least from a certain angle, and who in only that way had any use for me, had for a long time not concealed from her relatives her dim perceptions, her fears, and her psychological insights. It was she herself who had had the idea that she should be protected from me, that she should be placed in isolation, even declared legally incompetent. Sensibly or foolishly, she had wanted to be saved from herself. It was she herself who had instructed that my correspondence be read when the circumstances were important, but that it not be shown to her. Her doglike dependence on me and her fear for her own life, these had battled within her – she had conducted experiments no less than I. Alongside these experiments were the usual diversions, amusements such as befitted her age, her finances, and her social position, all falling under the rubric of *bridge*, of course not an adequate means of fulfillment. One day she had given in to her destructive or self-destructive urges, had come to me. That had been in the afternoon. In the evening, when I entered the apartment and camped downstairs in the study, she had called her daughter and her son-in-law and in presentiment of her fate had summoned the two of them. The strange telephone calls, all three of them (or were there only two?), were from these relatives, though they came too late in any case.

And I, as confident as a sleepwalker, had behaved more idiotically than any idiot! Think of it! I leave the scene of the crime without having scrupulously destroyed the most important piece of evidence. I fail to mention the fact of my wife's death to the servants, to the neighbors encountered in the street that night. And that's not all! I make the most unnecessary disclosure imaginable to my father, an entirely irrelevant person in this regard, and produce in him an equally idiotic reaction, namely, his flight to City X on the next Nordbahn train. The next day he fails to appear at work (for the first and last time in his life!). The noose tightens around my neck still more – through my own doing and his. If he had at least given me the money, if not a hundred thousand, then at least enough for me to get a cab and drive back, I would have been at the scene of the crime an hour earlier, would have destroyed the vial in time. Only the first four hours were critical. After that nothing could have been proven. I would have had to hold out with my wife for those four hours.

No, if the old man was at fault, it lay deeper, it went back a long time. What had happened now was incidental. Why accuse him – I could have hired a cab even with no money in my pocket and paid the driver when I got home. I always had enough money around for that. I had just had a fit of blindness and stupidity. For what else can you call it when a thinking person, one with such a high opinion of himself that he believes he is capable of discovering the invisible scarlet-fever virus, when such a person advertises the visible proof, the palpable evidence of his criminal act, even though what he wants to do, what he has to do, is conceal it. I had run to the old man to confess to him, thereby helping him atone for *his* old sins. And on top of that the experimental error mentioned above, one of the grossest type. What had happened to the vial containing Toxin Y? Instead of destroying it (washing it out under the tap, scratching off the label, tossing the empty vial out onto the street, along with the syringe) – instead of doing that, I throw the glass container, stoppered, containing a quite considerable residue of Toxin Y, into the toilet bowl in my wife's small, almond green private lavatory. And do I at least pull the chain, to wash the thing into the sewer main?

By no means. And the syringe? No, this too I fail to destroy. It remains in the bedroom, lying on a glass tabletop. I was so used to having it around, that precisely made, delicate little instrument!

So I considerately put weapons into my enemies' hands. My wife's sudden death, my unwillingness to prevail upon the neighborhood physician however reluctant he was to come at night, my refusal to attempt the recommended camphor or caffeine injection (we had camphor and caffeine in the house because my wife had become a hypochondriac after her illness and knew about their effects), the syringe with the slightly bloody needle on the night table next to the lamp, above all the little vial that now lay on the mirrored tabletop, conscientiously placed in evidence and open to official scrutiny, its label already half dry! – And the handwriting, becoming clearer every moment as the label dried, was mine and no one else's. – What remained of the whitish crystalline powder could be identified from my experimental animals as extremely toxic, as a first-quality coagulant poison; my wife's blood could and would be analyzed; everything pointed in one direction, and any amateur would be able to provide rigorous proof of the crime. That is, prove *what* had occurred. But to prove *why* it had occurred? That was the task of the court. But only the person who had understood all this could *sit in judgment*. Ultimately only I could judge this murder.

XII

The case was so hopelessly clear that lying was obviously not a practical response. Given that the crime was one that needed to be understood in psychological terms, it may seem that a more promising approach might have been to present oneself to the judges trying the case as an entirely bestial, pathological personality who had acted in a fit of unbridled rage and who therefore – and this is what rules out this at-first-blush viable approach – belonged, not on the scaffold, nor in prison or the penal colony for life, but permanently under lock and key. Many people would undoubtedly find the prospect of lifelong confinement in an asylum a better fate than execution or deportation. But I did not.

I lived through several weeks in the psychiatric observation unit of the remand prison infirmary. With the help of my lawyer, my father had seen to it that I be subjected to a court-ordered mental examination. I endured one grilling after another by doctors and intelligence tests that lasted for hours and made me appear an idiot; I attempted, while in constant visible, audible, and tangible proximity to raving, raging, shrieking, howling, babbling, self-lacerating, excrement-eating persons, in the presence of the authentically mentally ill, of persons with incurable intellectual and emotional disorders, I attempted, summoning all my strength and all my resources, to feign illness. But I did not keep it up long enough – and I will say: though their very lives may depend on it, ninety out of a hundred men are not capable of feigning severe mental illness, beyond a certain point, without falling prey to it.

For me the universe has never been built on entirely sound foundations. I have already said that in my youth I became, under the influence of my father, an anarchist, an atheist, and a negativist to the point of being a cynic. In addition to this the internal pressure (call it conscience or whatever you want, you will never grasp it), in addition lack of sleep, in addition the continuous observation, the formulaic questions, driven into an unstable person's soul as though with a sharp chisel, of the court psychiatrist, "court" being the operative word, in addition the bad food, the squalor, the latter all the worse the more one gives in to one's own destructive urges and wrecks everything there is to be wrecked in one's cell. (Who is not tempted now and again to smash everything in sight to bits?)

No one who has not experienced it could imagine the boundless exhaustion and enervation produced by being constantly face-to-face with oneself, the nights, the dreams, and nothing but a hostile atmosphere on every side – yes, Georg Letham the younger, did you expect a seaside holiday?

No matter, the day comes when your resistance breaks and you capitulate. Like a true madman I yearned to speak rationally, eat normally again, and it was high time. I was skeletally emaciated, and any force of mind I may have had was gone. My bones were poking through my skin, causing sores on the thin, dry, withered skin at the small of my back and beneath my shoulder blades.

Most terrible of all was that, one night, toward daybreak, I realized I had no hope of hope anymore. And that I had had no "hope of hope" since that rainy night. It was toward morning, at an hour when the truly criminally insane and the malingerers alike, through either natural tiredness or the effect of soporifics (usually scopolamine in powerful doses), grew quiet and slept. I was the only one for whom the effect of the soporific never lasted until breakfast (or what went by that name – a bowl of soup and a piece of bread, no spoon, no sharp-edged utensils). I was never able to sleep through until six. Ideas and words became a confusion then, thinking a sluggish muddle, difficult to describe.

That night I lay on my stomach to protect the skin on my back. It may be that the circulation in this unnatural position put particular strain on the cardiac muscle, burdened the pulmonary artery – I don't know why, but I had to get out, I couldn't stand myself any longer. I reported my "recovery" to the alarmed senior attendant, finding the words with difficulty, I wanted to have the doctor, the examining magistrate, my father, my attorney, you name it, I don't know who all, summoned in the middle of the night, but the management had its immutable rules, I was told to be patient. I was a confessed criminal, and alone.

But I didn't settle down, I couldn't. Bottled up within me were all sorts of things that are hard to put into words, I was driven to give vent to my hopelessness, impotently now, yes, I was a thousand times more impotent now than I had ever been! I shouted till I was hoarse and physically could not shout, only croak; only the truly raving mad had the hang of yelling all night without hoarseness. I, who had just confessed to having feigned madness, destroyed everything I could get my hands on. That was not much. Only my blankets, woolen, not too thin, had to go. I bit into them, tore off shreds with my teeth, at that time still in fine fettle, the primitive needs of the body made themselves felt – and I – I don't want to say it, any more than I have been able so far to describe specifically, in detail, the moment of my crime, I will only suggest that that morning I committed all the bestial depravities that I had heard described in paralytics as part of the lecture course on mental illnesses that I had taken as a young student. In others – and now I was seeing them, I was experiencing them in myself! My revulsion, in what lucid faculties I had left, against this animalistic raving, can scarcely be expressed, be communicated, in simple language. For one who has experienced this, the prospect of a quick punishment cutting things short, such as execution, will no longer seem so awful.

That terrible night and the next morning were a further step in the toughening process that my father had begun more than twenty years before. And it was me giving myself the lesson! To the staff – as in all such institutions, the staff was vastly overworked and jaded, had become cynical and dehumanized (and very likely had to be) – to them my case was clear. I had after all previously reported that I was of sound mind! I was no longer of interest.

Worn down and broken down (like so many before me), I had given up my hunger strike. I was therefore taken off the list of those who had to be fed through a rubber stomach tube. I had talked reasonably, and I no longer had to be given a shot of scopolamine in the evening. If I raged now, it was for my own pleasure. I attracted not a smidgen more interest than a dog in my laboratory attracts when it spins in circles behind the iron bars of its cage, howls frenziedly, and (after the experiment is over) tears the dressing off its wound. Thus do all things return in this short life! What would not return given an eternity!

I had had my father notified. He had been the one to suggest to me – not personally, through my defense counsel – that I be portrayed as mentally ill. In the interim he had requested retirement. The request was still pending, but he was supposed to be indispensable, irreplaceable. Now he had withdrawn from the world (though he was still continuously, without respite, pestered by newspapers greedy for novelty and sensation). Perhaps, in his rooms stuffed with art treasures and precious natural history specimens, he spent nights as sleepless and anguished as my own. All that is as may be, it may be that, his health weakened, a broken old man, he no longer felt strong enough to see me. He did not come.

My elder brother did come (evidently my father had only now given him permission, for what could have stood in the way of his visiting me long before?). He was frightened out of his wits when he saw me the morning after my "recovery," almost completely naked, smeared with my own excrement, starved to the bone. He had me moved to another cell. He was extraordinarily energetic (energy, the only thing he inherited from our father – and yet it was not the same implacable force of will) in arranging to be left with me day and night until I had regained a semblance of human appearance and understanding.

We had never been close before. He was a normal sort, the kind that come a dime a dozen, but here he mattered more to me than all of human society.

For the first time in years, I spent hours in conversation – no, they were something other than "conversations," they were meetings of minds, communions of souls, using the medium of words and simple human contact. If it can be said that I was in any way up to life again after that, I owe it to him. Let it be said to his credit, to the credit of mankind generally.

XIII

But I was far from being the person I had been before my crime.

I returned to prison from the observation unit.

During this entire period, that is, after I returned to prison and before my trial, I labored under a mental and spiritual paralysis. Past kept to a minimum, future to nothing, the main thing was the present, the moment. Possibly the life I was now compelled to lead was what caused this paralysis. Only things I could perceive directly concerned me – what I heard from adjoining cells, what filled the hours of the day for me and the others, what kind of food I was given, how I passed the nights, what visits I was permitted to receive, what my brother brought me, etc., etc.

One day my brother gave me some flowers, highly cultivated sweet peas, if I remember correctly. Formerly any kind of aesthetic beauty had enchanted me, I was a slave to the beautiful, the perfect, the unspoiled, as though under a spell – which may not be believable in view of my marriage and my profession, but so it was. Now, although the pale red flowers with their silken or creamy sheen aroused my interest, it was in quite a different way. I began to lay them out flat, to mount them using the pins from the tissue-paper wrapping, then to carefully dissect them, anatomize them, employing, for lack of a knife, the long nail of my right little finger, for which purpose I had given it an edge and a point as sharp as possible by honing it on the wall during my conversation with my brother, as he looked on in astonishment.

The anatomy of the sweet-pea blossom and stalk, the remarkable arrangement of the plant's vessels (like an animal, a plant has vessels), with this I was able to occupy myself for hours. My attorney, who took turns with my brother in visiting me during these strange days, was far-sighted, wore a monocle. I appropriated it and had in my possession a magnifying glass that was not half bad. Thus I spent an evening that was less dull and a night more tranquil than usual. This is just one example of the benefit my brother conferred upon me with his visits.

It was thus my brother, not my father, who succeeded in gradually ridding me of this derangement of sorts. It may be that immediately following my crime I needed a numbness of this kind in order to go on living at all.

But even now, in this less critical period, the idea of taking my life would not have appeared exactly absurd to me, and I believe there can be few lawbreakers who would recoil categorically from such a thought. More than one murderer or burglar or sex criminal would voluntarily put a painless end to his life if it were made sufficiently easy for him to do so. If gas valves were left within reach in the cells, so-called justice would be spared a good deal of effort, effort that is often very unproductive. But there can be no hope of such a happy solution immediately following the sudden change of feeling at the peak moment of the act itself. Later comes that stage focused on the present moment – that horribly passive, neutered, emasculated existence in the cell, which I now had behind me. And then at last comes the period of reawakening, of putting on the new man. And this "new man" now understands the awful turn that fate has taken and would be only too glad to exempt himself from its inescapable dictates.

This is of interest from the standpoint of so-called justice. During the trial, all the delinquent moments in a life will dramatically unfold once again. The crime will be committed *again* in the mind's eye. It will not be buried, even if justice finds itself played for a fool when the prisoner hangs himself before he can be tried! The crime will be resurrected, by the perpetrator's confession, his identification of himself, even his lack of contrition. And then, only then, as consolation for everyone else, comes the expiation, the neutralization of the crime, the "practical repentance" that is thought to be the proper punishment of the broken sinner.

My brother (I cannot repeat it often enough, so that the illusions I had about him will be understood), it was my brother who brought me back to life. And, why should I deny it, he did me good. Too much good. I awaited his arrival with longing, I liked to hear his voice. It was late summer, still very warm, especially in the narrow cell, a small window its only link to the outside world. He was perspiring, the philtrum in his upper lip, in the shadow of his somewhat stubby nose, filling up with crystalline beads of sweat that he wiped away with a self-conscious smile, stretching his broad shoulders and breathing deeply. On his brow, which was not exactly lofty, grew a great many tiny golden blond hairs (I had never noticed them before, and yet he had certainly had this peculiarity from childhood), coming to a little point at the bottom, a fairly dense down that, especially in a raking light, glinted metallically like mature crops in the distance. His teeth, which he revealed when he laughed (*he* still laughed, though now only rarely when he was with me!), were strong, with little gaps between them, yellowish white, short; the healthy bright red gums were broad. He wore his dark blond hair combed up *en brosse*.

But he already had lines on his forehead, quite deep ones, just below the downy little blond hairs. They were not worry lines, though. He said they came from spending every free moment outside with his wife and kids, preferably in the blazing sun. Knitting his eyebrows there had made the wrinkles carve themselves deeply between his eyes above the bridge of his nose, much too deeply for his age. I saw them when we sat together reading, bent over a book or a newspaper. Both of us silent and full of cares.

Was it any wonder? He must have known what it was to worry about putting food on the table, and not just by hearsay, given his low earnings and his rapidly growing family. My brother had as little money as I did. The fourth child was on the way. My father only laughed. No one would get any money from him before his death, he said. That way he could make his children do what he wanted.

My brother was often gloomy. The worry that his wife might work herself into such a state over my trial that she "deteriorated," that is, lost the child through miscarriage, preoccupied him more than he let on.

One day I had been discussing my case with my attorney for more than an hour. My attorney too lived in a present-tense delirium, if I may put it that way: neither past nor future events interested him except insofar as they bore on the present situation, on the pending trial in my case, and thus also on his reputation as a "legendary" criminal defender.

Thus he simply accepted the facts as the basis for his work, which very much facilitated our relations. He asked neither too much nor too little. He did not probe, nor provoke me. He was uninterested in my crime, did not pry into its psychological motives, but spoke only of the impression that the facts must make on the court and the jury – in a word, he was more a journalist concerned with current events than a philosopher concerned with the eternal, more a dispassionate natural scientist studying a pathological character than an interpreter and arbiter of a legal principle that had been violated. Unlike everyone else, he viewed my situation as by no means hopeless.

My brother often pestered me with stupid questions: For God's sake, how could you . . . someone like you! etc. All that was missing was for him to discover in me, as my feebleminded senile patient once had, a "loving heart." Thus he was mistaken about me. But was I, neither feebleminded nor senile as I was, not equally mistaken about him?

Only the attorney was unsurprised by anyone or anything. Since the thing had happened, it had had to happen. Facts = law, reality = necessity. As he saw it, my wife's death could be presented to the jury, men of modest intellect, as due to gross negligence on my part. In an unaccountable oversight, I had – on this basis he constructed his system, his plan – administered a second injection to my wife instead of the desired analgesic; in the dark, the excitement, I had made a mistake. Hence my panicky behavior afterward. As he would have it, I had always been a poor physician and had neglected my practice for good reason – the less I did as a physician, the more I was a benefactor of mankind. I had just made a tragic "mistake."

He thought anything was possible. I thought that only what had actually occurred was possible. The facts *had* to have a meaning, if only a terrible one. Whatever had produced the consequences that had in turn become efficient causes. But he was counting on my instinct of self-preservation. Inserting his (my) monocle thoughtfully, he told me he had never been wrong. In order to save myself, I would play before the court the remorseful offender breaking down on the stand, the clumsy doctor whose dear wife had suffered from his blunder.

A man whose neck was on the line would take the initiative and do everything humanly possible to avoid the death sentence, would he not? What could be more natural? I owe the reader an explanation, but now I want to discuss some other debts – claims by my old creditors for comparatively large sums, but also comparatively small bills for the rent of our apartment, my poor wife's burial, the plot in the churchyard, other routine amounts for servants' wages, for electricity, telephone service, etc.

My father no longer wanted to be my father. Son-in-law and daughter-in-law did not come through with a penny. They could not be forced to.

The office of my Herr Attorney for the Defense received monthly bills from the Pathology Institute for the upkeep of experimental animals. One evening, when the attorney had gone and my brother appeared (thanks to my name and my former social position, I had far more extensive visitation rights than most), I offered the good man my experimental animals – guinea pigs, puppy dogs, and some few goats and monkeys – as a small private menagerie for his boys. How his face lit up at my thoughtful gesture! Never before had I accorded my nephews the slightest thing in the way of a gift. But then he had concerns about the danger of infection and the maintenance costs. We gave the animals to the city zoo. He seemed happy to have snatched them from a death by vivisection. He had a good nature. How he could laugh now, sharing the optimism of the attorney, even here – even with me there! It was infectious and he made me happy for a moment. I imitated his laughter – and that made him laugh even more. That evening (autumn was already approaching) I did not dissect his flowers. Later the night was peaceful and my sleep deep.

XIV

"Defend yourself, dear doctor, I don't understand you!" the attorney often said to me when, during the periods of questioning by the examining magistrate, which could go on for hours, he had seen me sitting almost silent, seemingly apathetic, profoundly uninvolved, smoking one cigarette after another and rubbing the dry palms of my hands together. The rubbing produced a strange singed odor, particularly in dry weather. I breathed in this odor, bringing my palms toward my face mechanically. I was barely listening to the aggressive insinuations of the examining magistrate. Perhaps I was reminded of the odor my wife had had about her, which had also struck me as "singed."

The examining magistrates now suspected that I had not committed my crime intentionally – but the court psychiatrists had not found in my mental state the necessary evidence of certifiable insanity as defined by law.

Yet my father still, more than ever now, spared no effort in trying to have me committed as a mental patient. But my memories of the psychiatric observation unit were so terrible that I opposed this with all my strength. Better decapitated than decerebrated! Better dead than mad! My brother and my attorney backed me up. My brother's reasoning was based on his naïve belief in miracles; the attorney trusted that any circumstantial evidence would have sufficient shortcomings, and he was constantly warning me just not to say too much. What an unnecessary thing to ask! I had learned restraint. I was doggedly silent during the questioning periods, even though it is generally among the very worst mental torments to be harassed for hours on end by questions rephrased again and again. The judges, police inspectors, and so forth, traded off, I thought. They even set the chaplain at my throat, repeatedly. Events long past, such as the unsuccessful operations, were brought up and sifted through. They were described imprecisely and inaccurately, yet there was no way to object.

A half an hour of it is all right, you close your ears, you busy yourself with something, with voluptuously lingering over a cigarette, say, or with looking at your surroundings, the inkstands, blotters, faces, the sky that can be glimpsed through the poorly cleaned windowpanes. But then it becomes more and more difficult. Not that it would have driven me to a confession as the attorney feared. Not at that time. But the prisoner yearns for peace. Peace, quiet! A lie, some incomplete, equivocal utterance, would stop those probing questions repeated over and over and over once and for all. Or the truth would. The temptation to speak becomes stronger and stronger. Just so he stops! You bite down with your upper incisors as hard as you can against the lower – a not entirely natural defensive reaction, for, as anyone can verify for himself, maxilla and mandible normally meet in such a way that the lower row of teeth makes contact behind the upper, about three-quarters of a centimeter back, that is, not incisal edge against edge. Who cares? Why does it matter? But this is the kind of thing you work out, dream up, while the inquisitorial examining magistrate's drill buzzes into your brain, to no effect but still excruciatingly.

The observations you can make while getting the third degree in your chair are limited – silly ones of no scientific value. Eventually it became my only goal, in compensation for my loss of freedom, to make it through the many examinations without confessing, and without lying, either. For any lie would have turned into a confession. I have always had a sense of logic and coherence and I would not have been able to sustain an internally flawed structure. The facts were so very solid. Even though it was *my* crime!

The great difference in age between my wife and me, the marriage that had been contracted largely for financial reasons, the will benefiting myself, the insurance enriching the surviving spouse, with me needing those riches so very much and my wife almost not at all, my alleged propensity toward acts of cruelty, the outbursts of violent, ruthless temperament, and above all the direct evidence of my crime, Toxin Y, which on the fateful day I had taken from the locked reagent cabinet in the laboratory. I could have brought it to my apartment only by deliberate plan. My wife's sudden death showing signs of intravascular coagulation, the strokelike collapse. My father's sudden flight, etc., etc.

The gears meshed tooth for tooth, in fact they meshed too well.

I did not speak. They made me stand now. But I looked at the gentlemen and was silent. The gentlemen looked at me and were doubtful. At the end of the presentation of evidence, the examining magistrates and later the jury too had their doubts about the "truth," because it seemed just too simple! So this is how it was. Serious, but not hopeless.

I might still have been able to save myself after all, it is at least possible, if only I had been able to enlist people's sympathy. But I was not. I breathed a sigh of relief every time I was back in my cell after the interrogations. They were terrible, especially when I was dragged out of bed and marched off for questioning.

Over the long term it was not entirely easy for me to carry on extended conversations with my brother about things of less direct concern to him or to me than my crime and its consequences. But even where my crime was concerned I had nothing enlightening to tell him, although he was waiting for something and would have been overjoyed if I had told him, *lied* to him, that I was innocent, that it was all just a misunderstanding or heaven knows what. I couldn't! I couldn't!

He came to see me shortly before my trial. He brought me some clean laundry and put the dirty laundry in a briefcase. At the end of his long visit, during which I had said nothing serious or to the point for many hours, I went to signal the turnkey to let him out as he stood at the door (I have already said that visitation was very humanely administered in my case, in marked contrast to the period following the verdict). I saw that his hands, clasped over the shabby briefcase stuffed with clothes, were perspiring heavily and trembling violently. He had lowered his eyelids, his mouth was half open. The light from the bare electric bulb on the ceiling of the cell glinted on his thick, dark blond, clean brush cut, the style favored by so many good petty officials.

He wanted to tell me something, perhaps give me a word of advice, or perhaps he wanted to slip me a sacramental charm for my trial – to this day I do not know. He had always been very devout – like my father – and yet devout in a way quite unlike the nasty old man. It was only now, when I was in my fortieth, he in his forty-third year, that we had gotten to know one another. But he said nothing more, and I too was silent. When the guard's footsteps were audible in the flagstoned corridor (it had never been so late before), I told him he would hear something good from me yet. His eyes lit up, he spread his arms, the briefcase fell to the floor with a smack. But he did not embrace me, nor did we say anything more. But it seemed that he left me consoled.

Was it not a topsy-turvy world in which, on the eve of a man's trial, one in which his life is at stake, he consoles his older brother, instead of conversely? Though the "consolation" I offered consisted in something entirely material. The original medicine for "loving hearts" – money. It was the first time I had ever given someone a present of any magnitude, and the first time I had had anything to do with a person without making him the subject of an experiment. For my financial status had changed entirely as the result of my wife's death. To be sure, I had not become her heir. Whether I was condemned or was acquitted (but how could I be acquitted?), in no event would the tiniest fraction of *her* assets come into my possession. But the insurance was a different matter. I asked my attorney, and he agreed. The insurance policy dealt with the claims of the survivor, but nowhere in its many paragraphs were there any particulars about the circumstances under which one spouse became the survivor. The company could sue, of course. But my claim was incontrovertible. I had not taken out the policy. So there could not be anything "immoral" about the policy, whether I was a criminal now or not. I, or, in case I was convicted, my designated assignee, would have to come into effective possession of that very large sum. On the evening before the first day of the trial, I drafted a will, worded to be simultaneously a deed of gift. In it I named my brother and his children as my heirs. I could assume now that they would receive this inheritance after my "demise" under any circumstances. Even if I was sentenced to deportation or a relatively lengthy prison term, they would immediately come into possession of the money.

On the night before the trial, I slept like a log.

XV

The proceedings went as I had expected. For the murder of my wife, committed by poisoning, I was sentenced to hard labor for life in C. All the facts of my life were regarded as incriminating, with the exception of my zealous service on the military hygiene task force during the war. To this latter fact I owe the decision not to impose the death penalty. I will not recount here all the phases of the trial, which was, I might note, at no point dramatic, at best theatrical sometimes. What would be the point of bringing my stepdaughter from the wings to pointedly ask of the assembled court, "How can I live without my mama?" or my son-in-law to ball his neatly gloved fists and threaten to spring at me, at the man, that is, whose crime had brought him a fortune of millions? What would be accomplished by repeating my concierge's statements about my private life, or the account of a full-bearded, stammering, dark-spectacled department head from the Pathology Institute speaking evasively about my scientific work and, when pressed by the prosecuting attorney, ascribing to me (a) amateurish abilities and knowledge; (b) erratic interest in my scientific experiments – excessive enthusiasm alternating with laziness; and (c) a dark, withdrawn cast of mind in our personal dealings, something I had never thought I had? What would that prove?

It was certainly of greater consequence that my father, at that time long retired from the civil service and in every respect his own master, scorned to meet me face-to-face in the courtroom or testify for or against me. He gave evidence by proxy only, asserting his right to refuse to answer questions as a witness (did he have that right?).

But what was most painful for me was the fact that I did not see my brother, either among the witnesses or among the spectators. He had hardly figured in my past, but his role in my present was immense. I could not understand why he had not appeared.

I asked my attorney, who was astonished at my "impatience." Perhaps I was less "criminal," a person of lesser caliber, than he had assumed. He thought I must surely have had other worries.

Anyway he soon lost interest in me after the verdict. Though he did initiate the obligatory formal appeals procedure, clearly nothing could be expected from this step. He now came to the prison only rarely. All my visits were much more stringently monitored now, I wore the prescribed costume, I was subject to prison discipline, made my circuit of the yard, hands folded behind my back, on Sunday I heard (or did not hear) Mass, and time passed. The number of letters I could send was regulated, as was my activity, my cell had to be kept far tidier – but my psychological paralysis still had not entirely resolved. This circumstance was preventing me from regaining clear, responsible consciousness.

When I came from the mental ward to the prison, I was like someone entering a monastery after a terrible catastrophe. I wanted peace and quiet above all (or the death of the spirit); freedom was secondary. The import of a "sentence" had not yet dawned on me.

But the tedium gradually became very oppressive. I applied to the prison administration for work as a clerk. My request went completely unacknowledged. Perhaps I had not submitted it to the right office. The chaplain had the most influence on the premises, but I had never dignified his driveling missionary efforts with a response. Was I to bare my heart and my innermost motivations to *him*, when I had not bared them to my father, my brother, my attorney? But perhaps I had underestimated how helpful and also how dangerous he could be. It was on him that the type and quantity of reading material allowed to fall into my hands, classified by "level," depended. Any institution allows for small but over time very significant acts of preferential and discriminatory treatment. There will be loopholes in "house rules" seemingly covering every detail: unpleasant severities for this person, compensatory, palliative benefits for that one.

An intellectually responsible person bears up under solitary confinement, isolation, being alone with himself, quite differently from an intellectually lazy one. But – this was my good fortune – at that time I was not remotely among the intellectually living. Only very slowly did my past, from childhood on, begin to come to life in me. I had become a gloomy monk without a monastery and without belief. It took a long time for me to recall, bit by bit, my younger self, my childhood, the crucial experiences of my youth, my father, the house that had been my home.

I had often been sleepless before my crime. Also when I was in the observation ward among the mentally ill. But after that, even during the trial, I became hypersomniac, always tired, apathetic – heavy limbs, dull thoughts, no will, no pain – in a word, paralyzed. Hence, too, my yawning during the final statements. It honestly was not bravado, not a cynical gesture.

The date of our upcoming little cruise was uncertain. We communicated with one another as prisoners do everywhere. It was important to many to maintain contact with the outside world so that they could put their private affairs in order before they were deported to C., receive gift parcels, amass as much money as possible, and, as its possession was indispensable but forbidden, find ways to smuggle it onto the ship and to C.

There were frequent rumors about our departure date, circulated by knocking on the walls. Everyone prepared feverishly, but for administrative reasons nothing happened.

Now, when we were all under the authority of a state institution, we saw the injustice of every action taken by it, its mindless belief that it always did the right thing, its sluggish pace in getting anything done, its dreary self-importance, the sloppiness of its bureaucracy. Yet it was still a model facility, and commissions from foreign countries visited the building and observed the inmates, took notes, tried to learn things. To us such a visit was always a sort of change and thus always a pleasure.

We all yearned for pleasure, even if it was just malicious pleasure. I felt strangely gratified, if I can put it that way, when I realized that I had acquired a strong sense of schadenfreude. It was clear that misery loved company in my case just because at bottom I couldn't care less about the suffering of others and was if anything elated by it. It comforted me! I would never have believed it of myself before, but there it was. Perhaps my total isolation had had its effect.

I speak of total isolation, but I mean only being separated from my father and especially from my brother, my last and most unfortunate love. Most people start there, but that is where I ended, or thought I had ended. My brother's withdrawal, his lapse into silence. If only I had heard from him, even the tiniest sign of life! I knew that the prisoners around me received letters, ones that were permitted and ones that had been smuggled in. Now and then I heard my neighbors being taken to the visiting rooms for fifteen-minute visiting periods, particularly when a trial date had been set. I was never summoned.

Never? No, I exaggerate. My attorney looked in on me one more time, that was all.

On one occasion one of my neighbors returned sobbing to his cell. I heard him throw himself onto the floor, howling dismally. This was not permitted. He had to get up at once. The turnkey on his rounds showed military strictness in making sure the prisoners lay down neither on the floor nor on the bed that was supposed to be folded up into the wall during the day. But this man must have received bad news from home. Had his child, his sweetheart, his best friend kicked the bucket? I don't know. I knocked, I signaled to beat the band, but he did not answer. There was no distracting him from his animal howling and rolling about on the floor. It put me in good spirits.

So there were still people who were more miserable than I. People who were not as hardened as my father's son. Abruptly I thought of my brother. What could be the reason for his terrible silence? I evolved a lot of fanciful theories and yet never felt I had gotten to the bottom of it. Probably I understood him as poorly as he did me. Or was he dead? Dead? Of him I used the word "die," of the others "kick the bucket."

But the chaplain would not have withheld this news, though it would have been artfully put as always. Coming from him it would certainly have taken the form of a "lesson" for me!

I was sleeping less at night than had been usual for me. The fellow in the next cell moaned piteously and his bed creaked miserably. I heard everything clearly in the deathlike silence of the great building. Rats, those dear rodents, rustled and scurried as they had once in my parents' house. And on my dear father's ship, which I often thought of, stuck in the arctic ice during his voyage. I saw my father standing on deck, cradling two rats in his arms, his sons, my brother and me. I awoke in fright and lay there for a long time. At last I fell asleep again. I dreamed of an almond green, already somewhat wilted sweet pea, a flower similar to the one I had dissected and magnified using my attorney's monocle. The parts that had been cut to pieces reassembled themselves, sepals, nectaries, cellulose fibers, sap vessels, and respiratory organs, the male and female reproductive parts of the plant, and they turned into a living flower. It rose stiffly, oozing sap, from a piece of white blotting paper covered with black mirror writing, as though it were growing out of the ground. Unfortunately my wife appeared in the same dream.

Her image came into my mind for the first time since her death. I saw her, her face withered, wrapped in a crinkled, light pink crepe gown, looking out a window of my apartment. The window was framed by cream-colored, embroidered drapes. My wife was laughing with one half of her face, crying with the other, one corner of her large mouth turned up, the other drawn down as though squeezed inside. She was grinning, filled with pain and voluptuous feelings at once, as so often in life. Her teeth were falling out, she tried in vain to keep them in, push them back, with her long tongue. Then she sadly regarded the ruins of former magnificence, she spoke, I nodded and did not understand her, she suddenly stepped back behind the curtains, spread them across her strong dark breast, which was markedly chilly, deathly cold to the touch. But now I was behind her, more or less at her feet. I came up to her knees. The varicose veins in her calves had shrunken so much that the heavy golden brown silk stockings bagged. Someone had to feel sorry for this creature, and yet I could not arrive at any *remorse*. My crime had therefore been necessary, had come from the heart. I thought of my father, as of a judge. But even then I was not sorry. What can you do! What must be must be.

XVI

An imprisoned criminal is a wretched thing. The crime that he attempted, using every means at his disposal, has failed. Yes, I had gotten rid of my wife, and that was worth something. But I was beginning to understand that my freedom from her had come at no small cost. I had carried my plan through to her detriment, no doubt, but not to my benefit. Before that decisive moment, my life had been a very dubious business. Now it might become a very miserable one. In fact it certainly would and I needed all the willpower I had to keep from breaking down, as I had that night in the mental ward when the ghastly conduct of those around me had disturbed me so much that I had pronounced myself sane. I was now beginning to doubt my sanity with some frequency. I was as insensible as a stone, I devoured whatever was put in front of me, I relieved myself in a tub holding a few liters because our institution, wildly praised by the experts as it had been, did not even possess the convenience of a W.C. In sane times I had always set great store by personal hygiene. Quite apart from bourgeois decorum, a bacteriologist, a physician, cannot survive without the most meticulous personal hygiene. How low I had fallen! I was shaved once a week, got a haircut once a month. There was scant soap, a towel had to last longer than I preferred. I therefore took care not to get it dirty, that is, not to use it. And likewise with everything else! I began to suffer from dental calculus. One day a crumbly, foul-smelling crust fell from my teeth, calculus that had accreted due to poor nourishment. I felt with my tongue along the inside of my teeth. There seemed to be a decayed spot on the lower right premolar.

The prison doctor – not one of the worst, by the way, even if I received the same indifferent treatment that everyone else did – found no caries, though I tossed and turned almost all night with gnawing toothache. He had me brought in again the next day – and found nothing. The same story the day after that. Finally the overworked man, who was as pasty as his patients, directed the mirror to the place I described and found a decayed spot. I expected that he would treat the tooth, or rather the root. But without a word he showed me his primitive equipment, two pairs of forceps from the previous century. He gestured, again without explanation, toward the long line of emaciated, coughing, hollow-eyed prisoners with intestinal and skin disorders who all had to be dealt with in the next half hour. For this exemplary institution for the warehousing of human vermin had no paid full-time physician, but – aside from numerous higher officials inspecting and supervising – only this one frazzled, weary medical day laborer, who treated prisoners only as an extra job and received a pathetic starvation wage from the government.

He had me wait outside and when consulting hours were over again offered to pull the tooth. I recoiled. Was I so cowardly that I feared the pain of a tooth extraction without cocaine? Was I so vain that I did not want to have a gap in my otherwise beautiful, closely spaced teeth? Formerly I had visited my dentist every three months, I had tended my teeth with the greatest care. I shook my head and left the doctor's office, a small, artificially lit, suffocatingly smelly room full of the effluvia of scruffy, ill-washed men.

Three adjoining cell-like rooms were set up as sick bays. Only the most serious patients, the hopeless ones, were sent to the prison hospital.

That day I finally received another visit from my attorney, in response to my repeated requests. He was in a hurry, did not take off his overcoat, confused my affairs with those of another of his clients, excused himself with the explanation that he was swamped with work but gave me to understand in passing that he had been unable to collect his fee; my father had refused to pay for anything unless he could be held liable for it. The old man may have rhetorically commiserated with me, but at the same time he had announced his decision to apply to the Ministry of the Interior for a legal name change. I was much too dulled, much too wrapped up in my own suffering, to be affected by this dramatic gesture. For the time of our departure was approaching, I needed gear, I needed money. The attorney was astonished that I was asking *him* for money! Had he not already done everything humanly possible for me and done it all for charity, a wage unpopular with busy lawyers?

I suggested to him that available assets of mine had to exist in such an amount that the small sums of money for him and for me were negligible by comparison. Suddenly recovered from his befuddlement, he fired off figure after figure. Bankruptcy proceedings had been instituted against my entire estate, the expensive furniture and genuine carpets had been bought up from the bankrupt's assets for a minimal sum by my stepdaughter and her husband. My creditors had wanted to settle for an amount corresponding to fifteen percent, but it was doubtful whether this was attainable. My son-in-law and his lovely wife were too shrewd! And my insurance? The attorney, playing with his glinting monocle, smiled and shrugged his shoulders. (I was so unaccustomed to seeing a smile that I imitated it, much to his astonishment.) The insurance company had raised an objection that seemed to him, the attorney, very sophisticated: they had contested the policy – which the highly virtuous wife had taken out, not I! – as immoral. (I had expected this and still could not believe it!) He had lodged a protest, very much in his own interest. My brother had joined the proceedings. But the outraged public, in the figure of the press, had taken the insurance company's side against me. My brother had moved heaven and earth and made great personal sacrifices to at least bring the insurance company to a compromise settlement. But he had come up empty-handed, and his legal expenses had been greater than he would have liked. Fine. That was still not enough of a reason for his silence, but it would have to do. In all seriousness, was that all the attorney had to tell me?

He was the last link to my former life. In his beefy hand, covered with a great many blond hairs and brownish freckles, he worked the fluted rim of his monocle in a circle as though winding a watch. He was no longer really paying attention to me at all. He wagged his double chin, carefully closed (buttons and lock) his expensive briefcase smelling of morocco leather, glanced about to make sure he had not forgotten anything. When I tried to shake hands with him, he flinched, bowing so deeply that I could not pull my hand back quickly enough. I looked as though I was about to bless the bald-headed, pudgy, blond, elegant man in the ecclesiastical manner. Need I say that this was far from my mind?

Until the last day, I waited longingly, I declare it openly, for a sign of life from my brother, whom I credited with a "loving heart." Need I say that this sign of life from a loving heart never came?

TWO

I

The transports converged over the course of a day on a southern port that I knew from before (they came every few months from various cities). A hundred convicts or many times that – no one knew how many of us there would be – were going to be taken in iron pontoons to the battered but reconditioned transport steamer *Mimosa*. Where we were all going was, as I must have said, the penal colony C.

We had seen the low, beamy ship, with its small white protruding hump of a conning bridge and short, slanting funnel, lying at anchor offshore that morning as we were being unloaded from the barred cattle cars, each man shackled to another, and led up a ramp between two rows of bayonets to the freight depot. *We*, I say, as though I already felt like a seasoned member of our community.

For the moment this community was one more of bodies than of souls. I have said that before and after my crime I was in almost total isolation (my brother may have constituted an exception). It was an isolation so extreme that I unburdened myself to no one, indeed did not even believe any human soul capable of understanding me, my motives, and my fate, as it is called. Now I was quite literally yoked to another person.

At first I was stupefied by the heavy, seemingly spice-laden air, by the direct, glaring sun, by the noise, by the sight of the open sky, the hissing locomotives, the rumbling trucks, the clanking chains of the cranes at work, and so on – dust, sun, and palms everywhere – I could hardly grasp what was happening to me. You would have to have spent weeks, months, living a strictly controlled life, monkishly shut off from the world, to be able to understand what it is to take a long train trip and suddenly go from a cool, airless, sunless, silent cell into the bustle of a modern port.

The brilliantly sunny corner of the dock where we had been taken in a long column early that morning was thronged. It was a provincial town: the gradually silting harbor provided its sole industry, an old but insignificant one, though it did have a fairly strong garrison. Our deportation was an exciting event, something like the arrival of a large circus. The attention was flattering to many of us.

As remote as the town was, a few tourists had strayed here nonetheless. What a place to bring the Kodaks! I had been here once too, and there may even have been some shots of the area in my photo album. And now! What a sight we must have been in our puce-colored penitential garments, bulky sacks and heavy bundles on backs and under arms, prisoners' caps askew on shaven heads, coats with military-style hip and shoulder straps, covered with dust, our life stories written on our faces! We were just as exciting to the good people as a stage play, and much cheaper.

A newspaper photographer, apparently on vacation, was setting up his equipment. Before he was ready, we had gone past. I looked back.

Next to the photographer stood an older man, very like him, perhaps his father or older brother. As lightly dressed as they were, sweat was running down their faces, they were practically bathed in it.

As we neared the harbor, the two newspapermen tried to squeeze past the guards and follow us. I was the star of a sensational trial who had already been dragged through all the papers while it was in progress, and no doubt they were itching to get pictures of this VIP as he was beginning his sentence.

For doggedness and zeal they were nothing compared to the convicts' loved ones. They were surging rapidly from the many small streets and alleyways, down stairways, out of hotels and bars.

A crippled man of about eighty was being pushed in a wheelchair by a husky, sunburned lad. Another, younger, man seemed to be a little drunk. A thin, angular woman in black held her whey-faced infant in one arm and waved with her free hand.

The date of our deportation had been kept from us until the final evening. (Inexplicably, the cell where I would be spending my last night had felt like home to me.) But the loved ones must have heard. What they did not know was when we would be arriving. They had not expected us until sometime toward noon. Now we were there, and they were within range.

But it was no use. The guards were like a wall. They stood with their legs wide apart, holding their cocked and loaded rifles horizontally in their massive, brownish hands so that each silvery, glinting bayonet point touched a shiny, smooth-worn, chestnut-colored rifle butt. Every third man had an egg grenade on a strap to the left of his belt buckle. Almost all of us had been in the Great War and knew what a live egg grenade tossed from two or three meters away would do. But did they mean it? The fragments would have claimed as many victims among them, the guard soldiers, as among us. They feared us. We feared them. And, that understood, we were as docile as lambs.

The guards had the best intentions. They were going to protect us from love. All joking aside! Could it be anything but futile? What could parents do for their children, children for parents, brothers for brothers? What heavenly delights of love could girls and women bestow upon their heroes? Where would this belated excess of sentiment get anyone? It made no difference. Not anymore. Yes, go in peace! Good. Good. Possibly the "loving hearts" had forgiven and forgotten all our misdeeds. They thanked thanklessness with thanks and presented their cheeks to be struck as my poor wife had once done. But had the *crimes* been undone on that account? You who are entirely free of conscience, step forward! I am not among you.

True, most were unaware of their situation. Not all of them had the misfortune to have to live with their guilt forever, unable to stamp out every bit of human feeling in themselves. Most did not have analytical, ruminative natures like mine – not many were really even capable of thinking logically. Knowing that they could still scuttle about on the surface of the earth at all was very likely the most positive thing in their lives. And the "loving hearts" must have made this feeling, the only thing they had left, difficult to bear. Or was that true? Could they have brought consolation? Love in the form of consolation with no practical results of any magnitude – would that not make the punishment even worse?

My brother did not bring me consolation. He did not appeal to my questionable conscience. He did not make my punishment worse. He had now in all probability become a happy father once more. Very likely my father had given him financial assistance and asked in return that he leave me to my fate and to myself. I have no way of knowing that this is what happened, but it would be as much like my father as like my brother.

My brother struggled bravely through life with his mediocre gifts and had written me off. My father had tried to deny my name, a dramatic gesture, but I had still been able to see in it a kind of curdled love, suffering with its object and consumed by it. In my brother's disappearance, I saw only the coldest reason, coldest because the most guarded. I was happy that he was not pestering me, while at the same time (always that contradiction in me) I felt a terrible hunger.

II

Nothing in the world could deter the "loving hearts." And they kept coming. A late-arriving old woman, dripping with sweat under garments and flowing skirts that had been coffee-colored but were now caked with dust, raised her thin voice to a screech and, through the tremendous din, wailed out her mother's heart to a fat lout in our midst. I could see her in some peasants' collective, standing unsteadily in front of a tumbledown shack covered with rotting straw and shouting like this – stopping to cough asthmatically and then frantically resuming – to call a straying kid or a pullet feeding in a neighbor's yard.

She lifts the gift of mercy in her bony hands. A pair of new shoes, soles as thick as a finger and glinting with stout gold-colored hobnails around the edges. She swings them on their long russet leather shoelaces high above her head, on which she is wearing an ancient bonnet held on with large pins. Her heart is in the right place! No doubt the village shoemaker used special heavy-duty cowhide to make sure the prodigal son's poor feet would be protected up to the ankles from snakes and worms as he felled trees in the jungle out on the deportation island. May God preserve you, afflicted old lady, and may he preserve your dear son!

A drunken middle-aged man is apparently unwilling to let go of a half-empty schnapps bottle. It sparkles eye-catchingly in the sun.

Some old provincial, broader than he is tall, is standing on tiptoe; over his hoary head (bearing a sturdy, low-crowned derby) he is waving a sheepskin-colored flannel vest with neat piping. He has probably sewn his nest egg into the lining. What is the son going to get from the father whose love has so lately awakened? Very likely more than the spoils of the crime for which the youth (there are very many among us who are quite young) has been sentenced to deportation and hard labor. And this miracle vest is supposed to keep the body warm, to guard against liver diseases, intestinal worms, perhaps even yellow fever. I can see it now – the parish priest giving it his solemn blessing after High Mass; sexton, father, and priest shedding tears, all three of them. What a scene it must have been. As a man of scientific training and a former physician, I know, I can state with certainty thanks to my bacteriological expertise: if, on the other side of the ocean, on the island or peninsula C., yellow fever really is raging as fiercely as has been reported for months in both the medical journals and the daily newspapers, then prayer will confer no protection as far as science currently knows, nor will tears, and least of all a garment sewn with the needle of love and the thread of mercy from the vesture of the downtrodden like the one the distressed father on the dock is now waving about, a flag of Christian love, in the air that ripples and quivers in the heat.

Yellow fever is on the rampage down there. It follows natural laws that are not yet precisely known. No one knows how it comes. No one has any idea how it goes. The processions move slowly and the burials are done quickly. The hearses are busy day and night. And this sun of yellow fever shines on just and unjust alike. That is to say, it wreaks the same havoc and devastation among the penal colony guards who stand over the criminals as it does among the criminals themselves. Likewise at the Panama Canal among the white engineers and the dark-skinned laborers. No different in Brazil's great, thriving city Rio de Janeiro.

Nothing does any good against the epidemic. Nothing and no one.

Up on the rickety balcony of the small hotel, *Zum König von Engelland* – blue-washed, narrow-fronted, old (I recognize it: on my earlier trip I spent the night there with my wife, we had breakfast on that balcony, and I remember the enraptured and yet unmistakably lascivious expression on her face – only the eyes were expressive, the rest of her face was enameled like a porcelain doll's) – the newspaper photographer has stationed himself on this balcony along with his brother. He tirelessly holds a white umbrella over his head to protect him from the midday heat. He has put a telephoto lens on the front of his squat, boxy apparatus, a reflex camera. The lens is like a short, thick revolver cylinder (the little Bulldog revolvers have such cylinders) aimed at our group. Or, to be more precise, at me and my handsome blond companion, to whom I have been joined since this morning by an intimate bond (made of tough English steel). With a lock.

But now the sun is like the flames of hell. Twist and turn as one may to hide the skull between the shoulders, it cannot be done. Shade! Shade! Oh, for an hour in the dark prison yard on a winter's morning!

The brown prisoner's cap is my only protection. But, as dangerous as the sun is, I would rather hide from the photographer's lens. I spoke of twisting and turning, but my companion would have to help me, and I would rather not talk to him. Is my brother going to have to see this photo in the Sunday supplement?

What are external need, physical pain, moral abasement? Nothing to one who is hardened. This is what my father bequeathed to me, even while he was still alive. The last and most important freedom left to a man is the freedom to be his own master.

I have talked about myself for so long, I have told so much of my story, and yet I have left out the most important details. I am the son of well-to-do, unpunished parents (or is it a punishment for the old man to have a son like me?), I was educated in good schools – but life was my best teacher, as my father was the first to prove to me. Once he made me spend the night with rats in a locked, pitch-dark room, to teach me not to be afraid of animals. But of people? Should one be, or not?

Was that his entire curriculum? That is not for me to ask. But his calculation will turn out to be right. For good or ill, his calculations have proven themselves in the past, always and everywhere. One who takes for granted the basest motives in one's fellow men and in oneself, as he did, has never gone wrong, not in our time – and it is in our time that one must live, must prosper or perish.

Faith in God, which moves mountains? Goodness, which softens what is hard and sweetens what is bitter? Generosity, the noble heart of the crude clay figure of humanity? Three big Gs. Good! In our language, goodness, generosity, faith in God are untranslatable foreign terms. And knowing this as I do, why do I act as though I had something to complain about? No. I don't. Not anymore. I accept my punishment without illusion.

I have now been convicted for the murder of my wife. Given a commuted sentence of lifelong hard labor in the colony. Child of my father, husband of my wife, brother of my brother – off those jobs. Man without a job.

The sun is beating down even more strongly than I had expected. Its rays are like so many arrows entering the brain through the skin and the dome of the cranium. Scientists are still uncertain whether the harmful component of sunlight is the chemically active shortwave ultraviolet rays or the longwave heat radiation. Splitting headache, cramps, mania to the point of delirium, an agonizing death in a black sweat can result – and yet I am more afraid of the indiscreet lens of the intrusive photographer.

Whatever else I may be, I still know how to be ashamed. It would be terrible to see me that way, terrible for *him* to see me. Despite the blazing sun, I tear the cap off my shaven head and hold it in front of my face. Better to let the ferocious heat burn down on my unprotected cranium, better to breathe in the stifling odor of sweat and felt that assaults me sickeningly from the brownish, greasy lining of the battered but reconditioned cap. Yes, the government has to economize, and we're the place to start. The cute little cap has served many men before me and will do the same for many more after me if the yellow-fever epidemic takes me before my time. No. If that happens, this old museum piece will finally be decommissioned and incinerated, it will go the way of the suits, dresses, chests, furniture, beds, blankets, and linens worth many millions, all destroyed to stop the spread of the yellow fever. All for nothing. Beds and blankets incinerated. The epidemic goes on.

What difference does it make whether I die of yellow fever or malaria there or the relentless heat here? Three cheers for shame, the last remnant of a once virile character, long live honor, even if the hero dies!

Stop it, calm down. Why this mad outburst of ethical scruple? First live. In spite of everything, I still hold my life too dear. I submit. I give in. After this experiment (on myself), I phlegmatically cover my pate, the best and only one I have, and openly show my charming face. Go on, do it! Click, camera shutter, let my face be memorialized if fate wills it. I could be buck-naked, doing anything whatever, if that was what amused the European public and it was worth a twelve-by-eighteen dry plate. To me it's not amusing to risk my health out of a feeling of shame. It's the only health I have.

But I am more dead than alive just the same. My right hand is carrying everything. It has to do all the work, because, again, the left one is not free. It belongs to the handsome, tall but not very muscular, sweat-soaked, bony, flaxen-haired man with the not unintelligent, still childlike face. He has become listless, his small, heart-shaped, almost fleshless face sags, pale and tired. It tautens in childish pride only occasionally. The lips quiver defiantly but let out not a curse, not a sigh, not a word.

My left hand belongs to this man, in exchange for which I have his right. What acts might this right hand have committed? Question mark? Exclamation point! Dash – We have not introduced ourselves. Our only calling cards are the large Arabic numerals painted on our uniforms over our hearts. And what is interesting beyond that and distinguishes one person from another is revealed to the connoisseur of human nature in our faces.

Gallows faces or angel faces? Dwell together, beloved brethren, enjoy safe pasture. What more could you want? It is not good that man should be alone. This bond of love keeps us together, for as a pair we are weaker than each of us would be on his own.

Long live due process! As long as humanity exists, it will always be the next best thing to justice as our way of passing judgment on one another and serving God in the highest.

Hand in hand! Thus is the unruly individual brought together with his fellow man and molded to the most primitive, but truest, collective. Be thou blest! Amen.

III

Since the (to me no longer) puzzling disappearance of my brother, I have been firmly resolved to attain the greatest possible degree of freedom, both inward and outward. The first paragraph of this, my declaration of freedom, states that I shall close myself off from my fellow prisoners without exception insofar as possible. This will not always be easy. Thus there can be no exchange of cigarettes between me and my companion, and no conversation, though everyone around me is engaged in the liveliest discussions.

And now they shout to those beyond the cordon! They cry out for love – and what they have in mind is tobacco. But they do not get the latter and have none of the former. They waste no time moping, preferring to jabber and quarrel.

My companion, the tall, handsome youth, is unlike them. He is quiet. He is reserved. He radiates something, how shall I say, something plain to everyone, something inspiriting, something endearing, that might bind one to him. One might, if pressed, even conceive that this man shouldered his guilt for someone else's sake. Or that he acted out of some fanatically, childishly cherished, mad idea. For an ideal beyond price.

The man looks miserable now. He is suffering. He has suffered. He will suffer.

He fascinates me and yet I do not speak to him. We are two total strangers, thrown together by mere chance. Traveling acquaintances. We look at each other, we do have to meet each other's gazes. If he lifts his hand, I lift mine. If he goes somewhere, I follow. Constant brothers, more constant than nature makes them. For, let us be honest, the best brothers are not those nature gives us.

No? I remain solitary because that is what I want. That is what I want because I have no choice.

The time has come for me to consider my situation clearly. I have not done this in a long while.

What lies in store for me would be worse than death to most people. Nevertheless it is preferable to death. This is not the beginning, here on the dock amid the fieriest heat and the nastiest odors, inside a cordon of guards armed with egg grenades. Nor is it the end.

A look back, then a way forward.

The guards now stop their sluggish lolling about and straighten to attention: some ship's officers have appeared, beardless, fresh-looking young men and older men in a casual line, dressed in white or khaki, freshly pressed, with wheat-colored pith helmets on their heads. Accompanied by members of the fair sex and a great many factotums, they stroll past us pariahs and up the steps of the breakwater toward the official launch, which already has a head of steam so as not to keep the big guns waiting in the blazing sun. Steel gray, polished to a sparkle, its short brassbound funnel sending up boiling puffs of steam into air that quivers in the midday heat, pennants flying from the aerial masts, it rocks on the glassy surface of the sea, circled by screeching snowy gulls that resemble descending hydroplanes as they graze the water with one lustrous mother-of-pearl wing.

The hilly terrain of the town is hidden from view by the silver and green foliage of trees standing close together on the square. But through a gap some buildings on the outskirts are visible – lime white villas pillowed in gardens – then, farther away, tin sheds built out over the water, the barnlike hangars for the naval station's hydroplanes.

If only I have the will! If only I am ruthless and unflinching enough with myself and others in the midst of the battle for existence, the war of all against all! If I do as my father schooled me . . . then I'll never have to bow to anyone except when absolutely necessary. Then and only then. Then I will be equal to my situation to all intents and purposes.

By exacting its punishment, the state wants to deter me? No need for that. I will never repeat my crime or commit one anything like it. Never again.

The state wants to pay me back for the evil I have done to others? Because I have made others suffer, should I myself suffer?

Let the state protect itself and its "loving hearts" as it can. I have to protect myself. Let me hold my own! Let me last two or three years where countless others have perished from the hardships of the abnormal life, of the climate, despondency, and malaria.

The worst punishment is something else. To be thrown in with people and to see them, to have to see them, not as sympathetic companions in suffering but only as mortal enemies – I have understood what deportation, what prison mean. Here internal conflicts, there deadly epidemics. But to stand unbowed despite death and the devil as long as you have a spark of life left in you, G. L. the younger, is that not a task that must make life worth living to you, wherever, however? Yes, it is. I might survive. I might return from the prison island someday.

If only I were of one mind *with myself* at bottom! That's the thing! If only I could accept all of life. Could bow in uncritical worship before the "wonders of God's creation." Could pray. Could finally conquer the logical despair that unmoors me, but also lets me think clearly; that cripples me, but has also protected and shielded me since my father's crucial experiment on me as a child. So let me at the wheel of fortune! I'll give it a whirl. The dead do not rise. But perhaps I can raise myself up to a new life. No difficulty would be too great for me. I wouldn't be the first one lucky enough to escape.

In this burst of energy, I have pulled my left hand to my heart. My companion's right hand is forced to follow. He laughs out loud. But why does his feverishly bright gaze ignore me? Is that wonderful, heart-gladdening laugh not for me? No, his laughing nod was to the photographer, his laugh was grandstanding for the reporter: look, I'm in chains, sent up for who knows how many years of hard labor – and I'm *laughing*!

Vanity is paramount in his character too. Is it paramount in my own? In any case my inspiration ends in another shattered illusion. Next time I'll be still tougher, more hard-boiled. The old man was right. The way he looked at life after his unsuccessful expedition to the northern lands, that was the way it was.

Despite the terrible sun, my companion takes his cap off his long, nicely shaped, clean-shaven skull and throws it in the air. It twirls, a brown butterfly, and he catches it between his knees. Finally he straightens up like a gymnast on the horizontal bar. He pats at himself, trying to look neat – all this even though he seems to be feverish. Oh, all right. We know, *you* have the attention of the press, the public has its eye on you, not me. Laugh! Show your handsome, pearl-like child's teeth. That's what your astonished contemporaries will see in the Sunday paper. Heads up: one – two – three – now! The shutter finally makes its clattering sound, the plate has been exposed, the dramatic moment has passed – and the reporter has undoubtedly earned his five dollars (or ten, with reproduction rights). You can laugh and be happy! And if you wave your cap at the reporter, he'll answer you from the balcony with his handkerchief. Peace on earth. Goodwill toward men and, with luck, no scratches or halo on the plate and the viewfinder doing its job and the distance estimated correctly . . . Nonsense, all of it.

Once the picture has been taken, the handsome man slumps. I feel it, I have become "empathetic," close to him as I am. And through his loose prison uniform I note his elevated temperature. Never were patient and doctor closer.

The launch is back, and a tall, lean officer with general's insignia is the last to commit himself to the gangway. His storklike gait seems familiar: he reminds me of Major Carolus at the Pasteur Institute. But he is too far away for me to make out his face.

A little girl and her nanny, who seem to have come with him, have stayed onshore with a tiny, woolly dog wearing a sky blue bow and a twinkling little bell. The child waves to the tall general on the launch. He takes off his pith helmet to wave back, revealing a pumpkin-shaped bald head. It can only be Carolus!

The child leans forward in excitement; the servant holds her back by her silk waistband. The little dog barks spiritedly and whines, then breaks loose, runs, tail held high, excited like its mistress, to the shore and back, ready to jump into the water and follow its master, the old general or brigadier general. The child waves steadily. Her straw hat slips and she quickly straightens it with a toss of her pert little head. The little dog loyally returns to the child's feet and, out of breath from barking and running, extends its raspberry-colored tongue. The nanny holds a dark blue linen parasol over child and dog. She waves too, fluttering a kerchief in her free hand. Good-bye, good-bye, you brave man at arms!

No saber, just the épée, so this is no hero but only the rations officer or a brigadier general in the medical corps. What a touching family scene! And no less moving the scenes of parting staged by the prisoners' loved ones, the "loving hearts." I smoke a cigarette, the first of the day.

IV

What significance could these sentimental or idyllic scenes have for the ironic observer when thirst and the heat were making themselves more strongly and more agonizingly felt with every passing hour? It was nearly three when we received the eagerly awaited midday rations, of unusually poor quality but heavily salted to make up for it. And if they were bad, there was the consolation of their scantiness. Are we to suppose that the excellent judicial administration had been expecting fewer of us? Or had a few low-level pilferers helped themselves to some of our meager rations? Or did someone think that the sight of the ocean (deep indigo, rhythmically swept by short, quick waves, smooth swells shining with an almost metallic boldness), that this glorious view of the surging open sea would satisfy us hungry, hog-tied deportees? The little harbor is lovely, with only a few small low-draft coastal vessels bobbing in its silted-up basin, but many graceful sailboats with deep brown, saffron yellow, orange-red, rust-colored, often patched and fraying sails.

And, clanking on the rocks of the breakwater, a few ungainly cast-iron pontoons waiting for us. But as they are waiting for us, so we are still waiting for them. In vain.

The sails of the skiffs hang slackly from the masts and yardarms, the waves subside, total calm gradually spreads, and soon the stillness is oppressive. Your throat seems to close. You squat apathetically on the rocks (now unpleasantly hot, about body temperature) amid the disorder of bags thrown everywhere. Your rotting, sweat-soaked clothes stand away from you as though you have just come in from a thundershower and your skin is shriveled from the rain. You wonder where your emaciated body found that much moisture.

Suddenly a disturbance. A man has fallen over backward. His skull is concussed: he fell like a dead weight. The man to whom his wrist and his fortunes are bound went with him. He rolls over the fallen man as though trying to embrace him, to cover him with his body. The two men, chained together, are taken to the water's edge, to the stone steps on the shore. Why not the sick man alone? Is there a way to do that? The shackles don't come off for such petty reasons. Besides, the transport commandant, who has the key, is already on board with the rest of the aristocracy and may well be dining just now.

The man must have suffered sunstroke. He lets himself be carried by two guards, lying in their arms like a well-behaved big baby; the other man follows awkwardly like a fly with three of its six legs torn off. But now the prostrate fat insect attacks the hobbling thin insect. What a spectacle for the gods and the savages! Go on, don't be shy! Let your feelings out, comrades of better days. No, no sarcasm. To them it's deadly serious.

Why has this fight suddenly broken out, becoming wilder and more dramatic every second, far beyond the cordon of the guards, in the midst of the "loving hearts"?

The answer lies here among us. The thin man took a dim view of the fat man's "sunstroke," his way of making contact with his relatives. Earlier the two of them had made a thieves' covenant, but even on the way here conflict had arisen between these inseparable, faithful friends. And the thin man tried to extort from the fat man, the one who was "sick" just now, who could fake so well that he could even fool the retired physician Georg Letham, a higher percentage of the expected treasures, money, tobacco, clothes, valuables – everything the fat one was hoping, dreaming, that he would receive from his equally fat relatives.

And how did the thin one carry out his extortion? Did he appeal to the fat one's sense of fairness? Of course not. He twisted the manacle to try to dislocate his wrist. A little jujitsu between friends. If only it had been a prearranged fight! The supposed sunstroke victim bravely throws himself upon the aggressor and gives as good as he got – a terrible thing to see (and yet something is laughing in me!). To the laughter of the hardened guards and the horror of the screaming "loving hearts," roaring, cursing, and raging as one, foaming at the mouth like animals, the two of them try, each with his free hand, to box each other's ears, to twist each other's arms and legs, until they roll over the feet of their loved ones (who retreat slowly, unable to help their son or relative) and onto the stones that slope down to the harbor basin.

The guards, leaning on their gleaming bayonets (one of them playing with his grenade, but with the safety catch prudently left in place), phlegmatically adjust their helmets, spit, and wait for the two idiots to come to their senses.

No real blows are landed, nothing that could do any damage. The two of them rushed into the clinch, as boxers call it, and are too tangled up to really hurt each other. They start to go down, still locked together, but they catch themselves in time. Now they help each other up and trot back to the group with a few cuts and scratches. None of their relatives came close enough to slip them the expected articles. Now that they have both lost the day, the group is vicious and gleeful and someone trips them. The two fall, get up, and hang on to each other unsteadily. They look around in astonishment. Gloating on every side. What did they expect? Who could have any sympathy for them when they have none for each other? People are never more merciless than toward their fellows.

Or is that true? The high authority is even more merciless. It can only be called the most asinine mercilessness to make us stew here for almost twelve hours with bayonets hanging over us. All human feeling stops at forty degrees centigrade. We relieve ourselves when and where the opportunity presents itself, like animals in the pen at the slaughterhouse. The stifling heat makes this foul air a true torment to breathe. It would be a relief to pass out and sink to the ground, but that has to be avoided. Would anyone think it was a real fainting spell? Two, three men near us keel over with symptoms of sunstroke, then a few more farther off.

They all crash down with dismal groans, the same animal sound, a kind of gurgle, as though they were imitating each other. But this is no imitation, this is the real thing, this is nature. Bluish red faces. Limbs twitching and convulsed, eyes open and staring, with swollen lids and livid conjunctivae. On these no-longer-human faces an expression of dumb agony. Real! Real! But no sign of life.

My companion is already too far gone even to flinch when I shake him or respond when I talk to him. I don't even know his name, so I call him by his number. Ah, who needs numbers, who needs names! Shade! Shade! Shade for us, shade! No, no, once again no. And yet not even a hundred paces away, beautiful, deep warehouses, spacious, shadowy, dark, empty, smelling of coffee and spices. They belong to the government. The free port has hygienic facilities, including a W.C. Not for us. So must we do as animals do? Of course we must. For the warehouses belong to another department, Tax and Customs, and we belong only to Judicial Administration, Criminal Justice, Deterrence and Retribution. Tried under prevailing law, to be consigned through the usual administrative channels to the *Mimosa* for purposes of deportation, so many hundred head of morally wanting men . . .

I just want the sun to set on this terrible day. It seems to be moving in tighter and tighter circles in the whitishly blazing sky. If I could only cover my face, hold my right hand over my eyes, wrap my left around the back of my head – but how? Why don't they take us away at last? It must be infinitely better there on the *Mimosa*, which we can see sparkling and rocking gently on the sea. There it will be airy, shadowy, and cool, like a cellar. There are no real accommodations for us, only bunkers of a kind, stables originally, with iron plating for the dividing walls. At one time this glorious ark was used for shipping livestock. It was never remodeled, hardly ever properly disinfected. We know all this, the prisoners discussed it in the prison and on the train. But none of that matters, let's go! It can only be a thousand times better there, down below where the delightful sun doesn't shine, a thousand times better than here! Anywhere but here. Useless. Pointless thoughts, idle fantasies. Who is there to talk to? Who is there to complain to? I can't even curse. I don't have enough spit left.

V

My neighbor is beginning to babble. I hear something about a "cadet." His lips flutter, like the flews of a dog snapping at flies in the sun. His limbs twitch, arms and legs. He focuses his clear blue eyes on them wonderingly, seemingly surprised by their electrified movements. With his (and my) captive hand he grasps at his free one, which had the first spasms, as though he could stop it from twitching like a frog's leg, bring it to its senses, calm it down. His face shows no awareness of what he is doing. How many things people do of which they have no awareness!

The handsome face abruptly sags, the head falls onto the chest, as though something holding it up has been cut with a pair of scissors. His breath comes in laborious gasps, he brings up the wretched food, and his glazed-over eyes dart about.

I hold his heavy, hot, damp head as far away as possible; I have no truck with sympathy and for my own sake can't think of having any. His breathing is stertorous: I hear a rumbling in his chest like the sound of water boiling. I blow on him as though he were a saucepan of milk about to foam over. The pleasant breeze revives him a little, and he looks up at me strangely with the eyes of a loyal dog. *Now* would be the time to immortalize you in photographs, you suffering frog, you picture of misery! He shakes his head in surprise, as though he had guessed my thoughts. A little child, its kind father's index and middle fingers on its chin to steady the tiny, slack jaw, could hardly look more innocent. He wants to be a good boy and pull himself together.

And he does. He summons his strength, swallows hard. He keeps the rest of his food down. If only the ominous slaty bluish gray in his sagging child's face would go away! I loosen his shirt and coat at his throat, working around him with my hand (and his hand) in front of his face and neck. Meanwhile my free hand is occupied with holding his head – and everything becomes that much harder when he leans against me, his body close in the atrocious heat.

Luckily his sunstroke is not yet fully developed. He is not unconscious, only dazed. I am able to get him to stand up and gather his strength to stagger with my assistance to the edge of the crowd, where there are stacks of crates that will surely give some sort of shade.

The angle of the sun has changed. The crates are big, new, they smell strongly, of disinfectants, cresol and such. Perhaps they are on their way to the medical service in the colony. They are no hundred-year-old cork tree, there might be twenty centimeters of shade at best, but enough to lay a tired head in, or at least protect the eyes. His head and mine too. We are a community of interests, a collective. If I am an altruist, then I am an egoist. So I lay my head (which is buzzing alarmingly) on the filthy pavement next to his. Go ahead, brother mine! Relax and don't worry. Now pull the man's brown cap over his eyes, mine too, but be quick about it! Glowing sparks are flying now, I see them even with my eyes closed, and it was a close call – for him? For me! My ears are roaring like a hurricane.

But before long everything will be wonderful! Soon the sweet shade from the crates has crept down over the bridge of my nose, then over my mouth, neck, chest, hips, and knees, and both of us are as in the bosom of Abraham, lying in the promised land of shade down to our toes. We are not the only ones. Just the first. They come pair by pair. Without a word. No cursing, no mischief, no tussles, just breathing and quiet. The murmur of the "loving hearts" is like distant surf, and the surf is like the murmur of a restless crowd, no difference, same thing.

Suddenly a stir. Everyone wakes up with a start. The district commandant, the top dog, long awaited, has appeared. A deeply tanned bon vivant's face, handsome in a weathered sort of way and full of dash and charm. Bushy white eyebrows but black toothbrush mustache, neatly trimmed and shining like pitch or mustache dye. Truly there are no graybeards anymore. Very erect posture. Self-discipline or corset? In his tight-fitting, sky blue Litewka coat, buff-colored, wide, baggily elegant breeches, knee-length leather gaiters laced up in front with brass hooks and eyes, decorations across the pigeon-breasted chest, gleaming leathers and holster at his waist, monocle in his left eye, he stalks through our ranks, a god amid his brute creation, which is expiring while he shakes out the skirts of his tunic in back as though afraid vermin from us might be clinging to him. How would they dare, Excellency? He seems pressed for time. Two white-skinned (or powdered), red-cheeked (or discreetly rouged) young adjutants follow at a respectful distance. The big man and his handsome aides make disgusted faces as they race through a group of sallow convicts, many of whom are suffering from crusty skin conditions such as are prevalent in the tropics.

But these sallow penal colonists are no "common criminals," in the tactful words of the penal code. These are top-grade people, political offenders: misguided, but idealistic, spirited, self-sacrificing people who let nothing stop them in the service of their political ideal, not even the sanctity of government property, the invested capital of their country. Their judgment may deserve a question mark, but their character merits an exclamation point. And what do they get? They're down in the same muck with murderers and other felons.

The stiff-legged old stallion hurries on. It's all just a formality. No one has even counted the deportees.

One of the sallow political prisoners has a belt around his thin belly with his mess kit attached, and one of the armchair officers gets a spur caught on it. But no matter, he just flicks his riding crop behind him (there are no horses for miles around) into the poor idealist's rapidly reddening and swelling face, then continues on his way at a smart double-quick pace as though walking on hot coals, dragging along mess kit and do-gooder until one of the three has to give, and of course it's the poor devil, who rolls in the dust. Talk about a mess!

But this is what the young gentleman is paid for. He comes up with his boss in time to hand him his own fountain pen so the old man can sign some official paperwork that the junior officer on duty has set down on a crate. The boss makes no effort to read this official document. The junior officer did, so it must be all right. And as soon as he has signed his august name with a flourish, he faces about like a clapped-out parade horse on its hind legs at the circus, and the three minor deities hurry back to their car, a sleek, cherry red automobile six meters long. One of the adjutants holds the door, the general slips in with a gracious nod to the aide, who scampers in beside him, the third officer takes the wheel, turns the key, puts it in gear, steps on the gas, and off they go, the engine purring. Dust, and a bad smell. And *this* is who we've had to wait for all day. Had to? No! Been permitted to.

Two figures, not attached to each other, are now slinking back from the city under guard. Their former companions used a file to get away, but then had to be hospitalized. One got malaria following sunstroke, the other had epileptic seizures. But there were still others who got their eternal reward.

By all accounts things came to a merciful conclusion today. The "loving hearts" can give thanks to providence and rejoice. On the previous transport, on the same dock, in the same glorious, cloudless, windless weather, waiting in the same place for the same signature by the same general, no fewer than – no, G. L., old boy, pay attention! – no *more* than fourteen men became ill as a result of the heat, six fatally. So we can consider ourselves lucky.

The two unattached parties have teamed up. Were they unable to bear being single among all the exclusive couples?

One is a small, clean-shaven, lively, but horribly emaciated and constantly coughing man who could be anywhere between twenty-five and fifty, an old jailbird. The other is a bear of a man, a deeply tanned, broad-shouldered giant, black, greasy curls, an unruly mass of hair above the low, heavy, coppery forehead. He has an oriental look, and I hear people calling him "Sultan" or "Suleiman." He strokes the little fellow's sweaty neck with his big black paws, a brutish smile of almost animal sensuality on his thick lips. The little man tries to escape from the heavy arms, but the "Sultan," revealing a magnificent set of teeth, grins in a kind of bliss as though he were drunk or lying in the arms of a Persian princess. Far from it, fortune's fool! Believe it as long as you can.

VI

Now the general exodus is beginning. High-ranking officers are no longer present. The press photographer and his brother have disappeared. The junior officers are celebrating the embarkation in the docklands bars hereabouts. The military band has assembled near a church in a neighboring square, as it does every evening.

The sky begins to darken very slightly. The blue is becoming more penetrating. A gentle, wafting breeze, warm as though from a bakery, billows the sails in the harbor, which are being trimmed for night sailing. The crews of the iron pontoons are preparing for the short trip to the steamer. They are waiting for the launch to return with the officers' family members. Now the "loving hearts" are heard again. This is an important moment, the final one Will the long, expensive trip have been in vain? They shout for the transport commandant, hoping to make their wishes known to him. Even His Excellency the General would have nowhere to hide if he were here.

Most of my companions are equals, comrades in misfortune. For life. But how long is a life on the other side?

Suppose a prisoner had a lighter sentence, though, let us say five years. The barbarous regulations would still require him to spend another five years there on probation. This may not seem like much of a difference, but in fact it is immense. For what is the poor fellow who is "released" over there going to do? Without work, without family, without money? How terribly unlikely it is that he will ever return! No wonder the prisoners too are now erupting in moans and wails. The fatigue, the stupor, the general acquiescence are gone. The mindless facial expression produced by suffering greater than a certain magnitude when prolonged beyond a certain point has vanished. These emaciated, desperate faces are full of suffering, full of feeling. Everything but surrender to the inevitable. Some of the men shove the guards gently from behind, which earns them a rain of blows to the chest with rifle butts. They collapse and fall over their worldly goods (if the word "goods" is not too much for articles so meager). Others stand on the tips of their toes and ask their neighbors to lift them up. They promise a similar favor in return, but then forget or plead physical weakness.

Most rely on their own strength. But they are like white laboratory mice inoculated with tetanus and put in tall, straight-sided glass vessels so that their spasmodic leaps and finally their death throes can be observed. They jump, but never high enough to escape.

No use waving with both hands, shouting with voices hoarse from the heat and the dust, it only adds to the din. No one can make out a word. The wailing and raging of the handcuffed convicts even drown out the military music from the nearby post. No rattling of chains. The manacles cut too deeply into the flesh, the links are stretched too tight.

There are many dialects and a wide range of oriental languages. So many voices on the sweet evening air (with orchestral accompaniment) – if I could understand them all, I'd be able to write a detailed natural history of the sickly human heart. All these hearts speak the same language, they all sound the same. The palatals and nasals, the trills and sibilants, the vowels and consonants are beginning to run together: they are no longer the articulate expression of human yearning, human suffering, human pain, regret and outrage, despair and resignation. The sound made by this mass of men is the inarticulate, instinctual screeching and howling of penned-in, terrified animals.

My neighbor says nothing. He has almost recovered. His lips are somewhat fuller, his color is better: He seems a little delicate, perhaps, but he looks good. He buckles his coat on his own.

A cool breeze has come up. The waves on the harbor have whitish crests. The last fishing boats, sails taut, are heading out to sea, while the first are already far out on the horizon, their sails at the perpendicular and mirrored on the water, like butterflies hovering over a still pond with wings gently vibrating.

The fresh air seems to have awakened the appetites of many. If they seem so agitated, it may be because their bellies are as hungry as their hearts.

Yes, my friend, it must be hard to see your mother waving with good things to eat while hunger is gnawing at you. Reality is the only thing standing between mother and son.

So trust in luck! Packages are going airmail now, sailing through the air but not usually falling into the right hands. The shoes arrive, the flannel vest swoops in. Wild fights break out. Frenzied, clumsy brawling. Two partners in crime climb up on the medicine crates. They frantically shout and wave, stamp furiously, signal to their relatives with their long thieves' arms as though sending messages in code. One with his right arm, the other with his left. No good: an object that looks like a ham whizzes past them off to the right, something that might be a bottle of brandy off to the left. Finally they catch a package, open it, and find – a family bible. An especially jaunty fox-trot is heard, played with brio by the military band, and the two idiots, tired of all the excitement for nothing, link elbows and begin dancing like lunatics.

The first transport leaves, about sixty men. The barrage of going-away presents continues.

My companion lifts his beautifully shaped head, turns his gray-blue eyes in all directions. He has as little interest as I do in chasing after food parcels. So what is he looking for? Is he waiting for someone (the "cadet," perhaps?), to exchange last farewells with? Or is he so filled with trepidation about this radical change in his life? It's good-bye to home! One's native soil. Some shady corner in a courtyard of a city apartment building, or a meager autumn flower garden in a lonely mountain farmstead, or some other room or hearth or landscape or memory. A memory of being drafted and going to war, to a bedlam comparable to the current moment, and yet so very different. Country, family, a future to look forward to, the hope of continuous and blissful self-betterment, a hope that rich and poor alike willingly drug themselves with.

Now the desire for distraction and excitement can be seen in everyone. Bets are made, deals struck, currencies exchanged, this last quietly and stealthily, since money is forbidden. The brighter ones cheat, give bad money and not much of it in exchange for gold, and use their fists to stop the mouths of the ones they have cheated, who have no right to complain, because possession of the money of which they have been defrauded is against regulations. Barter, that primitive form of business, is conducted more honorably: wedding rings for smoked sausage, keepsakes for schnapps, beautiful objects for edible ones. People know what they have and are happy. Of course there is acrimony here, too. One man has illegitimately appropriated a food parcel and is strong and fierce enough to hold on to it. The legitimate owner would like to buy it back, but has no money and offers the brute his heavy wedding ring with the date of the ceremony engraved on it. Done. But just the food. He retains right of ownership in case there is also money or something of value in the package, and now the rightful owner, poor wretch, has to watch the thief rummage through his parcel, take out one thing and another and magnanimously hand back whatever is left. Where are the guards, the defenders of the commonweal allegedly based on law and order? Instruments of the state. They are no more than that.

VII

The motor launch has landed again. The guests have disembarked, and now the steel gray boat seems to leap away, darting like an insect on a pond over the now fairly open harbor, northward toward the hydroplane hangar, a gigantic shed covered with sheet metal on whose roof the evening sun is being refracted into shades of bronze.

The ocean is turning a deep blue with an uncertain, changeable violet tinge. Our ship, the *Mimosa*, stands far from shore like a house. A brownish cloud of smoke rises straight up from the short funnel, spreading like a tree, transparent toward the top. The slanting evening sun is still bright, covering everything like a glaze: us and our possessions, the filth and refuse around us, the gleaming bayonets and bandoliers of the guards, the façades of the buildings, the church tower, the dusty treetops, the wet steps of the breakwater, and the rippling, peaceful, seaweedy-smelling sea. Everything seems to have a kind of unnatural reality, lurid, unlike itself, dreamily close, and too clear; dull surfaces glow like velvet, smooth ones glitter like rhinestones.

My neighbor is preparing to take his leave of dry land. Not without a kind of pride, he again unpacks and repacks his things. Clothes – nicely washed, perhaps even a little perfumed, but tattered – a few bars of soap, a bottle of hair tonic, a tube of nail polish (!), and strangest of all: a small, scarred box with a crank on the side – a child's gramophone; also, tucked between the articles of clothing, a few small, cheap records of the kind that go with a miniature gramophone like this one. One of them is smashed, to his great sorrow. How touching when the big, strong youth first tries to put the pieces together and then hesitates, with a plainly heavy heart, wondering if he should toss them among the other debris and rubbish or take them to safety in the new life. No, he can't part with the useless junk. He wraps the fragments in some tissue paper that was used for the nourishing delicacies in the food parcels. I help him. Whether I want to or not. For we are a couple. It would not be believed how much someone accustomed to freedom is hampered in even the slightest movement when he has another person attached to him, when he can do nothing on his own. Already it frightens me to think how the two of us are going to climb onto the ship together without the free use of our arms.

It is becoming cool after the cloudless heat of the long day. Toward the west some coppery clouds ablaze at the edges are rising around the setting sun. The chalk white, cube-shaped little houses of the town are now especially brilliant where earlier they were in shadow. Or perhaps we simply paid no attention to them before.

Down on the beachfront, far in the distance, the huge door of the hangar opens like a stable door ahead of the farm wagon. A large, double-winged hydroplane slowly moves forward. It rocks on its pillow-shaped, slate-colored floats, the flat wings dip into the opalescent sea, first one, then the other. Now the sharp throbbing of the airplane engines starting up can be heard, even drowning out the military band, like the rattle of machine guns only not so percussive, and the hydroplane shoots into the open harbor, driving before it sizzling milk white water in broad billows; it rises into the air, its long dark blue shadow below it, climbs toward the evening clouds with its airfoils tilted upward, rocks again, sways drunkenly from one side to the other – and slopes down in a steep curve to splash clumsily into the water. Why did it go up? What a pointless maneuver! But a good distraction from the monotony of waiting.

No one is chattering now in our little group, no one is shouting.

It is becoming uncomfortably cool. My neighbor, exhausted from the strenuous day, is again squatting silently on the ground. Once more making a jumble of his possessions, he hauls from the depths of his bag a knit scarf and furiously wraps it around his neck as though trying to strangle himself. But he is not weary of life, he is only chilled. His teeth chatter like a child's after a bath that was too long and too cold, and he looks at me intently, devouring me with his blue-gray eyes. But he says nothing. His gaze goes right through me. If he touched me, I could discourage him. Against this look I have no defenses. I feel myself blushing. His gaze is unwavering. The hydroplane has taken off again, evidently a night flight. He ignores it. The band is playing a medley from *La Bohème*. He is not listening. He says nothing and looks at me. Has he taken a fancy to me? No, and let's not hear any more of that. I only turn my head as though my neck itches. Such a prosaic response to his "loving heart." Not that, anything but that! He understands me, though I have said nothing. Finally his look of silent solicitation releases me. He smiles and shows his fine, pearly, short teeth.

That's the way. Leave me alone and I'll leave you alone. I turn my head away. Good.

VIII

I want to think about something else. The past is on my mind. Methinks I see my father.

My father, that smart old bastard (smart of him not to come here!), made jokes sometimes. He had a sense of humor – detachment, in other words. From a distance he could take great pleasure (he knew how to enjoy life!) in watching the ghastly comedy of puny human beings in all their misery and baseness. But that detachment was not easily won, for anyone. You had to force yourself, and that was what he taught me to do. But when I suffered everything, literally suffered, without a whimper, then he was proud of me, a man and a tolerable companion at the age of thirteen. And when he had elicited that from me, achieved it, his way of thanking me was to bring out the jokes, and I was supposed to laugh.

Once, for example, during the period when I was going through the familiar pubescent struggles over the meaning of the world, expressed in my case in religious and social doubts, he feigned an eye condition and asked me to read to him from the newspaper. He had a sudden case of conjunctivitis, and I got an eye-opener.

I might have come straight from church that day. Could be. The religion teacher at our grammar school, a still-young man by the name of La Forest, the brother of one of the officials under my father at the Ministry, was not unintelligent, he had tried to understand me, to solace me, had commended my character (my "spiritual humility and fear of God") and my conduct toward others (my "helpful, self-sacrificing, energetic Christian love"). He traced the meaninglessness and cruelty of the world back to the original sin, from which anyone could free himself through the Savior's atoning sacrifice and his own strength of will.

How much I would have liked to keep these consolations from my father. But all he had to do was give me a cursory glance, eye trouble or not, or sniff my jacket – and he knew I had come from church, or from the schoolroom of an "illegitimate, pervertedly optimistic" humanitarian.

And what did he do? No hairsplitting discussions. No withering scorn. Quite the contrary! He still gave me nothing but encouragement – to attend Mass regularly, to go to confession, to pray. So what was so terrible about what he did that I apply the adjective "diabolical" to him? He only rubbed his eyes until they watered wonderfully, turned the pages of the evening papers with a helpless look on his face (he had always been a passionate reader of newspapers), called me in a fond voice (it never trembled, his deep, mellifluous, gentle, and extraordinarily clear voice), and asked me if I had time to read him the news. Curious that I still remember every word. At night, roused from a deep sleep, I can recite it all verbatim.

Headline: Night of Horror. Over Three Hundred Prisoners Burned Alive. Wire from New York. April 22. Late yesterday afternoon a conflagration broke out in the Ohio State Penitentiary in the city of Columbus, taking hundreds of prisoners locked in their cells by surprise. Terrible, he said. Please read more clearly! Or are you tired? Do you still have your algebra to do? Then don't let me keep you, I don't have to know everything. I continued: While some of the prisoners were reached in time through the prison yard, those housed in the old cell block were cut off by the flames. The guards and the prisoners . . . No, he interrupted, there's a part you left out. You're not that interested, I see! How had the old bastard guessed? And *how much* this extract from the annals of real life did interest me! I could not face losing the benevolence of the Almighty and the comfort of our Savior, I wanted to unite His divine mercy with some idea of reality. I wanted to be able to pray in good conscience! What was I to do? I went back to what I had skipped. Two hundred fifteen fatalities were announced at eight p.m. By nine p.m. the number had risen to three hundred five. We're going to pray for their souls, said my father, looking at me ingenuously. He knelt on the fine soft carpet, took a small wooden triptych altarpiece from his desk (behind it was a small microscope), and set it down in front of him. I was standing next to it. I did not kneel. I read on: The guards and the prisoners joined forces in attempting to extinguish the flames on their own. The fire department arrived one half hour following the outbreak of the fire. However, it was too late to free the unfortunates who occupied the four old cell blocks. In large print: Machine Guns Turned on Rescuees. Several hundred prisoners being held for minor offenses who were housed in a large common dormitory and three thousand additional prisoners from blocks somewhat farther away were led into the prison yard and kept in check by machine guns. My voice faltered, I had to stop. I could see it all. My father pretended not to notice. Just horror stories all the time in the yellow press, as though there were nothing uplifting. Enough brutality! The world isn't such a vale of tears. Speaking of chess, would my dear son have any interest in a game? We can play blind, or I will, anyway. Because I don't want to strain my eyes unnecessarily.

What was I to do? I controlled myself. So fully equal was I to the task he set me that not only was I able to hold my own for an hour in a game against him, a strong player, but I even finished with a draw. I have forgotten how he rewarded me for this triumph. Had I demonstrated enough detachment? Had I looked reality in the eye? Who knows? But I do know one thing, that the following Sunday I did not accompany him and my mother to Mass. There had to be another series of toughening experiments before I was outwardly master of myself, before I could dissemble, put on a face as pious and submissive to God's will as his own.

In his school, human nature and methods of managing people were subjects of vital importance. Here again he used practical examples, not books, and he put all his cold intelligence and diabolical humor into it. He refused to classify people as good or evil, humane or inhumane (he had a justifiably low opinion of this distinction), or again as successful or unsuccessful, for there was no accurate way to measure success at any given time, nor yet as smart or stupid, for the two are inextricably combined in everyone, but rather asked me quite casually whether people might perhaps be classified as frogs or – rats. At school we had just gone through Homer's poem "The Battle of Frogs and Mice" (a highly contested work, by the way). He had no interest in mice, to him they were colorless as characters, but rats he knew, rats he hated from the bottom of his heart, they were vivid to him, for they had shown their colors. The rats were the sticky personalities, the frogs the slippery ones. The first the murderers, the second the swindlers. The first cold, the second hot. He said there were few pure exemplars of either type among human beings; one must therefore attempt to figure out how much frog and how much rat a person had in him. A rat, according to my father, was a monarchist, a rat was a fighter and killed at the drop of a hat. A rat likes food and drink and lets others live provided he has enough himself. He acknowledges masters and leaders but would rather play the master and the hero himself, loves ardently and respects family; he is courageous, does not spend much time hissing but sinks his teeth right in. But the frog is a republican, he favors equality for all. He prefers to do the safe thing, even if it provides a living only after a fashion. He is therefore unambitious, praises the Lord, but lies and dissembles night and day, deep down believing in nothing greater than his own froggy majesty. He deposits his spawn quietly and doesn't know his children in a crowd. But he doesn't eat them, either, as rat fathers sometimes do. The rat thinks nothing of danger and faces it; the frog is always croaking his own name and jumps into the water at the moment of danger, saying it was too hot outside. The rat is bold and shows himself just as readily alone as in a crowd; the frog is shy and gives no thought to his fellows, shrugging his narrow shoulders. The frog has the more dangerous intellectual pride and would prefer to do nothing and have the stupid rat work for him, which the rat will not do. Unless he has to.

I don't know where he got these comparisons, nor can I judge how much of this was accurate. But for a time every visitor to the house came in for a diagnosis by my father, while he winked at me. Rats were supposed to have hot, dry hands and be unwilling to release the hand extended to them while they continued to look one brazenly in the eye. Frogs on the other hand would rather have their cold, moist mitts back even before they gave them, and looked away into a corner or toward the door.

It was best, said my father, who was the minister's left hand (the right one could never be allowed to know what it was doing), to be on good terms with both types of people. But if this should turn out to be impossible, you had to let a rat have it immediately, right on the head, and not even let him start taking too much for granted. You should deal with a frog by embroiling him in protracted negotiations, exploit him, tire him out, disparage him. If necessary, neutralize him by stabbing him in the back. True masters of their craft knew how to elicit the embrace reflex in these cold-blooded animals (imagine it's a woman, my father joked) – if you stroked a frog's little chest or belly with a finger at the right time of year (I saw the experiment done once), he would close his little paws around your finger with the most heartfelt froggy passion. He took it, the human finger, for a female frog. But not one in a thousand was cut out for such tricks! The frog was usually tractable when he realized he had been seen through, whereas the rat, when his vile behavior had been found out, only responded with still greater effrontery.

I recount this as it now runs through my mind: on the dock, chained to a silent man. As wretched as my situation is, I have to laugh. My laughter shakes me and my handcuffs, and I wake the handsome lad next to me without meaning to. He gives a start and looks at me with eyes wide. He does not join in my quiet chortling. I so much like to imitate the laughs of other people. He probably has no need of that, he has enough gallows humor of his own and a merry disposition no matter how serious the situation . . . He was simply brought up differently and has a different nature.

IX

The entire town, rising concentrically on a few hills, is now becoming a twilight tableau. The windows of a lighthouse on the north rim of the harbor glint now and again, unexpectedly, unpredictably, like heat lightning. Just reflections, not real beacons.

The sun is just at the horizon, so that great quantities of light are radiating eastward almost flat across the smooth ocean. The air is darkening rapidly. A bright expanse of crumpled fabric, gradually releasing its jumble of wrinkles and drinking in color, first at the center, then at the darker, sinking edges.

The brass instruments of the military band glitter distantly through the evening dust. The streetlights have come on. The band leader's baton waves: sharp eyes like mine can see it. The solid citizens, the officers, and the townsfolk stroll peacefully beneath the palms to the accompaniment of an evening concert of classical and modern works. Now the band delivers a high, triumphant trumpet note. The citizenry applauds.

The wind is not carrying in our direction and only the strongest notes seem to stand out. They fly through the air like severed heads. Grisly, yet comical, like everything bona fide in life.

Wretched as we are, a good many here within the guard cordon are proud not to be like all the rest out there. We broke through the cordon once. That happy accident must have been quite uncommon. Otherwise would we be made to pay so dearly for it?

Satisfaction of the scientific impulse can also afford exceptional happiness, of which the good citizens and officers can have no notion. But, of course, that happiness is not to be had for nothing, either.

The cordon that surrounded us all day has suddenly opened in front of me, an avenue is cleared, and before I realize it I am down at the breakwater with my companion and some other brothers in affliction. Hands full of baggage, pushed this way and that by the guards, we board the pontoon, which is supposed to be uniformly laden. Why does almost everyone hold on to the stern, look back toward the harbor?

In the haste of departure, I was too distracted to glance about me. It was already dusk when we got to the pontoons – people were crowding us, low voices were heard, there were hands waving at us in the shadowy twilight, and other hands were seizing our coats. Could I have made anyone out in the darkness? My old father, for example? I would have recognized my brother. Could he have spent the day waiting for this moment of departure, unseen among the "loving hearts" on the dock? As unlikely as it is – I hug myself at the thought. Unlikely?

Impossible . . . Just the same . . . I follow the example of another of my companions and wave, wave back toward the shore of my homeland, with a (formerly) white handkerchief.

The pontoon pushes off. The rudder blades pitch heavily into the water. We move toward the *Mimosa*.

Gulls have accompanied our transport, screeching indignantly. The illuminated portholes of the *Mimosa* are close now. Lone officers in white can be seen aboard the ship. Lone, every man for himself. Prisoners in dirty brown crowded into a mass.

A Jacob's ladder snakes down from above, black and glistening, either steel or rope that has absorbed seawater. Rope would give a better hold.

The houses of the town are already low and distant, somewhere far away, at my feet. In a valley of the sea. The church bells ringing for evening Mass reach us only very faintly. Fishing boats slip by. The patched sails rustle as they catch the light breeze; the tautened lines creak. The boats heel over. A bearded young man at the side of a barge lets his hand trail in the water. His cigarette glows. He does not look at us.

We are now directly beneath the *Mimosa*. Above our heads a galley worker shakes food leavings out through a round porthole. He holds the white enameled bucket away from him to keep the refuse off the clean dark gray hull of the ship. The scraps pelt into the still water beside us, crusts of bread, chicken wings, empty tins, fruit and peelings. The gulls, which have been flying around us in ever tighter circles, plunge into the sloshing water covered with white foam, pecking about them with their bills. They fight, pushing each other away from the food, screeching and scolding like market women. They seize the morsels with one slash of their bills and launch themselves into the air and away, or push them on the surface in order to eat them in peace at a safe distance. Their strong wings slap the water. Finally only a few champagne corks remain, floating in the light from the ship above.

X

I return to my father.

Among my father's subordinates at his office was a certain La Forest, whose brother was the aforementioned secular priest and religion teacher at our grammar school. I have forgotten what my father's reason was for casting odium upon this man. He, La Forest, must have shown himself superior to my father at some highly inopportune time. How, why, this did not become public knowledge. But my father detested him as he detested rats. Yet at the same time the man was virtually indispensable to him. He was a person of unusual abilities – energetic, discreet, and knowledgeable, possessed of indefatigable industriousness, unshakeable composure, very great and yet utterly controlled pride, and amply blessed with a dry sense of humor along with everything else, a combination rarely met with. He partook of neither rat nor frog. He was a man.

For a long time my father was unable to get rid of the rats in his old house. They defied all efforts to exterminate them, but he did not give up the fight. Later on I will recount the final chapter of this fight. At this point he had set himself another goal, to expel young La Forest (young – about thirty – for the high rank that he already held) from the office. And this was to be an opportunity to expose me, his son, already long familiar with the intrigues and horse trading of the Ministry, to one more example of practical anthropology and management of people. Ill-gotten gains profit nothing. But for my father, to whom La Forest was too virtuous, even fairly gotten gains could prevent one from profiting.

The goal was to induce La Forest to realize that there would be no point in staying on in the office and take his leave on his own.

My father's first approach to this problem was to question La Forest's colleagues about him (pledging them to the strictest discretion) while he was away on vacation. My father said nothing about the reason for these inquiries; the intent could just as well have been to further La Forest's more rapid advancement as to oust him. But subaltern creatures have a sharp nose for the unexpressed wishes of their superiors; the office guessed what my father wanted, and, by the time La Forest returned from his pleasant days off, the sentiments of his staff had turned against him and he had difficulties to contend with in his department. Important documents were sent to the wrong places. Periodically collected statistics went undelivered, and when matters became urgent, the subordinates excused themselves by saying that they had been waiting for La Forest to give them a specific instruction and had not wanted to remind him.

But La Forest was a good organizer. He spent nights at the office. He was not performing his subordinates' tasks himself but devising a work calendar that would allow absolutely nothing to be overlooked. He did not reprove any of his unruly colleagues and subordinates but merely set up his agenda and carried it out.

My father had failed. He went back to the chessboard for his next move. He gave La Forest new tasks that he hoped would be beyond him. He knew that someone like La Forest would never back out, but would take the assignment as a commendation, and he anticipated that

La Forest's ambition would exceed his ability. "You can set your own deadline." The task was indeed too large for one person to cope with alongside his regular duties. But La Forest found help, I surmise his brother, the priest, who would come to class deathly pale and utterly exhausted during that period and was now unable to give any of his pupils "private" attention. The two of them did what was necessary. From that point he (the priest) treated me with extreme reserve, limiting himself to his duties as a teacher and no more.

My father made his third move. He gave La Forest an assistant, a known careerist (and a regular frog). "You ought to have a lighter load, you need to take better care of yourself," he said with his friendly smile. "Don't you think?" La Forest was to see himself reduced to a figurehead. The consequences were easy to predict. And yet my father was mistaken; for La Forest never resented the man, he stuck to business, neither pushed himself forward nor gave any reason for conflict. He was so levelheaded that he pulled off the most difficult stunt and even made a friend out of the ambitious frog. When my father learned of this, he tossed the frog back into the lower depths, transferring him to an insignificant rural post with no possibility of advancement.

La Forest was strong. My father made a fourth move.

He provoked him. He annoyed him. He found fault, made pointed comments without justification, disparaged La Forest's work before he had looked at it.

"But you haven't read my reports yet," La Forest objected.

"Please let me make the decisions," my father responded patronizingly. He made vicious personal remarks, mollified him in the same breath, belittled him, used sarcasm, so that anyone else would have exploded in anger.

"Today he nearly pounded on the table," he said to me, to whom he reported all the phases of this bureaucratic duel, "nearly! Unfortunately I was called to the minister's office just then, and La Forest was in good spirits again by the time I came back. He offered *me* a cigarette."

"Did you take it?" I asked.

"Why not?" said my father. "But I'll write in his file, 'La Forest regrettably often lacks the reserve necessary between subordinate and supervisor.' I'll leave the dossier in an easily accessible drawer, seemingly by mistake, and then we'll see if he reads the document marked 'strictly confidential' in the folder with his name on it."

The idea never crossed La Forest's mind. He never read other people's mail, private files meant nothing to him, and "strictly confidential" did not tempt him at all.

My father tried another move. He invited La Forest to our house. I finally saw what he looked like. I found him extraordinarily appealing. My father had intentionally kept him waiting, and the man came up to me. He was a disconcertingly ugly, extremely taciturn person, but very clever with his hands, and he helped me repair an electrically operated toy that was broken. He knelt down on the floor with me and held the screwdriver between his teeth. Everything was in working order in half an hour. The expensive toy had never worked before and every repairman had given up on finding the hidden defect. La Forest was so methodical that he succeeded.

My father had intentionally left him alone with me for a long time. I asked La Forest all sorts of questions, including ones about his brother, the priest. He answered unselfconsciously, it seemed, without the least embarrassment, and treated me like someone his own age, which always pleases young people.

Now my father tried excessive praise. My father buttered him up so much that I was ashamed of him. But my father believed that a little butter never hurt anyone. Everybody could handle any amount of praise. But my father was reckoning on a specific effect of this fulsome praise, that the subordinate would start taking his recognized competence for granted and commit some blunder, or, even more abominably, overstep his limits, his authority. My father even went so far as to report La Forest's extraordinary competence, so as to be able to say to His Excellency when the anticipated failing came, "I expected *so much* of this man, as Your Excellency knows – how generous I was with him, and how shamefully we were deceived."

But, as strange as it sounds, my father met his Waterloo in this case. La Forest did not overstep the bounds of his position, however elevated it was now. He did his work; as a person he was modest, self-effacing, and cheerful. Both he and his brother had methodically worked their way up, overcoming great difficulties, and the result was that La Forest was recommended by the minister himself to the head of a large industrial concern that was seeking an organizer of unusual abilities. The perquisites of the position – percentages of profits, a house, a car, seats on the boards of other companies, etc. – were so extraordinary that it rankled my father that he had not been considered. Why hadn't he at least been offered the position? He would have said no (rich man that he was, power attracted him even more than money), but he would have liked to pose as the public-spirited, self-sacrificing high official who passes up a lordly salary in order to spend his life slaving on a comparatively meager wage for the sake of honor and country!

The priest was going along to organize the benefits system in the factories. He said his good-byes to us, all of us deeply moved, and gave each of us a book (approved by the estimable episcopal press office), which, when I brought it home, my father immediately hid in the back row, the second, dark row, of the bookcase. The cleric pressed the hand of each of us in turn, his eyes moist, and exited. I never heard anything about either of the brothers again – no, my father did tell me once that La Forest planned to return to the civil service. Whether that was because an effort had been made to bring him back or because he had soon had his fill of the overstuffed, indigestible sandwich of industry, my father did not say, nor did I ask. My father never found a replacement for him.

"Ah, La Forest," he would often sigh when he came home from work in a foul mood. La Forest was always a sore spot with him. "Never again!"

XI

Why these old memories? They are besieging me. For the first time in a long while. If I had my choice, I'd tell the story of how the rats were defeated. But there's no time for that now.

My companion and I are at the head of the line. We have to board the ship. Here as with everything else in the world there is only *one* practical method. I have figured it out by carefully observing the others, while most of the convicts in the pontoon, beset by hunger, were staring as though hypnotized at the gulls eating the refuse from the ship. In the eyes of many of the convicts can be read a literally burning hunger. They envy the birds even a scrap of garbage.

While thinking about my father and La Forest, I have worked out the best way to climb the accommodation ladder safely and practically, the best way to avoid slipping. Slipping would mean falling and falling would mean perishing. Or does anyone imagine that life preservers would be tossed to two convicts fighting for their lives in the waves, that a boat would be lowered for them? Sadly, I am sure the authorities would not put themselves out that far just to make sure the prisoners are fully accounted for.

But not to worry. The two of us will scale the thing like squirrels. The man whose right hand is free (me) will climb in front. With his right hand he will hold fast to the right rope, with his left foot he will pull himself from the gunwale of the pontoon onto the first rung. He will carry his possessions squeezed between his left arm and left hip. He will not look down, but only at the next rung, always taking great pains to make sure someone higher up does not step on his hand. His companion will follow two or three rungs below him and to one side, doing everything in the opposite order and not tugging too much on the arm of the other man shackled to him.

Does this need to be worked out in such pedantic detail? Let the reader of these lines try this. Improvise some fetters and bind yourself to your brother or friend or to your father. Climb up something with him, even a paperhanger's ladder that is not swaying back and forth or almost invisible in the twilight. Then consider that the joints of prisoners have grown stiff from disuse, that each man is carrying all his things, bedclothes and bags, everything that he believes essential for survival on the other side and will not part with voluntarily even at the risk of his life.

Now we climb up. Five rungs or fifty, we do not count them. The pontoon, the convicts in it gazing upward, their faces pale, sinks farther and farther away. Halfway up I feel a shooting pain in my left wrist. What is it? The fringe of my woolly coat has gotten caught in the handcuff ring and is rubbing the skin raw. Should I stop? Calmly straighten everything out? No way to do that when one man after another is pressing upward from below! And how to push that unruly sleeve back with my right hand? When I need my right hand to hold on to the rope? My companion could easily do it – not just for my sake, but for his own, too: I'll take him along with me if I fall. And he does it! Was it a considered action? Or was it out of pity? To thank me for my samaritanly help on the dock? In the same instant he has taken hold of me with his left hand and gently freed me while gripping the ladder more tightly between his knees. For with his right hand he has no choice but to hang on to his bags.

We brace ourselves with our knees and manage to get a grip on the rail. Covered with sweat and out of breath, at last we crawl on deck. A junior officer is standing there; finally, finally, he removes our manacles. He keeps a running tally as he tosses the handcuffs one after another into a basket.

What does everyone do with hands that are now free? It would not be believed! Many cross themselves.

The pontoon has gradually discharged its load. It pushes off. It is going for the rest of the convicts waiting on the dock. The oars dip metronomically. It is as steady as a child's toy, a wooden duck, perhaps, gliding on its four little wheels as the child pulls it across the smooth floor of the nursery, still playing after he has said his prayers, recited them for his pious father before bedtime.

The convicts are not allowed to sleep yet. They are still waiting. Most of them are chewing something. They smack and belch mightily. But they do not achieve satiety. Satiety of any kind slows and deepens respiration. But these men breathe quickly and shallowly like dogs being chased or giving chase. Even the feeling of a full belly is a kind of peace. There is no peace here.

It does not smell good. The tart aroma of the open sea, produced by seaweed and salt, is mixed with the warm smell of grease coming up from the engine room. But there is also an odor from still deeper down, perhaps from the uncleaned bunkers below, where livestock was once penned. It is a mingling of mildew, mustiness, latrine – no, it is none other than the true sharp, rank, stale smell of rats, a smell that decrepit old prisons and asylums have and (I recognize it now) that the beloved house of my childhood had, even though it was not an overcrowded coop for felons but a rambling villa on the edge of a city, its garden bordered by a sluggish river.

The house where I grew up had just this one flaw, that the rats were more at home there than people were. As I said earlier, rats had played an important role in my father's life. So he wanted to have the loathsome animals (loathsome to him, still more so to his wife, and most of all to us children) close at hand until such time as he was able to take his revenge on their kind. He did. Belatedly, but he did! That day I became an adult. Has it been worthwhile? I am not going to ask. I look at my companion. Could he become a comrade in the times to come, a substitute for the brother who is dead for me? I say nothing. My companion says nothing. Two mutes meet.

The night is starry. Very cool. Most of the men have unlashed their bedclothes and overcoats on the deck and wrapped them as tightly as possible around their limbs; many have even pulled them over their heads, Franciscan-style. Just the eyes, and what eyes! peep out from under the hoods of these strange monks. But each man acts for himself.

They do not associate. And yet two wrapped up together in two blankets, huddled close, would be twice as warm. As it is, much chattering of teeth can be heard.

The evening meal does not come. Many men grumble, curse wrathfully in the crudest language. But they lick their chops at the slightest provocation. When a junior officer comes near, they cravenly fall silent and bow their heads between hunched shoulders.

A lamp, its calm reflection on the water, glides toward us from the harbor: the navigation lantern of the pontoon with the last stragglers. And we hear that the *Mimosa* will be making another stop to take on more convicts. Now the men appear on board, one of them dragging a wet jacket; it leaves a damp trail on the deck, like blood. He and his companion, two wizened little old men, meekly hold out their thin wrists for the junior officers to unshackle. And what do they do then? With his freed hand, the older man, a mummy-like, yellow-faced figure, reaches under his shirt as though going after fleas. But all he does is bring out the rosary that hangs on his shaggy chest. He says his beads over and over, mumbling with loose lips.

Mosquitoes whine. An acetylene lamp comes on with a hiss, and the machinery in the engine room starts up.

XII

I have never believed very deeply in prayer or making the sign of the cross. Where ultramicroscopy, where microbial culture, where pathologic physiology rule, traditional religion usually has no crucial role to play. Sad, but true. Tragic, but that is the fact.

Science is what is intuitively convincing, built upon factual evidence free of assumptions. In order to do what it does, experimental natural science uses living material. In the area that interested me and people like Walter and Carolus, experimental pathology, intuitive conviction comes through vivisection of human beings and animals. Systematic experimentation – that is the only way. That is the only thing that counts. Suffering humanity is also helped in the process. But science leads the way.

Is it possible to combine science with affirmative faith in spite of everything? The world-renowned founder of the Pathology Institute, where I worked, could do it, he could, the man with the massive but smooth brow, with the crease at the root of his nose, with the penetrating yet humble gaze. He was a scientist who rocked the entire medical edifice of his time and built up a sublimely new structure – and was at the same time a devout Catholic. Revolutionary, bloody, and humane all at once. Pasteur.

At the Pasteur Institute, but long after Pasteur's death, I met the high-ranking medical officer who, wearing an open khaki-colored raincoat over his tropical uniform, has now emerged from his cabin below-decks and appears to be preparing to examine us. I look openly into his strange, long, worn, creased face, but he gives me only a fleeting glance out of the corner of his eye. I know you, Carolus, even if you don't know me.

The good man never was an observer of much distinction. He was a statistician, with a broad range of sources – a walking encyclopedia of the whole of bacteriology, pathology, epidemiology, and hygiene. Poring over heavy volumes, studying records, working with statistics, graphing incubation and epidemic control, this was what gladdened the heart of Dr. Carolus, this was where he earned his spurs. He was a major then, a brigadier general now. His knowledge must be stupendous, for he wanted to find out about everything.

He had no interest in hands-on medicine and never wanted to get close to living flesh. Even in the Great War he was engaged with statistical matters of the same kind. The precautions recommended by his office usually reached us too late at the front or at the epidemic sites in Russia or Asia Minor, where we were concerned not with science but with action, with going out and proving things by their efficacy in the field. He never was at the front, I see, for although he has many decorations on his left breast, there is nothing for bravery at the front.

His face is even more somber than it was when he was my colleague at the Pathology Institute. He too will have to live for at least four weeks on this galley, he too will probably not have undertaken this voyage very happily, but only because he was ordered to.

But one would hardly have sought out a man like him, with the rank of general, for a convict transport. An intern with the rank of second lieutenant would have been fully adequate for that. So does Brig. Gen. Carolus have some other mission? Is it possible that he will be taking charge of the bacteriological research on yellow fever instead of someone like Walter, who worked so hard on it?

The good man has my blessing. I leave you in peace! And why don't you leave us in peace, too! Why examine us wrecks: we're tired and hungry, that's the only thing wrong with us and the only thing that can be cured here. Give us some food to eat, a corner to sleep in! What's the point of an examination? We'll be delivered fresh and wholesome to the port of C. But what for? We'll only be fodder for the yellow fever.

The epidemic has flared up. Of a thousand new arrivals coming to a yellow-fever region such as the sumps at the Panama Canal excavations near the Central American city of Colón, five hundred are still alive six months later. But we are not even such unbroken freshmen. We are inferior material, we are broken.

If some unsuspecting person comes from a temperate climate to these swampy, torrid islands and beaches, which are drenched by daily downpours and have an average temperature of at least twenty-six degrees Réaumur, summer and winter, day and night, never changing, to these tropical regions where he must endure the most extreme precipitation on earth lashing down on him, an annual three meters of rainfall; yes, if he disembarks from the *Mimosa*, let us say, onto the soil of C., a place as intolerably humid as a steam bath, and if the possibility of infection exists at all (and would it not exist within the entire epidemic area?) – then it's a hundred to one that yellow fever will find that poor wretch so inviting that after two weeks nothing will remain of the silly boy but his death certificate, a lump of decomposed flesh, and the buttons from his prison trousers.

This fact does not keep a man like me up at night. I have been in mortal danger in a thousand experiments. For no one works with the most dangerous microorganisms that bacteriological science has been able to isolate without putting his life at risk: plague, tetanus, tuberculosis, glanders, cholera.

One must risk everything. One must think of everything. One must be equal to everything.

The great medical officer Carolus looks straight ahead, full of cares. The acetylene lamp above his bald head flickers, hisses, and reeks.

Behind his high, but not very domed, brow, are the lights on too? The good man glances toward the shoreline, receding farther and farther into the distance, and puts on his gold-embroidered uniform cap. A little while ago, on the way from shore, he had a pith helmet on. But now he is on duty and we are to kowtow to the general's stripes. Or is he just cold? What's on your mind? Has all your thinking had some result, are you on the trail of the yellow-fever pathogen?

My boyhood friend Walter, of whom I spoke earlier, worked on this epidemic. He had a serum sent over to him and inoculated guinea pigs with it, successfully.

It is important to understand what serum is. Serum is simply slightly stale, coagulated human blood that has been purified. Or animal blood. It is clear, like water, or a bit yellowish, like cognac mixed with water. It has none of the direness, the grimness, of blood about it. Under the microscope, normal serum is free of organisms, of microbes that can be seen, stained, cultured. Fine. But if, under conditions of extreme cleanliness, infected serum is injected into the bloodstream of guinea pigs, they sicken, their internal organs show effects similar to those induced by the yellow-fever virus "in real life," that is, in nature and in human beings, and the epidemic is transmitted with undiminished virulence from one guinea pig to another via the most direct route. If the blood of a dying animal is transferred to a healthy one, the mysterious illness goes with it. Could it not also strike a human being now and then? Certainly it could, if a human being possessed the superhuman courage to have a drop of infected guinea-pig blood or even human blood injected into his bloodstream.

But this *experimentum crucis*, as it is called, was never done at the Pathology Institute. Walter had to clear out his work space too soon, at a point when his experiments were still just beginning. The department head did not believe him – the compelling, unmistakable evidence was still lacking. And it is indeed possible that truly rigorous evidence can be obtained only on the epidemic's home soil, not many thousands of kilometers from the scene. Walter, who had married young, bore everything with stoicism, indeed with humor.

Perhaps, as a special-duty medic, to use the officialese, he followed "his" epidemic, made the exodus with his wife and child to the tropics, possibly even to C.

What is known about yellow fever – what do the absolutely unassailable scientific facts look like in black and white? That page is still a virginal white. Yes, it's blank.

There are theories galore, innumerable experiments have been done.

But there is no certainty. The pathogen is unknown.

If it were at least known how the invisible yellow fever microbe spreads, where it resides, and how it travels – then a great deal would have been gained. No one knows the route by which the epidemic propagates from person to person, or from person to animal and back again. Just as little is known about how to save the sick. Let them perish! But to protect the healthy from yellow fever in the future at least – *that* is the task, and no one is yet equal to it.

And this old fellow with the long, narrow face, who brings to mind a six-story building with only two windows facing the street, this man with his exceptionally long, sleepy eyelids, with pendulous earlobes covered with hair like rough gray lichen on the trunk of an old olive tree, this sallow man whose tired eyes have to squint in the light from the acetylene lamp, is this man going to unravel nature's secrets?

He'd do better not to put himself out, or us, either. But he has no such thought. He has a little table brought, a worn-out card table, flimsy, shaken by the vibrations from the laboring engine. His factotums have set up a nice chair for him and he makes himself comfortable, stretching his long, spindly legs in baggy trousers straight out in front of him and covering them with his coat.

He barely looks at us. In my day I would never have slighted the subjects of my experiments this way, the dogs, cats, rats, guinea pigs, and rabbits, even the white mice.

He lets his eyes wander into the distance.

Transparent colors appear at the horizon, the tops of gently rolling, bare hills magically washed in the first rays of the rising coppery moon, vegetationless hills on the windy seacoast.

On his knees, on the coat over his scrawny legs, he holds a voluminous register. Its pages catch the night wind.

A gentle salt breeze is blowing from the east. Or is it the west? It's night. We have lost our orientation.

The register, the grand inventory in which we are listed with all our vital statistics, along with our ancestry, criminal record, trial history, and personal evaluations by wardens and prison chaplains, rustles in the cool wind.

The brigadier general chews thoughtfully on a cigar. The night is fine. He is unable to tear his eyes away from a necklace of lights, evidently a small coastal city.

Cigar ash falls like dusting powder on the register. But it needs no blotting, the ink is long since dry.

At last the lights of the city sink back into the semi-twilight of the cloudless but somewhat misty moonlit night. The plume of smoke from the slanting funnel floats not far above our heads. Sparks glimmer in it for a few seconds, and the stars shine through faintly.

Our hunger is growing more acute. Are we going to spend the entire night here outside, looking at the stars? That may be a welcome tonic to a satisfied mind, but not to an empty stomach or overstretched nerves. The grumbling among the convicts is becoming louder, they want to get to their sleeping quarters, their evening rations. No use thinking about it. The doctor is proceeding methodically. His objects of study, their spirits, their complaints and pains are of little concern to him. At last he decides to begin. He authoritatively calls for rubber gloves. The factotums quickly bring some from the sick bay. He inflates them, examines them very closely. They need to be leak-proof. He doesn't want to touch us with his bare hands. Does he fear contagion so very much? But as sound as they are, they are not adequate. He calls for a basin of disinfectant sublimate solution. Filled to the brim, it slops over with the languid rolling of the ship.

Carolus, enough dawdling, let's get to it! Some hundred men are waiting for you, so tired they are about to drop, as ravenous as dogs that have been starved for twelve or fourteen days in order to make an accurate test of their carbohydrate metabolism. A little dispatch, sir, please! Why do you even want to examine us? Certainly there may be all sorts of infectious material among us future penal colonists. No, no cholera, no plague, no abdominal typhus, to name some of the lovely inventions of the Almighty Creator. But venereal diseases? Possibly. Or Hansen's disease, leprosy? Some of the convicts come from the tropics, they are nonwhite, and leprosy may be clinging to someone. With such a manifold, mystical disease, who knows? But a microscope would be needed to identify the pathogen, Hansen's bacillus, and the idea of performing such a meticulous examination out in the open, on the deck of a steamer in passage, at night and without good light, can only be called grotesque.

But not all that grotesque. My left wrist was scraped raw by the handcuffs. Do I know who bumped me in the crush during the trip from shore? The skin at that spot will be especially receptive to infection.

Our hunger is becoming stronger and harsher. It has descended from the belly to the small of the back, I feel it as a pain between the shoulder blades too, the front of my throat is constricted, my temples are pounding, my fingers are cramping. I'm so intensely hungry now that I'm actually nauseous. And I'm trembling with rage – maybe if I stamped my feet I could work off some of my anger. What am I doing here among these lowlifes? Are they my own kind? What am I doing under the thumb of this most mindless of all mindless medical bureaucrats? What a monumental lummox! I want to stamp, to break loose. I can't bear any more of this endless waiting. No more! But – what can I do? I can be silent and grit my teeth. This man with all his book learning still hasn't got the most moronically simple examination method straight. He riffles through his papers, all of them entirely useless; he moistens his fingertips, highly unappetizingly, with spittle from his thin, pursed, stupid lips, nervously flipping page after page. Stop it, sir, what's the point of this idiocy? If anything really needs to be examined, it's not our past lives and our crimes and mistakes, but we ourselves, and fast, for pity's sake! You beast, don't you see us, this pitiful lot of tired, emaciated, famished wretches!

More hesitation. He pulls on the gloves, but the sublimate solution is too weak for him. He has another sublimate tablet brought and dissolved in the liquid. *This* is how much he loves *his* life! If only I had taken mine a thousandth as seriously! Then I never would have fallen so far as to become his object of study. This fellow with the face like a wrinkly, jaundiced baby's bottom has no idea what it is to spend all day and all night on the hard floor of a cattle car, to sweat through an entire hot day out in the open under a blazing sun, nostrils full of one's comrades' filth and one's own. Does someone living in freedom ever know what it is to yearn for the bare necessities, the things one provides to animals, to dumb brutes? *Does* one provide them with those things, though? Did I? What were any of those brutes to me? Just what I am now to him, to Brig. Gen. Carolus, who raises his extraordinarily long eyelids and focuses his icy, impersonal gaze on me, who can't bear it.

XIII

Now one convict after another is being summoned. Those who are called are happy, thinking that as soon as the examination is over they will go down below, where warm food and a cot await them. No chance of that! They'll have to step back in line and wait until *everyone* has been dealt with. Carolus has given an order to this effect. "Order"? Where is order? How foolish it all is, how absurd. The mere appearance of order without order itself – this is the plague of mankind, enshrined in administration and government. And the mindlessness of the incompetent top medic! He clumsily everts the eyelids of one dark-skinned convict to look for trachoma follicles, but, as any blind man could tell by using his cane, the man's eyes are healthy, whereas his skin is diseased, covered with a pustular rash and crying out for a blood test, a "Wassermann." A second convict, the lively little fellow of a moment ago, aged somewhere between twenty-five and fifty, the old boy's immense, feverish, black, blue-rimmed eyes bursting with jailhouse tuberculosis in all its dreary misery, this man's skin he prods with particular care, though there's not a thing wrong with it. Then he taps the little man's kneecaps to test his reflexes, and all the time he's about to drop from coughing and hunger. And so it goes, for hours. Carolus is answerable to no one. No one is checking up on him.

No superior officer is present. Three junior officers are standing idly by. One of them, playing with his revolver, amuses himself by drawing a bead on an overfed ship's rat poking its head out from behind a coil of rope. I mentioned it before, didn't I? Rats, those disgusting, highly dangerous beasts, here too! Why doesn't Carolus think about ridding the ship of rats? He could get a few tips on that from my humble self. But what am I to the big man?

It would be the big man's job to see to the greatest possible cleanliness here on this run-down ship. But cleanliness! How would he know the meaning of the word, this man who hasn't once washed his hands in the sublimate solution, even after a good dozen examinations. For him the founder of the Pathology Institute where he did his studies, Louis Pasteur, the man with the mind of genius – and the affirmative faith – never lived. The man with little lines at the root of his nose from concentration and an unlined, massively domed brow.

Before that pathbreaking scientist's time, people were about as advanced as this miserable bungler Carolus still is. It was known that the dreaded condition of gas gangrene was infectious, but all suppurating wounds were uselessly and unthinkingly washed with the same sponge. As far as anyone knew, this was a prophylactic measure suitable for the poorest of the poor, though it was nothing of the kind. There was only *one* thing the physician did not wash at that time, and that was: himself. And when such a master of the healing arts climbed into bed beside his wife at night after a day's work, he folded his hands to say a little prayer, went to sleep, and snored, in the belief that he had accomplished something good and pleasing in the sight of God that day and done a vital job for suffering humanity. How fortunate his patients would have been if he had never lived! A terrible thing to say, but it could be said about me, too. And yet I hardly know which is the greater bane of society, the lawbreaker and renegade or a very different type, the character who is pleasant under all circumstances, free of conflict, and, of course, socially respected and guilty of no crimes, the good man of Carolus's sort. A man who takes hold of the world's horrors with clumsy hands. A man whose only response to the bleeding wounds of this most unfortunate of all worlds is to stamp bureaucratic file numbers on them.

What he is, his station in society, *I* could have had that. I would have!

But even now I don't envy him. If I did feel a twinge of envy toward this doddering idiot, it would never be for his gold braid, his "loving hearts" at home, his grandchild back on the beach, his high salary, or his pretty decorations – I could only envy Brig. Gen. Carolus his job, the job of investigating the infectious agent and transmission of yellow fever over in the tropics.

Is *he* really going to be the one, is Carolus destined for that?

Certainly he is, I'd bet my life on it if it were worth anything. Him and nobody else. Not someone like Walter. Carolus, so moronically stupid about the simplest hygienic procedures, was surely selected by those in the upper levels of the administration to head the yellow-fever research team because of his rank, his astounding knowledge of the scientific literature, and his shallow respectability. He is the right man for the job.

But am I so much smarter? I may seem bright, but I am even stupider than he is. A scientific undertaking of this kind was once among my aims in life, yet I deliberately and studiedly set about it in such a way that I would never get what I wanted. Everything had to happen the way it did, or am I wrong? I'm here, am I not? What doomed me was just that I was toying with myself along with everything else, that I did not value my own life and my future highly enough. Thus I squandered not only my considerable fortune but also my very self, completely and utterly. I was hardened, fine. But hardened even against compassion for myself. I myself was the vivisected animal, the bright, so very docile dog that willingly jumps up onto the vivisection table and holds out its paws to be clamped, stretching out on its back, between its clenched teeth the nickel bit and its slowly dehydrating tongue, and then opens its intelligent eyes, waiting to see what its masters the humans are going to do with it.

I have to accept everything now. I have to content myself with a bare minimum of possessions, I have to give up my name, have to jump when I hear the number 46984, I have to sink to the level of a dumb animal, yes, I am like a head of livestock to this wrinkly old fellow pawing me with his greasy hands, which even at the Institute were notorious for their filthiness and never served him for even the simplest experiment – this gray-haired, gold-braided oaf is prodding at my face, my ocular conjunctivae, with his dirty, sticky, rubber-gloved paws as though I were a low-grade steer. And if the old scoundrel touched a trachomatous conjunctiva a moment before, which is only too likely, or if Professor Hansen's leprosy bacterium is still clinging to his rubber gloves, endangering not his but *my* epidermis, there's not a thing I can do about it.

I'm nearly weeping with rage, and my neighbor commiserates with me. But the tears might wash the infectious matter out of my eyes. You're the beast, the monumental lummox! Georg Letham, in spite of all your ideas, your experiments, and your worldly sophistication, you're powerless now, the subject of someone else's experiment. You'll never get what you want, no matter how badly you want it. And what you want is to step on Carolus's long, silly face with the heel of your prison shoe encrusted with human shit, three times for each of the three syllables in his accursed name!

To be delivered into the hands of a physician, a man whose profession leads you to expect the best, the highest – recovery, solace, healing – and to see him as your *enemy*! An even more terrible thing to say, and again it could just as well be said about me, me, Dr. Georg Letham the younger, the physician, son of his father. Is *this* what they call remorse? Then the hell with it all.

XIV

Another rat has just scurried between my feet. Come closer, you dear little creature, I'm not afraid of you, and don't you be afraid of me, either.

I have known these animals from an early age, and, though I loathe them terribly, we have been on intimate terms. But this one is mistrustful and disappears underneath the ropes.

For my father they were fateful animals. No one made him live in a house where rats felt at home. But he wanted to show, to prove, that he was stronger.

They put in an appearance sporadically. There were hot, dry summers during which not one exemplar of the genus was observed. Then they would emerge in great numbers. In my early childhood they were the somewhat tamer kind with uniform blue-gray coloration on their backs; it was not until later years, after an especially rainy, autumnal summer, that rats of the other variety appeared, somewhat larger and stronger, with a dark stripe along the spine. The gentler kind were house rats; the other kind, the conquerors wiping out the weaker ones, were brown rats. Life-and-death struggle? War of all against all, family against family, like against like? What better way of demonstrating to me the laws of life as *he* saw it could my wise old father have found, that clever, cunning bastard, than to use these animals as an example?

July was stormy and blustery that year, like a November by the sea. Usually there were no rats in the yard while it was raining. But then they roamed the house instead. They raided the pantry, trolled through the cellar rooms despite the oak doors, they pitched camp in the servants' beds (empty because my father had let some of the staff go to save money) and staged races and athletic contests in the attics while the rains pelted down on the slate roof. Then when the rainy spell was over, every corner of the grounds was teeming with them, the valuable poultry were destroyed overnight, everything in the greenhouse was gnawed to pieces and pulled apart. My father was unwilling to use dogs to go after the rodents (later I found out why). Exterminators did their best but were no match for the beasts. As a horde they withstood anything. It was known that the previous owners of the property had moved out and let my father have the house for a song because they had been unable to beat the rats. At that time my dear mother was no longer alive. She was the sister of an important scholar who had accompanied my father on his expedition to the northern lands. But the geographer had not stayed in his native country, he had headed out a second time, had gone missing, and was never heard from again.

Now and then an animal was caught in a wire-mesh trap. I remember one such event. My father, looking down from his window with his eagle eyes, spotted something moving in a trap at the foot of the plane tree in the courtyard. It must have been late in the evening. He took me down with him. He gave me his silk-lined smoking jacket to protect me from the cool and damp of the night. I was still so small that it came down to my knees.

Under the rainspout was a large barrel for collecting the water. Back then rainwater was thought to be especially pure and especially suitable for washing one's hair. We went down, and he had me pick up the trap. It seemed so light that the little animal (evidently an inexperienced pup) might have been made of papier-mâché. The rat ran in rapid circles behind the mesh, looked worriedly about, did its business as it ran, gnawed with its sharp, protruding teeth at the wire, which was fairly stout and very rusty from the rain. Being an intelligent animal, it even jiggled the little door it had come through, shrilling now and then. It sniffed at the hook that had held a piece of bacon as bait, and then began running around again. Suddenly it made a great leap, clung to the roof of the trap with all four feet like a monkey, and looked up at us with its reddish black eyes, blinking now and then. Its long, dust-colored tail curled around the wires. I was weakening.

"Toss it in," said my father. "What else is there to do with it? Then I'll tell you the story of my voyage again." I could not hear this story often enough.

As much as I loathed the animal, killing it was not something that came easily to me. The windows behind which my brother and sister were already sleeping were dark. The moon shone brightly but was obscured by the edge of a mussel-shaped cloud moving eastward. More dark blue clouds were rolling by higher up.

There was a light on in the open window of my father's library. I saw the gilt-lettered spines of the books.

Grappling with its claws, the animal had let itself down onto the floor of the trap. It was not running now. It sat with its annulated, naked, ugly, very long tail coiled around it, swiveling its head about with great urgency and unease.

The wood of the trap floor was resting on the palm of my hand. I felt a vibration, rhythmic but very subtle. Was it the rat's heartbeat? The clouds had passed behind the treetops and nearby chimneys. "Now show what you can do, Georg Letham," my father said, with cool but tender mockery.

I lifted the wire trap in my right hand and, closing my eyes desperately, tossed it into the tub.

The water splashed into our faces.

"Good," my father said. He put his head back and laughed. He wiped the foul water first from my face, then from his, with a fine handkerchief that he took from the breast pocket of his smoking jacket, which I was wearing over my undershirt. I felt his long, thin hands.

Bubbles continued to rise from the barrel for a fairly long time, two or three minutes. My father's eyes were fixed on my face with an ardent expression that I never deciphered. Love? Hate? Was I everything to him, or nothing? Just an experiment? Did he mean well toward me? He had taught me how to take the life of a living creature. And yet I loved him the way he was – now more than ever.

XV

The rain barrel had to be destroyed after the rat's execution. The waterlogged wood was useless, even for heating. My father was sorry, for despite his great wealth he counted every penny.

Resourceful my father was, you had to hand him that, and I, his son, who looked up to him as though he were a kind of deity, handed him that and more. At that time he was having all sorts of trouble at his office (La Forest was still there and played a major role in it). He had always been a defender of high protective tariffs, but now the new minister believed in free trade. He had to adjust overnight, and that took some doing. He tried supporting a high domestic tariff while also coming down as a proponent of free-trade theory. Thus he was a patriot, a nationalist, yet international and liberal when it came to foreign trade. He could play any instrument in the orchestra. He played soccer with his feet while playing the fiddle with his hands, so to speak. And for all that, he was still unable to deal with the "enemies in his own house"! When he got some time off, he set to work.

How did he drive the rats from his house? Rats are full of passionate feeling, but they are clever, too. Indeed, they are so intelligent that one is inclined to credit them with ill will toward human beings, and this is the source of the great fury with which man has pursued them since ancient times, usually to no avail. But gods do not know fury. Only one thing helps against these animals, something for which man generally shows no affinity – the coldest reason, a scientific reason that tests and experiments, a *ratio* founded on the struggle of all living creatures for existence.

My father set about his work as follows. One fine day, assisted by the gardener and myself, he set up a great trap, this time one not made of wire.

Between the courtyard of the house and the grounds, in a spot where the rats gathered in great numbers when the weather changed, he constructed a square pit one and a half meters deep and a bit less in length and width. That year an old heating stove (from my poor mother's bedroom, which no one used now) had been dismantled, and the nice tiles, white porcelain tiles, were lying around in the courtyard. Actually they were not lying around, they had been neatly stacked among the peach and rose trellises at the south wall of the house and covered with old boards. These tiles were used to line the bottom of the pit. The walls of the pit leaned toward each other at a bit of an angle. It was quite a trick to get the tiles to stay together so as to create this pyramid-shaped cavity. It took us several evenings to adjust the tiles precisely. Perpendicular walls would have been easier, but whereas rats have been known to climb vertical walls when they are in mortal peril, ones sloping inward are an insuperable obstacle for almost any animal without wings.

My father put his heart into this work. He forgot everything, free trade and protective tariffs, the minister and La Forest, even his own frugality.

I can still see him splitting the tiles with a chisel to make them fit. Running to the kitchen after a day's work, then to the pantry next to the kitchen, and bringing down a side of bacon, slicing off a piece the size of two fists, having *me* light a great fire in the stove (what a delight for me!). I can still hear the bacon sputtering merrily in an old iron pot.

Finally the fat was rendered out, the cracklings floating on top. Then the pot was taken off the stove and brought to the open window. The marvelous bacon smell spread far and wide. From the pantry my father got a large, narrow-necked earthenware jar, a thick-walled, rust red clay vessel that no one had used in years and was covered with dust. It was cleaned, and my father took a funnel, shook into the jar's narrow neck some unused chicken meal (the chickens had wound up in the rats' stomachs, as we know), soaked this in some of the fat, and mixed it with the cracklings, arranging these nicely toward the top with an old spoon.

He poured the rest of the fat into the tiled pit outside, swinging the pot slowly and carefully to reach every corner. Then the jar was lowered to the bottom, and the preparations for the experiment were complete. He washed his hands, gave me some book or other to read, and left.

Here I must interject something that may seem irrelevant. This was the period when "inward urges" were awakening in me. They were not the least bit pleasant. Why bring it up now? Anyone who was ever young remembers what it was like: at first more anguish and trepidation than joy and pleasure.

I sat by the window with the book and controlled myself.

I had to wait for a long time. But then, toward evening, they came scampering out, the rats. They came running from all directions, as though pulled by threads, soundlessly. From the cellar door, through the narrowest holes, out from under the rain barrel, often three, four at once, large and small, pell-mell. It was the stronger species, all had dark stripes on their dirty-brown backs. They crowded around the four sides of the pit. They raised their pointed snouts, sniffing, the long, lighter-colored whiskers at their mouths bristling greedily, long hairs also visible above their gleaming dark eyes and at the openings of their bare ears. They gave off a nasty smell. They did not whistle or shrill or twitter in their usual way. In silence they raised their long-toed, almost hairless feet, pawed and scraped insistently at the slightly protruding rim of the white tiles as though trying to scoop out a path into the pit. They were looking down. They laid their shallow, conical ears back, seemingly watching and waiting for something. They gripped the rim of the pit; they were not about to back off. Then suddenly they changed positions, they thronged wildly, they put their heads over the abyss and breathed in the lovely smell; newcomers kept arriving and pushed and shoved from behind at the ones in front. But the ones in front did not let themselves be pushed down. They were too smart for that. They resisted temptation. They did not jump in.

My father stayed away for a long time. Or was he standing behind me and watching me? I made myself believe that he was and kept a grip on myself.

I fell asleep in my steamy innocence.

When I woke up, the page I had been reading was completely crumpled. I was very sorry. My father was finicky about the way his books looked and trusted no one but me with them. And now! I looked down. It was night. The animals were still crowded around the pit in great numbers. They were no longer so quiet. They were in a state of great agitation, constantly changing their positions. The ones in front tried to move back, the ones in back pressed toward the front.

Suddenly the first rat dared to make the leap. I saw its dingy gray-brown fur and the dark stripe along its backbone sharply set off against the snow-white tiles. The animal reached the bottom with a pattering sound. The kitchen staff, who had been following the whole thing from the window of the servants' quarters, erupted in triumphant laughter. My father was not there. The other rats fell silent, as though they were frightened. But they circled the pit, moving continuously around it from left to right. For a time the influx had stopped; now new arrivals surged forward once again, crawling on their bellies, following the scent, covered by the horde.

I saw the rat at the bottom very clearly from up above. It was so deep in the fat that its paws were almost invisible. At first it kept still, tried to pull its legs free one after another, swiveled its head like the one I had killed. But then it plucked up its courage and began to lick up the fat. First next to it, then farther away, as far as the corners that could not be seen very well from above. It was almost beyond belief, but in about half an hour the animal had eaten some two liters of fat. And was it satisfied? It cleaned its ears, licked its paws, and worried its claws with its tongue, but then – was it thinking about escaping? Hardly. True enough, it certainly would not have been able to. Our experiment had been designed too carefully for that. But the captive animal might at least have tried! This it did not do. It was still filled with nothing but greed. With its front paws it climbed up onto the upright earthenware jar, trying to tip it. When this first attempt failed, it threw itself headfirst against the strong, heavy jar from the front and then from the side, until it succeeded in toppling it. Then, with agile, delicate movements, as daintily as a squirrel, it fished a few bits of grain and chunks of fat out of the neck of the wide-bellied jar. It got no deeper. It poked its snout into the opening, ground its teeth against the ceramic (I heard a metallic ringing). But to no avail. Then it took heart. It was not in the company of its fellows. Its belly grossly full, it withdrew into a corner of the pit, the darkest one, coiled its naked tail around itself, made itself comfortable, pillowed its head on the soft parts of its lumbar region, and was soon asleep.

XVI

When I stopped by the pit the next morning, I saw a rat in it. But it was not the one that had eaten the two liters of fat. It was a much bigger one, with a lean, elongated body. It was uneasy and ran about incessantly. The pit was soiled. Instead of the fat, a bloody residue could be seen, not dark in color, but a pale, dilute red. Shreds of skin, claws, and the poorly cleaned remains of a spinal column were also lying about. The rat roamed among these repellent things, sniffed at the blood, vibrated its whiskers, cocked its head, bared its strong teeth, then threw itself against the heavy jar and rolled it into a corner, snuffled at it for a long time, and finally took up a position in front of it, as though to guard it.

I went to school. These were the last days before vacation, our lessons were no longer being taken so seriously. At noon I went home, but I deliberately avoided looking into the pit. In the afternoon I returned to school, where we had physical education and stenography, not compulsory subjects. Afterward I went to the tennis court. When I came home late in the day, it was as though the captive rat down in the pit were chasing me. The hole in the ground was easier to see from above than from the courtyard. Or so I imagined. I was pulled as though by magic into my father's room, where I sat down in the armchair at his desk, which I was actually not allowed to do. By the time my father arrived I had gotten up and was doing my homework. Evening came. I fell asleep with difficulty, late at night. I said nothing to my father. I believe this was the time of La Forest's farewell visit, but I may be mistaken.

As I lay in my bed, I heard nothing from the rats. But the treetops were rustling. The wind fell suddenly, and I heard the fountain splashing into the little basin. How far away it sounded. My father had forgotten to close the tap as he ordinarily did at night in midsummer. The water that was saved in this way could be used the next day for watering the lawn. Water cost money, something I was unwilling to believe for a long time. But my father, who otherwise did not shrink from lying (it just has to be learned, he said), never lied to me. He told no one what he thought, just me.

The birds stirred uneasily in the branches of the plane tree that stood in front of the windows. The air was heavy – though the sky was clear – and fragrant; nothing remained of the bacon smell.

A few minutes later I was awakened from a deep narcotic sleep (I believe it was almost morning and dawn was breaking) by a death cry.

When an animal dies, it makes a cry quite unlike its cries in life. An animal or a person may be wracked by the most extreme pains but never makes cries like the death cry until the end. The death cry has a singular inflection. A swell, I might say, a sort of terrible exultation. If I could only stop hearing it at last, the death wail of my poor wife!

Today I know it, as a man of ripe years, of more than ripe years. At that time it was only a suspicion I had, as an unripe yet overripe lad. But I had discerned it, even though I was still in short pants and sat on the school bench among boys.

It will be said that a child is not aware of such things, that no adolescent sees the world that way. I might say that myself if I heard my life story in someone else's telling. Yet that is how it was. What purpose would be served by lying to myself about myself?

I did have a normal child around me, my brother. That very evening

I had seen him take no interest in the "nasty" extermination of the rats. He gave no more than a curious glance into the porcelain pit as he ran past it with a deliberately stamping, jingling step when my little sister called him out of the yard. They had been playing their perennial simple game, in which my brother, a big, squarely built, very phlegmatic boy, would stretch a kind of leather harness studded with brass bells around him and play a "furrowbred." My little sister had once heard something about thoroughbreds and had recast the word. The harness had actually been for her and would have fit her – a chubby-cheeked, light blonde, blue-eyed, somewhat squinty (and thus always armed with distance glasses) little beast – to a tee, but she, quite the gal despite her youth, had gotten her much bigger and stronger brother to strap the harness on himself; his arms, held at his sides, barely fit, and his rib cage did not fit at all. So they were playing "furrowbred" and "driver."

My brother and sister were afraid of me. Yet it was they who jealously guarded their treasure trove of toys, which I was never allowed to touch, while I was only too glad to put my own at their disposal. They took them, but not when I was there. Stealing was more fun for them than receiving presents. Grotesque, but true. More than true, normal. Thus I was surrounded by normal, healthy, exuberant creatures. And my brother and sister turned into normal, healthy adults, too. So was my bloodiness not in the blood? We all had the same blood.

My brother and sister were now sleeping quietly in the two rooms on either side of mine, but I was at the window, looking out. It must have just started to rain. Through the veil of rain, two animals could be seen, one on top of the other. The moisture made their fur slick, dark. The top rat seemed to be riding on the other. With its front claws it was squeezing the throat of the rat below. I cried out softly. The animal raised its head, craned its neck upward, looked about. I was silent. Through the trickling of the rain I heard a soft wail like the meowing of a cat break from the throat of the conquered rat as the conquering rat calmly and deliberately hacked at the other's head. It bit through the easily cracked skull, gobbled the brain, then threw the carcass onto its side and went at the entrails. It worked among them with passion. The rain soon stopped entirely. The wind shook leaves from the lovely rain-wet plane trees into the pit. A perfumed surge of humid, almost tropically sultry, summer air came from the garden.

I fell asleep again – I might almost say I fell asleep against my will.

But the next day I witnessed something that had never been known to happen, two rats dwelling peaceably in the pit, a stronger one, a female, the animal from the night before, and a weaker one, a male, which had just let itself be tempted into jumping down, like so many before and after it. The male was shier, the female louder and bolder. Without fear of me or my father, it lifted its head and emitted high, unpleasant, vibrating notes – something like the whistling of an arrow through the air, that kind of sound. The female ran with short steps in circles around the male, or rather in semicircles, for the creature being courted was afraid and cowered in the corner. Romiette and Julio, my father said mockingly. The female did not slacken, sometimes getting up on its hind legs like a trained squirrel and dancing around the male, which came forward. I was not able to see the rest of the game (it was a ghastly and yet exhilarating sight to see, these horrible animals *playing*!). It was the day final grades were being given out at school.

My clever father's idea was that the animals would first be lured into the pit and then devour each other there, wipe themselves out. All against all. But now two mortal enemies were living, as it appeared, side by side, amicably and companionably. The fact that *his* law of life did not apply in all cases was, despite all the love I had for him, perhaps I will not be believed, a consolation, a freeing thought. Perhaps the world was not as bad, nowhere near as ghastly, as he made it out to be. Did he make it bad, or was it bad? I would so much have liked to teach *him*, to disabuse him. But what response could I make to a cynic who told me that blessed stupidity could not be learned and that even meanness had to be inborn? That was all he knew. He thought it the greatest good fortune to be stupid, which he was not, and a natural advantage to be meaner than the rest.

My father noticed that I was resisting him, perhaps consciously for the first time. As always, he was excessively polite when he was gathering all his strength in order to achieve a goal. He yielded to me in everything. He never contradicted me. And yet he never lied. I knew him the way he knew me. He thought the world would have been better uncreated. I did not want to believe that unless I had to. I liked being alive so much. I was a child. I wanted to be one for once.

But he wanted something else. In the evening, or, to be more accurate, at night, he would grow serious. My father was toughening me. He wanted to bring me up to be a courageous person.

I only want to report the bare facts. He took me down to the rat pit and left me there to watch the dreadful animals' shameless and repeatedly performed sexual intercourse in the beam of his powerful pocket flashlight, as though the light from the lamps in the courtyard would not have been enough. I am unable to describe it. My revulsion was indescribable, and my voluptuous thrill equally so. There was just one other time when I experienced both at once. The reader knows when and where.

XVII

I want to try to describe what went on in me, and yet I know I can't. There must be some connection with the passing of my wife, for that too I have been unable to describe. What sensuality there was in me was at the same time revulsion. The two were a mad muddle. My father took my hand in his, and I clung to it. Almost the way I clung to my neighbor's hand on the dock in the southern city a few hours ago. He spoke kindly to me. "While your contemporaries are ignorant urchins, you are already a man. When they are men, you will be so far ahead of them that . . ." He left the sentence unfinished. He had to support me. I twisted as though in convulsions, I held my breath in my chest involuntarily, my face became heavy and hot, something was roused in me, and abruptly the warm, moist night air shot deep into my leaden, narrow breast with a whoosh, something loosened, and with the most terrible fright I realized that I was grinding my teeth . . . They were grinding just as my father's did. That was how he had ground through an expensive gold crown on one of his molars in half a year, and to his fury he had had to pay the high-priced dentist a second time. But a boy has strong, healthy teeth. I did back then.

I stepped back to the side of the house. I clenched my fists. With my left hand I beat against the wall like a lunatic, with my right I struck out at the rain barrel.

My father stood next to me, having again switched off his pocket flashlight for reasons of economy. I had put my hands over my eyes, but my father removed them gently (how he could caress, with his beautiful, thin, but not hard, hands, marred only by an oval scar from an old dog bite) and said to me: "You shouldn't try not to look. And if you inherit nothing from me but the education I have given you, you will certainly become a great and successful man. You may be hated sometimes, but you'll never be laughed at. What else is there? You can laugh at them! If my father had brought me up as I have you, my expedition would have been successful, and I would have been one of the greatest explorers of my time. So: open your eyes and see! You believe in the omnipotence of feeling. I believe in the omnipotence of greed. Love makes the world go round – or does money make the world go round? Shall we make a bet? I'll put down a thousand ducats, like a king in a fairy tale, and you only need to put down the dried-out sandwich that you're carrying around in your satchel."

This was correct. As on every school morning, I had brought my two breakfast rolls, made into sandwiches and wrapped up in paper. Grades had been ceremoniously handed out, but there had been no lessons. I took the rolls out of my satchel and gave them to him. "That's your stake. I'm good for mine, I don't have that much on me." Good! He switched his pocket flashlight back on, swung one of the rolls in the air, and pitched it into the pit.

The animals were still coupled in their way, the way rats couple even as they wage the battle of the sexes. Their hatred for each other was nothing new to me. For I had studied it. The other thing, their brute love, was new. A few minutes before, I had understood for the first time what the "ignorant urchins" whispered about in the schoolyard or in the bathrooms and what, in my silly pride, I had always turned away from despite all my craving for knowledge. Nor had I wanted to be enlightened about human love. But what these "loving hearts" were doing was now borne in upon me, in a horrific, revolting, scientifically naked, and brutal fashion. Not Romeo and Juliet, but he-rat and she-rat. No matter, borne in upon me it was. I had grasped it. But, being a pathetic stupid boy, I was unable to grasp what happened next, the struggle of the (even now) "loving hearts" over the wretched dried-out morsel of bread. The rending of the "loving hearts" by the cruel imperative of the struggle for existence. This struggle was waged between the strong female and the gentler male with a fury, rapidity, and brutality that surpassed anything I had seen.

I will not describe it. Be grateful that I am drawing the veil over this scene as I did over that of my wife's death. A little gift! Enough of the horrors of the world, as my father said. That'll do.

The female won. It bolted the filthy roll in one bite and glared with its sharp, glittering little eyes toward the top, where my father was still holding the second roll. Most horrifying of all, the male of the two had not even been killed by its love-antagonist. The poor beast was bleeding, lying on its side, and was unable to protect itself against its beloved. Time passed. I was breathing heavily, my throat became constricted. My father breathed calmly. The female down below was quiet too. Finally, just as I was thinking that everything was over, there was a sound, soft and yet so bloodcurdling that I – I don't know, I don't remember what happened then. I saw nothing and heard nothing. I think my father took me in his arms later, carried me to the library, and waited until I awakened fresh as a daisy. When I opened my eyes, he was holding the big Andree atlas in his hand and, as he often did, was using the tip of the nail of his little finger to trace the route through the northern seas (on the "Polar Region – Arctic" map) that he had taken on his voyage so long ago. I stood up, bade him good night, and he answered: Good night. I did not spend a sleepless night. I slept like a corpse.

I had now become the person who could do what I have done and what has brought me onto this convicts' ship. I no longer dreamed. My father had awakened me, like Hamlet. Is not Hamlet a murderer too? He "only" kills Polonius, he kills his beloved's meddlesome father as though it were a lark, skewers him like a rat that is old and smart but still not smart and experienced enough, behind a curtain, to hear him squeal. And yet he is Hamlet!

Our war against the rats was progressing well.

One day the animals roused themselves to action. They had finally come to a decision. They no longer accepted the terms of the experiment, but left their home, the courtyard, the garden, the house. They must have gone to the river at night and launched themselves onward in a horde. Rat hordes were supposed to have turned up far downstream; whether these were "ours" is very much open to question, for traveling is just what rats like to do. Among other things they like to do.

There is no way of knowing how many of our rats had killed each other. We started to count, but soon tired of it. The remains of the animals were shoveled out day after day until suddenly there were no more. These mortal remains went into a hole dug for this purpose not far from the fountain, and they produced very good fertilizer. For flowers of a splendor, abundance, and beauty never before seen in the otherwise parched and excessively shady garden sprouted on this excavation the following spring.

My father took special pride in this miracle flower bed when he showed it to the buyer of our house. Now that the property was free of rats, its value had, of course, increased markedly, and my father thought it extravagant to have such a huge, valuable house for only four people (him, my brother, my sister, and me). He sold it for three times what he had paid for it. "Wasn't it worth the side of bacon?" he said, alluding to the lovely side of bacon from which he had cut a piece as big as two fists with his own hands. "I won my bet, by the way. Didn't I, my big, dear, foolish boy?" he asked, running his thin, dry, scar-adorned hand through my hair, which was brittle or soft depending on the weather . . . Yes, "my boy"! I was no longer a boy.

He reused the tiles from the pit, incidentally. They were cleaned with soap and soda, and with the gardener's help he reconstructed the heating stove in what had been my mother's bedroom. Only it was a little smaller than before, because a few of the tiles, the broken ones, could not be used again. The old stove had had a built-in oven in which apples and chestnuts could be roasted. This could not be done in the new one . . .

But the new owner of the house had no children.

THREE

I

If I am to explain how, because of my father, I became the person I am, I must begin with the story of my father, with the man who had a determining influence on my youth. He too once found himself on a long sea voyage that was full of privations, and, as I will soon relate, ultimately unsuccessful. This great journey, which entirely appeased his wanderlust, led him, not southward to the equatorial region, but northward. To the pole.

He was slender, muscular, with great endurance, had as a young man undertaken the most difficult and dangerous climbing expeditions, had reached summits never before scaled. He was scientifically well prepared, an outstanding geologist and a great botanist who, with other scholars, had helped lay the groundwork for the at that time new science of geobotany. Physical geography was his special interest, but he had written a doctoral dissertation on the terrestrial magnetic pole and the relationship between geomagnetism and variable air currents, proving himself a fertile meteorologist. All this before the age of thirty. Could anyone have believed that this versatile, promising scholar and naturalist would one day become an administrative official in the Ministry of Agriculture and the "left hand" of successive ministers? And the one to bring up such a promising son as I? Government support enabled him, in his thirty-first year, to equip a large three-masted sailing ship, taking account of the most recent experiences of northern travelers, and to choose the necessary collaborators – geographers, navigators, meteorologists, zoologists, botanists, linguists, and ethnographers. Where possible, a scholar was to have a command of several disciplines. An academy in miniature. In addition a select crew and a small dog, Ruru.

As the leader of the expedition, he had his name in the headlines at the time he set sail. People had faith in him. They believed in his star. The officially supported science otherwise known to habitually resist any true advance lent its assistance. He had himself blessed, along with his companions, before setting out. He was as handsome as he was intelligent, an appealing person. He knew how to command, all were happy to follow him.

The reserved, overly courteous man the world saw later, a man hugely vain beneath a mask of modesty, morbidly stingy though generous to all appearances, secretly buffeted by sensual passions, an atheist through and through yet a pietist and a churchgoer, an anarchist in his own eyes and a worshipper of authority in those of the world, unsparing toward others yet excessively indulgent of his own frailties, despising people from the bottom of his heart and dominating them with supreme ease, a Dr. Georg Letham the elder, who, beyond his career as a civil servant, his base passions, his instinct for power, and his psychological experiments, valued only his bank account and his second son – this Georg Letham was unrecognizable as the Georg Letham who set out before the turn of the century, pure of will, highly gifted, seemingly under the most favorable stars, to conquer the geographic North Pole. He was away for almost two years – but what years! The result was a report to the Academy of Sciences just five pages long, unfortunately consisting more of impressions and general propositions than of rigorous scientific facts. It was a catastrophe. The voyage cost millions. The result was a few phrases.

And yet there can be no doubt that he was masterful in managing people, and in turning circumstances to his own purposes when, beaten, returning after an atrocious odyssey, he was able to rescue himself even from this, to hold his own, indeed to prosper. He obtained a high post in the Ministry of Agriculture on the strength of his meteorological experience. He wedded the sister of one of his companions on the voyage, marrying money, though not very happily; and I was his second son.

This career and this "meteorological experience" did his soul no good. He had been so disappointed that the primary tissue of his being had changed. Beyond recognition.

It was not the failure alone that brought him down, but the gulf, the unbridgeable gulf, between his task and its execution.

To know what one lives for, and to be equal to it, that was the main goal of his life, his faith, which was not inconsistent with the Catholicism of his childhood. And that later on he knew, but was not equal, was that his doing? Was he at fault? What a question! Only the facts were at fault, the facts in his report. And what were these facts, what colossal catastrophes were recorded in this great report? If only some such thing had happened! But it was all just tragicomedy, it was all the doing of little animals, of sweet beasts that are only too devoted, of neighborly creatures that look upon people as kind, prosperous fathers and providers, of those children of God that even now are scurrying back and forth in the darkness between the ship's medicine locker and the ropes on the deck of the *Mimosa*, their long tails dragging behind them – have I not said enough, more than enough? – of rats.

From this voyage he knew them, and knew the world. It turned a naturalist into a connoisseur of human nature.

The North Pole lies beneath perpetual ice. It can be reached only on snowshoes, by dogsled expeditions, if at all. During the summer, the great expanse of ice is crisscrossed by fissures and crevasses that have emerged from the melting ice sheet under the weak rays of the sun. The breaks in the ice are frozen over during the winter, but then the rigors of the weather are too great. For four months, night is total. One must therefore make use of the short summer.

To reach the pole by water, daring explorers had occasionally entrusted their lives to an enormous ice floe! But they did not find this method a happy one. For as they moved northward on the ice floe (it was vast), the floe drifted southward, and all was in vain. But in those years, at the end of the nineteenth century, a world-renowned arctic explorer (it was not my father) came as close to that coveted piece of cold ground as was possible given the technical means of the time, that is, without the use of radiotelegraphic devices and without airplanes or airships. His method was the same as my father's; here, as in much else, there was only *one* practical way. For him it succeeded. Not for my father. Was the other more astute? Perhaps not. He merely had fewer rats on board.

Now what was the method? Many expeditions had undertaken the quixotic journey to the legendary pole without success. All had failed in different ways, at different places.

Years earlier one of these ships, the *Jeannette*, had come to a place north of the New Siberian Islands where it could advance no farther in the pack ice. Captain and crew leave the ship. Save themselves. The three-master remains. Masses of ice pile up titanically. More and more icebergs approach, irresistibly propelled; the entire horizon, the broad steel blue expanse of sea is filled with them. Gleaming greenish blue, hung with long beards of melted ice, sparkling in the northern lights, they gradually sail up to the ship's walls from all sides. The day comes when they join, soundlessly pressed together by tremendous forces. The little ship is squashed like a bug between two smooth fingernails. It cracks. It is done for. The dense ice mass stands like a mountain range grown up over millions of years. Polar bears, arctic foxes, arctic hares, seals, occasional birds, and many other animals draw near and pass by. The timbers of the ruined, abandoned ship, the yards and chains, the planks and chests, the ropes and sails, all are frozen into the ice. Snow covers them. Everything is silent. The moon, a glassy ball, then a half moon, then a delicate crescent, then back again – it never vanishes from the sky, except when snowstorms obscure it. Then the sky lightens: the stars come out and shine. The polar foxes pursue their scents. Solitary birds hang in the misty, somber air, their pearly wings outstretched.

The hulk is not released until spring, when the ice breaks up under the oblique rays of the sun and the warmer breezes. The sea is open now.

Does it follow that years later one would necessarily find all the wreckage of the ship in the same area? No. It is discovered far away from these New Siberian Islands. On the east coast of Greenland – that is, *beyond* the North Pole. A journey of thousands of miles. Blind, pilotless, the wreckage of the ship found the one practical route. Men with all their scientific knowledge and experience had been unable to find it. A slow but steady current must thus flow from North Siberia over the North Pole to Greenland. What was the conclusion? A ship must be so solidly built, the sides, ribs, and keel reinforced in such a way as to be able to withstand even the tremendous pressure of the masses of ice bearing down upon them. If the pole is not reached on the first approach during the short summer, one must allow oneself to be frozen in at the spot where the *Jeannette* went down. At the next thaw, the current will carry the ship into the region of the pole, close enough that it can perhaps be reached with dogsleds obtained from the natives.

The world-renowned arctic explorer Fridtjof Nansen succeeded in this. My father would have succeeded before Nansen, if not for the rats.

No ship of any size without rats. Even smaller ones have plenty of splendid specimens. New ships like my father's are not spared, they are no better off than old, run-down crates marinated in all sorts of harbor filth like my ship, the *Mimosa*. No reliable method of ridding the old tubs of rats is known, and the new ships are tenanted by these boldest of seafarers immediately, the moment they take on their first cargo. On long voyages their numbers increase in geometric progression, provided they have enough to eat. On sailing ships like my father's, which are provisioned for periods of years, they find colossal stores.

II

But an optimist expects only a slight loss from parasites; and my father, Dr. Georg Letham the elder, was one. An arrant optimist, though he became the darkest, most poisonous pessimist after his return from the north. Out of nature, into the office.

Such an optimist figures on a certain loss, but he imagines some rightful equilibrium between human dominion and the destructiveness and voracity of pests.

He had expected difficulties, he was not a fool, and he had great responsibilities. He was not a coward or a weakling and believed himself equal to his task. A night four months long did not frighten him.

All on hand were males; as far as any sort of intellectual cultivation was concerned, it was a desolate, dry company, which did not become much livelier when it was joined in a Nordic port by a volunteer passenger, a Norwegian Protestant missionary, for whom no space had been provided and who declared himself willing to replace the purser, the latter having fallen ill (or having decided to return home to his "loving hearts"). This was the company. In addition the crew, my father's dog, the parrots belonging to the geographer, later to be my uncle.

Everything has been heard before, the same responses to the same cues, stale phrases, questions and answers mechanically reeled off. The same reminiscences are rehearsed at random, the same remarks made. The same hopes and fears fill the hearts of all members of the expedition. Terrible boredom. Cards played for hours for no stakes of any possible value. No contact with the outside world apart from scientific observations and hunting, which becomes more and more infrequent at higher latitudes. No blue sky for so very long, scanty artificial light day and night. No flowers. Close quarters in gloomy cabins, not properly ventilated because of the cold. Fresh water only in minimal quantities: the fuel for melting snow must be conserved. Even the petroleum for the lamps has frozen solid and must be laboriously thawed. A warm bath in a wooden tub is a rare privilege, over which jealous fights soon break out; baths are taken in the most uncomfortable position, hunkered down, knees to beard-swathed chin. No fresh vegetables, no fruit (a ripe, yellow, aromatic butter pear, the "Prince of Wales," is the voluptuous dream of many nights), no green other than the pale green of the blotting paper in the herbarium folios brought with utter needlessness into these inhospitable climes. For what plants are there to be dried and pressed? Whatever sparse vegetation still grows up here, algae, lichens, mosses, is already dry and hard as straw. The pages of the herbarium therefore find "other use," much to the annoyance of the scholar, who finally brings the volumes into his bunk with him and sleeps on them.

Deathly quiet outside the ship, or, just a few meters away, the grating crackle of the ice plates, the grinding and creaking of the floes, the hollow roar of the frigid, knife-sharp wind, the explosion-like bangs of icebergs splitting, and the wrenching, sucking groans of the ship's walls writhing under the pressure of the ice.

The men (I am speaking of the time of waiting, of being locked in at the prescribed latitude) – the men groan too, but their groaning is not a human groaning, it is like the groaning of a board clamped in a vise. They forget surprisingly quickly how to listen, they forget how to speak sensibly. Lethargy, enervation, apathy. Tired, tired. They growl and snarl inarticulately, touchy from the moment they wake up, mute, grim, ironic, sullen to the depths of their uncooperative bowels. Only the Norwegian and my father are still in good spirits, the former with the aid of alcohol. One of the other men is always close to the edge, a gun has to be taken from him by force. Three days later he takes it back from someone else, and thus the revolver makes the circuit of most of the men. No one takes this seriously, it is just "playacting," an idea they are toying with, and it is even suspected that they are using this "playacting" to obtain the better rations that have been designated only for the ill and debilitated. Eventually my father is able to mend matters. At bottom they all still believe in a successful outcome. They just had not thought it would be so difficult. The cold is paralyzing. Dreadful, heart-gripping frost. The ship is finally frozen in at the eightieth parallel during the night. It no longer tosses, does not rock, it stands like a house, it is like solid ground. Good.

These were the predictable difficulties. They could have been overcome. But the rats! They were starting to breed with some rapidity. At the beginning no one had given them a second thought. One of the scholars had even experimented with taming two young ones, rearing them in a small, woven straw basket. He would laugh with childlike pleasure when they bit at his fingers or scratched his hand with their long front teeth. But rats were not playthings, they were unpleasant surprises.

There they were when one least expected it, sticking out their pointy, sparsely furred snouts and blinking their intelligent, sharp, malicious eyes, their drab heads adorned with long mustaches, their ears naked, hairless like those of bats. They made their presence known. They communicated with each other. *They* had not forgotten how to communicate. They raced hither and thither, purposefully. They were not apathetic. They did not miss blue and green, they did not sweat and did not freeze. They lived boldly and were bold. But at this time they appeared no more than very annoying, not dangerous, to the leader of the expedition.

These were the first months in the pack ice, the beginning of what might be a lengthy sojourn.

Even here there were men. Eskimos appeared, young and old, drawn from far away by the light in the cabins, courageous fur hunters who approached the ship in their kayaks or with dog teams, depending on climatic conditions. The missionary was as though electrified. The Eskimos were lively too. They already knew or learned very quickly what tobacco and schnapps were, and they also knew the way to these delights: conversion. They kissed the Bible, drank the schnapps, and chewed or ate the tobacco. And laughed uproariously.

These were people clothed in luxurious furs, stinking of rancid whale oil, with magnificent teeth in dingy faces; uncultivated, indifferent to danger and death, possessed by superstitions. Christianity was preached to them, and they related wonderful folktales and myths. The same men gave clear, scientifically precise reports of the weather conditions, the currents, the routes taken by the icebergs, the periodicity of the polar light phenomena. They could recount their hunting adventures, they knew a great deal about the habits of the arctic animals that they and their ancestors had encountered on their expeditions. Only about hunting shipboard rats did they know nothing, they were not even acquainted with the use of mousetraps, and to lure rats with bacon seemed to them wanton waste.

It was possible to communicate with them indirectly. The linguist and the Norwegian first learned their dialect, and their energetic sign language did the rest. Everyone listened with pleasure to their stories and enticed them with all sorts of delicacies, with harmonica playing, and especially with alcohol, which they prized in all forms and quantities, by the tablespoon and by the liter – and by the barrel. One evening, when they were particularly merry, two of them performed the famous drum dance. One imitated a frolicking seal, the other an enraged polar bear. They were paid once more in alcohol. After a time they vanished, without good-byes, without a trace.

At length another band appeared (mostly older men), who spoke a somewhat different dialect. They were not as garrulous and childlike as the first, but it was soon possible to communicate with them in a friendly manner too. One old man in this group made mysterious mention of a white man who wished to go to the northernmost north. A European? Surely not a European, a man like these scholars here, who, suddenly pale, gathered in a circle around the speaker? But yes. All fell silent in consternation. It was not a fur hunter. Not a seal trapper, not a whaler, not a skipper, not a missionary. It could only be another polar explorer.

My father was gripped by terrible impatience. He wished to consult with his comrades. He had to command, even the ship's captain had to obey him, but in this ship's council all had the same voting rights, officers and crew, scholars and nonscholars.

But he could obtain no advice, and he could give no orders. They had to wait.

My father changed, he became irritable, often insisted upon his authority, played the men against one another, became excessively courteous and moody.

Now all were suffering from living together so unnaturally, more and more with every hour that passed. The quarreling increased, my father had to adjudicate and perhaps often made partisan decisions. From time to time he wished to avoid making these judgments, have a bit of peace, not be burdened – but then something would happen without his knowledge, he became sensitive and withdrew, personally offended. The open, comradely atmosphere was gone.

III

It was at this moment that the plague of rats began to get out of hand, it truly stank to high heaven. The heavily constructed ship was stuck, held fast in the ice. The greatest cleanliness was required, the latrine rules had to be precisely observed by officers and crew, which often led to ship's hearings until there was a resolution. Only the rats paid no attention, leaving their filth and the sharp reek of their urine everywhere.

They set about tucking into not only the ship's provisions but also the ship itself, cool as you please they gnawed on the stout timbers, ate large holes in the strong, reefed, ice-stiffened sails, they set to work energetically on the stores, neither barrels nor chests were safe from them. Only the preserved foods soldered into tin cans, the wine bottles and rum barrels, and the ship's pharmacy were secure. Along with the weapons, ammunition, and the many scientific instruments. What help was any of that?

The entire crew began to sleep poorly. During sleeping hours the men rose, wandered through the ship's passageways, hunted for rats, fired carbines in the dark, and it was fortunate that no one was wounded.

Soon after the above intelligence was received from the Eskimos, the missionary, his face grave, appeared before my father. He took a conscientious view of his duty as purser and feared that the rats might have broken into a large portion of the provisions. At his urgent request, another ship's council was called. Some of the gentlemen could not be rousted from their bunks, many at this time were already leading a passive, entirely mindless and will-less existence, wishing only to be warm and well fed. At length an allusion to the brig succeeded in startling them and bringing them to the ship's council. The discussion went on for ten solid hours. The passions were finally awakened. The will to live had been rekindled. It was decided to smother the rats. My father undertook to prepare a particularly poisonous gas mixture. Poison gas warfare had been invented long before the Great War. Plenty of arsenic poison in solid form had been brought for the purposes of preserving valuable mammal and bird pelts. There was also sulfur in great quantities for sterilizing drinking-water vessels.

Every effort was to be made to snuff out the rats. Only two were excepted in response to the geographer's earnest appeal, the two tame males he kept, sharing with them his meager, monotonous rations.

He is to be permitted to keep the two rats provided they really are tame, which is doubted by all. But he maintains there are no animals that cannot be tamed through kindness, people included. Fine, as long as the two males do nothing wrong. The geographer is pleased. If my father can have Ruru, his dog, and the missionary the two small, ocean blue parrots that he brought from port, then he can have his tame rats. But all the others are in for pitched battle. The poison mixture (arsenic plus sulfur) is going to be volatilized on old leather, the remnants of snow boots and such. The yellowish white powder is spread here on a little tray of leather under the companionway steps, laid there in the magazine near one of the rats' breeding areas. This is known to be close to a rat's nest because the young rat pups can be heard twittering; they just cannot be located. But the poison fumes will reach all those places where men's eyes cannot. All the hatches are methodically sealed. Not the tiniest opening to the outside may remain. My father, the strategic leader of the operation, gives the rallying cries, all work with great zeal, things seem brighter, everyone sets to, sleeping hours are now punctually observed, people get along. Appetites are better, health improves. The teeth of some of the men have been threatening to fall out from the bland, monotonous diet and the associated scurvy, but now they decide to stand by their old owners, which gladdens the poor devils. Everything produces joy, hope of hope, true faith – in faith. Nights are calmer, the rats are seen and heard and smelled less, they are not as bold as before, perhaps they fear the fate in store for them. The two "tame" rats are a notable exception. The stronger male injures the weaker by biting his throat, and as if that were not enough, he craftily goes after the missionary's two parrots by squeezing his sharp-clawed feet through the bars of their cage. He comes to grief when the little parrots summon help with their excited screeching. The rat is caught and sentenced to death by shooting along with his innocent companion. The geographer is heartbroken, his eyes fill with tears, but, crouching in a corner of the ship's mess, he gives his silent consent to the death warrant for his two foul-smelling darlings, leaves the ship before the execution, and roams about with his lantern in the darkness out on the snow-covered floes, where the Eskimos have pitched their tents.

Two shots. Done.

While he is gone, the poison bombs are set off with fuses, a bell hanging from a yardarm is rung. This is the alarm, the signal: all hands on deck, officers and crew. The crew creep out, heavily laden. The arctic night is frigid, they have all their possessions with them, as though it were good-bye forever. The gentlemen have just blankets and furs, the missionary also his two parrots. He has thoughtfully covered their cage with a heavy fur coat, and their chirping is barely audible. They are freezing, this is their first time on deck in the cold. Earlier, before the assassination attempt by the recently executed rats, they were very loud, often fluttered screeching to and fro in their spacious cage. They have not yet recovered from the shock.

The crew sit on sea chests gnawed by rats, on nibbled-at coils of rope beneath the tattered sails hanging from the yardarms. The Eskimos, drawn by the unusual drama, are also on board with their strong, woolly, intelligent dogs, which sit together quietly, only growling softly now and then, straining at their leads, until a kick from an Eskimo quickly shuts them up.

It is not totally dark, this night, although the moon is new. Especially splendid northern lights spread in gentle arcs over the entire eastern sky. A multiply pleated, shredded band of greenish, magical, unreal light. It looks loose at the edges, hanging down in many layers. A blue star of particular lambency shines through the seething fog of the aurora. The cold fire undulates in the stiff, icy air and gradually subsides.

My father feels a compulsion to photograph the lights. He ventures down into his cabin, ignoring his own order, finds it still free of poison gas, and soon sets up a tripod on the motionless ship with the lens of the apparatus aimed at the phenomenon, requesting complete quiet from everyone present in order to avoid vibration. No one dares to light a lantern, a cigar. I still remember the photograph my uncle often showed us as children. All you could see was a washed-out band of light, a kind of diffuse halo; the rest had to be added by a child's imagination. But it was one of the first photographs of the northern lights, requiring a quarter hour of exposure with the shutter wide open.

The ice, mounting in terraces on the floes, eroded and fissured down on the level of the ship, boldly jagged higher up, can also be seen emitting a pale light. Nothing moves. Not the Eskimo dogs, not my father's collie. Not the northern lights. Not the ship. Not the men.

IV

While all is still locked in a strange somnolence, a small object suddenly falls somewhere down below, making a faint, hollow sound. Ruru, my father's dog, leaps up, turns her long, beautiful head this way and that and will not be soothed. My father too is startled, hastens to close the plate cover in order to save the precious exposure. The same hollow fall to earth is heard again. One of those cork shuttlecocks with colored feathers attached, the kind that children use to play a kind of table tennis, batting them back and forth with small rackets, makes such a sound when it strikes the tabletop.

But these are not children at play, these are adults, who are controlling themselves only with effort, whose hearts are heavy, whose eyes are beginning to tear, who are listening warily to the boiling and scurrying and stewing in the interior of the rat ship and now all long for light. The Eskimo dogs have suddenly broken free, they have pulled their masters along amid mad barking, snarling, and howling, and already the dogs are charging off over the gangplank and onto the open snowfield, their masters behind them.

The company and crew stay behind. Then someone begins to breathe with difficulty, to groan, he vomits, someone else croaks, racked with terrible throat irritation, tears gush from his eyes, his nose, his oral mucosa begin to be awash, twenty men complain of headaches, burning in their throats, choking, nausea, anxiety, fear of death, fear of darkness, fear of the northern lights, all throng to the gangplank, but this is no orderly retreat like that of the children of nature, the Eskimos and their animals; instead the civilized men stumble in the darkness, the steel hawsers slice the palms of their hands, they bump into each other, two of the scholars slip on the icy gangplank, slide sideways under one of the slippery steel hawsers and lie whimpering on the ice at the foot of the ship, all are as though gripped by madness. Only my father is not, he and the geographer, my future uncle, who had gone out for a walk on the snowfield with his lantern while all this was happening on board. Now he lights the lantern, which had gone out as he rushed to lend a hand, he helps the two men of science writhing in the snow onto their feet, they have only bruised their tailbones, assists the others in leaving the ship. Keep calm, don't panic! There's nothing to worry about! But only a few follow his orders, many more surge on deck in a confused mass, their fists pressed against their bellies, they are wading through their own vomit, and no one can see for streams of tears. The suffering becomes ever greater, the lantern illuminates a dreadful scene. The birdcage is also knocking about among the agonized men. Two small ocean blue balls of feathers are rolling lifeless on the bottom, on the bare metal (for there has long been no bird sand in this frozen waste) – whether frozen or poisoned, the parrots are no longer alive.

The dog Ruru circles my father tirelessly, snaps at his high boots as he tries to kick her away, a hundred times she runs ahead over the gangplank and back again, is so to speak asking him to follow. My father, as the leader of the expedition, has to be the last one to leave the ship.

What has happened? The poisonous vapors, arsenic mixed with sulfur, stewing slowly on damp leather, must have risen invisibly up through tiny chinks. The smell of the leather burning would have been a warning, but no one noticed anything. The men lie there groaning softly. Poison gas. The northern lights glow above them, traversed by silent flashes. Not a breath of wind.

All ashore. The most delirious ones first. They are in a kind of frenzy, stamp their feet, turn on their rescuers, hit their heads on things. Men of science weep and sob and – pray! The missionary, ordinarily a jolly fellow, always joking, reaches into my father's face, his own twisted with pain, pulls on his long beard, tears off his gold-rimmed spectacles, but my father and the geographer energetically take hold of the man between them, one seizes his arms, the other grips his legs, and quickly off with the heavy man, out of the atmosphere laden with invisible poison. Then the others follow, and ten minutes later the ship is finally empty of men. Let the poison do its worst, let the rats suffocate, perish to the last rat.

All now crowd into the Eskimo tents out on the ice, but the Eskimos are making ready for departure, they claim their provisions are exhausted, they say one thing and another. They have to be threatened with a good going over. The members of the expedition endure two days and two nights in the tents, fed extremely meagerly, freezing, plagued by the filth of the men and dogs, delirious from the effects of the arsenic poisoning, ill, either extraordinarily apathetic or extraordinarily irritable and foul-tempered. They hate my father because he has remained healthy. But he breathed the same poison fumes. Is he to blame for his good fortune?

They have to make an effort to restrain themselves, but they do it, gradually becoming calmer, hoping to find the ship free of rats upon their return.

Fifty hours later my father is the first to enter the ship. The planks echo hollowly under his high, heavy leather boots. In one hand he has a pike like those the Eskimos use to goad their dogs, in the other a lantern, he thumps on the deck, nothing seems to answer him. So the beasts are dead, thank heavens. His joy, his satisfaction cannot be described, he takes a white handkerchief out of his pocket, waves to his comrades on the ice: all is well. He lifts a hatch with the pike, its barb in the iron ring, he climbs down the main entrance to the provisions store. No sooner has he descended a few steps, shining the lantern about, than a second light appears behind him. The geographer could not let my father go down alone and has disobeyed his orders. While the two are arguing over which is more important, discipline or comradeship, a big fat rat darts boldly past my father's feet and up on deck, runs nimbly, whirring like a top, around the main mast and back again, leaping over my father in one colossal bound. My father and my uncle shine their lanterns into the depths. Good God! They are everywhere, sitting and slithering and darting about, the indestructible rats. My father's feet encounter a carcass, half torn to pieces, only four or five times. The beasts are there as always on the provision lockers and barrels, nibbling at things with their white protruding teeth or cleaning themselves, staring insolently into the light from the lantern. And the birdlike cheeping of the young rats is heard not just from one spot, but from many, indeed from every corner of the storerooms. The older generation has not cashed in its chips and the younger one is well on the way! What can happen now? How are they going to fill their bellies? The shameless rats have even consumed the fuses that did not burn.

Live, eat, procreate. Shamelessly! No, modestly. Equal to life, on the increase, a worthy adversary. How can they be eradicated without also eradicating the people to whom they have adapted themselves?

So this was the result: only thirty-two animals had met their maker. They had to be buried in the ice at some distance from the ship so that the dogs would not poison themselves on them. But most importantly: thousands upon thousands of rats are alive and flourishing. The ship is stuck in the ice. The renowned, venerable shipyard delivered prime work. The heavy ship withstands, groaning and creaking but intact, the masses of pack ice continually bearing down upon it.

The ship does not withstand the rodents in its belly. They merrily go on living. They are not looking for any pole. They are not interested in meteorology, not in dialects, not in Eskimo folktales, not in Christianity. Not facts to be taken down, but food to be taken in is all that exists for them. If a weaker, good-tasting creature is alive and they can catch it, then they kill it. And if it is dead, then they do not dissect it but gobble it up. They do not live lives without mates, full of privation, in the service of nothing but the lofty purposes and noble ends of theoretical science, like my father and his companions, but simply behave naturally. Male and female, father, children, mother, and grandmother, unto the fourth and fifth and seventh generation, all one family, huge and still not big enough. With their flesh and blood, their filth, and their scent, they overrun the artful structure built by men. Their uniform is everywhere one looks, that grayish brown body with its bottlelike swell, along the spine more darkly variegated, in front the sharp head and in back the wormlike, lighter, hairless tail with its two hundred transverse rings. They are happy to be able to gorge themselves. They rigorously obey the stubborn instinct to survive. They stake everything on their existence and know nothing else. Brown rats are known as *Wanderratten*, migratory rats, but they can also keep faith with a place as long as the place and the foraging there keep faith with *them*.

Here was where my father made his study of the animals that later lived as guests in his house.

But when a community grows beyond measure, can there be enough food for it in the long run? No. Fierce, passionate battles over food are already breaking out among the animals, infrequently at first, but nevertheless. And yet there are vast provisions on the ship, vast in the eyes of a single, comparatively small rat. But their greed is not small. Nothing is safe from them.

They no longer content themselves with the storerooms belowdecks. Having become a more courageous, virile race under the new living conditions, they advance up to the cabins of the scholars and the captain, they creep into the common ship's mess, first during sleeping hours, then even when men are present, for there it is always warm, it is heated. They find their way into the lockers, shredding even the thickest fur, mother, child, and grandchild move into warm winter quarters between the lining and the pelt of beaver hats with long earflaps. They have to be beaten with sticks, cut with knives, or they do not budge. They occupy provision lockers of all kinds as though they were houses and villages. Anything they can chew, gnaw, gulp down will do fine. Flour, grease, dried fruit, dried fish, sugar, tea, rice, tobacco, spices, but also wood, wool, leather, sailcloth – everything except iron, and rum and other alcohol. They have gotten into more than one cask of rum, but they did not drink, rather they drowned or were poisoned, much to the overjoyed satisfaction of the missionary. Alas – "joy"? Joy has long been unknown in the community of men, the atmosphere is never peaceful, and yet the men remain in each other's company for hours, for days on end.

My father goes about in silent fury. He is emaciated, his cheeks are gaunt, his eyes hollow like those of the others. He has very courteously asked not to be addressed unbidden, but his companions will not accept this order as legitimate, instead pestering him with every conceivable question, requests, reproaches, complaints. It emerges that they (all of them in an entirely abnormal state of mind) hold him responsible for the "impossible conditions" aboard the ship. He should have taken more precautions – but what would those have been? Others confide in him their darkest family secrets, still others their scientific plans and ideas, some, more fortunate, return to the realms of childhood, they play childish games, run races on deck, but stumbling backward, not forward – or on all fours, as though they wanted to compete with the nimble beasts – and these are grown men doing this, men with beards, with wife and child at home! My father does not dare order them categorically to stop, since he expects only opposition. What can he threaten with, how is he to punish anyone, how can he enforce anything? Others have taken up baby talk, converse like three-year-old girls, weave colored ribbons into each other's beards, kiss each other, progress to false, unnatural caresses, but also to grim, jealous battles.

And above all the rats. It's no good pretending that their numbers will diminish of their own accord or that they will necessarily destroy each other in their wild battles and vanish from the face of the earth. They are there. Everywhere. All the time.

V

But the time will come when the ship is afloat again. The great effort that will be needed to reach the pole is something that can only be imagined. And to know that then one will be trapped here on the accursed ship, which is home only to rodents, not to men! To be facing the prospect of hunger – for stores a hundred times greater would not survive the constant depredations of the armies of rats.

In this state of mind – this torment, this gnawing impatience, this awareness that someone else has gotten to the pole ahead of you and all is in vain – now anything goes. The last barriers fall between the crew and the scholars and officers. From this point the scuffles, the thrashings, the cuffs and the kisses, the fits of anger, the practical jokes, the fruitless and therefore forbidden mad rat hunts do not cease, and order, inward or outward, is now just an empty word, at which one can only laugh.

Among these men condemned to idleness and waiting and tortured by their boredom in both mind and body, compulsive weeping, compulsive laughter, compulsive praying begin to be heard. Nothing comes naturally. No one is now who he was when he set sail some months before, expecting quite different dangers and difficulties.

In all their battles for their daily bread, the rats remain cheerful and full of the joys of life. They have what they need, and if they do not have it, they get it. But how does man get what he needs?

Bibles in every conceivable language had been brought along in three large trunks, they too have fallen victim to the rats, down to the steel staples holding the pages together. But the hard-drinking missionary still had his private Bible, his confirmation gift, a personal memento – until it suddenly vanished. Who has it? Has one of his comrades simply hidden it as a childish practical joke, or has someone stolen it? Yet whoever took it would be able to read the word of God only at "Mass," that is the only place with enough light and warmth, and there he cannot bring the stolen item. A note requesting its return is attached to the main mast, but it too disappears after a few hours, either torn down or eaten by the rats. Still no trace of the Bible.

My father is silent. His face beneath his heavy beard can become no paler. What does he care about the Gospel *now*? It is easier for the others. The missionary solaces himself with alcohol, he throws the empty wine bottles at the rats in the magazine, but they misunderstand and play with them trustingly.

A new Eskimo band has come. They too have heard about the other arctic explorer, indeed seem to know something more, but will not come out with it. They are insatiable in their demands, behave greedily and calculatingly, watch their words, are deliberately unforthcoming. The oldest speaks for the others, who follow his lead.

Has the pole already been discovered? Have the *others* reached the mark? The gentlemen look at each other, but again learn nothing definitive. The expedition is no longer rich enough to buy an accurate report from the Eskimos.

A new mental illness has appeared among the scholars. They have finally devised the cruelest punishment possible under the circumstances. They are punishing each other with silence. Particularly artful practitioners move their lips as though to speak, but make no sound. They will not speak. Others have not produced a properly constructed sentence for months now, they are mentally at the level of one-year-olds and just as tearful. They cannot speak.

Purely physical health too deteriorates day by day during this period.

The cold is tremendous, the wind rages through the freezing darkness, no one wants to leave the ship. But an effort must be made to hunt fresh meat, there are ducks and eiders, polar bears, seals, arctic hares, arctic foxes in the area, their tracks can be seen in the snow on the ice sheet. The eye has adjusted to the murky twilight, the hunt could be successful. But who can be ordered to shoot if no one will leave the ship, even those in the most robust health? Only one possibility remains: to hunt the rats and consume their fresh, fatty flesh in order to guard against scurvy. But as gladly as the men fall to the forbidden chase, bang away like mad in the dark with pistols and carbines, they do all they can to shirk the official one. Why? Only the forbidden excites them. Kill – yes. Eat – no. They shun the repulsive animals like the plague, a plague of rats, they do not want to sully themselves with them, never mind ingest their loathsome flesh. But when hemorrhage after hemorrhage from the gums is weakening the men terribly, when gentle pressure leaves broad stigmata on their pale skin, when tooth after tooth silently falls out, when a foul stench emanates from the sick, miserable men who nevertheless mingle with the healthy, indeed have less intention than ever of leaving them – what then? Any other ideas? And on top of it all the silence of the arctic sky, the silence of the men among themselves.

The purser conducts a new inventory in the storerooms, white as a sheet he climbs up from the depths, kicking at fierce rats even on the ship's ladder. Something has to happen, the best, the most important provisions are dwindling; if it goes on this way, they can last just a few weeks, and the ship's cook will have nothing to make into meals. Starvation will take anyone who has been spared by cold, scurvy, and general hardship. But if it were possible to eat the beasts, that could save at least half a year's worth of provisions essential for keeping the expedition afloat. And after that half year, what good things might not come to pass? Might not heaven allow the ship to reach the pole (six weeks), and might the ship not then be carried back to the coastlines of populated lands by a current flowing southward from the pole?! It might! It might! Anything could happen. There is always hope – hope of hope – if only the rats were gone. My father thinks it over. He is in charge, it is his decision. He must make it.

VI

My father has so far remained healthy, his teeth are all there, strong and white; his skin pale, if you like, but not brownish, earth-colored, like the skin of those suffering from scurvy, nor mottled with livid hematomas. How is he going to inspire his comrades with the heroism necessary to eat rat meat, or, better yet, drink warm rat blood? That is one danger. The other is the inexorable proliferation of the disgusting animals. Neither is anything new, just the same old thing, but more intolerable with every day that passes. They must stop it, they must at least try to stop it.

My father has one last friend. He talks to this friend. He can no longer talk to his comrades. They would regard it as weakness, would view him with contempt for no longer being able to bear the silence.

This friend is the dog Ruru. She is an intelligent animal, full of optimism and unbroken in body and spirit. This beautiful, gray-eyed, tall, slender dog, covered with long golden fur in gentle waves, is not only magnificent to look at, but she still has her old fire, her pluck. When the men are boring each other to tears in the mess and a bold rat comes along, she wastes not a moment in thought. The men are already too apathetic to go after the creature. They are not true men. On the white patch on the map representing the unexplored area around the pole, the geographer draws made-up islands, mountains, glaciers, volcanoes, names a bay in his own honor and thus makes fun of himself. Or is he already so mentally enfeebled that he believes it? Other gentlemen carve toys out of nutshells for imaginary children or put dominoes end to end, playing games against themselves with the dominoes divided into two piles.

Another writes letter after letter home, letters that can never arrive, another takes the discarded dominoes and builds a little house with them, another prays ceaselessly, tabulating the number of hasty Our Fathers and so forth and timing them with a stopwatch as though trying to break a record. And the terrible, sharp, rancid odor of the rats is driven away by thick clouds of tobacco smoke and the penetrating smell of the arrack and rum that the gentlemen and crew polish off in enormous quantities without getting a proper glow. It remains a grim delirium, a chortling, an idiotic grinning, an awkward, tense embrace of an equally delirious comrade, it is unclear if this is unnatural love or if the intoxicated man is confusing his neighbor with his beloved bride, his beloved father at home.

What does reality mean to these men now in the terrible arctic night, nearly four months long! They do not wash, they do not comb their hair, and they are becoming animals to such a degree that they can no longer muster true hate for the rats. The healthy are becoming ill, the ill remain ill, traces of blood are seen everywhere on board, it becomes a torment to sit at the table where the men chew their food with painful listlessness, their mouths filthy and toothless. Only a very few are still on their feet, my father, the geographer, the missionary.

But the dog is still the same as she was at the start. If a rat is bold enough to sniff at the fur-lined, whale-oil-smeared boots of one of the stuporous gentlemen, Ruru dashes intrepidly after it. It went too far this time, and soon she has it by its darkly variegated, grayish brown, smoothly furred neck, a brief squeak, then she whacks its head three or four times on the deck and waits, growling faintly, tail wagging fiercely, to see if it has any fight left in it, if it is still kicking, then picks it up neatly with her shining white teeth and flings the carcass over the side and onto the pack ice. After my father has seen this I don't know how many times, he comes to a great decision. He will set a moral example. First he will prove to the slovenly men what a sacrifice he is ready and willing to make for the group, second he wants to teach the rats in the ship's belly a lesson so these disgusting animals know there is still something that is their equal. And through this moral demonstration he will inoculate his comrades with a new resolve: they will bravely drink rat's blood to get rid of the scurvy, and perhaps it will be possible to really bring the rats under control, to save the provisions at the last minute thanks to Ruru and rescue the fortunes of the heroic expedition.

VII

What a foolish experiment! To part with all one has left in the world, the only thing one can be sure of, with so little prospect of success! Can man triumph over nature? Never. He, man, is only an experiment on the part of nature, the terrible.

The dog will be sent below, into the underworld. But first she is to fast for a day, in order to spread terror and despair that much better among the beasts below.

Most of the men are quite apathetic. The only one upon whom this experiment makes an impression is the geographer. He gives my father his hand. If he is silent, that is not because he is punishing my father but because he is so moved that he is actually at a loss for words. The geographer strokes the fur on the animal's back. Ruru is so obedient to her master that she does not eat the table scraps thrown to her by the other scholars in the mess, but only sniffs at them. Hunger, fine! Ruru presses her flank against my father's boots, shakes her head so that her collar jingles, and determinedly lies down. But she resists being taken down into the magazine. Rats? No. She does not snap at her master's hand as he takes her by the collar and leads her down the steps, she only twists and pulls her neck away. So strongly that she chokes, she cannot draw breath. How terribly she must fear the world of rats down there. No use. The hatch slammed shut from above. Stamped on by heavy boots. A few words shouted down to the dog now madly charging about and barking: "Tally ho! All the best!" And then my father goes ashore, off to the hunt with shotgun on shoulder.

He returns an hour later. Even from far off, the piteous, almost sobbing, soul-lost howling of the dog comes to him from the recesses of the ship, horrifically amplified by the echo, like the voice of Hamlet's father from the bowels of the earth, his bad conscience.

The others are unmoved. Hell could open up beneath them and they, the scholars, would go on with their card games and eventually crap games, hour after hour, playing for bonbons found in a jar, preserved from the teeth of the rats. If Satan himself were howling below, the crew would not leave their bunks, where they have spent almost the whole day drunk and half asleep.

What is she in the greater scheme of things, what is she to the progress of the scientific expedition, this dog Ruru? Only one more victim, a needless one. She wails in her fear and suffering, accusing the man in whom she believed, the man who at his own cost has conducted a would-be moral experiment.

No one dares to go down into the hold. My father least of all. The geographer and the missionary argue over who will do it, finally they throw for it, the winner has to pay two bonbons and the loser has to go down into the hold, but is allowed to make his bitter task a little sweeter with the two pieces of candy.

The geographer climbs down the steps, he calls Ruru, coaxes her with a voice now truly affectionate. Ruru was barking furiously just now, it must be possible to find her?! Yes, he finds her, stretched out unconscious from pain and loss of blood, the rats have taken up positions at the head and legs of the poor creature, and even this vigorous man is barely able to drive them off with the most savage kicks, wrest the victim away from them, and bring her on deck.

He carries the animal in his arms. She is covered with blood and wheezing heavily. She opens her gummed-up eyes, blinks through the bloody bits, extends her long, narrow tongue, and whimpers heartbreakingly. He lets her down. Ruru cannot walk. Head, belly, and tail pressed to the planking of the deck, bleeding from the mouth, bleeding from the paws, Ruru crawls about on the upper deck and howls her misery to the icebergs and the polar sky, now tinged with a mild blue, no longer so sternly wintry. Hints of spring are in the air. There is light again, and the time of the "midnight sun" is approaching. The icebergs are shinier than they were, the dirt has been washed off the ice floes.

What good is this to the wailing Ruru? The rats have nibbled at her heels, a bit of flesh between lip and nose is gone forever. Ruru howls and extends her tongue as far as possible to lick the wound. Ruru will not eat. Or cannot. She has to have food poured down her throat with a wooden spoon. During sleeping hours she disturbs everyone with her belling, sobbing howls. Ruru is mean, scratches and bites all the men, including my father. She has willfully cracked the wooden spoon between her teeth, she refuses food, but lives on. No one wants to deal with her now, only my father comes every day, heart pounding rapidly, to the place where his pet sleeps, but he does not dare to come too close, speaks from a distance. His comrades laugh, a drunken sailor throws a glove at the animal's head. Ruru looks up and growls, bares her teeth. The sailor does not dare to retrieve the glove, which Ruru sits on and then tears apart in a frenzied rage.

The weather improves, the storms have abated. At night green-lit clouds in formations never before seen rush by under a soft twilight. Ruru barks to the sky, eyes closed. Her wounds glitter under the ship's lanterns, and when she moves across the deck, she leaves a trail of blood. But she is alive.

The gentlemen and the sailors have recovered. All who embarked are there. The symptoms of scurvy are almost entirely gone. Perhaps everyone has secretly shot a rat and gulped the blood as medicine. They are silent about that.

But the dog is in their way, they cannot get near her without being snapped at. They would like to snap at her, too, they hate her and scorn her because she has been beaten (for their benefit!). My father is very friendly, very gentle, and very unloved. The rations have become skimpier lately. It is not so easy to go into the magazine and bring up the provisions guarded by the rats. So the gentlemen would at least like an undisturbed night's sleep. This is not possible as long as Ruru is alive.

A ship's council meets. Now, since my father is the opposition, the gentlemen have found their voices, the silence is broken, they greet one another with gravity and solemnity, their full beards quivering, like men who have endured hardship *together* and survived. They stop being childish – or have they become childish in earnest? They charge my father in his absence with cruelty to animals and resolve, with two votes against (reduced to one once the missionary has been softened up with alcohol and bonbons), "Ruru shall be shot." Ruru is beyond cure and a burden on the expedition, a nocturnal disturber of the peace and a useless mouth. My father, summoned, eyes downcast, his mouth beneath his heavy beard twisted into an embarrassed smile, revealing his magnificent teeth, listens to the majority verdict that his dog be sentenced to a painless death on humanitarian grounds. He bows with the greatest respect, but he replies as the respondent that he will not fire the shot, and woe to him who lays a hand on Ruru. They believe him capable of anything and give up. Ruru lives.

My father sneaks out to Ruru in the cloudless moonlight and tells her, keeping at an appropriate distance from her sharp teeth, that those bad men have sentenced her to death. But that he will not hand her over. The wounds would heal and they would heal much faster if Ruru would just be sensible, if she would have the brains to let him near so that he could take care of her. Her only response is to growl, her sharp teeth are fearsome. Fur gloves can protect the hands, but Ruru could tear a person's face to pieces about the nose and mouth. She hates everyone, my father especially. She looks at him, her eyes burn, the once silky, now shaggy coat stands on end, particularly around the throat, and – most horrifyingly, Ruru wants to attack her former idol despite her wounded paws. Master and idol before, enemy now. And never has my father loved this animal more, never has he preferred her company to that of his companions as much as he does *now*. Now he has a suspicion what man is. But he and the dog do not make up. Day after day my poor father comes away, his eyes distant, letting the somewhat unkempt mustache soak up the flowing tears, attempting to whistle a cheerful tune to deceive the derisively smirking sailors about his frame of mind. The dog has gotten up on her wounded paws and, eyes glittering evilly, growling softly but almost without pause, continues to watch my father until he has vanished into the galley, where he discusses with the cook how to snatch the provisions away from the rats and how to prepare the food for the gentlemen and the crew and the freeloading, but now particularly indispensable Eskimos and their dogs. They all eat the same thing, it is bad and not much, but the lot of them are happy as long as their hunger is satisfied.

VIII

Meanwhile the weather has been improving steadily. Suddenly it is here: the midnight sun. The indescribable joy of the men, previously so depressed, is a sight to see, for example when one sailor takes off another's fur hat and holds his hand between the sun and the man's flaxen-haired head so as to admire for the first time after so long a *shadow* thrown by an object onto a surface, and then the *shine* magically produced by the sun's rays on his comrade's tousled blond hair. And among the scholars, what faith in a happy outcome, what confidence in success! Who will dare to enlighten them! The animals in the underworld are now nearly masters of the ship. If they become its absolute masters, then all is lost.

Now everyone drinks in the lukewarm air. Clothes and furs are put aside and aired out, pillows and covers spread out in the sun, under close watch.

The pack ice is moving. Vibrations have been passing through the now translucent masses of ice from time to time. A jagged fissure rips through the pack as it sparkles in the sun: a dark blue flash, and it splits thunderously. Great shards of ice send foam into the air as they plunge into the cobalt blue water covered with slabs of ice like fish scales. The ship is suddenly free – the sleeping passengers awaken, having felt it rocking beneath them. The ship? It is no longer a ship – everyone knows it, no one will admit while momentarily sun-drunk that it has become a traveling rattery. The warm weather has brought the animals out of its belly, they are literally ubiquitous, they are underfoot everywhere. They gleam in the sun, well fed and plump, their fur is smooth, and they actually have a kind of beauty, such as is produced even in ugly individuals by proper nourishment and a feeling of being at one with the world.

They hiss and snarl indignantly when stepped on. When wounded by carbine shots, they squeal bloodcurdlingly. Others remove the wounded creatures, whether to save them or eat them no one knows. The purser (unemployed missionary) and the ship's cook discuss the situation with my father, not revealing much to their companions. The rats allow no one near the casks and barrels, sacks and chests in which the last provisions are stored, except by force of arms. They are defending *their* property.

No more ship's council. There is only *one* solution. To temporarily take the food by force onto the immeasurably vast ice sheet, which stretches off to the east in front of the ship and which will break up in a few months – with luck. But without the ship, all are lost, only *on* the ship can they attempt to drift poleward – or southward, toward their native soil, toward their "loving hearts," toward home. Once the provisions are temporarily on the ice – up and at the horrible beasts with a vengeance. Carbon monoxide will be used. It *must* be possible to save the ship.

Carbon monoxide is reliable. It should have been used long ago. There are still some sacks of good coal. Now, in warmer weather, they are dispensable. They will char belowdecks on ironware basins, on copper pans from the galley. Carbon monoxide is absolutely lethal to all rodents. The gas will collect from the outset down in the rattery, in the deepest area of the ship, because it is heavier than air. It will not escape upward, like the disastrous arsenic.

So first, ashore with the provisions. The ship's watch, chosen from scholars and crew in equal numbers, enter the hold, some remove chests and barrels while others fire into the horde of rats. And if a bullet hits two or three or four rats at once – some hours later, when the job is done and the provisions have been removed as completely as possible in one of the two lifeboats and the missionary shines the lantern about belowdecks, there seem to be just as many animals as before. The coal basins are kindled in the deepest corner of the hold, and now: away from the ship in the second lifeboat.

Three groups are on the ice some three hundred meters from the ship: first the expedition's officers, crew, and scholars, second the Eskimos with their dogs, third Ruru, who was the last to drag herself off the ship, limping on three legs, leaving a moist trail behind her, and who has now settled down on the edge of the ice on an old, frayed blanket, rolling onto her back to protect her paws and licking her wounded muzzle with her tongue.

The ship stands there brightly, the sails, riddled with holes, are tightly reefed, all the icicles have melted off the rigging. A gentle breeze is blowing.

A tiny puff of smoke rises from the deck. Soon a dark fog from below is smoldering around the mast, dispersing into the air.

Ruru howls. She groans out her pain, mouth wide. The crew have brought a great deal of rum and arrack. They make punch in kettles under the Eskimo tents. The scholars have recognized the seriousness of the situation, they walk back and forth at the edge of the ice, there is a somber silence among them.

The geographer, the missionary, and my father meet at Ruru's bed of pain. They pity the animal. They do not pity the thousands upon thousands of rats slowly stewing and suffocating in the ship's hold. Nor would they pity the rats if they were all incinerated. And the ship along with them? Is it burning? Is it burning? Is the fire going out? The cloud becomes heavier and heavier, darker, sparks flash through it. Quarter hour after quarter hour goes by in the steady pale light of the arctic day, until with a cannonlike crack an incandescent flame shoots out of the dense, slate-colored cloud of smoke.

For the first time since human history began, and since the world as we know it came into being, and since snow and ice armor-plated the topsoil and the rock beneath it here below the eighty-seventh parallel, this wasteland of ice and water is seeing fire.

The scholars do not want to see it. The last kettle of arrack punch is heated by the crew using the last of the wood from the chests. This time the gentlemen drink too. Beneath their high, dirty fur caps, pulled down over the bridges of their noses, an abstracted expression appears on their dark or pale, emaciated faces, which might be a look of stunned horror or equally a dull-witted merriment induced by the hot alcohol. Many are toothless. Drops of the strong spirits hang from the unkempt beards. It is only despair behind it all. Mute despair as, one silently signaled by another, they turn their gazes once more to the ship shaken by flames: they see the rats so densely packed together that they are fighting for room in the water and one almost ejects its neighbor, a smooth-furred, shiny, darkly variegated back, onto *its* neighbor, and so on – the sharp heads stretched far out in front, the black rat eyes wide open – they see the rat community appear, without prelude, in one movement, as though the ten thousand animals were a single body, in the gap created by the spring thaw between the western side of the ship and the eastern edge of the ice. Hordes and hordes of rats follow, hurling themselves out of every hatchway, first onto the deck and from there into the ice blue and golden water, on which the reflections of the flames undulate.

The animals have a single goal, a single will, they swim with calm, measured strength. They push the little ice cakes forcibly ahead of them. They are heading for land. For the men.

IX

My father stands at the edge of the ice. He touches his chest. He is feeling for a case that holds an excellent cigar, the last of a large supply. The rats have demolished the rest. My father has promised himself that he will smoke this Havana cigar at the "critical moment." That moment has arrived.

The Eskimos plunge into feverish activity, harness the dogs, strike the tents. They look up at the reddish glare of the sky in which, as their superstition has it, the angry gods dwell. They have not a glance to spare the burning ship, the columns of rats approaching ever nearer.

The sailors, who have been drinking under the tents, stand under the open arctic sky, suddenly sober and freezing. Their raucous songs are suddenly stilled.

They surround my father, but at a certain distance. Between my father and his companions (the scholars and the ship's captain) and the sailors is a space of some thirty meters. In this space of thirty meters is the dog's bed.

Everything, the men's faces flushed with drink, the rolled-up leather walls and wooden pegs of the tents, the harnesses of the Eskimo dogs already standing in formation, the boats loaded onto the sledges, everything is burnished with the glow of the fire.

A crashing comes from the fiery ship. The murmuring of the sailors can be heard.

The two lifeboats are at the edge of the ice, in a kind of inlet. One is loaded with the last provisions and the weapons, the ammunition, and the blankets. The other, which brought the men not long ago, is now empty. Whoever has the first boat still has a chance of saving his life – if he can protect himself from the rats, if the provisions can be protected from their teeth.

The other boat is worthless.

The division of the camp has taken shape in an instant. The crew have huddled together. There is not room and food enough for everyone. There is space only for a small number under good leadership, only for the strongest "collective egoists."

The first rats try to land. They attempt to cling to the edge of the ice with their clawed feet, to climb up. Unsuccessfully at first.

My father is going to light the cigar. Before he can strike the match, he becomes aware of someone approaching behind him. A small, warm, square object with something that rattles attached to it is carefully placed in his left hand, between whose index and middle fingers the cigar hangs loosely. Surprised, he brings his hand up to look. It is the long-lost Gospels. The man who stole the book felt pangs of conscience at the critical moment. He wanted to give up the booty. He brought it out from under his shirt. I never found out who it was, the geographer or the captain. Between the pages of the little book is a rosary.

My father has to pull himself together. Reflect. Resolve is everything. His thoughts elsewhere, he opens the book at the place marked by the rosary. It is the Sermon on the Mount. His eyes scan the beginning of the fifth chapter of Matthew: Jesus's Sermon on the Mount. The first rats scurry over his feet. Their landing has been successful.

My father reads, but does not go on reading. He does not give himself up. He does not pray. He spits out the cigar, kicks at the rats, reaches for his revolver, gathers his closest comrades around him with a brief order. The social question has been broached, class warfare has begun. Here the officers, the scholars, and the captain. The leaders. There the sailors. The masses. Before them the object of dispute, the boats. The burning ship unattainable and useless. At their feet the rats. Above them the arctic sky and otherwise nothing.

The Eskimos are in wild flight, prod their dogs with long, sharp-pointed sticks, beat their flanks raw, they stand on the low sledges, legs wide apart. With a scraping sound the sledges move off on their runners.

And with the cracks of their whips coming again and again, but more softly, dying away, the children of nature race from the scene of the final battle among the members of the ill-fated expedition. Across the ice they came, across the ice they have gone.

My father flings the little book to the ground. Rats will eat it, as they have eaten the last cigar. Leaves of tobacco, leaves of paper, to them it is all the same in the struggle for survival. They escaped the carbon monoxide, death by fire too. Nor did they drown.

There is not a moment for sentimentality.

Something strange happens. The dog has risen from her bed, has limped to my father with neck outstretched, ears laid back, tail between her legs, has, for the first time since her return from the underworld of the rats, snuggled against him. What has taken place in the animal's soul (an animal too has a soul, if quite different from that of a person) cannot remotely be guessed.

What took place in my father's soul (my father too had a soul, if quite different from that of most people) cannot be guessed.

His narrative has remained in my memory as I have recounted it to this point. His words were precise and he never contradicted himself no matter how many times I heard the story. My mother, who knew about it from her brother, confirmed the facts for me too.

About the final battle between men and beasts, everyone kept silence, for as long as they lived. It must have been more terrible than any hunt in the heart of the wild in which men have faced dangerous animals and died glorious deaths. There must have been a truly indescribable contest as four-footed and two-footed creatures fought for survival, fought to have the last chance. My father won it.

He came to know man as he is. As I am.

Not only did he not shrink from the most extreme violence, he also certainly made exhaustive use of every psychological method of dealing with the men whose help he had to have in order for him to save *himself*. It speaks for my father's savage, boundless energy as well as for his virtuosity in playing the keyboard of the heart, working out every type of human behavior in advance with the utmost precision, like a surgeon with a scalpel or an experimental bacteriologist with a toxin test weighed out to a millionth of a milligram, it speaks for him that he . . . that as a collective egoist he . . .

X

Now there is a hissing over Brig. Gen. Carolus's wobbly little table. For a second his face, his salmon pink, rubber-gloved hands, and the thin hunched back of the prisoner he has just painstakingly examined are bathed in chalky light. Then a tongue of flame spurts from the old acetylene lamp's calcium carbide tank, which has cracked into jagged pieces. Fireworks, then everything is cloaked in darkness. The prisoners have spontaneously seized the critical moment. The charlatan general, rigid with fright, watches from behind his spectacles as they dash as one down the open ship's ladder, upsetting the basin of sublimate solution in the darkness, into the sleeping quarters, two facing halls or stables with strong bulkheads toward the middle, each with a veteran petroleum lamp swinging from its ceiling and peacefully smoldering.

I am no match for the others elbowing for the best spots, those in the corners. But my companion is. He pulls me along with irresistible energy, then pushes us both through the crowd while squeezing against me so tightly that I feel the warmth of his body, half with pleasure, half reluctantly. He twists and turns, presenting first his back, then the sack he is carrying, thumps and blows rain down, but he captures a corner spot, and once he has it, no one can wrest it away. As he looks at me silently, but breathing deeply, I have a rare feeling of ease. Home. Calm. Here? Now? With him? But so it is. Or is it only fatigue? I am unable to think clearly, and yet the image of my father will not leave me. Do I still love him so much? I don't know. But I want to finish with his story.

It speaks for my father's boundless energy and for his knowledge of human nature, which henceforth would take as its foundation nothing but the basest human motives, greed and vanity, cruelty and stupidity, that he was among the three survivors who were picked up by a whaler off Skovby. He, the geographer, and the missionary, the missionary troubled in mind, perhaps in an alcoholic delirium. My father was not in a delirium. He was only too lucid. A different man. He hated and hates people, except me and himself. Then again, he may not have received the best treatment from people. Fortune had not exactly smiled on him.

When I asked him to tell me the happier part of his story too, his rescue, he said he was too tired. He did not say no, in fact rarely did.

The bard also passed in respectful silence over his dog Ruru's end. An oval scar on the back of his left hand where the veins from the fingers snake under the skin in a soft ridge might possibly have been the traces of a severe dog bite; but I never found out whether this bite dated from before or after the reconciliation at the critical moment. It may be that the rats ate human flesh and the humans canine flesh, he did not say yes, did not say no, but ran his heavy left hand through my blond hair, at that time very thick, soft or rough, straight or somewhat wavy, depending on the weather. It is no longer so thick now and its pale blond has given way to a muted nut brown, but possibly my companion is tempted to run his fingers through it. I look at him in astonishment, but do not speak, do not say yes, do not say no.

I must have been a beautiful child. Not a happy one.

My father became an incorrigible misanthrope. Even my mother's brother (my father married six months after his return without fanfare from the far north) – even he was not his friend. He did nothing to stop him from leaving and never tried to find him. My mother grieved a good deal. He did not. *I* was supposed to be his friend.

When I was seven he wished he had a youth of fourteen, he didn't want to wait, he needed me. When I was fourteen I was supposed to be like a twenty-year-old, know what free trade, baseness, and victory over rats by cunning are, I was supposed to provide comradeship for him. I was his favorite son. Was? Am I that only now, perhaps? He experimented on me – and what notion can the experimental subject have of *when* the experiment is over? That is known only to the experimenter, and the good Lord.

He spared nothing so that I, his son, would be hardened to life, futile and merciless as it is.

I would like to continue recalling my youth, but my eyes are drooping now. I have a pillow that my neighbor has made ready for me, it is the children's gramophone wrapped in a coat. The inscrutable man has also covered my knees with a blanket. I am too weak to do anything, even eat. I see and smell the food, the flavor of the seasoned, nourishing soup is perceptible on the papillae of my tongue, but I can't. To sleep, sleep, and never wake up. Never wake up again as the son of my father – now he is standing by me, indistinct in the flickering light of the swinging petroleum lamp – never again as the widower of my wife, never again as the brother of my brother – now he has reached me at last and tells me in a whisper what has prevented him from coming since that last meeting . . . he caught yellow fever, he was saved, though he has not recovered, he shows me his wasted hands, but they gradually dissolve into nothing under the strengthening light of the petroleum lamp. He shakes my shoulder, lifts my head, lets it fall like a piece of lead, and, turning to look over his shoulder toward a crowd of onlookers or students, he pronounces my name, he, the Institute's founder whom I never saw, calls me Dr. Georg Letham the younger . . . Georg Letham, Doctor of Philosophy, was my father, he was . . .

FOUR

I

Who could my handsome companion be? Conceivably he was someone from the cultured classes. I reached for his hand when I awoke the next morning. Very much unlike his bony, noble face, it was somewhat flaccid, effeminate, but one wanted to take it. Stroking the palm was like running one's hand over a newborn baby's dry cranium, warmed by the spring sun, beneath it a pulsing where the bones are still soft, rubbery, not completely fused.

It was a pleasure to tickle the inside of his hand with my index finger as he slept, unaware of what I was doing. But the youth was not asleep at all, he had noticed it. Or I was not even acting spontaneously, and he had succeeded in tempting me to a caress.

He told me his name, March, and I told him mine.

Heavy iron heating pipes, like steam ducts in basement corridors, ran across the ceiling of our cage. Steam heat in the hold of a ship on its way to the tropics? Where now, in the morning hours, it was already as hot as a steam bath? Once the eye had adjusted to the half-light, it could be seen that these steam pipes were open at one end. Could they be attached to the boilers that powered the engines, for spewing out hot steam to make us see reason, should that become necessary? Discipline or scalding, that was the choice. It was not a choice. We would all be well-mannered and stay that way.

March looked at me, but refrained from caresses. He pulled out the gramophone, examined the records. He desperately stroked the one that was broken in the middle, followed the microscopically fine grooves with a sharp fingernail. The others cast covetous, almost fierce glances at the battered little toy. No one else had anything like it.

It was worth more to him than money. I would soon find out how much it meant to him.

He showed me something inscribed on the record, actually two signatures, one scratched on each of the pieces. Louis and Lilli. They were similar hands, straight up and down, regular, perhaps those of a brother and sister.

Meanwhile work had been assigned in Cargo Hold 3. Some of the men had to help in the galley, others had to clean out the filth in the holds while they were vacated during the "walkabouts," the half-hour promenades on deck. I will not speak of the arrangements for washing, which practically made one dirtier instead of cleaner. Let the reader take a shower in seawater and describe the result! But even these most primitive of facilities, which might have sufficed in the time of Columbus for the personal hygiene of his hydrophobic crew, had to be maintained.

The troughs for drinking water had to be rubbed down inside with metal shavings and seawater. The two together produced a corrosive acid, and the hands of the convicts entrusted with this cleaning job soon became unfit for work, or fit only if miserable pain were no object. I had this job.

I tried to laugh, but it was a false laugh, a croak. I resented this work too much! The others gloated as they watched me, and laughed laughs that were true.

It was not until the third day that I reported for a walkabout. I toiled along in the line like a beaten man.

The sea was frothing. The officers lay smoking, drinking, playing cards, red-and-white-striped awnings over their heads. Brig. Gen. Carolus was nowhere to be seen. Over our own heads were only the plume of smoke that wafted from the ship as it labored against the swells and the good, kind, vast blue and gold sky with its already almost tropical heat. The clogs of the convicts clattered in rhythm on the planks of the ship. The surface was slippery. Why was that? Many were seasick, unable to appreciate the fresh air. I lost my footing in the muck and steadied myself by taking hold of my companion's hand with my injured one. He squeezed back. Back?

My face was stony.

I had overestimated my comrade's age. I had taken him to be well past his midthirties, but he was only in his late twenties. One day soon I would find out more about the fancy he had taken to me.

I was very depressed, suffered greatly from physical symptoms, I was itchy inside and out. I had expected to be ordered to the sick bay, where I assumed life would be easier; I had believed that Carolus would show some human feeling toward his one-time laboratory mate.

I was mistaken, as it appeared. The days passed, and nothing happened. But I said nothing.

Silence is the most powerful magnet. One who contains himself, one who does not speak, need never fear rejection. He is safe. His position is good, or at least he is better off than the one who is driven to speak.

My handsome companion was one of those who must speak. On the dock he had been able to contain himself. For twelve hours we had been attached to each other, and he had not said a word to me. Now there was nothing binding us together, and yet I soon had an idea what had brought him here. This crime had to have some bearing on his feelings toward me.

March wanted to, I did not. It was so easy to scare him off – a frosty look, that was enough. When he launched into his confession for a second time, I mentioned my hand, on which there was now a painful eczema from the metal shavings and seawater. And the scab had come off the wound on my wrist, the place where the manacle had injured me as we were climbing the rope ladder. If only that had been the extent of it! My entire body was burning, as though I were wearing the shirt of nettles from the fairy tale. So had I had enough? Assuredly. But what did I do? I closed my eyes and yawned loudly.

The good March hung on me, his eyes drinking me in. Perhaps he thought he could appeal to *my* sympathies, to my warm compassion? Hardly. Nothing isolates one more than suffering. He couldn't take that away from me. I said nothing in response to his questions, I lay on my belly in my bunk, I tossed about, I could not rest. Not a wink of sleep.

At night the light of the moon came to me through the porthole. The petroleum lamp swayed and stank. Almost none of the convicts slept, a few dozed. One rooted through another's hair like a monkey. Others played cards, many told stories, but groups kept to themselves, there were sudden scuffles, boxing matches in the middle of the night, almost no words exchanged, only blows, bloody duels of unimaginable brutality. A master of the art of tattooing offered himself to the gentlemen as an emissary of the fine arts, demanding sums of money that no one could pay. But the most coveted object (after the leather shoes and the flannel vest that had somehow found their way aboard) was March's old children's gramophone. The gentlemen imagined that marvels would come from this music box. They expected the music of the spheres from the scratchy old records. March could have asked anything, and they would have given it to him. But he did not. What did he care about goods and chattels? He had no thought of such things. Feeling was his life.

And the proof of his affection for me? A kiss? A warm hand squeeze? A declaration of love, an emotional speech, a vow that he would be my friend forever, that we would be blood brothers until the two of us escaped from G. to Brazil? That he would care for me tenderly if I came down with yellow fever? No! Something much bigger and yet much less great. I will have to explain – no one will ever guess.

Almost everyone had three or four changes of underwear. After the long train trip, only what was at the bottom of the bag was still clean. But what if there was nothing there but two little books of the greatest cultural but no practical value, *Hamlet* and the Gospel? What if one had been relying on the excellent authorities to look after all one's needs, even those most intimate ones? If one had been counting on a dear blood brother, had calculated that he would come at the last minute to the embarkation point, the port city, bringing, aside from poignant words of parting, some clean drawers and undershirts? Yes? No? No! Then one would have miscalculated foolishly, and the idiot doing the miscalculation was me, my father's son, who had only a single good pair of underwear and two not very clean shirts to his name. Anyone who was a man tried to help himself: man and fate were one. A dirty pair of drawers should not be the cliffs upon which the intrepid experimenter was wrecked. There was enough time, what should he do? He should go to the tap and wash his underwear in plenty of running water, injured hands or no injured hands. Yes, that would have been good advice! If only I had tried to follow it from the outset.

I did do it the next night. And what was the result? Yes, some of the dirt came out at first, because, like a complete imbecile, I failed to conserve the soap that was so precious and for the time being irreplaceable. But, when I had finished washing my dainties, not all the soap came out, still less, unfortunately, all the seawater. And now these anything-but-sparkling whites would be dried on a line stretched between the frames of two portholes, or, better yet, ingeniously attached to the iron bulkheads. The next morning one would slip one's undies on and sweat through them. And fifteen minutes later find oneself in hell. But no, my dear Georg Letham, let's not exaggerate, it's only a mild condition known as red dog or prickly heat. What does the physician Dr. Georg Letham the younger have to say? He goes to Dr. Georg Letham the younger, listens to his tale of woe, looks the fellow over, and says:

"Red dog is a disease with which almost every newcomer to the tropics during hot weather becomes acquainted, usually even during the passage. It is an acute inflammation caused by profuse perspiration leading to excessively moist skin. The material of the underclothing is often an irritant, also sometimes soap that has been poorly rinsed from it during washing. Extremely small, slightly raised papules densely distributed over the skin form on those areas of the body where there is the most friction from clothing: initially the waist and the forearms, later also the shoulders and the chest, back, and neck. These are extremely itchy and hence highly detrimental to the general condition of the sufferer. In particular, nocturnal pruritus can lead to severe insomnia . . ."

Severe insomnia? Is there a mild kind too, Dr. Letham?

". . . Continual scratching generally aggravates the inflammation. Scratching to the point of bleeding will readily induce further inflammatory processes, infections by pyogenic bacteria, furuncles, and eczema formation."

Fervent thanks, esteemed doctor and benefactor of mankind! Where would we be without you, man of the spirit and custodian of medical knowledge? What do you advise? Powdering? With whose powder? Frequent washing with pure, nonsaline water? What pure water? Alcohol compresses would be excellent too, but to use alcohol for compresses, here in Cargo Hold 3, what a grotesque fantasy!

Oh, you loving hearts, I'm not laughing at you now! I'm not yawning. March had everything I needed, and he gave it with pleasure.

He had long understood my condition, he had powder, he had pure water, for he had saved up his supply of the fresh water we had been receiving, a liter ration poured into our canteens every day after the walkabout. He himself had suffered from severe thirst, and his tongue, long and narrow and purple like a dog's, had passed across his parched lips more than once.

He was capable of making a sacrifice, his ideal was worth something to him. But did he expect a reward? Was he capable of working pro bono in the service of an ideal?

Why worry about it? Shouldn't one just be grateful? It helps, yes! It's a balm, yes! It's a good deed. Let's switch roles. You be the doctor and I'll be the patient. In any event I slept well and deeply that night, very deeply.

II

That was when I dubbed March "Gummi." Rubber gum is wonderful, one of the things that make the world go round. To create the chicle plantations necessary for manufacturing rubber, broad swaths of land in the colonies are cleared, the natives' idle Eden is razed. The black plebs are worked to death, and if they rise up, if they want to return to their nation's way of tropical idleness, war is declared on the colony, there is not the slightest hesitation about using squadrons of fighter planes to drop poison gas. Man passes, rubber goes on.

What is the individual? March was lucky to be taken seriously as one, so seriously that he got a new name, no, two new names. For as soon as I saw his relentless sentimental smile, I named him not just Gummi, but also Bear, "Gummi Bear." His warm heart was never anything but a gummi bear. Step on a gummi bear, lick it fondly – it will always be what it is.

"Sweetheart, you bore me," I would say to him when, at night, he would resume his life story. I was tired, I had been saddled with duties. I had been released from the job of cleaning the water tub, but if a criminal suffering from typhus in the sick bay was pining for an enema, I was the one the guard called.

Thus my glorious achievements as a physician were being borne in mind. Was that not what I had wanted? It was thought that an old doctor like me was best suited for these delightful tasks. The guards, officially appointed and much too lavishly paid for their work, were so lethargic that they even fell asleep on their watch. For the heat was blistering. Even under the open sky, it was oppressive enough to take one's breath away. But all the more so where we were, down below or in the sick bay, that little room in which men lived cheek by jowl like rats! The less said the better!

When I returned from my charitable work one night, I felt an unexpected breath of fresh air. A gentle salt breeze caressed my brow. What a turn of events, by the grace of God! Gummi Bear, who had not been sleeping well because of the goings-on inside him, never mind the heat outside him, looked at me with swimming eyes. Suddenly I felt something wet and salty on my upper lip. What was there to cry about? But no! It was real, lovely, salty seawater, the porthole above my head had been smashed while I was gone. I had the marvelous godsend of a fresh breeze.

A thorough investigation. Who had broken the unopenable window? A tribunal loomed.

What would the punishment be? Who was going to be punished? How would it be possible to punish that miserable ship's passenger more than he was being punished already? Easy! Near the engine room there were some little rooms almost hermetically sealed by iron doors, true hellholes, outlet ducts standing on end, not much broader than an average man. If someone needed to be disciplined, he could be shut up in one of these and allowed to stew in his own juices. The stokers were relieved every three hours, and a Gummi Bear was roasted for forty-eight.

How had Gummi Bear carried out his crime? With the crank of his gramophone. Oh, that gramophone, what a marvel of technology! The most beautiful melodies in its innards. A poignant keepsake from the life before. And a tool now too, so that I, the bosom friend, might bask in fresh air.

Fine! Gummi Bear went to the steam room. That was his reward for his good deed!

But what won't love do for love! After forty-eight hellish hours, he staggered back, covered with dirt and almost blind from being in the dark so long, to all outward appearances hardly a man anymore. But in his heart more joyous than ever! Gummi Bear was despairing and joyous at once, submissive yet gifted with extraordinary energy, male and female – a mixture of contradictory psychological traits that an experimenter might find stimulating. "Poor little nipper," I said to him as I loyally returned to him the things he had left in my keeping, the gramophone and the rest of his possessions, "you poor dear pet!" And Gummi Bear smiled beatifically.

The ship was rolling wildly. There was no way to replace the smashed pane of the porthole during the voyage. The cool fresh air was a balm that would sustain me for the entire trip, but, since the battle with red dog that I had so ingloriously lost, I had the greatest respect for seawater. But why else did one have a Gummi Bear? When seas were heavy he stuffed *his* precious bag into the opening, letting the harsh, caustic seawater get into anything it wanted to. At least I would be protected and would lie tenderly in his arms. Yes, in his arms, I suppose that was what he wanted, but he would never have that. I swore that I would protect myself from *this* love.

I suspected that it was this love that had brought him here. No longer did I want him to keep his mouth shut, I wanted to hear his story. And once he had recounted the saga of what his brimming little heart had driven him to, then I was going to look at him, full of love, pucker up for a kiss, and say to him as tenderly as a wily anarchist and enemy of love can: No! You expect me to do *that*?!

Or was it better not to let him get that far? I wasn't going to be assaulted by *him*. I emphasized the word *him*, not *I*! Other men had been assaulted by other men here in this Cargo Hold 3 of the *Mimosa*, for I had seen it, and the others had seen it, and the guards had seen it, and there were cries and moans and murmurs and all the silly panting and sobbing eruptions of a sensuality repressed for months among these brute hearts, and the good Gummi Bear had tried to cover my eyes so that I would not see these abominations. Did he have four hands, to cover my ears too? Why worry about the eyes and ears? The soul! What did that mean to me!

The next morning the brigadier general glanced my way. He made no response to my meek and plaintive greeting, but looked away as I stared at him. Oh, Herr Brigadier General, *I'm* the one who should be disconcerted!

He was the king of the ship, but, like all kings, he was lonely in his exalted position. Even the ship's commander was many ranks below him, the commandant of our group was at the lowest of the officer grades, while Carolus twiddled his thumbs at the top.

I did not push myself forward. I bided my time. A single word from him was precious. Short of that, I hung on to what I had, this "loving heart," this March, who flattered me. I had no idea how it was that I, no longer young, no longer handsome, had "bewitched" this poor devil, to use his word, but it was so good to be pampered, to have the choice bits of food slipped to me, to be taken care of like a child! It touched me when he offered to start up the gramophone, which as yet had made no sound, for me. One of the convicts, Suleiman, the two-and-a-half-hundredweight man, the copper-faced colossus, his mouth protruding pinkly and fleshily beneath his bold, hawklike nose and taking up almost all of the lower part of his brutal face, a monster of a man who despite his baseness (rape and murder, child abuse) was not without a certain oriental majesty and cynical authority, had offered him a good sum of money for the machine. To no effect. Then more. People are children.

Not to be taken seriously. Gummi Bear was no different from "Sultan Suleiman," the colossus, the rich man. All impulse, nothing more. Why should I struggle against the love of Gummi Bear? Let's have it! Open up! Tell it, go on! Sing your song!

III

Gummi Bear's ambition was to be, not a gummi bear, but a diamond. His proud bearing on the dock, his reserve, lately again maintained with particular desperation, through which an irrepressible passionate nature always shone – it was unfailing. A criminal? No. But a dangerous child? Yes, he was that. His story was much less romantic than he thought. For he was one of the "loving hearts," and when he pitied others (such as me), he was pitying himself. When he lied to others (such as me), he was lying to himself.

He told the story of his betrothal. The girl is the daughter of a big shot (a high-ranking municipal official); he calls her sometimes by her first name, sometimes, as though inadvertently and then immediately correcting himself, Countess. The third party is the cadet, though in fact he is not an aspirant to high military rank but a prospective senior clerk or bank official who would still be attending business school now if he were still alive. *Quod non*.

Gummi Bear could not lie for any length of time.

Everything else is true. March's feeling is true. Gummi Bear's motive is true. The tragic outcome is true. The two pieces of the phonograph record entitled "Under the Bridges," on which the brother and sister, Louis and Lilli, solemnly scrawled their names as children, each on one fragment, are true. And he, March, who at first professed to be the son, the only son, of a manufacturer, an industrial magnate, eventually turned out to be just one of the brood of a pharmacist perpetually on the edge of bankruptcy. During periods when business was bad, March's father managed the books for a cinema owner or labored fruitlessly to concoct new shoe-polish compounds or herbal teas. But when the needs of the family became still greater, he also dealt in narcotics, at first obtaining real drugs and reselling them at high prices, but then substituting chalk and perpetrating such a clumsy fraud that informers turned him in. The informers did not have the clearest consciences themselves, the matter was dropped, the druggist could be punished only for violating the pricing regulations for pharmaceuticals; of course he hadn't been distributing narcotics.

And this is the way he always squeaks by.

In this atmosphere young March grows up. His father, at a relatively advanced age, has acquired a taste of his own for these narcotics; wised up now, he no longer sells them to others at predatory rates, but uses them himself. Haltingly the son recounted the stunts his morphine-addicted father had pulled, the great expense not spared by his mother, brave, competent, healthy, and entirely devoted to her sick spouse, in her effort to break the rapidly aging man of his craving.

Success at last. Rejoicing in the bosom of his family over the return of the prodigal father. But in the sanatorium where the pharmacist goes for withdrawal treatment, he meets a young woman, a star of stage and screen, falls passionately in love with her. He absconds again, this time for good, from the family, for which March, the oldest son, is now responsible.

March becomes a minor official, an organized, hardworking person aspiring to better things. Ten years of work, of scrimping and saving. Domestic tranquillity. Amen. After these ten difficult years his mother remarries, his brothers and sisters are working, a younger brother apprenticed to a watchmaker, a younger sister engaged to be married. Thank goodness – and March breathes again.

He is no shining light as a city official, but well thought of, welcome everywhere, a respectable, unassertive, retiring person who is already mentally in the bosom of his family at the close of working hours and who thinks only of providing security for them and giving them nice surprises from time to time. He does not yet feel very attracted to women. He has his mother, his sisters, after all. Fatherly feelings have awakened in him toward his younger brother, who is very delicate, perhaps conceived during his father's morphine phase.

So young March's life is taken up with his family. The passions, whatever they might be, have no chance to develop, the only perceptible abnormality is a childish vanity, clothes, underthings, personal hygiene; also a concern for a higher profile, a striving for greater prominence in society. And then a certain natural adulation and worshipfulness, a mental genuflection before male persons of high position, such as a young clergyman of lordly blood who left his "castle" to travel as a missionary to Africa, returned with a case of malaria, and replaced the priest of the parish in which the good March lives with his family. The abbé has nothing of the lord about him. He has a lean, expressionless face, the skin seemingly clinging to the bones, cold hands damp with sweat and limp to the touch, and his tonsure covers not only the occiput but the whole of his angular skull, for, despite his youth, this aristocratic Christ has not a single hair left.

This abbé is March's first love. March has not realized that he loves men more than he loves women. But he feels it. He sorrows over the abbé's somber indifference, he suffers from the emptiness and tedium of his bureaucratic existence. A change presents itself, no voyage to Africa to proselytize black children, only a regular promotion from Grade 6a to Grade 6b and, along with it, a move to a small provincial town in the north of the country. So good-bye to mother, stepfather, sisters, brothers, and the rest of the family, up and away! After his last confession, the handsome, shy youth, profoundly agitated, presses the hand of the brave reverend, who looks with astonishment into March's wide eyes, continues with his stiff, dry sermon, and wipes his hand with a rough handkerchief, whether because it is sweating excessively or because the handshake of a bourgeois, featherbrained civil servant disturbs his train of thought, or simply because he is preoccupied. Nothing more happens. If only the lordly abbé, with his knowledge of human nature and love of mankind, had earnestly taken the official to task on the spot (fond handshakes between confessor and confessant are definitely not done), poor March's aberrant tendencies might have been corrected in time and he might have attained salvation. As it is, however, a calamity will have to happen in order for the youthful March, so blind to this vital point, to understand the gift that Mother Nature has thoughtfully bestowed upon him.

And this may also explain the desire cherished by the poor frog, his fond wish to tell *me* everything – because now, much too late, he knew himself and because he felt a new passion stirring within him and because he wanted to protect himself and also (I can only hope, my friend!) myself from the effects of his wild temperament. But I can see you, little one! I do have some knowledge of human nature, even if I am no lover of mankind! I see you for what you are!

Wild temperament? You? Nothing but a misunderstanding. Children are not criminals, certainly. But to give free rein to everything in their dim little brains, that would be dangerous. The embrace reflex does not interest me. I am not a female frog. Prevention is the best defense. That way it can go no further.

IV

March rattled on in the sultry gloom of the subtropical night, but unfortunately did not command as much interest from me as he had expected. What was his abbé supposed to mean to me? What did I care about his private stirrings? Though they were no longer so private – the good lad made no secret of his thoughts, he posed no puzzles for me. He was tedious. He had been more interesting as a silent man chained to me.

So on with the story, you charmer of a man, you heartbreaker from the provinces, who is not satisfied with inflaming the passions of the daughter of an exemplary executive secretary and becoming formally betrothed to the young woman, a golden blonde, in the midst of family gathered from afar, but has also managed to wreak devastation in the heart of her brother, the dark-haired cadet.

How lucky this quite handsome, but not very interesting, man was with people! Here too, in Cargo Hold 3, he had already made conquests, without meaning to. The coppery oriental, the pasha Sultan Suleiman, cast fiery glances his way. Compensation for March himself would evidently be added to the selling price of the silly gramophone if he smiled upon the rich, crudely sensual criminal. So go on, March! I won't be jealous. Love in any form is beautiful and restorative for the average person, so go ahead and accept it, don't wallow despondently in old memories! Life beckons, it's made for pleasure. Let your Louis sleep the sleep of the just!

But a man like me was preaching to deaf ears, the good March was unable to tear himself away from his memories. For the tenth time he ran through his litany, which began with the pledge of eternal loyalty between the sister, Countess Lilli, and the brother, Louis the cadet, symbolized, much as in the ancient heroic saga, by a phonograph record broken in the middle, and which never really ended. During the final spring they both cling to March and shower the delirious fellow with love, possibly trading off on even-numbered and odd-numbered days. But poor March! What is pure torment to him with the sister, pretty as a picture, bursting with health and sensuality, luscious, golden blonde and gray-eyed, would be a much-longed-for happiness with the brother, dark-haired, pale, gangly, somewhat arrogant, his eyes sunken in deep hollows. He, March, does not hesitate between them for an instant, he plumped for the brother the moment he laid eyes on him, he is deferential to him, lets himself be tortured by his bored, languid smile, the tight curl of his lips, and he is tortured too by the tight curl of the sister's lips, the lips of the sensual, hale, good girl, his fiancée. She is much too proud to let on, but she is too much a woman to put up with this. Her vanity has been wounded. She neglects her appearance, a sign that she wishes only comradely feelings toward March, her fiancé, and that, in all innocence, she wants to live with him as sister and brother!

Whereupon he, March, delighted that the conflict has been so easily resolved, shows comradely candor, he reveals to her what he has not revealed to himself, that he is passionately fond of Louis, that he is "bewitched" by him. He expresses himself so poetically, the timid Grade 6b official. And she, Countess Lilli, strokes the hair of March, her fiancé-brother, she is kindhearted toward him, he is the apple of her eye, and she is all his, and when she spends entire afternoons at church, on her knees praying, she is kneeling only for him, praying only for him – and the frog sighs and believes.

Then abruptly she sends the engagement ring back. Unfortunately she loves him too much, she cannot settle for what little he can spare her. But the cadet remonstrates seriously with March, insisting that the wedding must take place, March must make up with the Countess, or . . . And for the first time the pale, arrogant youth toys with the idea that he might crush March, or possibly give himself to March – it might be high-handedness, it might be out of curiosity, perhaps out of pity, out of vanity, or just for fun. It is not clear. Perhaps out of real love for his sister, who is the most important thing in his life. And always will be. And March, who once expected a simple, untroubled life by Lilli's side, under the protection of the prominent father-in-law, is now, with his good heart, his weak will, his abnormal but strong urges, in a state of the most terrible confusion. He neglects his work. He no longer sleeps. Finally he goes back to the sister, and promises her – out of weakness, out of pity, out of Christian mercy – that, though he will not break with her brother, henceforth he will look upon Louis as no more than a future brother-in-law. Thus he pledges that he will see Louis only once a week and in Lilli's presence, perhaps they will dance, one of them will wind up the new portable gramophone, and he and March will take turns dancing with Lilli. Innocent, childish frolicking. Great solution, of Solomonic wisdom! But, of course, things happen otherwise. Lilli winds up the gramophone, but only Louis and March dance together, and suddenly it seems that poor Louis's mechanical daily work at the business school is no match for March's passionate, fanatical love, it has infected even the cool, languid, arrogant heart of a precocious, sickly, callous, already faded youth.

And Lilli is supposed to watch this? Is supposed to air out the smoky room afterward and tidy up while Louis and March go for a walk in the summer rain, sharing an umbrella, sit side by side later in a bar, a café, arms around each other yet gazes chaste, huddle in the darkness of a cinema. Louis and March love each other, yes, but purely and truly chastely, like angels or frogs.

Lilli, sensual, healthy, and young, unbroken, does not believe it. *She* won't share, not another minute. But her threats cut no ice either with the cadet or with her fiancé, and one day, while Louis is being visited by his bosom friend, yet a third man comes to his room, his father, the prominent municipal official, a man of principle. March flees on the wings of an angel. He is driven out of the office, he has to move out of his lodgings, he faces public opprobrium, and Lilli's farewell letter leaves no room for argument. And to make matters worse, his own father now appears, the morphine-addicted unemployed pharmacist: seedy, a beggar – March is supposed to help and has virtually nothing to his name, for, vain as he is, he has devoted almost everything to his appearance.

V

March paused. The other convicts amused themselves in the evenings according to their natures. Only the tamest played cards, or let off steam in their brutish way, or roughhoused. What most did, men among men for months starved for "love," this March tried to hide from me, he tried to enthrall me with his chaste tale, and when I asked him coolly, "Dear heart, why are you telling me this?" he dropped his eyes, nestled against me imperceptibly, and responded somewhat huskily: "So you won't think I'm one of *them*!" Ah, I wasn't supposed to think he was a common criminal like the rest of the bunch? I wasn't supposed to think he was a man of manly love?

I closed my eyes, I tried to snore. But he had sharp eyes and ears. Even in the semidarkness he could tell a mask of sleep from genuine slumber and real snoring from feigned. So I gave up. I raised myself on my elbows, looked out through the porthole, still lined with jagged glass. The lilac tropical sky was filled with almost abnormally bright, densely packed stars.

The sea was high. Now and then a fierce spray came showering in, onto my wild hair, my heavy, unkempt beard. March suddenly said something about a hotel room.

Because of the scandal, he is evicted from his cozy abode. No one in the small-minded little town wants to rent to him. And yet his love for Louis, the cadet, is so pure, so chaste, so restrained. A little more tolerance! Just a little bit of forbearance for him! And he, March, would have resigned himself to everything, would have become a good official and a good citizen – at least that was what he said now that the whole thing was over and done with.

Thus he lies despondently till noon in the same bed with his father, who is stuck to him like a barnacle. The weather is bad, he lies in his hotel room, propped up on his elbows. And looks at his papa. Affliction and inexorable decline are written on the features of the former pharmacist and drug dealer. Sharing a bed with him is no fun. Nor does this meet with the approval of the hotel staff. But necessity knows no law. Until now March has always sided with his brave, life-affirming mother; *that* was where he belonged, that is where his heart is. But now, when he is beaten and disgraced, when he feels within him, in his own sorrow-consumed heart, the misery of the mortal world botched by God yet not consigned by Satan to fire and brimstone soon enough, when people avoid him on the street, when he has lost his job between one day and the next, when he is refused entrance to the office, when he cannot imagine that he might see Louis and Lilli again – now he understands his father, and the two of them decide – to go to his mother.

March described his eyes falling on the brown-varnished sprucewood dresser, almost the only piece of furniture in the shabby hotel room apart from a rickety chair and a rusty iron washstand. On the dresser are two suitcases and a bluish cardboard box. One of the suitcases is made of leather, the other of pressed fiber; both are his. The leather suitcase is where the famous gramophone, "a present from the kids," is kept. The blue cardboard box belongs to his father and contains the last of the underthings that the old man has rescued from ruin. He has no washing things, but at least he has retained some idea of cleanliness (at someone else's expense).

March cannot stop him, his father, from using his son's expensive soap, his English razor, or his toothbrush. So did his father bring nothing with him? No, he has a gun (in addition to an ample supply of morphine), which, in better days, he obtained from a down-on-his-luck Baltic prince so that he would always have a "way out." Not a bad idea to sell it to pay for the trip to March's mother, but no one wants the old piece of junk. March has a nice gold watch. Without a solid cover, but genuine and monogrammed. But he will never part with this, the only gift from his dear mother. So every penny has to be saved. Father and son survive on rolls and, after their lunch from the bakery, sit in a public park and yawn with hunger at each other in the misty cold.

At night the son goes past the house with the father, showing him the windows behind which his Louis and Lilli live. But his father's teeth are chattering with cold and hunger, the hour is late, the train will be leaving in half an hour. They are going to spend the night on the train to avoid paying for a hotel room. So off March goes, accompanied by a castanet performance, gazing miserably back at the windows, stumbling over the cobblestones, his eyes full of tears and his heart full of cares.

They arrive at March's mother's house early. She is contented, meaning she is happily remarried for the time being, she is the wife of a dentist, a recent widower, and, quite frankly, she is disquieted and ashamed in front of her new family when her old family, in the shape of her distraught son and down-at-heels first husband, appears here in her respectable house, where everything smells of disinfectants and the vulcanized rubber of false teeth.

Neither son nor ex-husband dares to tell the whole truth. The two of them do give her to understand that they are in a fix, but all she does is nod and pretend not to hear. March is thunderstruck. This is the thanks he gets? For this he spent the best years of his life moping around the house, gave his mother every last penny on the first of each month, made it possible for her to live a carefree existence for almost ten years? So that she can cut them loose with literally a crust of bread!

But she has no use for him. Her main concern is to find an acceptable way to get rid of the two unwelcome guests.

The three members of what was once a family, father, mother, and child, sit together in spiteful silence, listening to the low drone of the drill and the suppressed shrieks of the harassed patients from the dentist's laboratory. As the morning passes, poor March's feeling toward *his* family, that of the executive secretary, takes over, it becomes overpowering, he is as though in a daze, can hardly wait for the end of lunch, which is being eaten at a late hour because of the dentist and his patients – March is in love, he is in love and must return to where the heart is. *There* he will be understood. The engagement has been broken off, his job is gone, his lodgings rented out, but he still has "loving hearts" back there, and Gummi Bear, tender and tenacious as he is, must return to them.

The old addict sees this with the cynicism of despair, hits his ex-wife up once more (his morphine supply is running low), and disappears from this story.

VI

Along with the old addict, however, something else disappears, which takes us further in the story of that great child March or Gummi Bear. The two good suitcases containing clothes and underwear disappear, and the cardboard box containing dirty underwear and the still usable, but unsellable, unpresentable, antiquated revolver remains. It is a wicked joke of the humorously inclined father to have added to these articles the son's "keepsake," the children's gramophone. But in exchange, the good son March's gold watch is gone. The father tenderly pressed his dear child to his shaggy breast, tears flowed down his thin cheeks, and he closed his eyes, the lids now swollen like sponges, but his hands did not tremble as they nimbly plucked his choked-up son's last valuable item, the gold watch, from the lower left pocket of his vest. Lament upon lament! Lament? What am I saying? Profound despair, vast disappointment. *This* is how people can be! *This* is how a father can behave toward his son! Beyond description how much he longs for Louis, for Lilli, even for the severe but morally staunch municipal official who drove him, March, out of paradise and now stands before him with fiery sword.

March gathers the last of his strength. Late that afternoon he comes again before his petrified mother and tells her everything. His mother stands with her fists clenched in the pockets of her blue-and-white-striped apron and, aghast, keeps whispering to her son: Shh! Keep it down! So that the good dentist won't hear. Only now does she grasp what has happened. With a man! Why? A man! What for? Aren't there enough pretty young women? And you were engaged! You were *all set*! I was, March admits in his despair. He is helpless.

His mother goes through the cardboard box. If only the gold watch were still there, "at least"! Perhaps Papa, her ex-husband, was only playing a joke, perhaps he hid the watch there. Nothing. March says not another word, he gnaws his lower lip and wishes he could leave, he distractedly feels for the watch in his vest pocket, although on this unlucky day he could hardly be less interested in what time it is. His mother thinks. Couldn't they set the police after her grifter of an ex-husband? No, says March, that would be no help and would destroy his mother's (at bottom highly problematical) marital bliss and happy home. So, what then? his mother asks. In order to have something to say, March says offhandedly: I'm going to America.

His mother seizes upon this plan. She sees a way out. That very evening she finds the necessary money for her son by dint of the most fantastic exertions, she washes and darns the prodigal father's undershirts and socks overnight, stealthily fixes everything up, and the two of them scribble ten penciled calculations in the margins of the newspaper to make sure the money, lent without interest by the wife of a well-meaning relative of her husband (the dentist), will hold out to the other side of the ocean. It will have to, March says at last, his eyes drooping with fatigue.

He falls asleep. He dreams of his friend.

The next afternoon, of course, he is not at the port, where the ship bound for South America is ready for departure, but waiting for his Louis at the entrance to the business school. They greet one another briskly, as though there were nothing wrong. First March speaks ironically of his situation, mentioning casually that he is going to America. Just as casually, young Louis says, Wish I could go, I'd be there in a flash. At this unconsidered statement, the utterance of a silly boy, March takes hold of him. He lays his arm around his throat, his voice trembles, but he does not weep. He tells him that he has always known what a difference there was between Louis and his own family, a promise is a promise, loyalty is loyalty, love conquers all, words once spoken, and suchlike malarkey, he could kiss Louis's hand, etc.; he talks absolute nonsense. In the presence of his dear one, who would like to hurry home for lunch, he has no control over himself, he could never ever live without him. He calls on all the saints and everyone else in the calendar, imploring him to come along; Louis, the cadet, could have the steerage ticket, March would carry coal, wash dishes, find some money somewhere, hock his watch. But his watch is gone. The youth is abashed. Despite his arrogance, this doglike adoration touches him, as my wife's adoration once touched me, he smiles indulgently, the way one smiles at a handsome, blond-curled child when it first tries to walk. They arrange to meet that evening by a monument in the park. March is there, Louis is not. March waits all night. He is hungry. Better to curl up his toes and die than turn his Louis's travel money into bread and sausage. Father and sister must have put poor Louis in chains, or he would surely have been there long ago. Surely! March learns what despair is if he doesn't know already.

The next morning he makes a decision to visit the home of his precious boy. His frantic ringing brings his former fiancée to the door. She is terribly surprised to see him, she sees the cares, the hunger on the features she once loved, she lets him in, makes him some chamomile tea to steady him. Compose yourself, Herr March, take it easy! Confused about how formal to be. If only March knew something about people, were a bit of a diplomat! In some dark corner of her heart, Countess Lilli is still holding out for him. But he suspects some treachery, says Louis must be surrendered to him, or something bad will happen. Surrender? Who? Louis. Something bad? Yes, and he lifts his box and lets it drop, the heavy revolver in it making a thud as it lands. They're supposed to tremble before him, the idiot! Lilli loses patience at last. She does not want to indulge him a moment longer, but she controls herself, she puckers her healthy red lips to blow scornfully on the hot chamomile tea, then says that March should "take his time" but drink up, have a couple of cakes, and clear out once and for all. Not without Louis. Louis is at school. Impossible! Louis at school as on every other day? He wants to search the apartment, Lilli does not stand in his way, but when this witless tour reaches the hall by the front door, without hesitation she pushes him, not exactly gently, out the door and – locks it behind him.

March related all of this calmly. His eyes became fierce only when he mentioned the door locking behind him, and I understood what had happened later that evening. March had fallen to his knees, beseeching Louis to come with him – or to shoot him. When poor Louis had begun to cry, March – who only a second before had had no inkling of what was going to happen – had brought out the gun and pointed it at his loved one's chest, and before the youth could push the barrel away, the old but still serviceable piece of junk had fired. Off went the first shot. Down went the poor love slave Louis. The second shot was aimed at March's own chest and failed. Obviously! Still more obviously, courage was lacking for a third. Sad, but true. Thus this chaste love story of a frog ended with twenty years of hard labor.

VII

Who would dare to moralize to such a pure heart? Who would be so unfeeling as to look into the furrowed face of the good March, smile sardonically, and tell him that this sort of extravagant love always made him (me) sick. I don't dare. I don't have the courage for such an experiment.

I must try to escape the vicinity of this overly ardent heart in some other way.

I'll be an attendant in the sick bay. Better to be hedged about by the ill than by the overly ardent love of a loving heart. How will I get away? Would money help, even here? Perhaps through the intercession of a certain seasoned junior officer grown old in the colonial service, whose family troubles would give him reason to make the crooked straight and the straight crooked for a few pieces of gold. He has very quickly grasped suggestions to this effect. Only the cash is still lacking.

So how to come by some money? My brother abandoned me. My attorney coldly stuck to business. My father took to his heels. But if fate swiftly sent me a "loving heart" in the form of Gummi Bear? And if Gummi Bear has in his possession a treasure with which he has only to part in order to obtain as much money as I need to get away? And to get away from him most of all, from March?

Come, dear heart. Don't tell *me* about your feelings.

It's morning now, and you have slept better than I, who was almost constantly awake. You pat my hand and return to your task of cementing the broken phonograph record. And what might clever hands not be capable of, what might a tube of fish glue not make whole again! When, at noon on the dot, we are led out on deck and into the atrociously scorching sun for our half-hour walk, you take your record along, carefully put it in a corner near a partly open cabin door; you happily pick it up on the way back to Cargo Hold 3, carrying it like a sacrament, a smile playing on your lips such as has not been seen in these holds, on this ship, for a long time, not even among the big guns and demigods, the ship's officers, the brigadier general.

When night falls (and night falls fast here in the tropics), you wind up your machine for the first time aboard the *Mimosa*, put the repaired record on the platter, and set the mechanism whirring. And the record plays. The music that comes out is not quite what it should be, for the halves are misaligned by one groove, so that the melody is limpingly disrupted every few beats in a highly amusing fashion. The crack runs straight through the center of the record. But what we hear is pretty much the same sweet tune, with the same syncopated rhythm, same saxophones, same drumrolls, and great delight is reflected in the faces of those in the audience, including the fat Suleiman, whose lips bulge lewdly like the inside of a luscious, dark red, overripe fruit, half rotten and beginning to ferment. The guards are gathering out beyond the bulkhead, too, and I am able to catch the junior officer's eye.

So now to business. The song is over, the convicts are waiting for more music and for their dinner. But I close the gramophone, pull March into a dark corner, I ask him in a low voice to be true to his word for my sake and sell the gramophone. Thus I am holding him to the boyish promise he so unconsideredly gave. He thinks. Thinking does not come naturally to him. Nor does he trust me completely, for March is not stupid. But when was a thinking brain ever a match for a "loving heart"? He straightens, pulls me too out of my half-crouching position. He wants us to be standing together at the open porthole, the dangerous mouths of the steam pipes above our heads, wants us to be looking at the sea, the lightening, violet tropical sky, just blissfully in love, and the silky curls of his thickly growing beard brush my hair with a soft rustling sound. And how subtle are the unfortunate March's caresses and how chaste are they in all their sensuality. His frog hand slides between my chest and my shirt, which he himself did his best to wash last night. He whispers to me that he has been thinking about becoming a tutor or getting an office job "on the other side." He has no trouble imagining everything. The bagnio is a fable. Yellow fever, malaria, and so forth, none of it exists for him. Nor do the thousand different kinds of misery, the fiendish climate, the milieu of criminals. I have said nothing about it – but he believes, he hopes, he loves.

Only one who has looked into my soul can have any idea how much these demonstrations of devotion horrify me. That they come from a man is not what is so terrible. Love knows no difference between natural and unnatural. But I can't now, I can't. He reminds me of something I hope to keep buried deep down, something that can never come back: he reminds me of my poor departed wife and her end. I can't be a brute, can't push him away, mistreat him, shudder in my own voluptuous fevers – I can't do it. Love and desire are finished for me, gone for good. I have to betray him, I have to break away, today. For he touches me, he affects me so deeply that perhaps something intolerable to me, something that can never be, may yet begin again. Not without reason have I been silent about my wife for so long.

If I loved him, I might push him away. But since I don't love him and can't love him, I leave him be. Get what you can! And when he turns away and looks raptly about, he encounters the lustful gaze of the Sultan. Let *him* have the gramophone, the keepsake, the memento of Louis! How generous March is. He doesn't have much. But he gives it all.

If only I could be like him! He lifts the gramophone from the bunk, unscrews the crank, opens the lid with his left hand while with his right hand keeping the box pressed against his heaving chest. You've bitten off too much, dear boy! The record that was just glued together with such care falls to the iron-plate floor of Cargo Hold 3 and shatters. No matter. Even the Sultan is magnanimous. There is no haggling over the price. The money in hard gold passes from the very unappetizing place where Suleiman has hidden it to March and immediately from March to me, and that very evening from me to the junior officer, and that night I am ordered to take charge of the care of convict 3334, a typhus patient. I pack my things and hope not to see March again before we land.

VIII

The sun is directly overhead in the cloudless sky. When I return from a short walk on the upper deck, the handle of the door to the sick bay is so hot that I need my handkerchief to touch it. Tar from between the planking is stuck to the soles of my shoes. Sleep is unthinkable during the day, even though the patient's condition is not as hopeless as it was when I came to the sick bay.

At night no one can sleep. Great schools of dolphins follow the ship, cavort in the moonlight, spray silvery water about. No land. But it must be close, for we have been on board for over two weeks. The *Mimosa* made a stop to take on a herd of livestock, sheep, swine, oxen. A small animal has been slaughtered every day, a larger one every two days. The herd is now down to a few animals. The sheep are woefully thin. They sullenly grind the dry hay with their long teeth, rake their parched tongues over the bottom of their water tub, bleat tremulously and miserably. The two cows lie breathing heavily, their bellies swollen, and they will die of exhaustion if they are not slaughtered soon. They are held fast with ropes and chains to keep them from slipping off the deck when the ship rolls. No one pays any attention to them except the ship's cook, who comes on deck to feel disdainfully along their thin backbones, and the convict March, who feeds and waters them as best he can. Food and fresh water must be conserved. But even if there were plenty of fresh food and plenty of fresh cool water, the rocking of the ship and the torrid heat would make this voyage an unnatural torment for the animals. Tormented or not, they serve their purpose. Their lean, juiceless meat is better than nothing.

The night is hot and clear. A large sea turtle drifts past on the open sea, carrying a silver bird, a heron, on its woody brown back. The turtle is about two meters long. Deftly yet placidly it paddles forward with its long webbed feet, extending its tiny head, dipping it into the gentle deep blue swells, and bringing it up again. The ship's cook points out the animal to the officers, who still make attempts to hunt at night by the light of the (repaired) acetylene lamp. But as eagerly as they blast away, this quarry escapes them.

The heron calmly rises from its swaying perch and is soon floating in the moonlight, turning in ever higher circles, its long neck outstretched, its sharp bill thrust forward, its great wings barely moving.

After a long while, far behind our ship, now the size of a butterfly, it lets itself back down with motionless wings onto its own vessel, the swimming sea turtle of the species *Chelydra* from the Galápagos or the Gulf of Panama. The turtle's tiny head has long since vanished in the bright, moonshiny wake of the *Mimosa*, and the officers, yawning, tired and sleepless, go back to the clink of glasses in the lighted mess.

Other signs of approaching land are becoming more frequent. Limbs of jungle trees as long as the ship drift by in the night. Gnarly treetops without leaves. But hardy creepers with lilac-colored flowers are still hanging like nests in the smooth olive or dark green branches. The tree trunks, which have floated to the sea from the great South American rivers, are covered with birds. Pink flamingos, standing on one leg, heads tucked under wings, asleep, travel on branchy rafts carried by the current under bluish white moonlight almost as bright as day.

If only rest were possible! If only sleep were possible! I have been a stranger to the deathlike release and celestial comfort of the deepest sleep since the first night here on the *Mimosa*.

No wind disturbs the hot night air. The chains of the rudder rattle, the little steering engine chuffs, the big engines work steadily, the screw propeller turns underneath the sick bay at the stern of the old steamer. From the mess comes the sound of the officers laughing and talking loudly, unable to sleep in the tropical night any more than I can. Nor is there rest down in the convicts' dungeons. March's gramophone plays constantly, the monotonous blare of the records does not cease. From my porthole, the one that the faithful March broke, the only one that is open, a white cloth is blowing. Perhaps laundry that has been wrung out and left to dry.

A rat scampers past my feet toward the restless, cruelly harnessed food animals and disappears beneath their bundles of hay. A soft squeaking, a weary baaing from all the sheep, a rattling of the chains of the cattle.

From the bridge can be heard the low, muffled commands of the officer to the helmsman over the ship's radio, answered promptly by the clanking motions of the long chains that work the mechanical steering, and abruptly the ship, which for miles has been making a beeline and leaving a straight wake, shifts its course to port in a long curve.

The drifting branches are gone. On the wavering shimmer of the horizon are the contours of something solid, either hills on one of the many islands or just cloud formations.

Just an hour of rest! To lie down on the deck, look up into the inexpressibly clear sky filled with stars, constellation next to constellation, the Milky Way a wide, swollen, luminous river, tender, all-redeeming, and full of deathly repose. Different areas of the inexhaustible light, power, and grandeur of the heavens come into view with the rolling of the ship.

A patient is moaning in his berth. I tear myself away from the sky and go to him.

But he seems to be the only one not awake on this almost palpably humid, starlit, moonlit night, the only one catching up on his long-denied sleep; and he will stay undisturbed. Die if you can, live if you must. You will not escape yourself, base yet pitiable heart.

Sky, stars and firmament, turtles and herons and branches peacefully traveling over the water with a crew of animals, a great school of dolphins dancing and playing and spraying fountains of water in the distance – who would credit this witchcraft! But this is only nature's painted mask. Everything beautiful, nothing true. The unearthly beauty of nature is just as excruciating as March's love. What does it mean to me, what could it mean? The dream of a doomed man before his execution. Morphine without an injection. If only belief were possible! Knowledge is necessary – belief is not possible. Not for me.

Better for me to return to the foul-smelling, hideous typhus patient, disinfect his sleeping area thoroughly, submit to the hardest physical labor in the breathtaking humidity and heat of this endless night – so that I won't be alone with myself for long.

Then, in a corner of the vestibule, the hall with doors leading to the patients' berths, the ship's pharmacy, and the patients' lavatory, make a bed out of blankets and an old straw sack, throw myself down, and seek the sleep of the just, the most wonderful thing of all, until, toward daybreak with its purple glow, the one bearable time of the day, it comes at last. For now, at five o'clock, a cool, refreshing wind blows, stronger, drier, one that gives some consolation.

At seven I am awake again and quickly get up to put all the areas of the sick bay in order. The lavatory door is unlocked, I open it, and there sits – the brigadier general on his throne, an unlit cigar in his mouth, deep in thought. He does not move. If such weighty, profound meditation could take the place of the work of a creative scientist, his voyage would be destined to succeed. God be with him! I gently close the door, wash and feed my typhus patient, the mugger, and think about nothing.

IX

The brigadier general is expending the sweat of his brow on a lot of little slips of paper, some round, some square, of various colors. He has been going through a mountain of medical journals and pinning the slips of paper (with the pins between his long front teeth, the good man resembles an old seamstress) onto a large map, to the horror of the captain, who did not permit the use of his valuable map for *this* purpose. But the rank of brigadier general is too godlike. Everyone bows in awe and deference.

Through unremitting hard work, the worthy Carolus has evidently obtained two results. No, he has not discovered the yellow-fever pathogen. This can be achieved only on the battleground of the most terrible, most dangerous epidemic since the bubonic plague. If it can be achieved. Nor has he discovered the epidemic's mode of transmission, its precise epidemiology. Here we have as many theories as there are scientists who work on this tropical enigma.

One of them, an old physician on C., even wanted to make mosquitoes the culprit. Without proof, of course. Mosquitoes! *Anopheles*! *Stegomyia*! As though this disease, the "yellow plague," were a kind of malaria, which is known to be spread from person to person by the bites of mosquitoes. What a difference, what a confusion, what a flight of imagination!

Carolus has at least one thing going for him. He has no imagination. He has clumsy hands, worse, he has unclean paws, he is incapable of isolating a pure bacterial strain, he is afraid of living flesh, of the pain of his victims! He pokes infectious material into the faces of poor, defenseless convicts, he forces them to wait for hours, exhausted and hungry, while he makes statistical tabulations of strictly academic interest – but he has one thing going for him: he believes only what he knows.

A simple principle. And yet this is the only solid difference between a man of exact science and an amateur.

The first of Carolus's two results has to do with the air temperature of all the places where cases of yellow fever have been reliably documented. Yellow fever requires an average night temperature that does not fall below twenty-two degrees centigrade and an average daytime temperature that does not fall below twenty-five.

The second result concerns the geographic range of the epidemic and its history, which he dictates to me as follows:

"Yellow fever, also called yellow plague, is an infectious disease, reports of which began reaching Europe soon after the discovery of America. The accounts of Father Du Tertre in the nineteenth century, when yellow fever was widespread in the Antilles, are the first in which the disease is unmistakable. It is, in fact, native to tropical America. From there it spread to North America, West Africa, and Europe. *Its primary zone lies between the two tropics*. That is, in the equatorial region.

"Within the two tropics – the area below the twenty-third parallel in the northern and southern hemispheres – it is the American and African coasts opposite one another where cases of yellow fever are attested. That is, the east coast of Africa and the west coast of America. To be geographically precise, the region of the Gulf of Panama and vicinity, and in Africa the Ivory Coast and Gold Coast. The disease cannot spread significantly in temperate zones.

"*Susceptibility* of the races: Europeans more susceptible than mixed-race individuals. African Negroes and Mongolians appear to be immune; that is to say, they may live in epidemic areas, may come into contact with the ill, and yet are not infected. The most susceptible" (what a sardonic smile, you old Pharisee – do you think your general's insignia is going to give you some protection from the disease that we poor felons don't have? Not likely!) " – the most susceptible is the newly arriving European, the more so the cooler his country of origin." (All of us! The righteous and the unrighteous, thank heavens!)

"Men more susceptible than women." (Too bad!) "Adults more than children." (Sad!) "Strong young people more than the old and weak." (Eternal lunacy of "kindly," "benevolent Mother Nature," as we like to call it, that painted old whore.) "The poor more susceptible than the rich." (From the circles of hell to the spheres of heaven and here too, preferential treatment for the moneyed classes!)

Finished, old itchbag? He drones on, mouth stretched wide, scratching himself with his apishly hairy hands, now on his chest, now on his long, columnar skull, with its patch of pale gray-blond hair seemingly in the wrong place, like a slipping toupee. No, he has a lot more theory to dictate, many more slips of paper to pin up. In one hand I have the pins, in the other the box of paper slips, and I'd need a third to write down all the important scholarly discoveries.

As the head of the commission, the brigadier general has the powers of a governor. If I can stay with him, everything will be fine, everything. I am going to be allowed to, will be, must be. He bosses me around sternly, orders me to join the other deportees when we land, but then to report to him. As a research assistant? Oh no! Only as a manservant, who will assist in autopsying yellow-fever cadavers and so forth. God does not forsake those He loves. He does not forsake them. So I'll be the first to be infected by the yellow-fever cadavers and will snuff it in no time. March, darling, you'll be avenged. Play your gramophone when they carry this old sinner to the grave. And don't cry for me. G. L. the younger doesn't deserve it!

X

My charge, the typhus patient, is fortunately on the road to recovery, and even the brigadier general is gracious to me. He addresses me again, from the depths of his narrow bureaucrat's breast. And what does he say? Does he thank me for my hard work? Does he commiserate with me? Does he marvel that a man of my background, of my (his) station, is a criminal convicted without possibility of appeal? Or is the good man thinking ahead, does he want to have a friendly chat about what he'll be up to on the other side in the near future? No, none of these. "You owe a great deal to your father." Long pause. His eyelids lift behind the smoke-colored, horn-rimmed glasses, he focuses on me, and says again: "You owe your father a great deal." That's it, and the tall, thin, impassive fellow, lightly clad, turns his endlessly long, stiff back to me, and with his storklike walk returns to his cabin to pore over encyclopedia volumes, study British, American, German, and French reprints, and copy out extracts from them.

But my troubles aren't over. Yes, the convalescing typhus patient has at last put his legs, sharp and bony, covered with black hair, over the edge of his bed, climbed down unsteadily, and taken his first faltering steps with my help; he eats solid food (in tremendous quantities), is mentally lucid (intent on thievery), keeps himself more or less clean – but the sick bay has a newcomer. The man who caught my attention during the chief's examination with his great, feverishly glowing eyes and hollow cheeks, their red circles the badge of jailhouse consumption in all its misery, has been hemorrhaging heavily due to congested pulmonary circulation, as is not uncommon in people with severe lung disease when they arrive in very hot regions. He is a young man, not much over twenty, a city kid, cunning, vicious, but fun, full of boisterous humor ("There'll be pie in the sky by and by!"), of irrepressible high spirits. Lie down? Rest? Take it easy? Keep quiet? What for? Delighted with his unaccustomed freedom (he spent long years in prisons, busily sewing mailbags), he roves about all over the *Mimosa*. He even intrudes on three men suspected of having leprosy who live sequestered in a room of their own in the sick bay, tending each other's nasty wounds, spending most of their time in a twilight half-sleep, and preparing their own scraps of food, as apathetic as animals at rest. They are even heard singing at night or early in the morning. But the lung patient wants things, he leaves me no peace. At night he stands at the rail and admires the sea, spitting cigarette butts down, almost asphyxiated by the smoke; during the day he scurries past the guards with a polite smile and into the officers' galley, where he begs tasty morsels from the chef. If only he could stomach them! But nothing stays down. Incredible that this man, doomed in equal measure by pulmonary and intestinal tuberculosis and with the signs of both of them stamped all over him, is still alive at all, talking and moving around. Why does this candle go on burning when it has neither wick nor tallow left? No matter. It is burning.

And yet he is still a man, that is to say, he is vain. He has rooted out his shaving things (a forbidden possession) from among his belongings and tries to beautify himself for our arrival in C. Are there women there? he asks. Are there ever! I promise him. Not women, dames, he means. More, you poor dog, than you'll ever have any use for. But he is happy nonetheless and hopes. There is no mirror in either the sick bay or the ship's pharmacy. But the clever boy finds a solution. Every microscope has a mirror that can be turned to reflect light into the light collector or condenser – and this the ingenious youth has turned to his own purposes. The microscope's wooden box was locked, the brigadier general had the key. But a thief as good as that, even one on his last legs, can find a way. A bit of wire and any lock opens for him. And there he sits on the laboratory stool, keeping his balance with effort amid the rocking of the ship, shaken by coughing and trembling with weakness, looking infatuatedly into the microscope mirror with his great beautiful eyes and doing himself up. Who would have the heart to stop him? Even the brigadier general kindheartedly looks the other way. All the tidbits the poor emaciated fool has begged fill the pockets of his convict's overalls. He likes to keep them around, he who cannot keep them down. But at least he *has* them.

He also makes music. On a well-used comb already missing some teeth – it belonged to the mugger, who lost all his hair from typhus – he plays stridulating, sweetly buzzing versions of popular songs, "Under the Bridges" and "La Carmencita," stamping on the deck to beat out the rhythm (his wooden clogs are loose on his emaciated feet). He smiles, he is happy, he sleeps peacefully despite the heat, despite the coughing that plagues him. He coughs and gags constantly, yet sleeps as though he were in the bosom of Abraham.

No other creature on the ship is so happy. The officers have given up the shooting at dolphins with which they amused themselves a few times. The ship's cooks struggle to concoct delicacies for them out of canned goods; nothing appeals to them, they just sit sullenly together in the mess, give the crew a hard time, avoid the convicts like the plague, drink whiskey, and play poker, their money passing from one to another in turn, all except the brigadier general, who never plays, never drinks, and is never bored.

The oxen up on deck have no interest in food, either. March, poor fellow, strives in vain to get them to accept some hay and water. They only pant, grunt reluctantly, lift their broad heads, strain at the tight chains binding them to the masts and other uprights. I want to be there when they are slaughtered so that I can use their blood to make a nutritive medium for culturing bacilli (blood flowing straight from the bodies of animals is almost sterile). We still have some days to go, and I have to work, have to keep busy.

March must have heard about my request to the purser. He has volunteered for slaughtering duty even though he has a horror of blood. To other criminals it would have been a pleasure: blood is blood.

And the unfortunate March, this man who is completely blinded by his infatuation and whom one is justified in barring from human society for that reason alone, tortures himself by butchering a beast that had once been a fattened ox but is now only a prisoner. Just to be able to see me and look into my eyes. But I do not look into his. I sterilize a tin basin with denatured alcohol, hold it into the stream of blood, and then take it away, leaving as I came, without a word. He is distraught. What was he hoping for? What am I supposed to be to him? He to me?

Hard-hearted, me? Only one who is equal to the world at last.

In the sick bay I follow my patient's example and check the mirror on the microscope before putting it away. The mirror is flat and beautifully polished on one side, concave and beautifully polished on the other. Precision is precision. I look at myself. And why not? I've been wanting to. I never found the moment for it before.

I look at myself. I see myself as I always was. I have not changed. My father certainly had a mirror on his voyage to the far north. Not on his way back. That I can look into this mirror, without love, without hate, face immobile, without a smile, without a grimace of pain, without hope, without feeling, do I have *him* to thank for this too?

XI

The lung patient has finally taken to his bed. He can no longer smoke and suffers painfully from doing without. "*You* smoke!" he says to me. I smoke a black cigarette that has almost entirely disintegrated from the heat and blow the smoke into his waiting nostrils. He turns away if the smoke is too strong (the paper is the main thing, the tobacco is incidental), but then he brings his wax-pale, skeletal face back, his eyes full of longing. He has no desire to eat. Or is now unable to eat. "*You* eat!" he says, and I eat, and he avidly watches my throat and yearningly inhales the smell of the food, his eyes burning. It irritates his throat, sore from laryngeal tuberculosis, just as much as the tobacco, but he is enthusiastic about the strong broth for which we can thank the world-weary ox slaughtered yesterday, and in his awkward, ludicrous voice, the dying man wheezes to me, "Go on!" He clutches at me with his emaciated hand, looks at me with his great, beautiful, dark blue eyes. He smells disaster coming but refuses to believe it. The bacilli demolishing his lungs, stomach, intestine, larynx, etc., secrete as a by-product a wonderful toxin, essence of euphoria, whose effect is that he *always hopes, always believes, is always happy, always laughs*! There'll be pie in the sky by and by. He dozes off. As he falls asleep, he asks me to open the porthole. But it has been open for a long time.

The night is blue, lit by the floating moon. Not the slightest breath of wind. The stokers shovel coal into the fireboxes. The ship's officers quarrel, then laugh, and singing is heard. In the convicts' catacombs, things are especially wild. But no music, just clamoring and scuffling, strident hooting, muffled crashing.

There is a gleam on the horizon like oxidized silver. The piled-up clouds are vast, complex edifices, like Indian temples with endless gingerbread and turrets, everything sharply defined, flooded by the bewitching whitish blue of the moon.

Down in the water by the sides of the old ship, a spectral shimmer is passing by. Tiny sparks flash, little flames strewn in a plane phosphoresce and die down. All in the shadow thrown by the ship. They materialize from some realm of light, tremble on the surface of the water, which gleams under the moon like a single piece of cast bronze, then fade behind the ship, where the smooth, shiny, silvery blue-green backs of the splashing, dancing, leaping dolphins toss in the wake. They reappeared this evening and have been following the ship in a large school. But little sea creatures play in the soft shadows on either side of the gliding ship, phosphorescent plankton and undulating medusae, squids on the hunt and being hunted, tiny organisms brought to the glistening surface of the ocean by the hot, still night.

The lung patient has awakened. His body feels the end coming. But his mind, addled by the happiness toxin, has only a blind sense of well-being. He asks me for his suitcase, and from the bottom of it he brings out scraps of illustrated magazines. Photos of naked and half-clothed young women, in candy-cane colors, posing provocatively. He turns the pages with his pencil-thin, tobacco-stained fingers, and suddenly he begins to cut the figures out with his nail scissors, laying them out on the grubby blanket in front of him. A children's game? You little lamb, white as snow! So this is a harmless person, someone who arrived on this convicts' ship just because of a moment of recklessness? Pie in the sky? Pie in perdition too, I fear. Just look at the dark red lips twisted with lewd destructiveness in the pale, gaunt face, their corners still showing traces of the blood he lost this morning! Look at the depravity in his pathologically glowing blue eyes as he carefully, precisely, dismembers the paper figurines with the scissors as though they were living, suffering flesh. Off comes the left foot, extended in a toe dance, then the right foot, then the delicate, supple left forearm. The typhus patient looks on, a smirk on his face. Take him away, off with him! But I leave the dying man undisturbed. Now he hesitates: should he first cut the paper head off straight across, or slice the slender lingerie-clad midriff top to bottom? Pure evil at play is an exciting thing to see up close. For him who understands it. Rejoice, poor soul! I do as he wishes and leave him alone. Fifteen minutes later he is again in a deep sleep, the blood gone from the corners of his mouth. The next morning he can barely breathe. "Am I going to die?" he croaks. He's dead already! There are no scraps of paper lying about. But when he is lifted from the sweat-soaked bed, there they are on the sheet. I give him the dismembered figures to take on his final pilgrimage. A man must have what he needs.

The brigadier general comes to view the deceased. He gazes at him with a sage expression. He touches the dead man's fallen-in chest with his black fountain pen like a Chinese medicine man with a chopstick and sends the deceased to his final repose. And a cross is entered in the rolls. Prisoner 4431 is no more.

We are near land. Possibly an island is not too far away.

A ring, now much too big, is taken off one of the dead youth's fingers. Imitation gold, with a fake stone. The junior officer checks his mouth for genuine gold crowns, but, what a pity, the boy still has all thirty-two of his teeth, gleaming white, flawless. So without further ado. The body is decaying from within, and one more hour on board in this hellish heat would be too many. Where can it go? Not to heaven. The other way, where we all must go. Down.

Scattered butterflies, the size of grape leaves and with the same ragged shape, crimson and sapphire blue, or dull mauve, float through the rigging on the forecastle of the *Mimosa*. They encounter obstacles and come to rest, their long, dove gray antennae vibrating, behind coils of rope, winches, chests, nothing giving more than the scantiest shade in the blazing equatorial sun.

Behind the ship is a frenzy of activity: the school of dolphins. Several hundred magnificent ones and more every hour.

Gleaming like niello, they are so densely packed that they almost lift each other out of the dark blue water; they spiral into the air, spinning like dragonflies over a brook. Broad heads, white snouts, small eyes, slapping dorsal fins, laminate tail fins lashing and reflecting the highlights in the water like mirrors. Above them gulls and pelicans: shrill cries, rippling wings, banking, powerful climbing, lightning plunges as they slash into the water, flinging up silver-bellied, finger-sized, slim little fish. Above it all the unapproachable grandeur of the sky.

This is the hour when the convicts are led on deck, in squads, double file: a boarding school with a prefect. Bayonets in front, on the side, in back. Quick time! Move! Move! A tender rifle butt in the back, a kick in the meager behind, forward, march! Flex those muscles! A little exercise never hurt anybody! I will not describe the gray faces.

No church bell tolls to announce the burial. The convicts do not care. Their faces are agonized, sullen. Many drag themselves along like sick birds, like lame animals. But what primal strength still lives within them! Strength to suffer!

With my help, the junior officer has wrapped the not yet cool body of the consumptive criminal in one of the typhus patient's sheets. Throw in a piece of iron bar, and then the whole thing into the sea! One, two, three, hup! But the piece of iron comes loose and flops into the water.

The featherlight corpse beside the ship is carried to the wake and then back to the dolphins.

They play with it: the fun-loving lad floats between heaven and earth as the animals in mad high spirits toss his mortal remains back and forth, until at last the whitish naked corpse disappears in the dark mass of silvery dolphins.

XII

I was awakened by shouting. I heard shots being fired. I say awakened, and yet I was unable to wake up properly. It was hard to breathe, there seemed to be a lump of lead the size of a man's head on my breastbone. I was dreaming about being awake, tearing off the few clothes I had on, yet they kept being there, clinging tightly to my sweat-bathed body. There was an unnatural, pathological longing in me, the half-sleep refused to lift, and I had to realize that the shooting and shouting had stopped (waking thoughts alongside the sleeping ones) before I could summon the energy to wake up. And this after close to three weeks of almost total sleeplessness.

When I finally became fully conscious a few hours later, I thought it was still night. My cabin seemed strangely gloomy; the ship was abnormally quiet. The horizon was completely draped with brownish black clouds resembling coarsely woven old sacks. The air was dark, the sun breaking through only at rare instants with an unpleasant gleam. Here and there on the horizon toward the west and the south, little rain showers sprayed down from the clouds, creating a fraying fringe lit by rainbow colors.

The sea is not turbulent. But abruptly whitecaps appear, the ship shudders as though it has run onto a sandbar – the throb of the engines stops, then sluggishly starts up again. A dense lilac curtain forms in front of the ship to the north and northeast.

The surface of the sea is wan, flat, dirty, gray. Without warning a cloudburst hammers down out of the low sky onto the planks of the ship. All decks are flooded. The junior officer and the black guards wade through tepid ankle-deep water, carrying an apparently lifeless heavy man on a stretcher.

The convalescent typhus patient, happy not to have to be below in the common area, makes himself useful, sets up a bed in the sick bay, blows the dust off the night table. The heavy man is Suleiman, the Sultan. He is breathing heavily, wheezing, his head moving beneath a bloody rag; he prods with clenched, bloody fists at his face – a shapeless, bloody mass, a seething, twitching expanse of raw flesh. The men carry him carefully into the sick bay. He twists his head back and forth, unable to see.

His face is unrecognizable. It has been leveled, so to speak. Where the bold hooked nose once was, the pride of its owner with his manly beauty, now there are only lumps of flesh and the two nostrils. A warm, sickening stream of blood, air, and discharge pushes out of the nostrils, jagged bones have broken through, white ruins of teeth guard the entrance to what was once the oral cavity, and there is a steady trickle of something flowing down through the wild beard. As strange as it may sound, this is tears! The nasolacrimal duct is torn. There is no way to stop this out-of-character stream of tears.

The rain pelts down with the force of a hailstorm. With his dirty fists, the injured man tries fruitlessly to lift his eyelids, swollen and bluish with bruises. Is he blind? he rasps out. He is fully conscious.

He was trampled in a brawl in Cargo Hold 3 during the night. He may have lost his sight, or he may be lucky. His good friends were among those who stomped on his chest. Three ribs are broken on top of everything else, and he is coughing up frothy blood.

It is so dark now that the light has to be turned on in the sick bay. The man lies on the improvised operating table. He is in the hands of fate. Not much can be done. The bone splinters can be deftly removed with forceps, the wound can be dusted with iodoform. It is terrible to see the sausagelike fingers, covered with more bruises, clench during the painful procedure: the criminal who has been savaged by his fellows suddenly raises his hand in fury and shakes it at the physician. The physician notices now that the left thumb is broken too, dangling from the plump, blue-tattooed hand like a branch snapped by the wind and held on by a bit of inner bark.

As the wound is being carefully cleaned and the finger is being splinted, the rainy gloom outside the porthole suddenly lightens. In the distance the heavy, bluishly livid murk lifts like a curtain, and the vast sapphire blue surface of the sea can be seen again.

The overcast lifts, the sun shines.

The planking on deck steams with evaporation. An ox, the last of its tribe, lifts its glossy, heavy head, lows loudly, and clanks its rain-wet chains, the sheep shake the moisture out of their dense dirty-gray wool and bleat, and – March appears, to tend the animals as he does every day. He is sweaty and pale, and the sunshine only makes him look even more miserable and more grief-stricken in his lovesickness. Oh, those wistful glances!

A commission consisting of the brigadier general, the commander of the guards, and the captain conducts a hearing with the injured Sultan Suleiman. But he is uncooperative. He shakes his wild head, spits a bone fragment out of his lacerated mouth now and then or shakes one inelegantly out of his ruined nasal structure, curses savagely, but he will not name names. Will not give his comrades away. He only wheezes, lisping with his swollen tongue, "Bathtards, bathtards! You wait till we meet again! You wait!" That sweet baby, the *s* is too hard for him to pronounce. Even this brute of a man has become an innocent child again. We all have.

March, who crept in after the officers abandoned the futile hearing, looks him over nervously. His tread is gingerly in his heavy, hobnailed shoes. The Sultan cannot see him. Whether he will ever see again at all is the question. The giant may be fallen, but he still terrifies March. Are we to believe that it was March (along with the others, but their true ringleader at bottom) who trampled on this no-longer-human face tonight when there was no other way to fend off the bestial assaults of a pathological criminal, a satyriasis case?

Dozens of small storms have appeared on the horizon and passed over within a short period. The air has become still more oppressive. After each cloudburst the heat seems to be worse.

The authorities are nervous now. With good reason? I don't know. The steam pipes running to the cargo holds are going to be tested. When the alarm is sounded, the convicts rush on deck. Scalding hot steam is diverted to the cargo holds below. The convicts are made to hear the hissing, it is impressed on their innocent young minds what awaits them if they revolt, if they kill where there can be no killing. Only fate can kill with impunity. The state: war. Nature: yellow fever, typhus, cancer, pulmonary tuberculosis, and other fine inventions of God. Hunger and the struggle for existence. All will continue as long as the world exists.

But the test of the steam jets has had one good effect. The steam, at a hundred degrees centigrade, has roasted a good two dozen plump rats. When, in the midst of another storm, the all-clear signal is sounded, the convicts toss them into the sea, holding them cautiously by the tails so that the cooked skin will not come off the bodies. The convicts laugh and go back to Cargo Hold 3 while 1 and 2 receive the same lesson.

Four days later we arrive safe and sound. You can come back now, March! Now I can come back to you. On solid ground I'm safe, and we'll be the best of friends as long as you stay sensible.

FIVE

I

I will not describe the life of the deportees in the archipelago. Much as I would like to, others have already described it better and more movingly than I could.

Disembarking from the ship was less exciting than boarding it had been. Suleiman was still alive; he was half blind and unable to walk. He was carried down the gangplank on a stretcher, cursing a blue streak. March was pale with anxiety and clung closely to me.

When we arrived, the epidemic of yellow fever (which, for the sake of brevity, I will henceforth refer to simply as Y.F.) had evidently passed a peak. Among the convicts – who lived in large camps far from the city of C., as well as on the other small islands of the archipelago – it had not yet wreaked its havoc. The civilian residents of the city had been affected to a much greater degree. But a rainy period had recently begun – that is, one of the many rainy periods that took the form of titanic downpours of short duration, followed by torrid, insalubrious heat and malignantly luminous gloom – and the Y.F. had abated.

At the last census, five years earlier, the city had had a population of about twelve thousand. Thirty years before that it had been forty thousand. Its fortunes were like those of a person of whom one says at age twenty: A genius! At thirty: A man to watch! And at forty he is simply a name.

Late in the evening we were led through the squalid streets, which were filled with almost blackish rain pouring down in torrents. It was evil-smelling, dark, dank, and almost deserted everywhere.

Conditions in the camp where I spent the first night, the faithful March at my side, were not much different from those on the ship. The convicts were awakened at four in the morning and they began their work at five, felling and trimming trees in the mangrove forest and removing the trunks, clearing land and putting down log courses for a road across the great woodlands (laid out many years before, it had never progressed very far), and so on and so forth.

But first a few men were taken out of the work gangs, either for office work in the very large administrative corps or, as in my case, for "special service" in a field hospital. Weak or strong was irrelevant. It was accident or caprice. March was also among those selected (because he had been an official?). No protest was possible. We were not asked about our wishes, talents, or capacities.

The most interesting diseases were rampant in the camps – skin conditions of all kinds, malaria in the most beautiful forms, tuberculosis, and the insidious condition of intestinal worms, whose victims wasted away, becoming true skeletons – but, by a happy twist of fate, not a single case of Y.F. had been found recently in any of the numerous convict camps.

March did not leave my side. He knew that Carolus had designated me for very hazardous work as a morgue attendant in the epidemic hospital that stood on a rise in the center of the city. It was a large-scale catchment hospital primarily for Y.F., dating from the city's better days and run by nuns.

No doubt that good child March had no idea what this meant. Otherwise his handsome face would not have been shining with delight on the way. Or else he trusted in his star.

And why would he have left me? He had given himself. And whether I accepted him or not – he stayed. They would have had to shoot him, or cut his hand off, the hand that clutched my coat. But the administration did not consider such barbaric measures. Despite his childlike nature, March may have been able to look out for his own interests properly. He had not banked on his past as an official. God knows how he had obtained more money. But he had some. Those minor officials who kept the rolls also kept a sharp eye for the main chance, and were no doubt every bit as impressed by his generosity as they were by his devout wish never to leave me.

Thus we were brought arm in arm to the old convent, which, with its yellow patients, was at least as well guarded up on its hill as the camp with its convicts was down below. For everyone was terrified of the epidemic and helpless against it.

Now, during the day, the city almost looked bleaker than it had the night before. Dereliction and crumbling walls everywhere, many churches, few shops or restaurants, here and there a warehouse or shed by the shore, crates, barrels, and bags lying outside unguarded in the alternating rain and steamy heat. Hungry dogs, ravenlike vultures looking for food. Muck and refuse all around, wretched paving, ragged people hurrying along, heads down. Magnificent plantations, avenues of palms and breadfruit trees and so forth. But we ran into four funerals on the short tramp that had taken no longer than forty-five minutes. What devastation the epidemic must have caused among these people in the worse times that had just passed! Suddenly the rain stopped and the sun burned down. The sea gleamed, the dogs scratched, the vultures soared, and the vegetation between the cobblestones gave off a scent that seemed ambrosial, or feral.

We passed a burnt-out area, deserted and still smoldering. I learned that the people there had tried to protect themselves from the epidemic by setting fire to some disease-ridden buildings after buying them from the owner for a high price in hard cash.

But the epidemic took no notice of this extravagant prophylaxis, it slipped nimbly around corners, a house here, a house there, three cases here, five there. And the entire city would have had to be burned down, from the harbor to the farthermost houses already sinking into the slopping, bile green swamp, from the barracks to the administration buildings, from the bank to the theological college, everything would have had to go up in flames like Sodom and Gomorrah in order to conquer the Y.F. The city? What am I saying? The entire coastline, as far as the eye could see, and much, much farther beyond that, to the Pearl Archipelago, the region of the Panama Canal to the north, and an equally vast distance to the south! And even that wouldn't have been enough!

As we panted up the hill, we saw hordes of ragged, hollow-eyed, deathly pale, half-starved men emerging from dark little side streets steaming after the downpour. These were freed convicts who had hidden from the epidemic in some corner of the jungle, living on raw fruit and orangutans that they had hunted, and who, now that the epidemic had apparently abated, were seeking the way to the imaginary fleshpots and shot glasses of the city. They envied the two of us as we climbed up the narrow little zigzag road to the convent hospital side by side, preceded and followed by guards, or so it seemed as they twisted their scrawny, naked vultures' necks and watched us. One of them even began to run after us to beg, but the others held him back from this foolishness. Certainly they assumed that since we were wards of the state, that loving, faithful provider, we were being given the necessities of life. They did not know that something scarcely enviable was in store for us.

The bell at the hospital gate rang. Two old black women and a stern-faced white nurse in stiff blue cotton, all with large silver crosses on their breasts, came out tiredly with a stretcher. They were very surprised to find healthy people seeking admission. The guards on duty as a quarantine cordon could hardly get over their astonishment either, laughing so uproariously that the whitewashed, pungent-smelling passages and corridors of the old convent rang.

But it was not us they were laughing at. An old man had come with us and joined us on our walk to the examination rooms, a man wearing a costume more original than anything at a carnival. About seventy, tall but stooped, narrow-shouldered, olive-skinned, with a leathery face and dark, deep-set eyes of unbroken fire of which one never had a direct view. For this vigorous and characterful old face was hidden by a faded yellowish green nun's veil. A veil? What am I saying? Two of them, one behind the other, stiffened in front with semicircular wicker strips, so that no unchaste glance could offend this maidenly granddad. Ah, but it was not indiscreet glances that this elderly he-nun was afraid of, but, strange to say, mosquitoes! And perhaps not even that. It was morning, and mosquitoes never bite in broad daylight. So it was something else: a show.

For this striking aristocratic gentleman was none other than the pharmacist and municipal medical officer von F., the renowned originator of the mosquito theory of Y.F. He was just now paying his first visit to our Herr Brigadier General, the head of the commission, and the army medical officer Walter, its scientific director. The news that Walter had arrived here astonished me greatly. This was the greatest coincidence, the most unfathomable of the many unfathomable things that had befallen me in my lifetime. And yet it was logical. Meeting this man here! But what role should I assume? Old comrade? Fallen man? Eternal sinner? Scientist with a thirst for knowledge? I was apprehensive. But everything seemed to happen naturally.

We all went into a clean room, formerly a convent cell, where the two top men already were, surrounded by splendid, spanking new equipment. That is: Brig. Gen. Carolus, the mastermind, the state dignitary, human knowledge personified. Then Walter, my old comrade, the idol of my youth. He recognized me. I bowed, and he nodded. He was very worn, not unmarked by time, but still the same good fellow as before, a man with all sorts of degrees who was much more knowledgeable and capable than he let on. The pharmacist and retired municipal medical officer Dr. Felizian von F., the man behind the veil, shook their hands warmly after much ceremonious bowing and flowery language. He had brought them some mosquito eggs in a matchbox as a small token of his esteem. They looked like coffee grounds. He smiled quietly and proudly, as though this was something of the greatest interest. Then he extended his hand to March and to my humble self. The door was closed, the chapel bells tolled outside, we looked at each other. The commission had been convened, and the great sphinx known as Y.F. lay waiting for us to penetrate her secrets. I was tired and yawned discreetly.

II

The hospital director was at Mass. (A weekday!) His aide, a young resident, was away on vacation. But pharmacist von F. was in his element. The son and nephew of physicians, though his children had left the trade and gone into business, he had been begging the authorities, learned societies, patent offices, and physicians to take his theory seriously for years. But anyone who looked this comical fanatic in the eye could hardly help laughing. His bearing solemn, not really stooped but stiff as a poker despite his sagging, crepitating knees, the little box of mosquito eggs in his gloved hand, he led the way along the twisting corridors to the autopsy room. But could this be right? Stop, friend! Instead of telling us all about how you carefully culled *Stegomyia* mosquito eggs from marshy pools (painfully bending your bad back), watch where you're going, don't take us into the waste room, where there must be reeking offal in a state of the rankest decay. But he turned his wise face to us, holding his veils together, bowed, every inch the Spanish grandee, and ushered us into the dissecting room.

A stench for which there is no name, so nauseating and intolerable that the demonic imagination of a Dante could not have conceived it, assaulted us from the small, electrically lighted, relatively cool underground room. March clutched me with a low cry. Even the leathery, phlegmatic Carolus trembled all over. Only Walter and I did not lose our composure.

Lying in its perfume was a blond corpse, quince yellow, poison yellow, wearing white gloves and a shirtfront, a once white but now very unsightly dress shirt, on its concave chest. In its gloved, graceful, long hands a silver crucifix.

In this place, at that moment, I was encountering Y.F. in nature for the first time in my life, and I silently paid it due reverence.

In fact my life changed fundamentally that day. For the better? In any event it was different. And that was a great deal for a man so dissociated from himself and from the world as to be convinced that he – twisted man of the spirit and man of doubt – and it – the world of futility, of misleading appearance, and of undeniable tedium – would never be reunited, and that his existence would therefore go on being the most superfluous thing in this superfluous world . . . But why these thoughts and memories? Back to the present, that was exciting enough.

I would be lying if I said my dignified bearing was entirely genuine. The smell, an outrageous, abominable stench utterly beyond description, something purely sensory yet beyond what the nervous system could make sense of, made me, believe it or not, cry. Shed tears, to be more precise. I wanted to vomit but did not allow myself to. I had to manage that much self-control. I needed to live up to the upbringing my father had given me, and I did. And, as strange as it may sound, at precisely that critical moment I became aware in every nerve fiber of the mysterious spell of scientific investigation. A thousand reasons for controlling myself and doing my best to will the nausea away, even if tears were shed.

It was as though I had an inkling that I would soon need all my strength of will – that I would need it to master fate lest I be mastered myself. I overcame my revulsion. I pressed March's hand, which was trembling with horror (he had perhaps never seen a dead body before the death of his beloved Louis). A feeling of sympathy for him awakened in my heart. Reluctantly, but nevertheless. There is something to be said for having a living person by one's side at a moment of crisis.

And another odd thing happened in that instant. I saw not only that golden yellow corpse in its ugly, stained dress shirt, not only the heavy silver crucifix in its gloved hands, the gloves just pulled on, not buttoned, but also, through a strange association of ideas, a scene from my childhood in which my father and three or four rats (as big and as distinct as he was) figured, and then a scene from the happy period with my wife of which I have not been able to give a report as yet. And what finally appeared in my overly scattered (or concentrated) thoughts was the grand, blazing night sky I had seen on the *Mimosa* before our landing, which had put me in mind of the illusory, all-too-beautifully painted mask of nature.

At that moment the pharmacist, who had let down his portable mosquito netting to chest height, dropped his little box of mosquito eggs. I, gentleman that I am, stooped at the same time as he did, we bumped heads, I found the box first, and, as the old grandee was excusing himself profusely with a thousand baroque old formulas, I put the little box in the breast pocket of my prison livery.

But enough of these trivialities. The work began.

Not for nothing had Walter gone through the Institute's rigorous methodological training. He had spared no effort in preparing the ground for our bacteriological research; there was a good microscope, there were incubators. But when Carolus mentioned that he owned an especially powerful instrument equipped with all the latest innovations (dark-field illumination!), even two eyepieces, whereas the microscope that belonged to the epidemic hospital was not a recent model, it was agreed that he would go get his own while we did the first culturing experiments. *We*, I say, for the second time. I used this wondrous word the first time to express my fellow feeling for the deportees, who, by virtue of their common suffering, their common ejection from civil society, had constituted a we of sorts. But a we full of boredom, full of spitefulness, rancor, cynicism, piggishness, an appetite for brutal fisticuffs, full of unnatural love and unnatural hate, futile snarling at the authorities, though they frankly deserved no better. Here, on this first morning on C., as initial preparations were being made for a systematic and exacting epidemiological study amid the pestilential stench of the Y.F. corpse, there was also a we, but a different one. Neither on that day nor during the days to come did I hear among *us* a contentious word. Nor an overbearing one. Everything happened naturally, at an excellent pace. We were frankly not always of one mind, perhaps not ever. But we worked together nonetheless, and did our utmost.

I personally did not believe, could not believe it would be possible to get a grip on the Y.F. pathogen using ordinary methods. Too many investigators, ones who had been too good, had failed, Pasteur among them. Nevertheless, from the first moment, as soon as March and I had disposed of our highly disagreeable clothing, I was a zealous participant in the bacteriological investigation. For the first time in years, I was absorbed, knew no fatigue, I had a truly pervasive feeling that there was a constructive reason for me to exist, and the others too. If only fate willed it that this go on! That was all I wanted! Was it too much to ask?

So, down to business. There were two primitive incubators in the adjoining laboratory. More than a hundred cultures were started in short order.

The departed had been the director of the city of C.'s small power plant. He had passed away during the first stage of the disease, on the fourth day following initial symptoms. He had arrived three weeks previously on the packet steamer with a group of various administrative officials and the like, had paid his first visits to important personages such as the governor, and was just beginning to get the rather shabby plant into some sort of shape when he became ill with Y.F. and died. To go by his fair hair and skin, he must have been a Scandinavian, perhaps a Swede. His name, Olaf Ericsson, suggested the same.

III

I return to the first morning. This must be an orderly and methodical report.

"Let's write, please – and clearly!" Walter said to the somewhat astonished Carolus when he returned with the microscope, expecting God knows what respectful thanks from us. But let it be said to his credit that Carolus neither sulked nor assigned this menial task to me, the convict, but sat down at the little table, took his black fountain pen out of the breast pocket of his uniform, and wrote: first the precise autopsy findings on the Swede, which were typical, and then the sequence of bacterial cultures to be produced from the blood, the devastated liver, the affected gastric and intestinal walls, the inflamed renal cortex, and so on.

Would luck favor us in this Y.F. problem where so many had failed, including none other than the great Louis Pasteur himself? Miracles may happen, but not in bacteriology. Over the following days, weeks, and months, not a single bacterium grew. The flasks containing liquid culture medium kept in the incubator at a constant thirty-seven degrees centigrade would remain abacterial. For us as for all researchers who had worked on this disease.

All four of us, Walter, March, Carolus, and I, had been busy with this one case until midnight, and the black nurses whose job it was to look after us came repeatedly to call us to eat something. Eat! Nothing could have been further from our minds. Let the reader try working for an hour in the deadly, pestilential stench characteristic of Y.F. and then sit down to eat. Even with nectar and ambrosia on Limoges china in front of you, that hellish perfume will have taken up residence in your taste buds, in your oral mucosa. The choice was either to get used to it, by denying it, or to get out and stay out. For me, as for the others, the first alternative was the one that prevailed in the long run. I ate, I bathed, I changed my clothes, I slept, I began my work early every day and did not finish until late in the evening. The waning of the disease was short-lived, by the way. It was all gong and no dinner, as the saying goes. But the strange fact remained that not one case of Y.F. had yet been reported among (for example) the recently arrived criminals. What was one to make of that? The only thing to be made of it was the theoretical result that the wise Carolus had already obtained from his books – but all in due time!

However mysterious the pathogen and however puzzling the pernicious disease's mode of transmission, the clinical picture was classically beautiful in almost every case. High fever out of a clear blue sky (clear blue sky? downpours in incredible swarms, separated by radiant tropical sunshine and humid, leaden heat) with extraordinarily rapid onset, jaundice. Seeming recovery after the third or fourth day and then all hell would break loose, vomiting, dreadful abdominal pain in the region of the liver. Throat, gastric, intestinal symptoms. Headache. Lumbar pain. Overwhelming feeling of illness, blazing red eyes with vividly inflamed conjunctivae – everything was there, shall I say unfortunately, or shall I say *thank goodness* in the interests of our research? The contagion appeared as implacably as it had for centuries, then subsided again, war and peace, no end in sight.

The authorities had to add their two cents, of course. The wire chattered, Walter and Carolus put their heads together over brusque telegrams. "Give special attention to matters related to the cause of yellow fever and its prevention." If only! Eventually we had examined eighteen cases, from head to toe, inside and out, we had scrutinized patients at all stages. For purposes of control we used the famous double microscope in pairs – Carolus and Walter, March and I. We stared until our eyes were sore, and at the end of those terribly hard days knew no more than we had on the very first day, the day of the yellow Swede who had long since been buried in his white gloves and dress shirt.

Walter and Carolus would not have been the classically trained doctors they were if they had not done animal experiments. Monkeys from the nearby jungle, guinea pigs (easily obtained at home but here a resource difficult to come by), rats, mice, parrots and other exotic creatures too, even a world-weary nag housed in a shed in the old ruin of a convent, all of them received injections of blood from patients, of blood from cadavers, of extracts prepared from dirty laundry. The four of us seemed to be equal participants in these vivisection experiments.

But our roles had changed, in a way that was quite perplexing and will undoubtedly appear very curious to the reader of these lines. Carolus, who had formerly always shunned living flesh, who had always avoided vivisection experiments, was now fired up about them – and I, I, Georg Letham the younger, was now unable to overcome my inner resistance to them. I did not directly refuse, but I was adroit enough to pass these distressing tasks on to my colleagues and contented myself with the other part of the work, the culturing experiments, the staining methods, the preparation of histological organ sections, their fixing, hardening, enhancement, and precise sampling.

I am unable to say why. But I did not touch an animal. Not even rats, although this species stood on the debit side of the ledger in my life and I continued to find these creatures a bane of creation, a misbegotten horror that had unfortunately been allowed to exist, one of nature's mistakes. I preferred to have old Carolus do the guinea pig injections when necessary, and the result was not long in coming. One of the guinea pigs perished, the sole casualty among the animals in this series of experiments. But was it the unknown pathogen of Y.F., or simply the uncleanliness and poor technique of the brigadier general, whom the good Lord had wrathfully made a bacteriologist? Was this the way it had to be? Did I *have* to have this bias against him? I will speak more of this.

But, by way of compensation, the entirely professional Walter received unexpected assistance from – March. No one who has not seen that brave, handsome little fellow at work can have any conception of that unbroken young person's cleverness, of his thirst for knowledge, of his manual skill, his tireless industry, indeed his passion for the work that surely must have repelled him, disgusted him.

Nor was he deterred by the negative result of his work. Every day he rose to do it knowing his appetite would not suffer because of the stench, whereas Walter and I both lost a great deal of weight during this period (it was July, always an abominable time in the equatorial region) and were often near tears from exhaustion. But we held up.

For all March's help, Walter had to wire the result to his higher-ups – the result that he had nothing positive to report.

Cases of the disease continued to vary in number and severity, but material was always there.

We worked. It was often enough to drive one to despair.

But, apart from Carolus's one casualty, the inoculated animals enjoyed the best of health.

IV

From the beginning we had all thrown ourselves into our research with the greatest passion. The setback had to be correspondingly great, and so it was. I said before that all the inoculated animals (except for a single guinea pig) survived the introduction of infectious material without any perceptible deleterious effect attributable to Y.F.

The brigadier general was looking around for something else to do and remembered his statistical tabulations; with these – here as in Europe – he was in his element. He felt at home wherever there was a box of paper slips, a chart, little flags and pins, the old fool. But when I say "the old fool," as earlier I called him a "lummox," I must ask myself if this is not the voice of envy speaking. Envy not just of his military grandeur, his general's insignia, but envy of his sheer philistine certainty. Of the fact that he had borne life as it was. But the brave Walter had done the same, and I do not call him these things.

Here there may be an internal contradiction in my character, a self destructive false foundation, which gave way when I committed my crime, assuming it would support me, and would probably give way when I came to make any important life decision. It was something unfathomable, but with the force of a natural law. That is to say, ultimately just as incomprehensible as any law. I would not speak of it at such length had my antipathy to such a person as Carolus not cost me a great success. But all in due time. Here I will restrict myself to our old medical statistician's conclusions, alluded to earlier.

He observed (always on the basis of his maps, charts, and statistical methods) that a case of true Y.F. occurred, let us say, in the third house from a certain corner in the city of C. (on the right side of the street coming from the harbor). The next (luckily it was possible to make a precise observation of this now, when cases were relatively sparse) – the next case was found not in the house next door – that is, not in the second or fourth house from the corner – nor directly across the street, but around the corner on another street, perhaps, or even around the block, separated from the first epidemic center by a large vacant lot covered with piles of refuse, cisternlike pits full of water, pools and puddles, piles of rubbish and empty cans, bodies of animals and sawdust, hutches for small domestic animals, and relatively small run-down planted areas. It was determined that there had been no contact between the first case, that of the Swedish engineer, let us say, and the second, the wife of a senior administrative official; they had never seen each other. How had the contagion spread? On the wings of angels? I asked sardonically. At the time none of us was able to draw the correct conclusion. No doubt it was *too simple*.

Secondly, it was determined that people in the hospital became ill relatively rarely. The building was situated on a rise. At this time of year it was exposed to a particularly blistering sun – what idiot had decided to make the Jesuit convent a hospital? The sickrooms were thus true hellholes comparable to the "steam rooms" of blessed memory, the torture chambers on the *Mimosa* (do you remember, dear heart, fair, dear March, is that why you're smiling at me?), and some of the examination rooms had to be located in cooler basement areas, where it was necessary to work by artificial light, preferably in the evening hours or the first few hours of the night.

But who could always arrange this so conveniently? It was frightful in the sickrooms, especially the ones under the flat roof. And yet it was very seldom that transmission occurred within the building. The staff remained healthy, as did the black women who dealt with the mostly dreadfully soiled clothing and so forth. So: why was it that the nightmarish contagion lost its infectious power here within these walls, where the chapel bells tolled death knells often enough? Crossword puzzles are easier. We had no answer.

The third observation was that the patients often came in waves. There happened to be a lull when we arrived. Then there were three or four cases; then there was a lull of about ten days; then the epidemic resumed with renewed virulence. Could it be some plant that took ten to fourteen days to bloom and then sprayed the poison of the yellow-fever plague from its resplendent, showy stamens? Carolus's statistical curve was very distinctive. But what did it distinguish from what? Connoisseurs of these things such as the good pharmacist von F., the old man with the portable mosquito netting around his patrician head, were consulted. He was questioned closely about these three matters. But all he had on his mind was his mosquitoes and their fine points. These he had observed and studied in minute detail, but he had neither made his own observations of the three particulars of interest to us nor had his attention drawn to them by others; nor yet was it possible to induce him to attach any special importance to them, no matter how hard we tried. Not that he really grasped our problem. The eye of an inspired statistician was needed in order to see these three points at all – and Carolus was one. And he was even more than that. By no means the lummox I had called him in a moment of abject envy, not in all situations. For, to my discredit, let the following be reported at last.

It will be recalled that the sole casualty of our many experiments was one of the three guinea pigs he had inoculated. I had gone through the corridor into the basement rooms where there were ranks and files of animal cages. All the animals alive and well, except for this one guinea pig, a male with rust red and yellow-white spots, that would not eat, had yellow conjunctivae, and seemed to be feverish. I took its temperature: thirty-two degrees centigrade. Was it any wonder? The clumsy hand of a Carolus had wielded the inoculation needle; everyday contaminative microorganisms had evidently gotten into the bloodstream. The animal whined softly and piteously and shortly died. I told Walter, who nodded gloomily at my (false) report – general blood poisoning with hepatomegaly – and seemed very depressed by the negative result of all his (our) efforts.

"Is that all you've found?" he asked.

"See for yourself!" I replied, producing the specimens. And he, who had himself once determined or at least rendered it very probable that guinea pigs could be inoculated with Y.F. serum, was satisfied with my superficial finding. He put terrible trust in me, and I wanted to put my trust in my preconceived idea. But I could not. I was more conscientious than that. I stained the guinea pig's greatly softened, inflamed liver, placed the tissue sections under the microscope, and found, instead of the usual pyogenic organisms, suspicious microorganisms, pale objects more intuited than really precisely detected, with a spirochete-like form, that is, shaped like corkscrews – and this in one spot, in one section out of six. Now the most obvious thing to do would certainly have been to report this problematic finding to Carolus and Walter. To pursue it. To give the specimen special attention. To repeat the staining, try all known methods, from flagella staining and osmic acid mordanting to the familiar spirochete tests, as it is the duty and responsibility of every honest, respectable bacteriologist to do.

Did I? By no means. I was too ashamed to admit that my first report had been inaccurate. I also begrudged Carolus, whom I knew to be a bungler, his success. So quickly was the team sundered. In dealing with a lummox, I thought, anything was permitted. I preferred to convince myself that what I had seen had been "shadows" of bacteria, remains of spirochetes from another case. For the administration was thrifty, and the glass plates on which we stained the smears had been used before; March was supposed to have washed them carefully in hot caustic soda liquor, but, pigheaded as I was, I had my doubts. So out of antipathy to him (a natural reaction to his unwanted, importunate love) and hatred for Carolus (a reaction to his indestructibly assured, parochial, stolidly happy nature), I neglected everything that should have been my duty. I was every bit as frivolous and small-minded as so many mediocre researchers, and hence what I was looking for eluded me just as it does them.

V

Had I done what I should have done, and had I not done what I did do, I would have been spared many hard lessons. I am not softhearted. Not even toward myself. But, after all that had happened, I had believed that my capacity for suffering was exhausted and that now I would – but let's not get carried away. The facts and nothing but the facts are going to have to go on doing the job of conveying my joys and sorrows.

So far I had dealt only with nonliving material – and with the animals. When (thanks to my failure) the futility of our efforts to date had become fairly clear, I had to expect that I would be put back in a camp with the other felons and from that point on do hard physical labor, such as road building. In the best case I might hope to be sent to one of the municipal offices as a clerk or bookkeeper. In the environs of the city and on the surrounding islands, there were rubber plantations of no mean significance; there were deposits of gold-bearing quartz, which, though sizable, had not been adequately worked due to the climatic conditions; the precious woods in the immense and to some extent still virgin forests on the peninsula were traded internationally by a wood-utilization company. Even within the numerous convict colonies, which included a leprosery and a few more or less primitively equipped hospitals (also a modern one), there would have been plenty to do for a man with an academic education who was willing to work. And yet it was decided that I would remain in the old convent hospital, the collection point for Y.F. – and why? I had said not a word, I had made no requests, but my highly placed father had brought it about that when deported I "be employed in my profession where practicable." My profession was primarily experimental bacteriology. Experiments were being done here in C. They had to do with bacillus X. Would that do? Of course it would. And when there was no longer enough for me to do in the laboratory, idleness being the very worst punishment for a man like me, I was put to work, as I had been aboard the *Mimosa*, caring for some severely ill patients.

I had always had the ill-fated ability to awaken trust in people. And now the hospital director, who was old and not overly bright, but capable and experienced in his specialty, had me brought to him, looked at me for a long time without saying a word, and then assigned me to take charge of medical care in one of the many sections of the hospital that stood empty these days more often than not. It was understood that this would be a test. And so it was, though not at all in the way he and I expected. He trusted me. I saw that.

To approach the disease from a clinical perspective, that is, from the standpoint of bedside observation, I was to study fresh, recent cases especially. Smiling politely, I bowed deeply before the old gentleman (sunburned, with snow-white hair and beard), while he sat smoking his good cigar. As I did so I brought my chin down onto the neck of my lab coat, and in the breast pocket I felt a rectangular object. In the sickroom where I was taken, I realized what this was – it was pharmacist von F.'s matchbox of mosquito eggs, some of which had now hatched into little mosquito young. Later I will describe these curious insects in the depth these strange children of promiscuous Mother Nature deserve. Here I note only that one of them had inquisitively forced its way out of the box through a tiny crack and was producing its peculiarly high, piping, piercing sound, like the buzzing of a string, as it sought to make good its escape. Which it did not succeed in doing. The room, the sickroom I mean, was in semidarkness. Not only had the green wooden shutters been lowered, but the windows were also hung with red woolen or silk fabric. At a minimum I would have to remove it in order to perform the initial examination of the sick child. For it was a child, as the hospital director had intimated. There was one more person in the little room (its construction, the high Gothic vaulting and so forth, indicated that it must once have been a residential cell for inhabitants of the convent).

Before I laid eyes on the partly hidden, fearful patient, the chaperone, her ayah or nanny, came to my attention. This was a woman in her midsixties, in claret-colored Sunday best, with freshly starched white cotton petticoats, broad white gauntlet cuffs around the worn, gnarled, coffee brown hands. The close-fitting bodice was buttoned to the throat; around the shoulders, hunched with age, was a small, triangular fringed shawl. Long earrings made of green paste in gold filigree settings hung from the earlobes, which were greatly stretched out. The wide, rubbery mouth was tightly set with emotion. The bony fingers moved agitatedly, a strange rosary made of large silver spheres rattling between them. Her eyebrows were shaggy like an old man's, as gray and coarse as grit. The animated, sparkling black eyes moved restlessly from the director and me to her charge, of whom only the neck could be seen at first, as the child had buried her head in her sky blue satin coverlet out of fear of me, or perhaps to avoid the strong light. As one neared the bed, by which the old woman was standing, one noticed first the rather sharp odor characteristic of the mulatto's black race, somewhat reminiscent of the perspiration of animals, but then one noticed another smell, stronger every moment, like that of the old Swede and the other corpses that had come to our basement table, only not so penetrating. Y.F. There could be no doubt after all.

The director told me briefly who this was. She was a girl of fourteen and a half, Monica Zerlina Aglae, etc.; the family name, a Spanish-sounding name consisting of many individual names, is irrelevant here. He gave me to understand that the young thing was the only child of very well-to-do Portuguese parents. The father had worked for three years here in the old section of the city as the director of the large wood-utilization company. The child had been brought up in a convent in Europe. But at the fervent request of her unreasonable, doting mother, the old nanny had brought her here. Here? Certainly! She was lying there before us, was she not, looking at us with beautiful, velvet brown eyes already inflamed by the disease and smiling imploringly.

Her mother had known of the danger of Y.F. Indeed, she herself had long been in constant fear of it. So why stay here? And why in the devil's name bring an innocent child into this atrocious climate, this hell for criminals known the world over? Her husband was putty in her hands.

He had no choice but to stay, and he could not live without his wife. And she not without her Monica. Logical, no? He needed to earn a lot of money. The wife had led a life of luxury in Paris in recent years, had bought crazy amounts of jewelry and so forth; it was precisely here, in such a perilous post, that the husband could hope to recover a large fortune in a short time.

The child had evidently been in good hands in Europe. Everything going swimmingly, had not the foolish woman been afraid every moment of catching Y.F. And of having to die without seeing her one and only again, her child! And the husband weakened as men often weaken toward women they love, even to their downfall, and gave in. He accepted the mad notions in the doting mother's simple, stupid doll's head and had the child come. The ayah missed her little girl and had pushed for it, too.

When the ship was already en route, the epidemic, then in a quiescent period, broke out again with renewed virulence. What to do? Send a wire? In vain. There was no way to call it off (or was it that no one wanted to call it off? Any ship can be reached by wireless telegraphy!), but vows were made. The fearful mother (afraid for herself? for the child?) promised heaven everything, ten years of her husband's earnings, all her splendid jewelry (I would make the acquaintance of some of it). But heaven showed no consideration. Why should it?

VI

Heaven showed no consideration, I say, but did I?

I must speak, I must tell how it all happened – and for the first time I am seized by a diffidence inexplicable even to me, I don't know what to say, what not to say.

My innermost feelings are now responding for the first time since the death of my wife, I am speaking of the only human being toward whom I have felt what I have heard described as "love." Ill-fated love? I don't know. So positive a feeling as love can never be ill-fated, if it is genuine. Such an enormous test of the human heart can never be all for naught. What a load of sentimentality and slippery ideas. I have pledged, I have promised myself, that I will speak only of facts.

The first sound I heard from the child was a low, brief cry of pain. What I now saw of her was a small, brownish, plump, but long-fingered hand, feeling about on a slender neck beneath dark blonde pageboy-cut hair. But she did not find what she was looking for. All there was on her fingertips was a little blood, at which she gazed in wonderment with her large, still quite childlike, yet already womanly eyes. A mosquito, no doubt one of the young ones from my matchbox, had bitten her and, disturbed before it could finish its meal, not satisfied with that little bit of blood, was still humming about the bed, taking that unpredictable zigzag path that is familiar to us from moths in our climes and is so frustrating to hungry animals. The little insect, gleaming silvery and black, pleased with its newfound freedom, circled quite unconcernedly about the night table, upon which lay all sorts of fruit, little dishes of compote, bottles of mineral water, and a small bowl of ice chips in fairly large clumps. Finally the mulatto was able to shoo the mosquito away with one of her cotton kerchiefs. The insect flitted out the window and into the hospital courtyard, where its wings flashed in the afternoon sun and it vanished.

The little Portuguese girl had sat up and was looking at me. Despite her feverish condition, she was amused by the chase after the mosquito. Her strawberry-colored lips, which were swollen now and perhaps for that reason had a somewhat sensual appearance, with a shadowy suggestion of dark fuzz over the mouth, curved in a smile. She seemed to be mocking herself for having taken seriously something so trivial as a bite on the neck by a mosquito. It was just this pluck, this mischievous irony, that I found so captivating. I couldn't take my eyes off her, and she returned my gaze. Or was she only looking at her new doctor with childlike curiosity? I have said that I had the gift of being able to awaken trust, and what could be more important for such a young creature, one who is seriously ill, than to find a doctor who inspires trust at first sight? Then she will hope, believe, and trust.

Many physicians have this ability. It can be seen in pediatric clinics when an exhausted tiny creature, in the midst of its suffering – suffering that can only be bewildering and thus all the more terrifying for it – will instantly stop all its wailing at the sight of a certain doctor, wipe away its tears with hands almost too weak to do anything, and with an indescribable expression of pure submissiveness, of courage, indeed of faith and even delight in the midst of distress, give itself up to the physician who, responding to the illness, not the gaze of the sick child, is preparing to examine it.

I was given this ability, as are many others. I don't know why. The venerable age or imposing beard or practiced manner of the physician or friend to children cannot be the reason for this mysterious trust, this devotion, this touching absorption of the suffering little creature in the strange doctor.

But why the theoretical discussion? All because I am unable to bring myself to report my love for the child. Let the reader fear no new horror stories! Let him expect no weepy fiction, either. What is at issue here is the typical medical history of a girl somewhat older than fourteen, and the futile efforts of an older man disillusioned with himself and the world to save her and become at one with himself and the world once again.

It was, as grotesque as it sounds, love at first sight. Can that have been an accident? Or did I, Dr. G. L. the younger, sentenced to lifelong hard labor on C., embark upon this absolute self-abandonment, hopeless from the outset, because I suspected that it could never be fulfilled? That Monica was just as doomed in her way as I was in mine? Or was I still hoping, in some corner of my heart? That is the question.

I don't know, and I didn't think about it. I had no thought of the future. My heart beat, I was with her. It was that simple.

I stood on the left side of the bed and began the examination. The mulatto on the right side, breathing heavily with agitation, watched tensely. She wanted to be in the room at all times, would no doubt also want to improvise a bed for the night here on the cotton-covered reclining chair of the kind often provided for convalescing patients. Whenever I was with Monica, she was there. We were never alone, even for a minute. Or no, we were, before the end – nearly alone.

My examination yielded the following picture. She was a girl of normal development and stature, of the southwestern European type, with good, strong musculature and gracile, regular bone structure. The dentition was complete and well-formed. The fever was moderate, 38.9°c, the lips and pharynx swollen, though only slightly at first, the tongue coated, dry, the conjunctivae reddened and highly sensitive to light. Hence the red cloths over the windows. The liver was only negligibly enlarged, not sensitive to pressure, but the abdomen was somewhat distended, with dull pain. The onset of the disease had probably been three to four days previously. Carolus's statistical findings – the particular vulnerability to infection of new arrivals from cooler regions, healthy, strong, muscular types, white people – were borne out here, except the fact that men tended to be more susceptible than women, which I had cynically regretted on the ship. At that time I had been sorry that men, the more highly organized of the sexes, were more sensitive to Y.F.; now this injustice angered me. For *now*, seeing this blossomlike, chastely sensual, truly enchanting creature with the slightly frowning, strawberry-colored lips and the downy shadow above them, when I had this creature afflicted by the great misery of Y.F. and the small misery of a mosquito bite before me, close enough to touch, and when I felt: here now in your life is what you have always yearned for and always dreaded – now I would have wanted all men to be subject to the epidemic and all women to be safe. What madness feeling is!

But what can words convey? For the first time I see the meagerness, indeed the factitiousness of what at the beginning I called my "report." "Close enough to touch," "chastely sensual" – what drivel that is, fraudulent, sentimental drivel. For the thing that really happened and happened with outward banality, yet with inward unfathomability, here as so often in life, I am unable to put into words. I doubt now that anyone will have any feeling for me in this part of my story, very likely with good reason, for I know that very likely no one will understand me.

The child had fallen back onto the hospital pillows without taking her eyes off me. The plump down comforters with embroidered cambric covers that she had brought with her into the hospital were sprawled on the reclining chair, which, covered with bright repp or cotton, stood in the corner of the room and which I have already mentioned.

The eyes were glassy, the conjunctivae bloodshot, as one sees in drinkers in a state of advanced, blissful alcoholic befuddlement. I have already reported this, have I not? But drinking! Befuddlement! This was remote from Monica. Not even fever was befuddling her now. She was lucid, and answered my questions in French as precisely as she could. She was bright beyond her years and perhaps had an idea what was happening. Speaking was already difficult for her. But she even raised herself off the pillows as if to make herself more clearly understood, pulled her cream-colored, brightly flowered chiffon pajamas, which were held around her throat with a green ribbon, still tighter, so that her somewhat too thin neck emerged like the stalk of a flower. The carotid artery could be seen throbbing beneath the fine skin with its blond down. The pulse was rapid, 125 beats per minute, the heart within normal limits, strong, as is generally the case in the flower of youth.

Presently she put her hand to her brow, behind which she felt severe pain, and I hastened to fill an ice bag with ice chips for her, first crushing them as finely as possible, and then placed it on her forehead. Crushing the ice chips required some strength. It is usually done with a mallet, not with the hand. But it seemed to be easy.

I had acquired new energies since entering this room.

VII

Someone in the full bloom of youth – could I not hope to save her? If it was humanly possible. Nevertheless I was not able to devote myself to this patient alone. Two more Y.F. patients were brought in on the same day, or rather one Y.F. patient and a second man whose symptoms were similar to those presented by Y.F. sufferers, but who in fact had a different, less dangerous ailment.

This was a man in his late fifties, worn out before his time due to alcohol and nicotine abuse, a tavern owner from the docklands. His establishment was said to be small, lucrative, and disreputable, as it was frequented by the most dubious elements of the city, freed slaves, thieves, and scoundrels, usually swindlers rather than murderers; also lepers – who furtively traded the poultry bred on their (officially) hermetically sealed leper farm for absinthe and whiskey – half-caste women, and the like. He had the best relations with the administration, for which he acted as an informer for love and money both. For who if not he was so knowledgeable about what the dregs of the population were up to? Needless to say, he took advantage of the trust placed in him by the authorities for the purposes of extortion of all kinds practiced against his peers. He shamelessly cut people's throats and then boasted about it later; he was one of the richest but most despised men in the city. He was proud of the livelihood he had created for himself and did not hide it from me. He had, by the way, also provided us with some of our experimental animal material and had not made a bad profit.

When he had suddenly fallen ill with ague and hematuria and a yellowish tint had appeared on his bloated, flat features, he had been hospitalized involuntarily. He was in a state of high anxiety that his house might be torched while he was gone or that he might or would become infected here. He ranted and raved, spat incessantly, would not stay in bed despite his patently serious condition, and his raucous presence had the quiet, gloomy hospital in an uproar. Bellowing like a chained bull being burned alive in its stall, he wanted to fly at the director, at the old nurses, and it took all the art of calm persuasion I could muster to at least get him to permit a thorough examination.

I have said that I possessed a certain power of suggestion, both with children and with raging patients. Here again it did not fail. No doubt it lay in my gaze and my laconic but strong-willed nature. He yielded to me, mastering himself only with the greatest effort. His limbs still twitched. He rolled his eyes like a ham actor playing a villain; his head, with its oily, slicked-down hair, jerked back and forth on the bed under my hands while at the same time he strained to pull it backward away from me. But the instant I made the first exploratory maneuvers, he grew visibly tranquil, like a mesmerized rooster. Yes, he grinned at me, took my hand, looked me in the face, and he was off and running. He took me for one of his own kind, had known right away that I was not one of the hospital's staff physicians, but rather a convict (as he himself had been), and that (like him) I enjoyed the undeserved protection of the authorities. His eighteen years on the island, where there were always more sick people than healthy ones, more people dying than being born, had practically made him a doctor too. For the region was just not a healthy place to live. He took me by the wrist, guided my hand beneath his left costal arch, and had me feel a moderately hard mass jutting out into the middle of his left upper abdomen beneath his skin, which was feverishly hot and covered with dark hair.

At the beginning he had blustered, raving, spluttering, shaking off spittle, had balled his fists and gouged furrows in the soft wood of the night table with his long, cracked nails. But now, quickly soothed, he had silently guided my hand.

He was a criminal, a vicious parasite upon human society, but by no means stupid and, even with a temperature of more than forty degrees, he was in control of himself.

And he was right. What he had was anything but Y.F. In all likelihood it was a severe tropical malaria that had made him ill, and, as would emerge, neither his first nor his last bout of it. What to do? Honestly tell him that? For was *he* honest, did he even understand what the word meant? He was not without experience of tropical diseases, as I said, for anyone who has lived (if you can call it living) for long years under the hellish sky of this jungle region, in an area where epidemics take turns with each other and have worked out a peaceful coexistence, is familiar with all the plagues of this blessed Eden. What he had had me feel with my hand was, he believed, an enlarged spleen due to severe malaria, and so it was.

Again, what to do? Could he be discharged? Rightly or wrongly, he was now within the Y.F. cordon. If he were allowed to go, who could assure the custodians of municipal health that he was not bringing the unknown microorganisms with him down into the city, perhaps in the black grime under the cracked nails that had dug into the wood of the night table? If they were bacteria, might they not lurk there and elude all attempts at disinfection? One question after another.

And keep him here? At his peril? Who could assure *him*, who was after all a human being, whose morality or immorality could never be permitted to have any bearing on his suffering or the decisions made about it, that he would not contract Y.F. here in earnest? Could one say: Look here, you old extortionist, you trafficker in human beings (retired), trafficker in animals, bloodsucker, you filthy brute, you criminal who may have been punished but are by no means reformed, you engorged tick on the poor, sick, afflicted body of civil society, listen, we who work here in the hospital are just as exposed to the danger of Y.F. as you are. The following have sacrificed themselves. Brig. Gen. Carolus, a high-ranking military dignitary, irreproachable, a man of the spirit and of science, has readily put himself forward for the sake of the commonweal, with no thought to his wife and child and grandchild at home. Likewise Walter, a man far above the common standard, a scholar and humanitarian, also a husband and the father of no fewer than five children, a man of the highest worth, both as a human being and as a scientist. Quite apart from the director of the hospital, the chaplain, and the altruistic, entirely selfless nurses, everyone from the old mother superior down to the washerwomen who have to clean the dirty sheets and pajamas of the Y.F. patients, for someone has to, and down to us, March and me, we have all taken upon ourselves the risk of Y.F. Why don't you follow our example and do the same!

What to do, I repeat. Compliance could have been expected from a person with any philanthropic cast of mind, in his silly muddleheadedness (if I may be blunt). Not this man. He was in the right, that was certain. He had been done an injustice. For he should not have been brought here by force (and in the meantime have had his belongings rifled through) without a thorough examination.

But there, it had happened. I shrugged my shoulders, freed myself from his flattery, bald assurances, and crass attempts to creep into my good graces, and left. I asked the hospital director. He could not be induced to make a decision (although there must often have been such cases here), but referred the matter to Carolus. Carolus would not have been Carolus if he had been able to bring himself to a clear, resolute decision. So on to Walter. Walter had been my youthful ideal, I credited him with all that I myself lacked in unbroken will to live, positive attitude, and affirmative belief, but today my expectations of his high-mindedness were bitterly dashed. He said nothing, put the tips of his index fingers together, looked at us with his serious, masculine gray eyes, and then, still without having said a single word, went back to his specimens. He had equipped this laboratory with everything that was needed, and exemplary order prevailed. If the matter had had anything to do with *him*, he might quickly have come to a decision, for he was one of those devout, heroic men who may be called upon to do great things and actually do them provided their own interests are involved. Not if those of others are.

But he withdrew into himself, shrugged his shoulders; he took off his wide gold wedding ring abstractedly, putting it between the pages of a notebook bound in red leather that he kept in the breast pocket of his white coat. This unconscious, mechanical movement of Walter's suddenly reminded me that I still had pharmacist von F.'s box of mosquitoes (*Stegomyias*). I interrupted the discussion and asked Walter for permission to breed the mosquitoes. He had nothing to say either for or against it, and, with the help of March, who had been listening silently, I readied a wide-necked stoneware vessel, closed at the top with thick gauze, for the pretty naiads. Then I went back to my three patients.

VIII

What a pleasure it had been in the old days to play the god of fortune! This had now palled a great deal. I humbly returned to the old tavern owner. He looked at me with a cocky but worried expression in his feverishly glittering rat's eyes. He should have become truly hardened to all the horrors of life on earth during his eighteen years on C., but he was frightened of nothing so much as of contracting Y.F. in the hospital. Did he want to live forever? As far as the welfare of the lovely city of C. was concerned, whether he was permitted to take off or had to stay came to exactly the same thing. Since no one had the remotest idea how Y.F. was transmitted, the cordon around our building could be freely lifted, the guards could be sent home, and, for his part, this good man here with his pleading eyes fixed on me could be restored to his noble profession, his dear family, his "loving hearts" down in the old part of the city.

Until such time as he was released, he would give the poor nurses and me no rest. He would be a constant disruption; his angry, vengeful clamor would be worse than the delirious clamor of the Y.F. patients who were actually seriously ill. So off with him! If for no other reason than to let poor little Monica in the next room have some peace and quiet and get a little sleep.

I had another feeling, one new to me. No longer did I ask myself whether I was even capable of love. My life had changed. I even used a different tone of voice with him. Was it true? Could it be? Was it thinkable, had it ever occurred in the annals of the human heart, that someone far past midlife was still capable of so radical a change? Or was I deceiving myself again? That someone past forty might feel and suffer from and delight in something he has never known in his eventful life?

Responding to him just as if he were a human being, I asked the innkeeper if he felt strong enough to be taken home. For if he was without a doubt free of Y.F., well, he did have severe tropical malaria. His tobacco-stained, widely spaced but strong teeth were chattering with fever – but he did not hesitate. He wanted to be off no matter what, if only to die down there. If he had to die, he didn't want to die of a disease that had been imposed upon him here, even inflicted upon him, for the sake of human society at large.

So arise then, gird your fat loins, and clear out!

What happiness, what rejoicing!

If only fate willed it that the charming little creature in the next room leave this accursed building alive, alive, alive! This was all I asked of fate, which had so far mercifully protected me from the worst! But could I believe in a reasonable fate? I, who had had to recognize the unreasoning, impassive horror of the way of the world from my first lucid moment? Had my father taught me what life was like for nothing? Had he dwelled among rats for nothing? With all his intelligence and energy, was he still wretchedly inferior to them after all, to this aspect of nature?

Suddenly the lights went out. This had been happening occasionally since the director of the municipal power plant, Ericsson the Swede, departed this life. The convicts who operated the machinery at the edge of the forest under the supervision of junior officers and kept the plant's boilers running with freshly felled timber did not always understand the voltages and control panels, and the lights often flickered, sometimes going out for minutes at a time.

I hurried to the young girl, but even at the door I saw the twisted filament in the little green hospital table lamp blaze up again with golden light and, after a bit of wavering, go on calmly burning.

May it be a good omen! And I, who had never been superstitious, grasped at this insignificant portent, I rejoiced that the child seemed to be sleeping quietly, while the old mulatto continued diligently working on her knitting without lifting her eyes. Occasionally she fluttered her needlework to shoo away the flies circling around the light and the little one's head.

Meanwhile the tavern owner had already set about getting dressed. He fumbled into his clothes, swayed on his short, bearishly clumsy legs, and attempted his first steps. Suddenly, cursing under his breath, he seized the beefy Bordeaux red roll of neck that bulged out of his narrow, grimy collar. An insect seemed to have stung him, he had grabbed for it, and the little beast, besotted by so much fine blood, had chosen to be squashed rather than give up its prize.

He now held the mortal remains of the mosquito between his sausagelike fingers, muttering something about his sweet blood, whose allure neither the girls nor the mosquitoes could resist. But what did they mean to him, either of them? He had plenty of money and could buy himself the best quality love (by his lights), and as for the mosquito bite, otherwise so dangerous, the mosquitoes had already given him a token of their esteem, he already had severe malaria, which was known always to be spread from person to person by mosquitoes.

This last mosquito bite would not hold him up. He, who had vanquished, had given the knockout punch to so many episodes of malaria with plenty of quinine and whiskey, was hoping that this time too he would be back on his sturdy feet after a few days – or else in the grave.

A third patient had been brought in along with him. I had had the least to do with him so far. Firstly because the diagnosis of Y.F. was unmistakable, and secondly because he seemed beyond human help – beyond medical help, that is.

It had struck me when I first arrived at the Y.F. hospital that there were very few physicians, though there were many nurses. The old hospital director, who was swamped with administrative work, was supported by only one young resident, and he was on vacation.

For it was characteristic of this disease that the work of the nursing staff was often much more important and meaningful than that of the physician. I had not wanted to believe that human ingenuity and science could be so utterly powerless against Y.F. And yet they were.

There were a substantial number of nuns, older ones and the candidates known as postulants. And that was good. For the physician had to content himself with giving general instructions. The clever helping hands of the nurses, the efforts of the hospital kitchen, the provision of ice and so forth – these were the main things. Science had nothing to offer; everything came from the ministrations of the compassionate heart.

And spiritual comfort! In his first hours here each patient received spiritual comfort in the form of the sacrament, whether his condition was critical nor not. The tavern owner ran into the chaplain at the door. But imagine the smirk on the face of the man, full of merriment and insolence despite his fever, as he escaped the nonplussed white-haired father's clutches.

IX

Two old nuns took the innkeeper to the hospital office; the discharge formalities took some time. Meanwhile his family had been informed and he was to be taken away. But how? Still gripped by terror of Y.F., he refused to get back into the hospital ambulance (drawn by a donkey and a mule), and so there was nothing for it but to bring two burly fellows up from the harbor, released criminals, to literally carry the idiot to his domicile. The next day, after taking three heavy doses of quinine, he would be back behind the zinc bar of his smoke-filled tavern.

I still had to finish with, I mean take care of, that man whom I had given up for lost and whom Walter too, after a summary examination, regarded as hopeless. This was a man of only thirty-four, but already aged in personality and appearance, white-haired, emaciated, skin and bones, homeless, unemployed, the bare ruin of a man who had worked for a time on building the Panama Canal. He was saffron yellow from the roots of his hair to his deformed toes and was now in a delirious state.

When he was asked about the primary location of his pain (for one wished to and was required to provide palliative care even if any true curative treatment appeared hopeless), he pointed now to his low brow, now to the lumbar region; his scrawny, hirsute legs twitched, as though he had calf cramps. The conjunctivae were yellow, shot through with distended scarlet venules. He too gave off the foul, carrion-like stench that is characteristic of the disease. Every slurred word hurt the poor wretch, any intake of food or liquid was associated with raging pain. And no wonder. For when one opened the mouth beneath the wild, stringy, matted gray beard and found that the tongue and oral mucosa were unspeakably raw, as though the top dermal layers had been removed with a grater, taken down to the bare meat, then one understood the extent of his suffering.

And if only he had at least been able to suffer and make an end in peace! But the heaving in his belly was unremitting, the abdominal musculature, pressed against the backbone, underwent paroxysm after paroxysm, and the stomach, tortured by constant vomiting, retained nothing, not even the ice chips that the hospital aide offered him. The vomitus was initially watery, later tinged with thin threads of blood, and finally brownish like coffee substitute, dark and granular.

He was allowed not an instant of peace. The chaplain came in and, wishing to administer the last rites, spoke of the gravity of his religious mission.

The canal worker was not listening. His exhausted features, altered beyond recognition by the disease, showed only complete cachexia, if anything at all.

With the greatest effort he raised himself from his bed, lifted himself up, his joints crepitating, as though he might have an easier time of it in a sitting position. He even tried to stand, clutching the night table with both hands, a yellow skeleton, bloody mouth beneath bloody beard, staring out of red eyes, retaining of the nobility of the human spirit only the ability to suffer. A grim, no longer manlike thing.

He was tormented by intense thirst, and it was poignant to see him vacillate between the desire to drink and the fear that he would have to vomit everything again amid the most wretched paroxysms.

The chaplain, filled with divine patience, a man well acquainted with sickness (also a man with a peculiar past, by the way), held out a crucifix for him to kiss. The poor devil put his bare lips on the silvery metal and cooled his raw tongue, stripped of the top dermal layers, on that emblem of human suffering.

I could no longer bear this sight. Honestly, did I want to? My presence was unfortunately superfluous for the time being. I repaired to my bedroom, expecting to be called during the night for the poor fellow's last moments.

The little Portuguese girl's room was quiet. Only the soft rattling of rosary beads could be heard. I did not go in.

Carolus and Walter, who were still absorbed in their investigation, working with undiminished interest though entirely without results, also retired late that night.

The two of them occupied the room of the vacationing resident, while March and I were housed in a basement room that was also used for the storage of wood, coal, vinegar, oil, and the like.

March was touchingly tender toward me. Why speak of the many kindnesses he did me just when I really needed them, the silent services of his hand and heart! I would have to enumerate every detail of our daily life in order to convey how he took care of me. I had never known anything like it. And I will say frankly: I could never have done anything like it!

And nevertheless I did not love him. I was fond of him, I thought highly of him, I needed him. I took his hand in mine and stroked it – but my gaze and my thoughts were elsewhere, they went right past him. Before I could doze off, I got up to check on my patient again.

She was not asleep. The black governess nodded in her corner, dozing in a sitting position; her sweat-bathed, copper-colored face shone among the many fanciful lace pillows and doilies. I woke her and barked at her impatiently. If she was going to take it upon herself to look after her precious one, then she couldn't sleep. She murmured something in her lingo and began rattling her silver rosary beads with her hard fingers. I took them away from her. Didn't she understand anything? From the adjoining room I heard the muffled clamoring and restlessness of the laborer and the ministrations of the nurse and the urgings of the old chaplain, who had not yet retired.

My patient's appearance was fortunately somewhat better than it had been late that afternoon. It was now getting on toward eleven at night. The fever had fallen, the pulse was full and regular, the pain bearable. She smiled at me, as though she had awakened cured. On her lovely brow – no, I do not wish to speak of her beauty. There is no way to do justice to the essence of beauty, just as it is impossible to put into words the essence of music. What is more, even if I could convey this moving beauty here, I still would not be able to put into words what went on *within me*.

The most profound despair: my bleak situation, that of one deported for life, my entire frightful past, the impossibility that my feeling could ever be understood by this child in her purity, never mind requited, I a relic of more than forty, she a spoiled, charming mama's girl of little more than fourteen. Enough said. End of story.

But everything would still have been wonderful had a severe disease state not existed. Or was it severe? Was she not lying there like a little nun in a casket, the ice bag made of white rubberized material spread across her lovely, velvety, cream-colored brow? Was it sleep, was it fainting, was it the marvelous calm of the beginning of convalescence? Against all reason, my life and hers seemed to join together and I felt a sense of happiness.

I was happy at that one instant when, for the second time that evening, the lights went out. I had leaned over the child to change the ice bag. I was still standing there, my head bent over hers, when I felt her outstretched arms reach around my bare neck in the darkness – I had stopped getting fully dressed in the evening because of the heat and was wearing only my white coat over my undershirt – the sleeves of her chiffon pajamas slid back to the elbows with a swishing sound, and her face, the somewhat pouty lips half-parted, slowly but distinctly came up toward mine. But long before her lips could touch my forehead or my throat, her head sank back onto the pillows, the thick, silky, loose hair unfurling, and at that same instant the lights flashed back on, brassy and steady as ever after a few current fluctuations.

We had not said a word to each other. To this day I do not know whether she did not kiss me because she was afraid of giving me her disease or because her strength failed her. For only too soon I would see to my horror that I had underestimated the seriousness of her condition.

Her improvement was only apparent. Was mine real? I still did not know.

I now did everything that lay within my power. This was, of course, not much. Then, with the heavy heart that can be produced by great joy just as much as by great, inconceivable suffering, I went back to March.

I did not weep. I did not say what had happened. I only took March's hand from the coarse pillowcases as he was attempting to smooth them, and I said to him: "Stand by me, March. I'll stand by you."

They woke me that same night, and I had to go, making my way through silent corridors and stairways – not to the canal worker, but to her, who had called for help and asked for me.

X

Will I be believed when I say that I set out slowly and with hesitation? I had a bad feeling about it. But I should have hurried. I did not.

To get to the sickroom on the third floor, I had to go through the basement corridor containing the animal material. It was getting on toward morning, the electric light was burning, most of the animals lay sleeping quietly. The monkeys, in adjoining cages, had lain down in such a way that their heads on both sides rested on the bars between the cages, and some had even put their long fingernails through, into the next cell. The dogs too (some very handsome ones among them), which were housed individually, slept pressed against adjacent walls. The smaller animals were kept in common cages. They were identified by small rectangular metal tags tacked through the cartilage of their ears. The guinea pigs, now only two of them left in a very spacious cage, had been awakened, they nibbled on what remained of their food, glanced curiously at me with their glistening little eyes, then silently went back to their slumber. They rarely made their whistling noises in captivity. A dog howled with a hollow, infernal sound, but this was not an expression of suffering; the animal was in a deep sleep and was vocalizing as dogs do when they dream. A rhesus monkey craned its neck, turning its flat, naked, brown nose and conspicuous wide black nostrils toward me. It lifted its left leg and briskly scratched off a bug. As it did so it brought its round, clear, amber eyes up to look at me, its strange gaze so remarkably like a human being's. Some time earlier we had given it a painful injection (which had not had any consequences). But it seemed to have forgotten this, or it did not recognize me as one of its tormentors. (I had only been an onlooker – but does that distinction matter to an animal?) As the long bare toes with their horny oval nails felt for and crushed another bothersome insect, the monkey's circular eyes, standing out brightly against its dark brown face, closed sleepily. It twisted and turned its neck with supple movements so that its head was again by the wall of the cage. And with a languorous sigh indistinguishable from the sigh of a weary schoolchild, it prepared to go back to sleep. It breathed slowly and deeply, bringing the hot, heavy air of the basement corridor in through its nostrils. Thus I left the animals all sleeping peacefully. Only a couple of rats, restless as they are known to be, were nervously active in their wire cage and suddenly began to run about in circles behind me in their prison, scratching and biting furiously at the wire.

The windows of the sickroom corridor looked out over the old part of the city far below, the fringe of palms and plantain trees at the edge of the restlessly heaving sea, the buildings with their flat red roofs, separated from one another by more allées of trees. All in the pearly, opalescent gloaming that is usual in the tropics just before sunrise. For the transition from night to day is very rapid here. Farther away from the city, army regiments could be seen on the beach, around them the security forces' barracks covered with glinting sheet metal. And now, when the light from the east was suddenly reddening more and more, one could see in the lifting mist, within the territory at the edge of the vast woodlands, the huge colonies, the hutments of the camps in which hundreds and thousands of convicts dwelled more or less peaceably under the shadow of loaded weapons. Off the coast a craggy island of black rock gleamed faintly.

It had not been long from the time I left March's side until I reached the patients' corridor, yet I had seen all this, the repose of the animals and that of the archipelago and the slate blue ocean gently surging to the shore, the buildings on the harbor, the chain of islands in the misty distance – did I have some suspicion that I needed to prepare myself for a terrible sight?

Monica's appearance this morning was no more dreadful than that of the canal worker with Y.F. had been the evening before. But what can I say? It was more ghastly than death.

The girl's condition had worsened dramatically. She had Y.F.'s well-known brief intermezzo behind her: in almost all cases the fever abates for what is unfortunately only a short time, the pain eases deceptively, lucidity returns as though in mockery, and the temperature falls. The heavens are thanked. For the patient believes he is saved.

That was the moment when she reached out her arms to me. She had thought she was cured, was with her mother in her heart, with her boarding-school friends, with her dolls, I don't know. Who can interpret an impulsive gesture? Was she thinking of her foolish, doting mother, from whose arms she had had to be wrested by force a few days before? Or did she want to cling to me, trusting in my help? For the sudden turn for the better had come when I appeared.

Only too sudden, too brief. The course of nature was only too diabolical. The fever was invincibly on the rise once more, over forty now. The suffering began again.

When I saw the column of mercury above the red line indicating forty degrees, I knew that all was lost – short of a miracle.

But to believe in miracles now, when I had never been able to? I had, needless to say, known the typical course of Y.F., had learned and had not forgotten how one dies of it. And yet I did not want to believe that now. I took refuge in childlike faith instead of science, neither the first nor the last to do so. But the first vomiting bringing up only water had already begun. The child was astonished. She had just taken peppermint tablets for ozostomia, and now her gorge rose with a clear fluid smelling strongly of peppermint. She was unwilling to vomit, she fought it, she was ashamed, well-bred as she was, in front of her nanny and – in front of me. She had hardly a minute of rest. The old ayah had been using a silk handkerchief to dry the now markedly pale lips, which stood out against the canary yellow face, but had not yet finished when the nausea began again. No! No! No! She wanted to take a deep breath and recover from an agonizing exhaustion that must have been new to her experience. But it didn't let her. Before long thin filaments of blood appeared in the vomitus, soon mixed with black granules, and in a very short time I saw that she was already vomiting almost exclusively blood.

She was unable to complain, could only whimper – without forming real words. And who could form words with a bleeding, swollen tongue?

I provided the assistance, the treatment, that the head physician of the hospital had suggested to me the day before. But this treatment was palliative only, it could not really help. I would have been delighted to be able to ease her symptoms at least. But even this was too much to hope for.

Any heart, any heart that was not yet completely dehumanized, would have ached to see even a low fiend like Suleiman suffer as this blooming, enchanting, innocent, childlike creature was doing now. I gritted my teeth. I answered the fearful, imploring, desperate expression of the doomed creature with a hideously grinning grimace that I meant to be a consoling smile.

Since a poison had invaded the bloodstream, every effort had to be made to eliminate it by flushing the renal system as thoroughly as possible. Would serum be used to combat the vomiting? No. Medication? No. Just horizontal positioning of the body. That was the treatment! And when paroxysms still came up from the distended abdomen, when more retching convulsed it, I gently held the child down on the bed in the vaunted horizontal position, the only proper one. What a joke! Y.F. and a temperature of forty-two – and horizontal positioning and ice chips to swallow are the best I can offer!

I spoke encouragingly to the child. I did not stint on promises that I knew to be false. The mulatto, who had been watching these terrible things and whose face had become as pale as a black person's can, would not leave the child. I pushed her out the door, chased her off to the hospital kitchen to bring up some chilled lemonade. In the kitchen area there were special vessels with finely chopped ice between the double walls (this was neither the first nor the last case of its kind). The child refused it. I sent the nanny, who had not yet had a real break, back down for champagne from the director's private cellar. With a table knife I cut the wire that held in the cork. The child had as little interest in it as in the lemonade. Perhaps the carbon dioxide in the champagne, the acetic acid in the lemonade caused more irritation of the inflamed, raw membranes of the mouth, throat, and stomach. The nanny had to go down again. She muttered and looked at me spitefully with her brown dog's eyes. This time I had a sorbet brought and patiently fed it to the child after having to take the spoon out of the nanny's clumsy hands. I tried to keep the spoon from touching her lips and swollen tongue.

I was called to the other patient, the canal worker, who was somewhat better, but still wretched enough. I did not go. March turned up, wanted me to accompany him to breakfast, I said no, he went, and then (that boy!) he came back with fruit and a freshly washed handkerchief. I sent him away. I thought about nothing, was unable to think about anything but the little creature whose fever continued to climb, though her hands and feet were cold to the touch. More than forty-three degrees.

The little Portuguese girl seemed to want something. We, the mulatto and I, were unable to make out the stammered word formed by the bleeding tongue amid the constant retching and vomiting. The black woman hung her silver rosary around the child's neck and also Mama's valuable pearls – the foolish, godforsaken mother had given them to the victim of her doting love to take along to the hospital. But none of these things was what the child wanted. A last wish – and unsatisfiable like all true wishes!

Or is that not so?

XI

For a long time we – that is, the mulatto, the Portuguese girl's former nanny, and I, her doctor – couldn't understand the stammered word. We finally did. It was *wine*. In short order I obtained a bottle of soft golden wine instead of the champagne. But she only shook her head, vomited with effort, and, already half dazed, repeated her request in a failing voice. At last we understood. She wanted not *vin*, but *raisins* – grapes. Possibly the juice of freshly pressed grapes would be especially mild, sweet, easy on a tongue that had lost its epidermis – or possibly she just thought so now. Perhaps she had been comforted by freshly picked grapes while under the weather with some innocuous ailment at the Swiss school. Grapes thrive in the sunny parts of Switzerland, particularly the Vaud region. But here, practically on the equator?

Could it be completely impossible to get hold of such fruit? The people in the hospital's business office just shook their heads at this odd request. It was all I could do to make sure someone at least tried to find grapes at the produce markets. What was the use? They came back with everything but grapes. Giant yellow mangoes that looked like Calville apples, a few thick, sticky drops oozing from their lacerated, ruptured skins like resin from the bark of a tree. Fine stuff. Terrific fruit. We mixed its juice with bits of ice, but the child refused it. We brought fresh local sugarcane, almond green, fibrous, somewhat woody stalks a yard long, which had a strange fragrance perhaps most comparable to wine (the native population believed it quenched the thirst better than any alcoholic beverage, and without increasing the perspiration). She refused it. She began to weep. It was an unnatural, drawn-out crying, from the chest and throat. Babies cry like this, but from their loose, slobbery lips – weary of the world and of life even before they have come to know them in their full glory. It rang in my ears, it was ghastly. It was not the weeping of a half-grown person. It was the sobbing – soulless, mechanical, perhaps, but for that reason all the more poignant – of a completely childlike being. My heart broke with the bitterness of it. I thought I would do anything to at least make this weeping stop. So still more fruit from the Eden-like gardens. We brought her West Indian bananas – here they had none of the insipid flavor of the unripe fruit imported to Europe, but tasted of honey and cloves. She only opened her mouth to vomit; she wanted neither the bananas nor the fresh bluish dates with a tinge of white bloom, a rarity here in the tropical zone, that the head nurse had gone to great lengths to obtain. We offered her pineapple, freshly picked that morning from plots outside the city, still with its corona of spiny sap green leaves. The mulatto sliced it with a silver knife. Grotesquely amid all this misery, her own mouth was watering, the rubbery black lips were dripping saliva, for she had eaten nothing in forty-eight hours, so absorbed was she in the care of her darling. But we had no luck with the fresh pineapple, either.

Someone had also brought a lovely flower, a wild orchid with an exquisite vanilla-like scent and marvelous coloration on the long, pendulous, bannerlike lilac pink blossoms and the blazing, saffron yellow, luxuriantly brimming pistils.

That sunken eye was blind to the wonders of this terrible world.

The worst was when we had done everything we could think of and had nothing left to try.

The monotonous, aching, endless sobbing filled the cramped, humid little room, broken only by the buzzing of the insects that had been attracted by the strong smell of the fruit. They harassed the poor defenseless patient so much that the fruit had to be removed. The mulatto woman, a "loving heart" of the first rank but only a mediocre nurse and not someone who could get used to order, flung some of the fruit out the window into the courtyard, where it fell with a slap. The matron came in and gave her a severe look. The mulatto blushed and tossed the rest of the delicacies into a pail. In other respects too there was not as much order as the matron thought necessary. The mulatto sullenly buckled down to work. The heat was frightful.

Now the disease's smell of decaying flesh – which came from the loveliest mouth I had ever seen – mingled with the scent of the rapidly wilting orchid. No one bothered to water it, for why should it live when the child had to die?

Beyond saving, and me a doctor – even God couldn't make sense of it, I said. But now in my despair I clung to the idea that there must be a way out "with God," some act of violence, some thunderclap that would lift the world off its foundations – and save her. Foolishness! Madness! This was the megalomania of desperation, no more. Smash the thermometer on the edge of the table, the fever would remain. We looked on and said nothing.

Walter appeared, and just his standing next to her gave me a glimmer of hope. Had I not always justly looked up to him, thought him capable of things I myself was not? For me he was the European archetype of the brilliantly practical man, equal to life, unsentimental yet benevolent and humane; more than I, he exemplified natural, clearheaded human understanding, the sum total of all medical knowledge and skill. He represented the lucid mind dominating the vicissitudes of nature, the genius of the great physician. But all he did now was use his four-color mechanical pencil, held in his left hand, to enter the patient's temperature on her chart in red, her pulse in blue. And while these two lines described the oscillations of a steep wave whose excursions continued to climb, the curve for urine output, in black, fell with every new tabulation.

Intoxication was increasing. Detoxication, in black, was decreasing. It pointed downward like a finger.

On the evening of one of these days (eventually I no longer knew how much time had gone by, whether the sobbing and retching, the fever and deterioration had been going on for three hours or three days), Walter asked me if I had done the usual blood test. A blood test? How could that help? So why do it? For the sake of knowledge? For the sake of clinical and scientific exactitude? I was supposed to puncture the arm of someone I loved more than I loved myself? Yes, even now, when the signs of death were becoming unmistakable and when, with its poison yellow mask, the face that had been so lovely had taken on a ghastly ugliness, yes, only the silky dark blonde hair still held a little of the Monica of the first day – everything else was abysmally ugly, repulsive, abominable, the cracked lips covered with bloody scabs, the skinned tongue, the swollen, bleeding gums, the mouth that I saw gape like a corpse's amid the endless sobbing, there was nothing lovely, nothing adorable left in this apparition; she was no longer a sentient person, her suffering was heavy, wordless, a ghastly spectacle, her sobbing not an expression of conscious affliction but an automatic reflex of the vagus nerve, made oversensitive by the Y.F. toxin – and yet, even now, when everything was as it clinically had to be, I prepared the blood lancet to draw some blood as Walter had instructed me, I had the nanny squeeze the thin, saffron yellow arm above and below the crook of the elbow to pool a little blood at the puncture site – but I did not press down. I did not prick the skin.

I cheated for the sake of appearances. I took a tiny drop of the blood flowing from the gums and spread it on the glass slide, to simulate a specimen for Walter.

That evening Monica often reached for her throat, sometimes with her left hand, sometimes her right, gasping as though she were suffocating. The nurses took the valuable pearls from around the child's neck and washed both with warm water, first her neck, then the necklace, then put the necklace back on her.

It had great value, it was real.

I remember that in my old life I once called money the best medicine.

It was another person who said that, another mind that had believed it.

I want to say something else, since I promised myself that I would be completely honest, as honest as the human spirit, deceitful from the womb, can be.

XII

It was at bottom quite an insignificant matter. I mention it here more for the sake of completeness than anything else.

Adrenal extract is recommended by many physicians for hemorrhaging from the mucous membranes, as in this case those of the mouth, pharynx, stomach, and bowel. So that nothing would be left untried, I had the preparation brought from the hospital dispensary. I had filled the standard Pravaz syringe, holding one cubic centimeter, with the colorless, crystal-clear liquid. I had placed the syringe on the night table with the bevel of the needle facing upward and outward and had begun cleansing the injection site.

At that instant the poor little one's dreadful sobbing had increased. I could have borne anything else more easily, even the shrillest screaming and the most furious struggling. Anything but this monotonous, soulless sobbing. I couldn't bear it, couldn't bear it anymore.

I stroked the child's hair, I fed her a little vanilla ice, melted, yellowish, with tiny particles of vanilla in it, which ran back out of the corners of her mouth mixed with bloody froth. Fruitless effort, fruitless torment.

I saw that all was lost. I saw something else. The pharmacy nurse, who for want of a staff pharmacist was the one who took care of the prescriptions in the hospital dispensary, had been unable to decipher my handwriting, had prepared a solution ten times the proper strength, and had conscientiously noted the abnormally strong concentration as such on the vial, with an exclamation point. I immediately sprayed the lethal dose through the needle into the air, and because I wasn't careful enough, a droplet of it got the label wet, so that the black ink of the pharmacy nurse's handwriting ran. One zero too few or too many – it was illegible now. Good poison – or useless medication?

At that moment I thought of my wife. I saw before me the vial of the toxin that I had used to murder the poor woman, I saw the finely made old syringe that I had used in my crime glinting on a mirrored tabletop with the bevel of its slightly bloody needle pointing outward and upward. "All things return in this short life" – this thought flashed upon my mind. Flashed like a light, and I saw.

For a second I hesitated. I understood my fervent wish that this dreadful sobbing, this mindless animal suffering of a totally doomed being simply cease. Whatever the cost. Why not fill the syringe again, give this wasted yellow arm a jab – a split second, one deep breath, and it's all over. Horribly over, but over. Only those who have sat with someone beyond help for weeks or even just days or only so much as a few hours, with ears and eyes and heart and soul rebelling furiously against this useless torment, will have understood me.

But I did not make this split-second movement, and will that also be understood? That I, Georg Letham the younger, let fate take its course?

I almost believe that the meaning of my punishment flashed upon me at that moment. I was the only one who could sit in judgment upon myself now. I was the only one who could punish myself. Part of the punishment I had to serve was to have to watch my darling's agonizing death and be unable to help. Never in my much-too-long life was it ever so difficult to do something as it was now not to lift a finger. But I understood that a human life has an absolute worth. I understood the connection between what went before and what came later. Was that so difficult? It was difficult. So difficult that until that day it was impossible. It was not until I had set my foolish, blundering heart on such a person, unalterably, against all reason (what could I expect of the beloved child, what did I know of her but the long since wasted face, the ravaged features – I had scarcely heard the sound of her voice, had never seen the child walk, dance, be happy!), not until now, when I had taken my place among the infinitude of suffering, *pointlessly* doomed people, as one of their own, that a loss could wound me, that I could do penance. Could? Could? No! No! Had to.

If I had not murdered, I would never have come to this point.

I gave the world my consent. I had to. I kept to the straight and narrow, did not stray. It had to be.

By the time I had diluted the solution properly, the pulse had already become imperceptible. The injection was now evidently useless. And thus I let it pass. The child lived several hours more, for she was young, had never been seriously ill – she had come to her parents on C. unbroken in body and spirit. It took many hours for the Y.F. poison to break the little Portuguese girl's body and spirit. I sat and watched her. I stifled my wish to act, to do something. I put my hands in my lap. Not on the dying girl's brow, not on her morbidly bloated, bright yellow body. Had there really been no way for me to leave my late wife, even her, without doing what I had done?

Why give one more stab to someone in biological decline from the first day of her life, who from earliest youth, from the womb, was wilting and dying? Why murder, why make someone suffer? Leave it! Leave well enough alone! It wouldn't be worth all the treasures of Golconda.

Murder is for nature the merciless, or for God. Look on, you excellent physician Georg Letham, you winsome, well-loved son, husband, and lover, fold your hands and keep silent! Despair, be silent, and die! Things are the way they are. You no longer pray, because you can't, and no one helps you. And why beg for sympathy later? What good are these silly tears flowing from the mulatto's red-rimmed eyes and down her velvety brown old lady's cheeks?

I am unable to weep. I had made fate an offer, I had been ready, provided the bargain was kept, to sacrifice myself for my beloved. Sacrifice, what a sentimental, pompous old notion! But all right! Was it not an experiment too to stay constantly by a patient who had a high fever and was passing contaminated blood and so forth, that is, was infectious? And not an unhazardous one? But fate had not favored me (as it had not favored my poor father). My offer to fate had been: Let me have her, cure her, and give me hell – and it gave me hell. But it had not actually hurt me. For it had not accepted the object of exchange, Georg Letham the younger, as valid, and *I* stayed alive, I left the sickroom, broken, yes, in despair, yes, as though I had been hit on the head, weighed down by unspeakable fatigue. But fit as a fiddle.

What did she mean in the greater scheme of things, the little Portuguese girl? What did she mean to the progress of our noble scientific mission? No more and no less than Ruru did, the good dog that went with my father to the region of the North Pole.

I wanted to, I had to find meaning in my life, indeed I sensed it, I believed it was there to be found, was confident that it could be understood, and yet I went off mutely, head down, teeth gritted, yes, so help me, as I ducked out I ground my molars, as my father had always done at critical moments in his later life. The room was filled with the old nanny's primitive and uninhibited howling as I escaped from it, leaving her with the dead child. To clothe her in a dignified manner for her final repose.

Shortly thereafter I inevitably ran into the chaplain. He looked at me, and I nodded. I looked at him, and he shook his head and smiled. *He* had devoted himself with special love to the care of the old canal worker. Now it seemed the latter was on the road to recovery! Yes, the chaplain had a good line to the man upstairs, as was evident in his "blessed touch." The laborer would live. What good fortune! Thus the childless prole, senile at thirty-four, would leave the hospital in one or two weeks, pale but cured, restricted to a light diet, and very much in need of rest and recuperation. Yes, a light diet. When the man didn't even have enough dry crusts of bread to keep his scrawny body from starvation, no roof over his shaggy head to protect it from the downpours of the coming rainy season – no matter, no matter! He had to be restored to humanity, and she . . . she!

. . . I said nothing. But the chaplain seemed to understand me. He drew me into a corner, one safe from spies and eavesdroppers (the building's regular guards were tramping up and down in the flagstone corridors nearby because it was cooler here than out in front, where they actually belonged), and there he revealed to me – his secret? No, not quite. He only batted open his no longer entirely clean, well-worn cassock, opened his rough shirt at the collar, and showed me the word tattooed in blue letters from left to right across the base of the throat: *Amen*.

Not a word was spoken. I could have said something, and what stopped me? Another word: *Omen*.

He quickly did up his clothes, eyes downcast, and climbed the stairs I had descended, to make arrangements for the child's consecration and burial.

XIII

Why hide it? I was ashamed of my misfortune. I holed up in my underground cell with the oil and vinegar bottles and left the treatment of new patients to the resident, who had just returned, and the head physician.

First I slept for nearly twenty hours straight, I believe. When I woke up and awareness of what had happened returned to me, I would just as soon have given up in despair. Would have?

Nothing on earth could have rid me of my mortal despair, I believe now. I ate nothing, drank nothing. I sweated, was silent, and suffered. The notion lives in many very unhappy people that, if they weaken themselves to an extraordinary degree through fasting and deprivation, their mental suffering too will become much weaker, more moderate, easier to bear. But unfortunately there had long been no question of moderation. During the second, completely sleepless night (and why had I idiotically indulged my exhaustion so thoroughly on the first night?), I ground my teeth so much that the faithful March woke up and sat down next to me in his pajamas. How could I explain to him this desperate love for a totally unknown dead girl? I realized that, had I heard the whole story told about someone else, I myself would have listened in silence and never understood it. And why should someone like March understand me? And even if he did understand me, how could he console me? How could he take the place of the one upon whom I had inexplicably focused all the feeling I had in me?

There was no light burning in our cell. Not much illumination came down through the high basement window. He wanted to see me. So he lit his cigarette lighter and shone it in my face. His sleep too had no doubt not been the most restful, for he had had bad news from home about his youngest brother, the watchmaker's apprentice. And he had thought of him fondly so often, had soaked the stamps off all the foreign mail for him, had dried and pressed orchids between sheets of filter paper for the herbarium that his "bitty little brother" kept. Now the bitty little brother was sick or had debts or had stolen something or was out of work, who knows? Did his distress make me feel better? As cynical as it sounds (the cynicism of hopelessness), even his disconsolate manner was no help at all. It gnawed at me and plagued me cruelly to consider (my mind was working whether I wanted it to or not) that I lived in a room directly below the one in which she had died (not true, by the way, but I was connecting everything with her), or that my white coat hanging on a rusty nail on the basement wall still bore traces of her terrible days of suffering. And yet I was silent and said not a word to March. He saw my brow knitted tensely, forming the usual two deep furrows above the root of my nose. So he patted down the skin there, or rather he tried to. No sooner had he, in his childlike, foolish goodness, smoothed my brow (as though that could wipe away the cause of my frightful pain!) than it automatically knitted again. What could I do? Did I want to do anything?

He had tact. What he had never shown in his relationship with his cadet, this he now showed toward *me*, who had not asked for it and to whom it meant precious little.

He asked no questions, for he knew I would speak if I had anything to say. His stupid lighter crackled and shot off sparks as he waved it about and read me something from a letter that had some importance to him. I understood nothing of his gabble, but simply nodded.

Why was it that I had no peace? I never had any.

Meanwhile daybreak came. I watched the demijohns of vinegar with their wickerwork wrapping and the fat, dust-covered little drums of oil take shape in the shadowy gray light.

He got up, dressed, got water in a tub, reached into a vat of green soft soap for two handfuls of the slippery stuff, dissolved it in the water, and was on the point of putting my coat in it, the doctor's white coat that I had worn at her deathbed. I gently took it from him. We stood there half-dressed like a couple of imbeciles, and suddenly *he*, who had understood none of it, began to weep. Perhaps at the thought of his foolish little brother, who could not help him and whom he could no longer help. Or was it on my account? A harsh contempt gripped me. I contorted my facial features as he did his.

Weeping, as is well-known, involves the same grotesque facial distortions as grinning, differing from it only in the shedding of tears. I mockingly imitated his blubbering, as, in better days that would never return, I had sometimes imitated the laugh of a happy person – I have already spoken of this. And, do you believe it, this grimace, the despairing grin of Georg Letham the younger, turned into a true weeping, a sobbing! The unending sobs of a heavy, half-insensible soul suffering unto death. It was like the weeping I have described in the throes of Y.F., representing the curious reflex of the vagus nerve under toxic stimulation. A moment of laughter for all of us now. After everything I had seen and experienced in my forty-one years, the only thing I could do was imitate the little Portuguese girl who had sobbed herself to death before my eyes two days before.

The good March had primly looked away from my outburst of excessive feeling (is there any other way to describe it?). Amid tears he had soaked the white shirtlike garment in the foaming, greenishly lustrous liquid. Bubbles boiled to the surface. He rubbed the sleeves of the coat together with the front so that the pearl buttons clacked, scoured the bottom parts with the top parts to get the dirt out. Suddenly he gave a yelp – he had cut his finger on something. It was the slide with my darling's blood on it. This little sheet of glass, wrapped in white blotting paper and labeled in blue pencil with the patient's name and the date the blood was drawn, had been in my breast pocket. The strangest memento that a lover had ever kept in remembrance of his departed fair Juliet, or rather would not keep.

My tears ebbed, I got up, dressed, went upstairs, bathed, had breakfast, and set to work in the laboratory as I had done before my vigil at Monica's bed. In a corner I saw a preserving bottle of mosquitoes. March had taken the *Stegomyias* out of the stoneware vessel, perhaps at the request of Brig. Gen. Carolus, who had suddenly become orderly, or because the inquiring Walter wished to observe the cute, truly adorable insects, the object of such vile calumny, through the glass. But what was there to see? There seemed to be nothing out of the ordinary about them.

I note in passing that Walter's heart was in his work just as little as mine was, though he said nothing. For when scientific work has gone on beyond a certain point without yielding the slightest positive result, the researcher is gripped by a sort of paralysis, an intellectual despair, a stubborn apathy. One sits diligently and steadfastly over the microscope, assiduously checks the cultures, or, to be precise, the dishes of abacterial medium that one removes regularly every morning from the tightly sealed incubator kept at body temperature; only to find, again and again, that cipher, that nothing. The sterile internal organs, the untroubled expanse of broth, the smooth, virginal surface of the solid, gelatin-like culture medium still showing the slight scratches, like old ski tracks on a glacier snowfield, left by the platinum inoculation needle. A very pleasant sight, but eventually an infuriating one. Sterile work, literally.

No wonder the good Carolus's nose, long enough by nature, was becoming longer every day, though he personally had made the greatest use of this time. Under Walter's brilliant tutelage, he had absorbed exacting, scientifically rigorous bacteriological research methods from alpha to omega. Should he have to leave C., where the epidemic was again gaining strength, with empty hands, even if he had to leave that instant, he might conceivably be able to use these skills in the future to achieve something fruitful in another, more easily accessible field.

But for now the mission's bad luck weighed so heavily upon us all (with the possible exception of the indomitable March) that a piece of news brought by the fateful pharmacist von F. came as a thunderbolt that left us practically devastated. For, as in the case of my father's expedition (all things return in this short life!), here too a competing commission was underway, provided with strong financial backing and a capable scientific team; it was in transit from the States to the American epidemic centers in order to get to the bottom of Y.F. once and for all. The epidemic was costing so many precious human lives in Havana that there was no way either to colonize additional areas or to build the all-important canals that would transform the continent until something definite was known about this enemy of the American people. Yes, the American people! The American nation, noble sister of those of Europe and their great competitor! What a feather in Uncle Sam's cap if the Y.F. pathogen were discovered under the glorious Stars and Stripes! And we – empty-handed! Ignorant we had come, ignorant we must go!

XIV

There was thus a great danger that our little commission, consisting only of Carolus, Walter, and us underlings, might be forced to regard its business as finished. There was laboratory work for another one or two weeks, why not? Another hundred or five hundred sections of diseased, inflamed livers, gastric walls, kidneys, and so forth, could be fastidiously preserved in formalin, tricked out with all sorts of sophisticated staining methods, labeled, and then scrutinized by the sweat of our brows under the microscope at a thousand times magnification (never was the Biblical brow-sweat so literal as here in this continual steam bath, which was never less than thirty degrees centigrade but very often more than forty in the "shade") – we could methodically do all that, record the negative results as systematically as we would have recorded positive ones. And if Walter was the great master of experiment, Carolus was nothing less in the systematic statistical integration of the results. But zero plus zero never makes one.

Everyone but me was in communication with the outside world by mail, Walter by telephone too.

Not a single sign of life reached me during this period. Not so much as a picture postcard in kitschy colors from my brother, on some steamship tour with his wife and children! Whenever a mail boat was spotted from the elevated vantage of the hospital, tacking carefully through the archipelago and steering among the buoys in C.'s marshy harbor, the faithful March looked every bit as glad as the two top men, and even if the mail that March waited for with such longing (thoroughly censored, by the way) contained almost nothing but the joyless news that his family thought it should not keep from him (the breakup of his mother's marriage because of the scandal about *him*, the ominous illness of the youngest child, the "bitty little brother," the money problems of the other siblings, and so on) – he was at least not as completely cut off from the living as I was.

I made no attempt to break through these walls. I could certainly have begun a correspondence. Yes, mail was screened and had to be cleared by the director's office; but, like every deportee, I was permitted to send one letter per month at the expense of the penal administration. Not once did I exercise this right. I had even given away most of my stationery, to March, whose joy at this proof of my sympathy is beyond description. Never was a gift easier for me – and never had anyone thanked me more.

At that time I was lulled by the belief that the slow-witted youth's affection for me, which, though it got on my nerves, was profoundly comforting in its persistence, would go on forever and that I could toss him a crust of bread from time to time like a pasha. He was so very grateful for everything. When, for example, I advised him about how to advise his *mother* to help out his unemployed brother-in-law, an insurance agent – yes, this big fat zero's worth of love, was this not something for which *I* should have thanked *him*? For it represented a connection, however crude, with the world beyond our four well-guarded walls. It kept me from complete inner numbness.

As incomprehensible as it may sound, so it was: my present condition, down to almost the last particular, resembled the mental lethargy, the psychic paralysis, that had enveloped me immediately after my crime. But that was a crime with serious consequences, taking from me at a stroke my position in society, my scientific reputation, my respectable calling, my financial means, my erotic relationships, and very nearly bringing me to the scaffold, to use that sententious expression – whereas this was nothing but the commonplace death of a velvet-skinned fourteen-and-a-half-year-old Portuguese girl with whom I had never exchanged a single word other than strictly medical vocabulary. I was as innocent of her demise as I would have been of her providential recovery.

What had I meant to her? What could she mean to me?

And yet when I watched the canal worker, the convalescing Y.F. patient, hobbling along in the hospital courtyard, or sadly regarding his greatly emaciated, bony, myasthenic arms, which were tattooed with blue and red anchors and naked women and over which a conspicuous bile yellow shadow still lay – then my gorge rose. It took all my not inconsiderable strength of will not to imitate the Y.F. patient's retching and vomiting out of spite just as I had imitated the poor little one's weeping some days earlier in distress.

If only it had been possible to at least seek distraction in *work*! But this was beyond me. I was not permitted (the deportation authorities demurred!) and frankly did not want to return to the sickrooms. And so I stood around half or entirely inertly. Despite all my friend's love and tenderness, I floundered more and more in the atrocious heat.

I need not detail what has been noted by all observers with regard to the opium-like effect of time spent in the humid and perpetually overheated regions and climatic zones of the tropics. For many constitutions (and whether ours might not be among them, particularly Walter's and my own, was not yet certain), the equatorial regions are felt simply as an illness, and a deadly one in the long run. An illness even when those affected remain free of tropical diseases, that is, ague, dysentery, malaria, and on through the entire alphabet of ailments to *Zuckerkrankheit* or diabetes mellitus.

This was known not only to me, but also to Walter's wife, whose acquaïntance I would soon make in an indirect fashion, that is, by telephone.

There was a telephone booth in a corridor adjoining our large common workroom (formerly the refectory of the nuns in the convent). The lady was, as I heard, a woman of over forty (that is, the same age as our good Walter), the happy mother of five. She lived in the old city, or rather she was penned there like an animal, for what problems did that quarter not have? The absence of laundry facilities! The filth that lay on the crumbling brick stairways! The repulsive bare-necked vultures that boldly patrolled the streets, cleaning them as no one else would! Nowhere to buy quality linen goods, stockings, dresses, stationery, cologne, insecticide! The criminal riffraff, turned into beasts by their lives of poverty and vice, that prowled about just outside the door, begging, mooching, and threatening! I heard it all thanks to Frau Walter's powerful, sonorous voice and the good acoustics of the imperfectly soundproofed telephone booth, whose doors had warped from the damp and did not close completely. Her husband too – otherwise moderation and calm incarnate, patience itself, the very model of a high-minded gentleman – often raised his beautiful voice to an unbecoming volume in order to make himself understood to the mother of his children, who was unfortunately deaf.

Because she was hard of hearing, she screamed her head off into the receiver. As if volume mattered! But he caught the bug too. As paradoxical as it sounds, when he spoke slowly and accentuated the final syllables, while keeping his voice down, we would hear only his wife's voice from the telephone booth. Then we did not understand him, but his wife evidently did, and that was what counted. But if he began to shout, the wife's "What? What? Sorry?" would come out of the hallowed chamber, far away but distinctly shrilled in the highest piping tones. Muffled by the walls but still understandable or easily guessed. Walter, resourceful as always, would occasionally hang up and sit down to put the substance of the thing in black and white for his wife in his clear but somewhat careless handwriting. Gently but resolutely he would push his colleagues' voluminous papers to one side of the desk and neatly stack up the medical books into which the incorrigible slob Carolus habitually and obstinately stuck his used toothpicks as bookmarks. And if only unappetizing toothpicks had been as far as it went! But Carolus even put culture tubes there, and if these had not been as chaste and untouched as a fourteen-year-old virgin, then the greatest disaster could easily have resulted.

But no matter, the good Walter would hardly have sat down to write than the telephone would ring again with brazen insistence and Walter would have to go.

The good wife and devoted mother left no stone unturned in trying to induce her husband to break off his fruitless work. She knew there was still no result up here. That gave her words such weight that Walter would emerge from the little cubbyhole cowed and perplexed, and would seem to be wordlessly asking us what he ought to do. Another call! Not enough housekeeping money. Threats of divorce. Bulletins on his daughter's bad complexion, the poor progress being made by his son, once so promising, in his private lessons. And the horrendous prices of groceries and clothing. The "horrible people" she had to live among – criminals and their overseers. The miserable apartment. The wife's yearning for her husband. What was he to do?

And what about us? What did our mission mean? Our duty?

XV

Mission and duty were not necessarily the same thing in Dr. Walter's case. As far as the mission was concerned, to him, as to all of us, though we had not discussed it lately, it appeared to be probably infeasible by the available means, that is, those of bacteriological science as currently constituted. As far as duty went, however, that big word necessarily meant something quite different to us, I mean March and me, than it did to those two men of spotless reputation Walter and Carolus. And even between them the roles were not evenly divided.

Carolus could go on doing what he had been doing until his dying day. He had earned the right to leave wife, child, grandchild, the fine library he had begun building, and the superb cactus collection he had tirelessly, patiently nurtured to obey the beloved fatherland's glorious call. He had taken on the cause with all the commendable application and enthusiasm of which a man of his stripe is capable. Whether he was successful or not, he could be sure of a respectful reception when he returned home.

He carried on a lively correspondence with all the learned societies of general pathology, bacteriology, and biology, both domestic and foreign (March collected the stamps for his "bitty" brother); upon his return he could expect to be made an honorary member of those august organizations. This courageous citizen could also be certain that the top public-health authority, the Ministry of the Interior, would be among those bestowing such honors. He could even expect citations and decorations without so much as lifting a finger. And in the end he deserved these signs of favor from a magnanimous nation (happily generous as long as it costs nothing) just as much as any office poobah who spends thirty years sitting on the round leather cushion of his rotating desk chair until it's as flat as a pancake, but not as fragrant. Not that rank acquired through long service and devoted administrative work means anything. I knew how my father had disdained such men. He called these people turtles and said there was no way to get rid of them. You had to sit on them and ride them.

Walter's situation was quite different. For him there was much more at stake. But he – and, curiously enough, cute little March – kept at it, almost pigheadedly, no matter how unproductive their efforts were.

Walter's life was not easy. With a good head like his, he of course had more doubts, less confidence, than some full-of-himself nitwit would have had. No doubt he told himself that he might be wasting his time, and certainly he was often short of money. The excellent Carolus worked full-time; his salary, augmented by the "tropical bonus," kept coming in. But Dr. Walter's official position was not entirely clear – I never really understood his actual administrative grade ("attached" but not "assigned" to the shore batteries, or the other way around). Our commission was a voluntary one. There were, of course, allowances for expenses. But Walter was not financially minded enough and was too wrapped up in his work to apply himself to carrying out the tricky calculations of hours lost, increased outlays for the family, and so forth, in such a way that they came out to his advantage.

Yet the value of ready money was not unknown to him. He was perfectly aware of his responsibility toward his wife, who, after ten years of untroubled marital bliss, was becoming excessively hard-headed. Thus he found himself in conflicts of all kinds, and this was only the beginning of his difficulties. The "loving hearts," if that fine phrase is permitted here, both made his day-to-day life difficult and took from him the drive and great intellectual persistence that he needed in his work.

But what a lucky dog I was! I was so constituted that nothing took from me the drive and great intellectual persistence that I needed in my work.

Yes, I saw that now. And I saw something else. I saw the last moments, what am I saying, the last hours, of my departed sweetheart, lying in excrement, soddenness, and filth. And I had stood before this still living and sobbing corpse. And had stopped any man or woman from disturbing it.

No flights of feeling! Let us come back to reality! Walter's wife desired only that her husband finally discontinue his futile efforts. That he return as quickly as possible to the fleshpots of the civilized world along with her and the children, who could not be given a proper education at this remove from any sort of culture, indeed could barely be provided for decently. As a good, much-sought-after practitioner, he would always find opportunities for scientific work at home, would be able to relax at his microscope after his day of toil and trouble if he preferred that to playing bridge or having family members over or chatting with his wife about household matters or about how to find apparel that is both cheap and attractive. Intelligent, mature woman and faithful helpmeet that she was, she allowed him every freedom except that which he was now exercising, as she believed, to his family's undoing. But Walter, with all the love and tenderness he had toward his Alix, was not a man who gave in.

He turned a deaf ear. His wife's were deaf already. Thus it got to the point that the woman screamed raucously on the telephone and we all became unwilling witnesses to these petty squabbles.

Walter made it through his ten or twelve working hours day after day. Anyone who has spent a few months in C., whose climate is a sweaty, suffocating steam bath from which one never emerges and where dry laundry, a good night's sleep, adequate digestion, and a cool hour of leisure are things one knows only by hearsay, will understand what that means. Not without reason was it a penal colony.

I was glad I had already made the acquaintance of "red dog" on the

Mimosa. I took precautions now, I did whatever was necessary to take care of myself. But what could be achieved in the end? Anyone can guard against cold, with fur-lined coats and boots and hats (I am thinking of my father's stories). And if it becomes impossible to continue on the ice, one can crawl underneath, where the stinging snowstorms cannot reach. One digs tunnels beneath the surface and waits them out.

But here there is no protection from the heat and the extravagant humidity. There is only escape from it, to a cooler, drier climate. To the highlands, the mountains. Or into alcohol or morphine.

But one had only to observe a man like Walter for an hour to realize that anything of the kind was profoundly abhorrent to him. If he escaped, it was to the bosom of the church at worst. Every Sunday, wearing his white tropical uniform that the hospital nurses had washed and ironed for him, he went to the Mass held in the chapel of the old hospital, to return an hour and a half later, his linen suit with all the starch taken out of it and his red, haggard face dripping sweat, but inwardly fortified. A pious man who had remained true to the religion of his youth and would remain so to the end.

To what extent this faith sustained him in his inner conflicts was beyond my ken. He discussed this with me as little as I told him of my unremitting suffering, my never-ending thoughts of the poor child. Not until just before his death did he share his problems with me.

With God he was always at peace. He was easy to help. He would have been easy to help, I mean.

He was invariably friendly to me. He called me Dr. Letham and shook my hand when we met in the morning. But otherwise not a word of an intimate, personal nature was exchanged. It was not that he was too proud. He was much too self-effacing to bother someone else with his private affairs, even a lawbreaker such as myself, convicted for the murder of his wife without possibility of appeal. Nevertheless the rest of us were as well-informed as he was about his private affairs, in fact rather better in certain respects.

I said earlier that we learned more from the caterwauling of his wife, who often strained her voice to the limit because of her deafness, than might have suited the proud and reserved Walter. But things soon changed.

Our poor doctor was getting two or three calls a day from the start. The quiet of the workroom (normally interrupted by nothing worse than the sounds of the experimental animals) was broken by the ring of the telephone, which seemed particularly harsh in this context. Plenty of calls. But after a while his wife seemed to be answering his questions evasively. At first broadly and rhetorically, but then with only a stock "I don't know." Whether the doctor was inquiring after the health of his oldest boy or about whether his second-oldest daughter's dreary pruritic skin rash had gone away or whether the household money had been adequate over the last decade (all public-health officers think in decades) or how things were going in the hardware business that supported the dear wife's family back home – he received the same deadly, vacuous answer every time: *I don't know*. Although it had nothing to do with me, it filled me with a kind of horror, and when I saw the happy husband and father hurry back from the telephone booth to his lab table, outwardly melting in sweat, inwardly not heartened, as he had been after Sunday Mass, but distressingly drained and troubled, I privately compared his state of fulfilled love with my own of ill-fated love. His wife, that dear woman, had not even been able to resist answering the doctor's good-bye with "I don't know." He was agitated, in despair, he might have wanted to curse, to slam the door of the booth, but that gentleman was in control of himself in all situations. He closed the door quietly, said nothing, set about his work with gentle hands, and, it will not be believed, he submitted to this game many times a day with the most good-humored expression in the world. Instead of having the number changed, which could easily have been done from the head office, he always yielded to the shrill ringing of the telephone. He did not believe it was right to let his wife think he was not there. He preferred to acquiesce to her diabolical attempts to manipulate him. He tried to understand her. Not vice versa.

Or did he even think she was right? It was her belief that, in the interests of the family, a family that was going to wrack and ruin, anything was permitted, even required, in the face of his stubbornness. That was just what she believed, and people with unshakable beliefs always have the advantage.

Why had Walter brought his family here? Was he any better – that is to say, was he behaving more rationally than Monica's mother? Was it not madness, the whole thing? Walter's wife was someone of pure, more than that, of practical, rationality. And she was someone with lively female wishes and desires.

If she was a normal woman, then she expected a normal man in Walter. Had she not made enough sacrifices, and had she not always been told that this was absolutely the last one she would have to make?

Thus he listened patiently to her infernal "I don't know" and then went back to his work with silent dedication, to find for the thousandth time that yellow fever was a terrible disease, but its nature and its mode of transmission still entirely unknown.

XVI

Sometimes the chaplain paid us a visit in the late afternoon, bringing the news from the city; he would invite us finally to play a card game, puff-puff, if I understood correctly. He was very concerned about our health and state of mind, we not so much about his. We would listen to his talk with seeming raptness, but soon one and then another would edge away and go back to work. What choice did he have? He would take his leave in his quiet, polite, impenetrable way, the way that elderly priests have about them. He did not disturb us, for, what with the fruitless yet very hard work in the oppressively hot, indescribably humid laboratory reeking with every horror there is, a brief interruption was always welcome.

Another visitor sought out the doctor during these days, behaving with rather less delicacy. This was an agent, who called himself a general agent but was really only a subagent, of the various shipping companies that would berth a foundering tub like the *Mimosa* in the city of C. every so often. He was also the representative of some large North American life insurance companies and had made a not inconsiderable fortune through all sorts of more or less legal deals (with the criminals here or against them, needless to say).

The subagent had come on a business mission. He would not be deterred from entering the laboratory. Everyone knew him, must surely know him! He was fearless because he already survived Y.F. during a great wave of the epidemic three years earlier compared to which the current one was a trifle, and since that time had not traveled. For if one leaves the soil of the Y.F. site, one's immunity disappears and the whole farce can start all over again. But the dandified gentleman, decked out in a diamond stickpin, gold cuff links, and similar gewgaws, was protected from this danger. He was a knight in shining armor with a pith helmet, for he was exerting himself on behalf of a lady who had been slighted, threatened, who was in peril. And this lady was not a widow, her children were not orphans, it was Dr. Walter's wife herself who had sent him here, even if he denied it in his genteel way, as an emissary of reconciliation. With a palm branch in his beak, but a poisoned arrow concealed under his left wing, if I may put it that way. The palm branch was the greetings that the good man conveyed from the languishing wife and helpmeet. This was not a surprising piece of intelligence in view of the quarantine under which the husband had been kept for almost two months now and which would continue for an unforeseeable length of time. The business was soon settled, and Walter ushered the literally oily little gentleman out the door.

But, even behind the glass door of the laboratory, he shot his poisoned arrow. This was the insurance policy that the able subagent was formally canceling in the name of his company. Walter, prudent paterfamilias that he was, had taken out a policy providing his wife and children with fifty thousand American dollars in the event of his death, at particularly favorable, exceptionally low premium rates, as the subagent had ebulliently claimed.

So the current premium hasn't gone unpaid, has it? Of course not, acknowledged the subagent. All right, what then? We don't have a lot of time, said Walter with a trace of impatience. No wonder, when an experiment that was in progress had been temporarily halted and, if the moment was not seized, would have to be repeated the next day. The subagent bowed. He hadn't closed the lab door, he had a foot in it. He wasn't about to go, he was just getting started. The insurance company cannot assume this risk, he said as earnestly as a psalmist, gesturing through the corridor window at the courtyard of the building, where at that very moment a Y.F. corpse wrapped in a white sheet was being carried to the basement autopsy rooms.

Walter understood. But he said, No, I don't understand, I thought it was the company's business to assume the usual risk of a physician in an epidemic area and the terms included that. Yes, but just the usual risk and no more, replied the subagent. If someone goes tumbling over Niagara Falls in a leather kayak, my insurance company might possibly, possibly assume that risk, but it has to know about it *beforehand* and will set the premium accordingly high. Anything else would be commercial suicide and could not be expected of any business. The fact that you would be willfully and deliberately exposing yourself to the most dangerous contagion for months on end was not known to the company when, through me, it signed this document, he said grandly, indicating the bumf he had under his smelly armpit. "Fine! I'll guide myself accordingly," Walter replied, and bowed. The subagent finally had no choice but to leave. The guards in front of the hospital door greeted him with great respect and stood at attention, for he had spared no expense in order to be allowed into the quarantined research areas. He was a "pretty man," a half-breed, and like many of his race afflicted with social ambitions. What did we care about his beauty, his race, his ambition, his business? Walter's face was very somber nonetheless. But he said nothing and went back to his work.

XVII

I empathized with our collaborator Walter all the more easily because my own experiences along the same lines with my wife were still fresh in my mind. For it was at that very time that I was preoccupied with an absurd but nonetheless very intense interior monologue in part to do with my late wife and my old father, in part with the late little Portuguese girl. What would have become of these people if . . . Is there anyone unfamiliar with those annoying obsessions that will not loosen their grip on one's poor tormented heart and mind no matter what one does? So too are those cobweblike draperies known in the lands given to poesy as "gossamer" unwilling to let go of the hair of a person out walking, even in the strongest autumn storm, or of clothes whipped by autumn winds. They do not let go voluntarily. One has to use gentle force. But what kind of gentle force is there against terrible memories?

The good March's love and trust were only a mild consolation. If he had at least been able to do without any sort of requital, if he had left everything to me, if he had made things easy for himself instead of difficult – what might not have happened. As it was, however, all that happened was that I tried to bring it home to him for the thousandth time that I could not reciprocate his absurd feeling, now less than ever. And why, he asked naïvely. What response can you make to that? Only to stroke his hair and look away over his shoulder.

But for Walter, the love of his good wife, that exemplary normal woman and mother who wanted her husband to return to her and her children, was every bit as painful and crippling. Dispatching the pretty man, the subagent, was not her last attempt. She found a much more vulnerable spot than his material interests – total altruist that he was, other people were the only ones who ever got the benefit of his worldly goods. Money was just money for him. Of what percentage of the people of Europe, among whom money is absolutely worshipped as something holy in life, can that be said?

The telephone conversations were now becoming very brief. The lady indicated that she did not want to detain her lord and master, she was much too lowly, too small, too insignificant, much too much a domestic drudge to disturb her husband at his important, public-spirited, promising, earthshaking work. As cheap as this irony was, it wounded the doctor, both hurting his pride and damaging his feelings toward his wife. Nevertheless, though at first glance he seemed softhearted and considerate, he was someone of indomitable character who knew just what he wanted to do and pushed it as far as it would go.

As far as it would go? Or only as far as he was permitted? The wife, availing herself of almost diabolical means, was beginning to distract her husband from his crackbrained, time-consuming, life-endangering experiments. On this day, for example, she demanded, quite coolly and even with a kind of gay composure, her passport. Her passport? She had never had one. There was only one passport, the one issued in the names of Dr. Walter, his wife, Alix Rosamunde Gabriele Therese, and their five children. Yes, that was the document the wife wanted. She no longer threatened divorce, or suicide, she indicated that she and her (her!) children felt they could not cope with the grueling climate, though it was quite good enough for convicts, that she wanted to move abroad, go to her mother and her brother, who were carrying on, after a fashion, the old hardware business that had belonged to her father, now three years dead. He, her husband, shouldn't worry, he'd be kept posted and would now be able to finish his humanitarian researches undisturbed.

As may be imagined, the good doctor, cut to the quick, did not have a snappy comeback. This tone, so calm, so composed, so acutely calculating, contrasted utterly with his wife's usual impetuous manner, which was the only one he was hardened to. For the plan did not come from her own foolish brain but from the brain of the subagent, who knew more about human nature than the doctor had at first assumed. But the subagent was hardly mentioned, except when the wife casually let fall that the doctor need no longer be unduly concerned about his family's financial situation, the subagent had relieved her of the most pressing household worries, was taking care of everything for her and the children, for she herself was fully occupied with preparing for the move to London. And that was that. Bzzz – gone! The good Walter was so stunned that he fairly slumped (by the telephone) and then sat mutely in front of the microscope, his face grim. It was the microscope of recent manufacture, the one with twin eyepieces through which two people could observe and examine the same field of view at the same time. The brigadier general had brought it from Europe, and Walter had more than once used this splendid instrument to demonstrate to the good Carolus a beautiful (but uninteresting) bacillus specimen.

Now too the tall, gangling, rawboned Carolus went to Walter, gently took him by the shoulder, and leaned against it so he could see the field of view. But Walter could not bear being touched, or he was too apathetic to work. He stood up and left the microscope with the double eyepiece to Carolus, though Carolus had no clue about how to use it. But Carolus was more tactful than I would have given that "lummox" credit for. He did not ask and also restrained March from asking any questions of the poor husband and father, who did not compose himself until late in the evening, after he had played a match of puff-puff with the Reverend Amen and had lost in style. For his thoughts were elsewhere.

That poor martyr was going to be roasted over a slow flame. His time spent in the accursed telephone booth was probably as harrowing as

March's in the notorious steam rooms on the *Mimosa* where he had been locked to stew in his own juices as his reward for his true love. For now there was another phone call, this one of laconic brevity. We heard only the doctor's startled exclamation, and thereupon his wife's two words: I know. The good Walter, thunderstruck, had the receiver in his left hand; he had opened the door to the booth with the other and was gazing at us all. I know? What *did* the wife know? We looked away. We were ashamed for her. There could be only *one* secret that a wife whispers so confidently into her husband's ear – we had guessed it long ago. A *sweet* secret.

Now it was all as plain as day. An ultimatum. Either abandon the experiments and the research immediately, depart the epidemic-swept island with its calamitous climate, particularly so for expectant mothers of the white race, and return to temperate zones – or the consequences were unforeseeable. Unforeseeable? Actually not. One could foresee exactly what happened.

To leave his theater of activity with only the entirely negative results to date, which would not have taken up even as much space in the learned journals of general pathology as the results of the remarkable expedition of Georg Letham the elder to the North Pole had taken up in the learned journals of descriptive geography – to exit and leave the field of research to the second commission – that was one alternative. And the other? Was there another? Was there anything left untried?

Walter wandered restlessly about among the microscopes, the two incubators, the bottles and dishes of experimental material. He threw into disorder the rows of books that the excellent Carolus had now learned to keep in splendid order (only a tiny ear curette made of cream yellow horn protruded from an encyclopedic handbook of bacteriology).

He, Walter, opened the lab book, cast his eyes upon it; in his loose, untidy, flapping, broad-sleeved coat, he roamed about like a soul-sick priest among the cages of living animal material (only too merry, and in unbroken health), and it was very affecting when one evening he let a dog, one that had been barking at him particularly piteously that morning, out of the kennel and took it for a walk in the hospital garden, still waving his hands and carrying on a silent dialogue with his wife, or with fate. The dog barked, leaped, and rejoiced.

Pharmacist von F. had not been around for a long time. I can still see the dismayed grimace on Walter's face when the telephone jangled once again. But it was a false alarm. Pharmacist von F. was promising to come with an important piece of news, that evening if possible, otherwise the next morning.

It would be the next morning, and that was perhaps for the best. For that evening Walter was completely worn out (there must have been another of those infernal telephone calls, I don't know), he was deaf to reason and logic. He probably would have decided to break off the investigation and return to his family and to a bourgeois, orderly life, leaving us. After all, his wife had reproached him especially for choosing, of his own free will, or rather out of callousness, the society of "avowed murderers and bandits" over the "devoted warmth" of his "loving hearts." What won't people do for love?

XVIII

The irrepressible doctor and pharmacist von F. (for whom the quarantine rules seemed not to exist) appeared this time without his famous mosquito veils. But he could have dressed as Salome and not gotten a rise out of us. Even Carolus turned away in boredom, Walter listened with half an ear, and March only had eyes and ears for me. I alone, on my face the indulgent smile with which one submits to the harangue of a monomaniac, had time for the ancient gentleman's story. His report had chiefly to do with himself. Like many very old people, he assumed that everyone else was vastly interested in his private affairs. Walter was listening for the telephone, which today was noticeably quiet, Carolus was digging the remnants of some fruit from between his incisors with a toothpick whittled from a match and regarding the stuff he brought out with tender attention (which, God knows, would have been better applied elsewhere). The atmosphere was thus not promising for the old pharmacist. But there he sat, reciting his pensum.

If one had been able to muster a certain sympathy, it might even have been worth the quarter of an hour. For he was making his will before us, just as if we had been four witnesses. The last will and testament of a humanitarian medicine man grown old and yellow in the tropics who was, regrettably, a mediocrity, and had long since been overtaken by the modern era. He had seen much; his father and grandfather, long-dead doctors who had left various writings (as he told us), had seen still more.

Each son in this family of doctors had stood by his old and infirm father in his final illness, had prepared the author of his days for the coming end – only pharmacist von F., whose children had other worries, had had to make a self-diagnosis (chronic renal atrophy and arteriosclerosis). But he was fortunately free of sentimentality. His composure in the face of his demise, which he expected in about three or four months (he was not mistaken), won me over. I must admit that I (green-eyed as I am) envied the children of this comical old tropicalized humanitarian – they were lucky to have such a father. They did not understand him. And did we? I took his mosquito eggs, which this time, to be on the safe side, he had packed on cotton in a pillbox edged in gold foil, and weighed the featherlight thing in my hand.

If only we had been able to understand each other! There was a clinical tradition in his family. His observations, at least those concerning the life history of different kinds of mosquitoes, had all the precision to be expected of a modern natural scientist. He carefully distinguished his mosquitoes, the Y.F. mosquitoes, *Stegomyia fasciata*, from the *Anopheles* mosquitoes, the well-known carriers of malaria. He knew how these sat, how those jiggled their hind legs, and so forth. The two subspecies also deposited their eggs in very different places. Such keenness, such minuteness of observation, brought to bear out of what must have been pure idealism, on top of the old man's professional activity, so difficult to carry on here in the tropics!

Touching in his senile naïveté, he inquired about the fate of the first mosquito eggs. At that time I knew only about the one insect that had escaped in Monica's room and had bitten her. Possibly it was the same one that had later attacked the tavern owner and drunk his sweet blood. If he had then fallen ill with Y.F., the pharmacist's absurd theory would have been proven. Yes, "if"! It would have been a giant step forward. But was not. Out of curiosity I asked him about it. He didn't know a thing. We even pursued the matter, thorough as we were, and telephoned down to the city. The tavern owner was healthy and fit, apart from some scratches and superficial wounds that he had received from his cronies in a scuffle three days before. So it was a dead end. The old fool's bleak face, with the stamp of death already upon it, was something to see.

All that was left of his first lot of mosquitoes was the mortal remains floating in an oily liquid in the gauze-covered glass vessel. Particles of the powdered sugar that had served as food for them were still sticking to the walls – and at the bottom was the residue of the chloroform that fun-loving old Carolus had used to send them to the better Kingdom Come of God's dear creatures.

I must say that even the slightest reminder of the Portuguese girl (the bite from the mosquito and her sunny, mischievous, courageous nature) still upset me every time. I had not recovered from this love. I still felt it. And thus it was difficult for me to resist the pleading eyes of the old man, who wanted his fondest wish fulfilled before he died. "At least have the insects feed on the patients, and then put them under the microscope. Could it do any harm?" he asked. The memory of the Portuguese girl had put me in a tender frame of mind.

But my response was not what the expression on my face had led him to expect. "Why haven't you let yourself be bitten by the *Stegomyia*?"

"Haven't I tried often enough? Unfortunately I didn't think of it until I was already too old. What can I do, they don't like my blood, and I think such experiments are against our religion, too . . ."

As he uttered the word "experiments," a strange association of ideas flashed through my mind. I had always told myself that he did not understand us. But then again we did not understand him, either. For us, what he said was nothing but unproven and unprovable twaddle, and he in turn, that old practitioner of direct observation, had no clue about our statistical findings on the transmission of the disease, those three peculiarities that old Carolus had worked out, the sparklike leaps . . . "Sparklike"? What does that mean? Get rid of it! And "leaps"? "Flights"? Can this metaphorical language capture the essence of a natural phenomenon? I am a man of reliable memory, and the ironic phrase I had used, "On the wings of an angel," came back to me. What was that again? Yes, no, it was not on the wings of an angel, but very likely on the wings of a mosquito that the disease might, come on now, "might"? – *must* be transmitted from a sufferer to a healthy person, and if the tavern owner had *not* been infected a thousand times by the bite of a mosquito, how many things might not explain a negative? Had the tavern owner had Y.F. before? Might he be immune? I asked pharmacist von F. But I did not wait for his answer. I did not want to know. I wanted to shed some light on the problem by doing experiments.

Stop dissecting! Start doing experiments! I pulled him by the sleeve of his thin, blue silk jacket, beneath which I felt the coarse weave of his net undershirt, to the worktable where Carolus and Walter were once more diligently but fruitlessly examining the same field of view together, each at one of the lenses, and said quietly to my comrades: What Herr von F. suggests might tally with our observations after all. The illness might be transmitted by something that flies through the air. Across a courtyard, perhaps even from the east coast of one continent to the west coast of another that has the same warm and humid tropical climate, twenty-five to thirty degrees centigrade, neither the north, nor the desert, nor Europe. That addresses point one.

And if nurses and washerwomen and so forth remain free of the disease despite the unappetizing things they handle – and that was your point two, Herr Brigadier General – that proves that the clothes and the excretions of the ill don't contain the invisible virus. Or if they do, then in an inactive form.

And if, point three, the cases come in waves, that might mean that the invisible virus matures in the body of a mosquito, as is known in other epidemic diseases, specifically malaria and hookworm.

This was very simple. Hence difficult to believe. The gentlemen would have laughed in someone else's face. Not in mine.

I have already related, have I not, how beneficent Mother Nature gave me a healthy dose of logicality to make up for goodness, cheerfulness, and beauty, and for a good, warm heart with human feelings. But it would have done me no good had I not also received the gift of the ability to awaken trust. Among ill and healthy alike. As now.

XIX

The gentlemen, who had just been joined by the chaplain with his deck of cards for a very ill-timed session of games and chitchat, looked at me with surprise and said nothing. I continued: "What I have said is just theory. It needs to be proven."

"What? Proven? How?" asked the foolish Carolus.

"What a question. With experiments, of course!"

"But haven't we already done enough experiments? Monkeys, rabbits, guinea pigs, dogs, rats, what else is there?"

"What else? People!"

"People?!"

Little March, who evidently took this remark for a joke, gave a silly laugh. I found this very unpleasant. The other gentlemen were on the point of going off to consider the matter by themselves. If that happened, I would have to drop my plan. This was impossible for me. I was, I felt at that moment with certainty (but not too much shock), just as fanatical, as blinkered, as credulous as old von F. was. I had gotten hold of something. I was not about to let it go of it: this clue was worth making an effort. It was mine, it was *my private war*, as they say, or, expressed less grandly, my job to do.

I found their weak spots. First Carolus. "Animals in nature are certainly immune to Y.F. But people aren't. So sooner or later, any commission, no matter what its nationality, is going to have to do human experiments. As you know, Herr Brigadier General, the American mission is disembarking even now. It's government-supported, has unlimited funds. We have to expect that its members, imbued with true patriotism, are ready (not to put too fine a point on it) for anything!"

Carolus was less thick-skinned than I had expected. "If that's all it is" (namely?) "I'm prepared to let myself be infected by one or two bites from *Stegomyia* mosquitoes. If the theory is right, we'll be accepting the risks of success and will obtain a positive result. If the theory is wrong, it's a mosquito bite, and let's not waste a lot of words over it." Well roared, lion. You'll get your medal on your scrawny hero's chest, a sword-and-enema-syringe war decoration on a golden breast band. That takes care of *him*!

"But this is impossible, gentlemen!" croaked the servant of God with the blue "Amen" tattoo on his throat, an earnest look on his face. "Think a minute! You've seen what this disease is. The death rate is forty-five percent to . . ."

"Oh, isn't that old news?" said Carolus irritably. Here *he* was the expert.

Pharmacist von F. sat toying with his matchbox like an old abbé with a snuff tin. His eyes moved in bewilderment from one person to another; he apparently understood nothing. "Be that as it may," said the man of God emphatically, and no one could mistake his tone of voice, except March, who was still grinning, the idiot, "be that as it may, I can only regard it as a sin, for one may not do experiments on living human beings, one may not interfere with Divine Providence."

"Where in the Gospel is that forbidden?" I asked. And when he made no reply – doing up, then undoing, the worn cloth-covered buttons of his cassock, which was either gray with dust or green with age (it varied between the two) – Walter spoke, his words like a shot from a pistol:

"I'm in."

"'I'?" I repeated thoughtfully. "*We* don't want to carry out this experiment as individuals, nor can we. Either we all agree or it won't be done."

"Dr. Walter," said the chaplain, "I'm not speaking on my own behalf. If, with my insignificant life, I can render a service to science and to the general welfare of humankind, I'm ready to do my part. I suggest that you restrict yourselves to those among us who have no dependents, no family, no obligations. I'm alone in the world. The families of the two of you at home" (he indicated March and me) "have no expectation that you'll ever return [?]. But you, Dr. Walter, have a wife and five children here, down in the old city. What would be permitted for the rest of us, perhaps even a moral imperative under a charitable interpretation of Holy Scripture, if that would leave your family helpless after your death, for you it would be . . ."

"One, two, three, March, you, and me, that's not enough," I interrupted shortly. "We'll never wind this up if we start getting into personal matters. I propose that each of the six of us take a match. If he wants to be in, he'll toss it just as it is into this marmalade jar where the dead *Stegomyias* are floating in sugar water and chloroform. But if he has any reason to exclude himself, then he'll tear – no, he'll *snap* the top of the match off and toss the rest into the jar. The vote will be secret. Here are the matches, one, two, three, four, five, six. There's the jar in the corner. If all five matches (six, including mine) aren't intact, we'll drop the whole thing; unanimity is required. Each of us must speak for all of us. All of us must speak for each of us. Very simple."

"Very simple," echoed the steadfast March.

At that moment the telephone rang. It was the time when the dear wife usually called. "Would one of you be so kind," said that gentleman Walter, his voice trembling with emotion, "as to tell my wife that I can't come just now and that I'll call without fail very early tomorrow?"

"With pleasure," Carolus said. He proceeded to the telephone booth, closing the door behind him. Very soon the chirping of the hard-of-hearing wife, the human annunciator, came to us, her usual "What? Eh? What?" low in the distance, but clearly discerned. But Carolus was not one to lose his calm. Someone who is able to do statistical studies of a few hundred dog-tired felons by the light of an acetylene lamp on a ship en route does not lose patience too quickly. He nodded his long yellow head like a bent fire lily (also called Turk's cap), but by the time he left the telephone booth he had fixed everything.

It was evening, and the lights went out as they often did.

"Wonderful," I said, "a sign from fate! May it always smile upon us. Now each of us can vote without being seen by the others. Just one thing. These matches don't all have the same weight. My vote will be cast by a man sentenced to lifelong hard labor for the murder of his wife, that of my comrade March will be cast by someone who cut down his friend as one butchers a rabbit. Why mention it? I only want to anticipate this argument so that no one makes it against us later. We're playing for keeps. Ethical scruples can be raised now, there's still time, but not later."

In the marmalade jar were – five matches, all with their russet heads. Not six? Was the decision not unanimous? Of course it was. That ninny March had thrown in his lighter instead of his match and was now fishing it out, a smirk on his good-natured face. To proclaim his willingness, he had tossed not just a match but an entire lighter into the ballot box!

I could not deny myself the pleasure of giving him a good box on the ear out of sheer joy (I was as though inebriated and did not come to my senses until later) – I believe the only one I have ever given anyone in my quadragenarian's life.

XX

I have no wish to make our decision seem more momentous than it was. Physicians have experimented on human beings from time to time for as long as medical science has existed. It has not been exactly the rule, but by no means the exception, either, that physicians have ventured to experiment on *themselves*. We were not the first and will certainly not have been the last. Whether this undertaking would involve murder (voluntary manslaughter?) or suicide in legal terms was our (my) ultimate worry.

We were prepared for difficulties. But only for difficulties, not for something that was plain unachievable. Our task did not require genius. Only courage. Method. Discipline. Were these too much to expect from the six of us?

Unfortunately they were. The initial obstacles came from the man of whom I would least have expected such a thing. From old Dr. von F. His mission and his duty coincided, and yet he shirked them. He could have perished honorably for his idea, but he preferred to wait out the final consequences of his chronic geriatric disorder and drink the cup of life to the dregs. He did not have courage, nor did he abide by the method, nor yet did he evince discipline. I said that he had appeared to me to be free of emotionalism. But the sentimental tears that now flowed down his sunken, leathery cheeks set me straight on that score. Pasteur certainly did not cry before his experiments. But let the old imbecile von F. have his effusion, we were in his debt for the crucial hint.

Of greater importance was another point. It goes without saying that absolute secrecy had to be maintained as far as the outside world was concerned. The fact is that the average person, burdened by preconceived ideas, responds to such *experimenta crucis*, as science calls them, with ethical scruples. Further, financial considerations (such as the matter of the insurance) were involved; opposition from the high authorities was to be feared. Now that we were really going to poke our noses into the yellow plague, no one needed the goodwill of the gentlemen in the bowels of the bureaucracy as much as we did.

So were we not our own masters? Of course we were. But our experiments on ourselves were only the start – we all understood that. A problem like this one was not going to be solved by a series of experiments on only six specimens of *Homo sapiens*. Sooner or later we would have to have recourse to other "human material," as one must bluntly call it, and if the voluntary decision to give up one's life on the altar of science should perhaps become something not entirely voluntary or clear-cut in one case or another, then the issue of murder would become more salient. What could happen to us? To me not much, certainly. Far more to our work, which we wished to finish, had to finish. March and I, individuals lost to civil society, admittedly had nothing to fear, for the threat of disciplinary action could not intimidate us. But the other four? One of them was a man of the highest social position whose rank of general meant that he had to bear responsibility for everything, a second was the husband of a faithful, unprovided-for wife and the father of five, humane, a gentleman, and a Christian, the third was a man of the cloth with old-time qualms of conscience and an inadequate understanding of the ethics of bacteriology, and the last was the old pharmacist von F.

I had called him a humanitarian. And until then he may always have been one – at least nothing to the contrary was known. But I had not reckoned on his vanity. And I had given far too little consideration to the fact that the experiment we all faced was one he could have done on himself long ago, while his noble hidalgo blood was still fresh and sweet and would have been pure nectar to the hungry *Stegomyia* mosquitoes. He had not done it then because his fear of being infected had been even greater than his vanity and his desire to make the name von F. world-famous. We will not speak of his humanity. For he never put it to the test. And whether one believes it or finds it fantastic, the very next morning after the matchstick ballot, this man at the mercy of death from a chronic incurable illness fought tooth and nail against our plan to include him in our series of experiments.

I could have gotten over it. Even five is a good number to start with. But the accursed man could not manage to keep his triumph to himself – that he had at last been taken seriously. While his mosquito eggs were still hatching in the incubator and we were racking our brains behind closed doors and windows about the proper way to set up an insectarium for them, and while the deeply distressed but resolute Walter was evading his wife's calls under always novel but ever more implausible pretexts, that old blockhead von F. had long since spilled the beans about our plan down in C. Walter found out from his wife that his intention was known. He, and we too, had to listen to the pregnant wife threaten in utter despair to throw herself and her children out the window and onto the street. What choice did he have? He swore to her by all the saints that it was all mad talk on the part of the pharmacist. That we had wanted to indulge the old sick fool von F. during his last days, but had not taken his fantasies seriously for a minute, and as proof he proposed to meet with her in three days if she found the courage to get near him. Yes! Was she thrilled! She'd love to, that dear, faithful wife! He'd help her in making the long-planned move from C. She'd finally be allowed to take the children and leave this awful place. He suppressed his sighs, sketched out the travel plans with seeming coolness. And the wife was happy, overjoyed to hear this. At bottom she expected that she would be able to take her husband with her when the time came. She had every confidence in the power of her love.

So then one day, after a long private talk with Carolus, the good Walter disinfected himself from head to toe and, resplendent as a bridegroom, freshly pressed and bemedaled, but reeking of cresol instead of eau de cologne, he tried to leave us, to hie to the waiting arms of his yearning wife. For the time being the children would not come into contact with him, until he had proven to be free of infection.

How long should he wait to press his father's kiss to their brows? Not a living soul in the inhabited world knew. Each did what he felt he could accept responsibility for, and it was left, how shall I say, to the divine grace of God or to chance.

The good Walter did not promise us that he would be back punctually in a week's time (the wife had already bargained the three days originally granted up to that much). He had never been a man of particularly many words.

We expected that the insects would have pupated and matured in six to eight days (though it took longer) and be ready to feed on the blood of the Y.F. patients and hungry enough to bite five people after that. That is: since each of us could be used only once in the important experiment, others would have to be present to carry out the necessary observations, tests, and examinations, record the findings, and so on. So at the last minute, while Walter was already looking impatiently out the window at the sea, the ship, and the islands, a plan was devised whereby first March and I would deliver ourselves over to the experiments while Carolus and Walter made their observations of us and took charge of our care. The chaplain was conceived as a reserve. He would step in either as an experimental subject or as a record keeper. But he could not replace even a Carolus, never mind a Walter.

What I am going to say will sound brutal and repugnant. But I cannot express it otherwise than comports with the facts. Our plans were unfortunately disturbed once more by the foolish, garrulous pharmacist, who did not even understand what damage he had done. We suggested to him – Carolus, that is, with the gentlest, mildest face in the world, while the rest of us shrugged indifferently and looked down – that upon further consideration we had thought better of our decision to do the experiments. So he was released from his promise. Go in peace! Give us your blessing and clear out! But the dismayed face of the old fool when he heard the bad news was something to see. He had been so sure we would stick to our guns and make his name known the world over.

Walter stood up at last, after he had asked March to get one of the experimental dogs out of its cage, the same one that he had walked. He wanted to take it to his children. What a kind heart! Pharmacist von F. smiled, but he did not go. Pharmacist von F. stayed. We looked askance at him, but he was not ashamed of his intrusiveness. He even became a pest. If there was anything good about it, it was that at least he was able to tell us about his latest, most exhaustive observations of the life history of the insect under suspicion. If these had been no more reliable than his self-control and discretion, they would have been unusable. However, it became apparent that a weak personality and a vain and craven character have no bearing on the precision, fidelity, and subtlety of one's observations of nature. We checked his statements about the biology of the *Stegomyia* mosquito insofar as we were able. Almost all were dead right.

We passed the time with these things. We had to wait for Walter. He was coming back. Of that we were all certain, without having said a word.

He needed us, we him.

SIX

I

Needless to say, I slept very little during this period. Our plans were on my mind constantly. If I dozed off now and then, I was awakened by ideas about the best design for our experiments. It was clear that the stakes were as high as they could be. A lot of things could go wrong. Everything might. But one thing was certain: nothing could be allowed to go wrong due to our own carelessness or absence of mind. Yet only someone who has carried through from start to finish an undertaking of this or a similar kind knows how difficult it is to guard against mistakes, how nearly hopeless it is to try to foresee all foreseeable problems while there is still time to prevent them.

So many ideas seem attractive at first! Here's the solution. Thus and such is the way to do it. This is how I'll set things up, there's no other way. A word to comrades and collaborators and my plan will seem plausible to them. But only a few minutes later doubts have appeared in my own mind. One has misgivings. One considers. Hesitates. Vacillates. Every thinking person is a bit of a Hamlet when it comes to action.

One is uncertain – and uncertainty is the only thing forbidden to a man with a task he must carry out. And may one take counsel? Give someone else a word of advice? Of course! Share responsibility? Gladly! But only Walter would do for that. Herr Statistics could be counted on for nothing but passive industry. A hundred percent conscientiousness. Not even one percent initiative.

Was it possible that I thought far too highly of Walter? Not that I would have doubted his spirit of sacrifice, his heroism, whatever one wants to call it. We were in accord on that score. No one had doubts about anyone else. No one suspected anyone else of wanting to get a better deal, meaning a safe experiment. (There have been, there were, such experiments!) And what was better, when you came down to it? Was it worse to be the first subjects, or the last, who would have to witness the suffering and possible death of the earlier ones? The risk borne by a given individual depended on his physical condition, his resistance to the Y.F. virus, but who could calculate that in advance?

Details of much greater importance had to be worked out. The longer and more thoroughly I considered the business during those sleepless nights, examining it from every angle, the more complicated the edifice of our theory became. Here I was always alone. It was no easy matter, and I breathed a sigh of relief when I finally had a working plan that seemed practicable, with the advantage (or disadvantage, depending on one's point of view) that it started simple and moved toward complexity – that the problems still to be solved increased in number with each increase in certain knowledge. "There is a direct relationship between *Stegomyia* mosquitoes and the transmission of Y.F. from person to person": this theory, which I will call Axiom I, was the beginning, the foundation, the first step.

But can we imperfect human beings accomplish anything of which it can be said, "This is how it is. This is how it will remain. All questions have been answered. All mysteries revealed" – even if we have put our very lives into it?

We still had not lifted a finger.

We all needed a rest after the long series of experiments with negative results. When we (March and I) came into contact with deportees, as we occasionally did, and compared the state of our health with theirs, we had to say that one was as bad as the other. Whether one did horrible, grinding backwoods labor or soulless office work in the penal administration – or whether one spent one's time in the sultry laboratory areas and the underground autopsy room as we did, the result was much the same: sunken cheeks, severe weight loss, general physical deterioration, extreme irritability provoked by the most ridiculous things. Fortunately we needed only a word from Walter to soothe us. At the moment we were frankly very much in need of one.

We were tormented by thirst almost constantly and were never really hungry. We were tired when we woke up in the morning and exhausted, physically wretched, night after night. Often we were in a state of despair so great that sleep was impossible.

I had no clue how the other deportees were coping. What could I do? I could only be glad that I did not have to live and die with them.

Though it was not yet clear that in the end I would not be facing death among them after all. But the decision was not ours to make.

This could only be a matter of indifference to me. What mattered was that Walter return, that I and my mainstay, my assistant March, remain fit, and that Carolus, persevering in his very pedantry and as patient as an ox turning a mill wheel, fortify himself sufficiently that he would be equal to the moral and physical demands of the coming time.

Walter had left on the *Mimosa* with his wife, to accompany her to a nearby island that was free of Y.F. In his absence Carolus had ordered that the laboratory areas be open for only one hour every day. That was enough to permit us to follow the biological and anatomical development of the *Stegomyia* mosquito, as we wished to do and were required to do.

We took specimens at various stages of larval development out of the jars, killed them with alcohol, cold, heat, steam, sulfur vapor, petroleum, or chloroform (testing all these methods systematically, in order to have guidelines for mosquito eradication in the future), dissected them, prepared slide after slide. We were not supposed to be spending more than a full hour a day on this preliminary work. We had set ourselves this rule, but we could not abide by it for even a single day.

Otherwise we spent all our time resting. We received permission to visit the nuns' little jewel box of a garden, which was kept locked, and we strolled in the shade of the trees there; in the late evening hours and very early in the morning, this was truly restorative. The hour was precisely specified so that we would have no contact with the nuns who might be there in their leisure time.

The exotic botanical luxuriance of this oasis is beyond description. But we were not in the mood for it. Certainly I was not, although formerly I had taken the greatest delight in the beauty and supreme power of nature. Just as little could one ask a passionate gambler, while the roulette ball was rolling, to appreciate the grandeur of *Hamlet* or the wisdom of the Gospel or even, to cite something closer to hand, the fragrance of the flower gardens of the Riviera. I had no eyes for it, and when March effused like a poet, pointing out this flower, that star, these moths, or those clouds, I let him talk and listened to him with the same attention that I might have paid to the twittering of a little bird. In my mind I was composing a scientific description of the most important features of the *Stegomyia* mosquito. I arrived at the following picture.

As Carolus had determined from his books, the insect, whose scientific name is *Stegomyia calopus* or *Stegomyia fasciata*, belongs to a family of mosquitoes, the Culicidae. (They have families and clans, just as we do!) It is a graceful, lively insect of brown to blackish brown color punctuated by conspicuous white parts. Particularly characteristic are the vivid lyre-shaped markings on the thorax and the ribbonlike stripes on the long, thin, spidery, many-segmented legs. The first two segments next to the body are a uniform black, but the next segments have white stripes. This very important feature, both necessary and sufficient for the insect's identification, is clearest on the last of the three pairs of legs. And this remarkable last pair of legs vibrates continuously in the air while the mosquito is sitting. Thus the *Stegomyia* sits on only four of its six legs. The rings around the mosquito's abdomen have silvery bars and spots. The wings are folded one atop the other when the mosquito sits. They are somewhat shorter than the body. They iridesce in all the colors of the spectrum. The male is distinguished from the female by a kind of mustache. Allegedly (according to von F.) only the female animal bites, not the male. It can be somewhat over two millimeters long; counting the long legs, about five millimeters. When the insects pass from the pupa stage to the adult stage, they are immediately fertilized.

The geographic region inhabited by this family of mosquitoes lies principally between the tropics, but it extends farther. The mosquito is found in Japan and East Africa.

The studies that the good Carolus had undertaken on the *Mimosa*, with his little flags and pins, to establish the geographic extent of the epidemic proved not to be as entirely useless as I had assumed. But he was off the mark in one respect: the disease Y.F. did not appear wherever there were mosquitoes.

As against the converse: there were always mosquitoes where the disease appeared. These facts, of course, supported the theory of pharmacist von F., our Axiom I, but that in itself would never have sufficed even to achieve scientific probability.

Experiments were needed in order to get to the bottom of the matter. The initial difficulties were as follows. A fresh case of Y.F. had to be there when the insects hatched. That was the first thing. And Walter had to be back, for we could not carry out our plans without him.

He had intended to be back in four to eight days. He was not. The steamers operated according to demand. We had already calculated the most unfavorable schedule. And soon my nights were spent thinking about what would become of our hopes and plans without him.

No one could give me any help or advice. I was very surly toward March, who irritated me terribly with his silent tendernesses and ill-timed attempts to comfort me. Toward Carolus I behaved no differently than I had on the ship, which astonished him greatly. The chaplain kept me company, which, despite the boredom that the good father spread about him, I tolerated better than I had expected. Associating with him was like eating soup that has gotten cold. His best years were behind him. But that very fact made him more bearable than someone like March, who boiled and stewed as though over an open flame.

II

The chaplain had conceived a confidence in me. Evidently he wished to impart one to me. But if I had had the patience on the *Mimosa* to let the good March "sing his song," I was not capable now of playing the father confessor to the father confessor. I did not say no straight out, but I put him off until quieter times. What a muddle! I, a murderer, a doubter, an atheist, and an anarchist, I was going to be the mainstay of a comparatively unsicklied-o'er man like March and the confessor of a morally elevated priest dedicatedly fulfilling his samaritanly offices in a Y.F. hospital! And was going to be sharing the intellectual stewardship of important experiments on human beings with a sentimentalist, a man who was high-minded but softhearted, with Walter. Walter finally returned, looking much more frail and miserable than when he had left. But you had to hand him one thing – and I realized that I had begun to hold him in awe because of it; I had not thought too highly of him. In four words: he was a man.

He kept his counsel. Only little signs betrayed the extent of his suffering and the reason for its persistence. The telephone had only to emit its first shrill rings and Walter would tremble like an aspen leaf. And yet his dear wife was many miles away on a "lonely island," in the words of the song, an isle without a telephone connection. Only a telegraph line brought her to him.

He was wearing his wedding ring again. Presumably he had made up with his wife and gotten her to promise to believe him when, probably for the first time in his life, he lied. For she would never have let him go if she had suspected that he would return with the same resolve as when he had left our laboratory: not to budge from here until our protocol, which I systematically laid out for him within the first hour, had been carried out from beginning to end, on human beings. On us. And on him. But there was no hint of anything personal from him; it was not until much later that I got a glimpse of his thoughts. How beautiful his marriage had been, how difficult. Walter was at the service of humanity. His wife and children were deprived of his all-embracing love – but he was giving his all!

He wanted to settle his financial affairs before the experiments began, that is, on the morning of his arrival. He sat down with Carolus at a laboratory table by the window that overlooked the harbor and the ship on which he had returned at daybreak. It was not the *Mimosa*, but some other tub. The *Mimosa* was en route to Europe to fetch another batch of deportees to these blissful shores.

Carolus showed Walter the slides of the anatomy of the mosquito, particularly some nicely stained tissue sections of the insect's biting apparatus, proboscis, and salivary glands, but Walter's mind was elsewhere. All things considered, how the lovely bug's mouth parts and biting apparatus were put together was somewhat beside the point at the moment. These were matters of secondary importance – we knew mosquitoes could bite! So down to business!

This time it was Carolus, animated by a lively intellectual curiosity, who urged haste, and Walter, the real scientist, who was still hesitating.

Scientific work is a joy the depth of which can be compared only to love (not to being loved!). I, Georg Letham, have known both in my life, and when I say this I am speaking the truth.

But why all the rigmarole about the delights of intellectual curiosity and its disappointments? I could more easily make this vivid with an illustration, by describing, say, what an isolated proboscis looks like under fifty times magnification, and the remarkable fluid that seeps out of the insect's ruptured tissues instead of red blood. But no matter. Like the joy of love, the joy of research, whether primitive or brilliant, must be experienced to be understood.

Even such a phlegmatic person as Carolus, grown old and sallow at his desk and among his boxes of paper slips, was fired up now that he saw before him a promising series of experiments. So why not Walter, the born experimenter? Because he was weighed down by financial worries. Worries about his family. The "loving hearts" needed money, and it was short.

His earnings were limited. His expenses were not. He looked ahead. With a heavy heart. He considered the experiment on himself, and though he was not a trained statistician or a pessimist, he was able to say that the chances of death were greater than the chances of life. He believed in our Axiom I. He hoped, finally, as does everyone who is still alive and breathing and enjoying the sunshine. But in his eyes it would have been a crime to leave his family without bread.

Carolus was very rich, perhaps a millionaire. Personally he was without wants. His children were more than generously provided for, his relatives were entitled to the most sanguine expectations. His financial situation was truly excellent, to go by his bank statements. For he had still not spent a penny on himself here, and his stocks had been going up. He was in the chips.

Walter was anything but. His father, the discharged war hero and retired lieutenant general, lived on his high officer's pension, but spent half again as much as he took in annually and from one year to the next got involved in riskier business deals, racing bets, short selling with unpaid shares and other obscure financial affairs, which the son did not find out about until they had fallen through, as unfortunately they usually did. Warnings by letter or telegram were no use. The father did not want advice, and it came much too late, anyway.

And Walter, if he should leave this house of Y.F. on the hill overlooking the harbor of C. feet first instead of alive, was going to be entrusting his widow and five (or six!) young children to the care of this father? No. Relations with his wife's family were no better, in fact were more uncertain still, since to the lack of money and property was joined the family's dislike of Frau Walter, who had married her husband against their wishes. They had even considered it a crime that she had followed him to the tropics with her children. And was her family not correct, from their standpoint? And then the child on the way, too! Was that all? No! On top of everything else the cancellation of the insurance, or rather the subagent's proposal that the agreement with the company be renewed only under quite different, more unfavorable terms: Walter's premium would be twice as much from now on, though he had been hard-pressed to squeeze the old one out of his earnings as it was, and to make matters worse, there was a very complicated determination of a "damage event" or whatever the insurance term is. Should he sign the new policy? Or let everything stay as in the old one? In that case the current situation would not be covered.

This was the reason Walter looked so miserable, and not the moist, unhealthy swamp climate and the wretched living conditions that he and his family, as he reported, had encountered on the delightful mountain island, allegedly so hygienic. It was money worries and nothing else.

He had come to an understanding with his wife that, if the climate did not agree with her and the children, she would go farther south, to Rio de Janeiro, to a famous hotel at an altitude guaranteed safe from mosquitoes. And he would follow her there. Yes, but when? How? Time! Time! Time! Rio de Janeiro was seven days away.

Money, money, money. Even before he left, Walter had gone to Carolus and asked for a loan. Carolus had hesitated, but had then come across without resistance. In the meantime the first of the month had arrived, their payday. Both Walter and Carolus drew their salaries at the same time. Carolus not only happily pocketed the large-denomination banknotes in which he received his high salary, but he also took the small-denomination banknotes of Walter's monthly earnings without much question. He had the nerve to accept repayment of a debt that Walter, like a gentleman, had decently offered him despite his family's distress. Making the offer was hardly the same as wanting it to be accepted! Didn't Carolus have eyes? Actually, he did. He was not the lummox I had taken him for.

He was a man like any other, to use that banal truism. Carolus wanted to risk his *life* for science, humanity, the glory of the fatherland. Not his ducats.

Such was our frame of mind as we embarked on our first experiments on the afternoon after Walter's arrival.

III

The first experiment was to begin in the late afternoon. Conveniently, a fresh case in the first stage of the disease had just been admitted. Our failure to settle all the details in our first meeting with Walter after his time away came home to roost.

Should the glass jar of young mosquitoes be taken up to the sickrooms? Or should the patients be secretly brought down to the laboratory?

How would we manage to get the mosquitoes to feed properly to begin with? And how would we induce them to bite a second time immediately thereafter (or later)?

Would it be best to do the transmission experiment immediately on No. 1 (March) and No. 2 (me), or should we immediately differentiate? That is, should we keep the experimental design unchanged until the first positive result was achieved, or modify it at once? For example, not have me bitten until the second or third day? If we had had at our disposal hecatombs of experimental subjects, a few hundred rabbits, perhaps, or thousands of mice or rats, we would not have had to work out the experiments ahead of time to the last detail. As it was, however, we couldn't be too careful, and every contingency had to be thoroughly pondered before we dared to do even one experiment.

It seems only natural that everyone should have been uneasy. But I wonder if the feeling that filled us should be characterized as *anxiety* in the ordinary sense. We all wanted to do the experiment, after all, and as far as I myself am concerned, I must say that my first bright moments since the demise of the beloved M. came when I was climbing the stairs to the sickroom, the jars of young mosquitoes in my arms, followed by my friend. Were these moments "bright" because I was not No. 1 and still had a grace period ahead of me? At that time I was still as though in a delirium. Later on it was different.

Walter was not the Walter I had known. Any little thing could throw him off balance.

And was it more than a little thing, was it anything but a trifle as compared with our great plans, when there was conflict with the resident? The young physician had returned, had dutifully assumed responsibility for the patients. He worked hard and wanted his rest at night, his comfortable mattress. But, as I said, the brigadier general and Walter were now living in his official apartment, which he had equipped as cozily as any petty bourgeois with covers, pillows, photos on the wall, a twee lamp with a silk shade on the night table, a fan, and even mosquito netting around his bed and over the window. Now he had returned to find his nest occupied by other guests. He had been given makeshift accommodations elsewhere. The matron, a sanctimonious, combative, but very capable person, had done all she could to satisfy the young, spoiled, handsome, and not even entirely incapable physician, whose work in the epidemic hospital was not the easiest. But could anything really be done? Everyone had to be patient, and a few polite words from Walter might perhaps have done wonders. But Walter, when the resident had visited his former abode and tried to take some articles for himself, books, the fan, the lamp, writing materials, and so forth, had abruptly lit into him. Yet it was *he* who was the guest, the other the one who really lived there! It had come to heated words, and perhaps we had one more adversary now. And this young physician, who had direct charge of the care and treatment of the Y.F. patients, he of all people would have been very useful. But we had underestimated him. He later proved to be closemouthed and decent, helped us and bore no grudges.

How much we needed every true helping hand would become clear the moment we entered the sickroom. The patient was a half-grown youth with very pronounced symptoms. Jaundice was still absent, but the eyes had the familiar inflamed, watery appearance. He was stupefied, almost somnolent, and it was not even easy to undress him properly without help. There was, of course, no question of explaining our intention to *him*. Finally we were ready. His slender upper arm was bared, the veins stood out. The skin showed not only the slight bluish-tinged redness that is common in Y.F. but also the somewhat rarer urticaria-like weals that very severe cases have immediately, in the first stage.

We drew the curtains over the windows. The room, which faced west, remained bright.

Carolus had drawn up a chart for No. 1 and used his lovely fountain pen to record the first subject's name, age, and so forth. The pen would not glide over the rough paper. So Carolus, in all his naïveté, licked the iridium nib and – now the pen worked. He could not be broken of such habits, any more than he could be gotten used to closing the door properly behind him, for example. Whether it was the W.C. door on the ship or the sickroom door here, he left it open. This had been without consequences on the ship, for it was no secret what he was doing there. But here?! Unfortunately Dr. P., the young resident, was just then passing by and, through the crack in the door, caught sight of the sizable group of us, this foreign congregation of doctors and assistants with jars and so forth, in *his* area, with *his* patient, intent on God knows what meddling. What was he supposed to think, knowing nothing of our plans?

But Dr. P. had the gentlemanly tact not to concern himself with these imponderables, with whatever it was he had witnessed against the wishes of the participants. He looked at us candidly, even bowed slightly to all of us, but then closed the door gently from the outside and left us undisturbed. In the future we would have in him an ally who at first only helped discreetly but was later keenly engaged in our cause. Without him and without the hospital's old matron, to whom I will devote some words later, we would not have overcome even the first, the most trivial difficulties. It will perhaps be thought that we had achieved a great deal merely by getting onto the right track. But this right track was so far nothing but an unproven theory. We would soon see how difficult it was to prove it rigorously.

It was a curious state of affairs in which we were virtually champing at the bit to deliver ourselves over to a disease whose dreadfulness had just been demonstrated to us *ad oculos*. *My* heart at least was now in my throat with anxiety, even though it was not I but only March who was at the head of the line, and the world might end or a miracle happen before the next experiment, mine. From the standpoint of experimental research, it was nothing out of the ordinary.

Finally all the preparations were complete. We found a female mosquito (again, it is allegedly only the females, which are very clearly distinguished from the males, that bite or sting) and placed it initially in a glass test tube of the kind used for urinalysis and chemistry experiments in universities everywhere. The mosquito hunkered down on the smooth wall of the cotton-wool-stoppered test tube and moved its last pair of legs rhythmically up and down. We had made sure it had been given no sugarcane or sugar, etc., in two days, and presumably it was very hungry. Then I removed the wad of cotton wool and held the test tube with the open end down on the skin of the patient, who was breathing rapidly and shallowly amid the characteristic carrion-like miasma of his terrible disease and barely noticed us. Carolus held his hands fast while Walter helped me. March, No. 1 in our series of experiments, stood by with his arm bared and smiled at me, as though to buck me up.

But I had no moral scruples. The technical difficulties absorbed me totally. The insect now glided down to the patient's skin, as quickly as though it were falling; it maintained its equilibrium with even more rapid jiggling motions of its last pair of legs. It held its white-banded abdomen somewhat higher and lowered its tiny head. The little antennae, like branches with feathers, pressed onto the skin, the needle-shaped proboscis drilled into the tissue. The *Stegomyia* pierced it effortlessly, and while the only apparently unconscious patient jerked, so that we had to hold him down, the *Stegomyia fasciata* fed.

Stuffed to the gills. Excellent. It was five thirty on . . . , 192 . . . , a weekday: Tuesday, I believe. The room was the one in which my Portuguese girl had stayed, by the way.

IV

The difficulties, soon to mount unexpectedly, began. Should we allow the mosquito to drink the blood of the youth, who was becoming impatient, until it was full to bursting, or should we immediately have a second, third, fourth, xth insect feed on him? I was in favor of not waiting long, Walter opposed. Perhaps he had an inkling of what was coming. He wanted to leave it at one mosquito and spare the sick lad, now restless and resisting clumsily, a second bite. Apparently Walter had never done experiments on human beings, or else the commotion the last time around had daunted him unduly. So I took the mosquito off after about three seconds, using a little scrap of paper to remove it gently from the skin, swollen with weal-like eruptions, of the young Y.F. patient. This piece of paper came from the English pocket edition of *Hamlet*, which I had happened to find among my possessions that morning and had brought along. They were the words at the beginning of Act II . . . But why quote the thing, enough, it did the job, and the insect had to desist perforce. Its abdomen was now a rounded form through which the blood shone with a rubylike glow.

Act I – curtain. Curtain up for Act II. Namely, the bite on March's bared upper arm. The insect now had ample Y.F. blood in its body, in its salivary glands, its biting apparatus. A bite should thus carry blood to the strong, healthy March.

I carefully brought the little creature, holding it with the wad of cotton wool from the test tube on one side and the scrap of *Hamlet* on the other, to March's upper arm, and we all waited tensely (even the patient, despite his fever, was looking on with interest now that the mosquito was gone; his somnolence had diminished) for the *Stegomyia* mosquito to bite a second time and transmit the microorganism – from the blood, through the blood, into the blood?

It sat there. The last pair of legs did not jiggle. It had lowered its head; the tiny stinger, finer than the finest needle, touched March's skin. But it did not sting. Is it biting? one of the gentlemen kept asking. They smiled, perhaps only out of nervousness, but I was furious. Evidently they had doubts about our experiments deep down, or perhaps I was imagining it. I often had doubts before an experiment and just as often afterward, but never while I was putting my plans into effect. Carolus, that dry fellow, could not refrain from making the silly joke that the mosquito, a female, would certainly find such a delicious man irresistible. March was, in fact, a handsome man, comely if somewhat effeminate, whose well-cared-for and presentable appearance, even now, was always certain to awaken the sympathies of others.

But the fact was that the mosquito perched there motionless for almost two minutes without biting. Suddenly the door opened and the matron came in. The wretched Carolus had again forgotten to lock the door behind resident P. as Walter had expressly directed. The dignified lady could not suppress an exclamation of surprise, and, truly, what a sight! Here was the youth, sitting up in bed, eyes blazing with fever and curiosity, glad that now one of the doctors (he took March for a doctor) was going to be bitten as he had been. Then March and Carolus and the chaplain and I, all gathered around a tiny, blood-engorged insect, imploring it to pluck up its courage and bite.

I had now entrusted the test tube to Walter, to hold over the insect so that it could not escape. But, as I have said, the nasty family saga had unmanned him, he was not even competent to act as a proper assistant, and as soon as the old nun or matron or whatever she was came into the room, he forgot himself, looked up, and involuntarily lifted the test tube; the beast flitted away, its precious cargo inside it, without having bitten March. What confusion! Now we all went chasing after the mosquito. It whirred back and forth in the unbearably stuffy room, zigzagging and making hairpin turns like an old-timer, young as it was. With us right behind it, to the amusement of the matron, who put her lovely, manicured nun's hands in the pocket of her freshly starched habit and laughed heartily.

Needless to say, we did not catch the beast. We turned on the light (the sun was going down), we shone flashlights into every nook and cranny, but the creature must have had enough of us, it had holed up in a dark corner to digest its meal, was safe from us there in its minuteness and did not emerge. What to do? I asked the nun very politely, very ingratiatingly and firmly, to give us another fifteen minutes, and ran up against more regulations. I realized now that either we would have to abandon the entire series of experiments – but I would rather have committed suicide than let go of my idea – or else I would have to take matters into my own hands.

What was I? A condemned criminal exiled for life, an entity without rights, an obedient subject of the penal administration. But, oddly enough, as soon as I worked up my energy (and there was still a remnant of the old strength of will in me), circumstances yielded to me, as did people far above me both socially and in the eyes of the law. For I still possessed something else besides my energy, namely, a logical mind, unbounded intellectual curiosity, and undimmed judgment. I am able to say this in all modesty, for my view has proven itself. Perhaps only a man like me, the son of my father and the product of the upbringing he gave me, could have done the job.

What was at issue was simply the following. Should we break off the experiment? And if not, should we now have other hungry young female mosquitoes feed on the little lad here? Or under these circumstances would it be better to use other patients?

I was in favor of sticking with the youth. And for the following reasons. This was a fresh case. I had the notion (based frankly not on logical considerations but on intuition) that the dangerous, pathogenic, contagious virus would be found most reliably in the blood of those who had recently fallen ill. If any blood was suitable for causing an infection to spread from one person to another in an experiment, theirs was. The business with the little Portuguese girl had been not only a sentimental romance but also a close medical study.

I have discussed how an apyretic period follows the period of onset, and is in turn followed by a kind of intoxication. I said: intoxication rises, detoxication falls. I remembered the ascending lines for temperature and pulse and the falling curve for urine output. Every observer to date had noticed these facts, or rather had not noticed them. For only I drew from this remarkable behavior the conclusion that the microorganism must necessarily be circulating in the blood in a fresh and active form *only until* the initial defervescence (which, in a good many cases with felicitous courses, can be followed by full recovery). Then they are killed by antitoxins in the body, and these killed Y.F. microorganisms, the mortal remains of the microorganisms disintegrating in the blood, only these produce toxins. The patient suffers from this intoxication in the third stage. And thus he perishes with symptoms of intoxication like the poor Portuguese girl.

But if one wants to have living microorganisms fresh from the source, if one needs them for transmission as we did, then one must stick with the fresh cases, and such a one was the youth. He was tired? The matron was knocking on the door after twenty minutes exactly? He did not want to be bitten by one mosquito after another? He wanted to sleep, satisfy his needs, get an ice bag for his forehead, have some cooling lemonade or ice cream? Swallow his medicine?

So sleep, eat, drink, see to your needs, but later! Anything you want, but don't interfere with us!

I was adamant. Walter shook his head in annoyance. He did not agree with me. I saw it clearly. The brigadier general offered passive resistance. Spending any time in this room under the roof was dreadful. For everyone. But I did not rest until I had brought no fewer than ten young mosquitoes to the well to drink. Then we slaved for hours more trying to induce one of those ten mosquitoes to bite March's upper arm. Not one did our will. But that was the least of my worries. Hunger was the best cook. And if today it was satiated and snubbed us, tomorrow it would be ravenous and bite.

I advised March to consume plenty of sugar, fruit, and the like, in order to sweeten his blood.

V

The first experiment had, to some extent, begun in failure, and the skin of the good March, who had put it on the line so bravely, remained unpunctured by a mosquito on the evening of the first day. Thus we had to change our plans after we had already begun, which is never very pleasant. Carolus could always be counted on. He did his best to give up his self-will and submit to our dictates. But who was going to be doing the dictating, Walter or me? Would Walter still be the equal of the youthful Walter I have described, my neighbor on the lecture-hall bench that June morning, who had ended the failed dog experiment the way it had to end? If so, I would have put my hands quietly in my lap and done nothing, or submitted to the will of God and held them out to be bitten by the *Stegomyia*. But I doubted that Walter's vitality was unbroken. I did not know whether he had thrown off the burden of his soft heart and the bourgeois atmosphere around his wife to such a degree that he would be able to act with authority.

I would have bowed to discipline at once had I known for a certainty that system and method lay behind the orders Walter gave. But it appeared to me that he was wavering. Not that he ever would have refused to work with us, either actively, as a research bacteriologist, or passively, as an experimental subject. He was too much a man of duty for that; he had given us his word. He kept it. But when I saw him looking out the laboratory window at another small coastal steamer laboring through rough swells, picking its way among the many craggy islands into the city's marshy harbor, when I saw how longingly he was waiting for news from his family (which never came), I made up my mind to take charge myself. I may have been only a déclassé lawbreaker and he an impeccable, ideal character, but this was irrelevant at the moment.

And the little experiment I conducted told me I had made the right decision. I proposed to my comrades that we depart radically from the original plan. Even before I could explain what I thought this change should entail, Walter stood up, mouth working, began to pace back and forth in front of the window, still gazing at the coastal steamer, and at last said I could give the orders, fine. But in that case I would also have to take responsibility for everything. Of course I would! Why wouldn't I? Anywhere, anytime. If we worked *within* the law, that was fine with me. But I was game even if our human experiments went outside the law. Since the Portuguese girl's death, nothing frightened me anymore. Walter was astonished that I had accepted his proposal at once. And that was where the matter rested.

I found it no more than an odd surprise later when Walter reproached me for usurping the supreme command, which he had after all suggested that I do. Not that he would have interfered with my plans. They were too practical, too much in line with the facts. But at a personal level he withdrew from me. He no longer shook my hand. He always used "Herr" in addressing me, that is, using neither my old academic title (I may have forfeited it, the world may have been that silly, but he was just now recognizing my abilities as an experimenter) nor my name, Georg Letham. But why agonize over such trivialities? No matter that he banished me now from the common table, forcing me to gulp down my meals by artificial light down in the oil-and-vinegar room in the often puerile company of no one but March (even if this did permit me to read one of my two books at my leisure, while March merrily did his best to disturb me), no matter that his only response to my innocently friendly greeting was to look away. Of much greater importance was the change in the battle formation, if I may put it that way, in the midst of the battle, which always gives one pause, though it was only a battle against mosquitoes. First I changed the sequence in which we were to be inoculated. Now I wanted to put myself at the end of this initial but most important series of experiments. No one will be able to call me cowardly on that account. I maintain that waiting to be inoculated was much more of a psychological strain. I endured it. The waiting nearly shattered me. Anyone facing an important, risky decision will want it to come *at once*, if come it must.

But I knew why I was saving myself until later. I had to arrange everything down to the most inconspicuous detail and be constantly on hand to supervise, until I delivered myself over to the disease. I had to map out everything, preferably in writing, so that the experiment would be able to proceed systematically after my demise or while I was ill.

The second change was that we would do the inoculation by mosquito bite at intervals of at least two days, not twenty-four hours at most as previously planned. There were not many of us. We had to make the best use of our material.

The blood-engorged mosquitoes were now being kept in separate jars. Later we put them together if the experimental conditions were the same and labeled the jars precisely with grease pencil.

They could be seen through the walls of the test tube, some of them whirring up and down in steep spirals in their narrow prison, others sitting down at the tip and calmly jiggling their hind legs. We fed them, but only with very small quantities of sugar, so that they would not lose their appetite for human blood. Sugar and the like could never satisfy them anyway; since they were true bloodsuckers, particularly the females we were using in the experiments, blood attracted them more than anything else.

This experimental design proved its worth. On the third day after we had begun the entire undertaking, March was finally bitten by three specimens one after another, and very substantially. Whether it was because he had eaten a lot of fruit or because the mosquitoes were ravenous or because, having unfortunately learned in the course of their lives what hunger is and what blood is, they wanted more of it – no matter, they were unable to tear themselves away from his soft skin with its blond down, they fed and fed, fluttering their antennae, and would perhaps have liked to remain till the end of their days on March's upper arm, ever beefier as he continued to put on flesh here in captivity. For March had gained weight despite the tropical heat, as had Carolus, while Walter and I had lost weight. This was irrelevant.

We allowed the mosquitoes to bite Carolus on the fifth day, and on the seventh it was Walter's turn.

He had now finally received word from his wife on one boat or another. But he was silent about what the fat letter contained. Or was it from his lawyer? It was not our concern. But if the mosquito or its appetite was any measure of the "sweetness" of his blood, much had to be laid at the door of the wife, who had made his life a bitter thing. The mosquito sat morosely on his wasted upper arm, wagged its head back and forth, jiggled its last pair of legs, and would not bite for all the tea in China however hungry it may have been. This was taking too long and we killed it with a drop of chloroform, replacing it with another that was evidently as hungry as a lion in the jungle. Whether poor Walter's blood was bitter or sweet, it swooped down on his arm, drilled in with its stinger, and fed until it was full, so that its bloated abdomen was like a tiny ruby. Thus it ingested blood, healthy blood. But in this blissful feeding did it also discharge any? Infected blood? Blood containing the Y.F. microorganism in pure culture? One would have to assume so with fair certainty if our logically constructed theory was correct. Give blood, take blood – this was the only way the disease could spread according to our theory. Was it true? Was it not true? No gambler has ever waited with greater anxiety to see where the roulette ball rolls. And here our lives were also in play.

But all three men who had been inoculated, that is, bitten by mosquitoes impregnated with Y.F. blood, were so far as hale and hearty as minnows in a clear stream.

I may have trembled for my life. Certainly for our plan.

VI

The eleventh day, my day, the one on which I would be bitten by a *Stegomyia* mosquito, was a Sunday. Carolus, Walter, and the chaplain were against performing an experiment on that day. And I, I went along with them. Why? Out of consideration for the religious twinges of my collaborators? By no means. To be frank: out of cowardice. Out of a wish to put off being bitten for one more day. I was afraid. I would be even today. At that time I already knew very well what the disease was. Although my life was wretched, I feared for it. I dreaded the waiting, particularly. Had I not waited long enough already? Those eleven days were not days of rejoicing. I shuddered at the thought of the retching, the vomiting, the terrible diarrhea. My sleep was disturbed. I was deathly pale when, on Monday evening (the mosquitoes were most inclined to bite in the evening), my collaborators had me take off my white coat and told me to have a seat and keep still. This was not an unusual command; it was the normal procedure that I myself had directed for all those who had been inoculated previously. And what a huge difference between what one asks of someone else and what is done to oneself. The one is an experiment. The other is reality. Or does it come to the same thing? No matter. Thus it was that my upper right arm was covered with what is called gooseflesh. The little insect scurried back and forth on my skin. I trembled with cold. At the laboratory's temperature of more than thirty degrees centigrade, my teeth were chattering. Because of the gooseflesh or for some other reason, the insect would not bite. It sat there and did nothing to me. My collaborators asked me, Carolus very dryly, then March in the quavery voice that he always had at important moments, whether the mosquito had bitten. I could not lie. I shook my head and looked with anxious vigilance out the laboratory window over the archipelago, at the little island made of black rock, known all over the world, to which the worst criminals were deported and where, shut off from the living, condemned forever to silence, to the sight of the shadowless sea, and to the company of no one but themselves, they would limp along to the end of their lives, which were not lives. And yet I would have traded places with any of them! What was the use? There was no going back. Walter, who had watched everything in silence, removed the insect that was disinclined to bite and took another, the last of this series, out of the insectarium. The room was dim. He had not been quite steady on his feet lately. I suspected him of not being averse to a good swig of whiskey now and then. Whiskey? Walter?

And yet it was so. After his belated little honeymoon with his wife on the "lonely island" (it was a black rock with only three palms and otherwise as bare as a hand, but a flat isle, free of infection, somewhat marshy, yet covered with luxuriant vegetation), he had returned completely distraught. Though he had always been so scrupulously well-groomed, so impeccably neat, now he neglected himself. Much to my consternation. For it is a known fact that the first step on the way to moral dissipation in the tropics is the neglect of one's dress. Next come inadequate personal hygiene and poor table manners. The penultimate step is the use or abuse of alcohol and morphine, which are generally extraordinarily conducive to the morally destructive action of this deadly climate, going far beyond what these poisons do in temperate lands. Such a debauched gentleman is sent over the edge by entering into one of the temporary marriages with the native black women that are stigmatized by the English especially. In so doing, these men take their leave of the respectable world and fall to perdition among the blacks.

Even now I did not think that this complete gentleman and faultless spouse would be capable of such a step. But would I have believed even six weeks before that he could run around in a crushed, open lab coat, unshaven, his hair full of dandruff, with untended, black-edged fingernails, could wipe the sweat off his stricken face with a handkerchief that had already seen a great deal of use?

Was there no end to what all the waiting to hear from his "loving hearts" did to him? The fruitless hoping and pining had caused him to degenerate so far that now, in the late afternoon, under the influence of one or more whiskeys, he was no longer steady on his feet and was stumbling. Stumbling? Would he stumble? Fall, break the test tube containing my mosquito? I was so addled by anxiety and dread that I imagined this with the fondest hope. But then he stayed on his feet, he pulled himself together.

He was surprised at himself. He did not recognize his condition. He thought it was an attack of malaria, whereas it was only the alcohol and the sorrow of his heart. Could I be feverish, he was thinking as he held the test tube to the window and shook it to rouse the quiescent insect in it a little. "I just took my temperature, and it was normal. Well, give me your arm, hold it like this, please." Then he held the mouth of the test tube down on my forearm.

"No, not there, higher up," I said. "We want all the experiments to be completely uniform."

"As you wish," he said, and cautiously slid the test tube up my arm to a point just below the shoulder.

What I went through in that moment is difficult to describe. Just a mosquito bite?

But the moment of hesitation, of uncertainty, was past. I too had gotten hold of myself. The fit of cowardice, the wave of dread, was over. No gooseflesh. I smiled. I yawned discreetly. I must have been a strange sight. My blood may not have been as sweet as sugar, but it was palatable, and the mosquito was unable to tear itself away from the feast that flowed beneath my skin.

Carolus logged the experiment, and I retired very early that evening.

How long Y.F. needed to incubate was still unknown. It might have been two, four, even six days. Even more. There are diseases, such as leprosy, whose incubation period, the interval between infection and the appearance of disease, is months or years long. During this time the infected individual goes about his work as usual, he lives as though he were healthy. He acts like a healthy person, but is not one. Happy is he who knows nothing. I knew too much. That made my lot more difficult.

There were only two possibilities. Either our theory was correct, Axiom I was valid, and we, or at least one of us, must contract Y.F., provided we continued to abide rigorously by our methodology. Or everything was wrong, and in that case I saw before me nothing whatever to sustain my life. What more could I hope to do here? Vegetate in the deportee camp (which was unbelievably poorly run), among the dregs of humanity? But I would not even be able to vegetate *among* those dregs, I would be *beneath* them, inferior to them in every respect – would any man like me be able to tolerate that for more than a few days? I shuddered to recall my first days on the *Mimosa*. I have held my tongue about the details. And I will continue to do so.

By my side I had only a sentimental, maudlin man like March, who loved me and was my friend, but who could never satisfy me. With no real work, without freedom, in a dreadful climate – and without hope of hope? Even before my crime I had found life hardly bearable! And this! The only thing that had sustained me lately – now I understood clearly what had kept me from suicide after Monica's death – was my belief in our experiments.

As I went past Walter's room that evening, I saw on the table an open seltzer bottle and an empty glass. In a corner between his bed and the window, where the evening sun could not reach, was a half-empty bottle of Scotch whiskey. No one was watching it, and it would have been easily replaced by its owner. But I left it undisturbed. No inebriation! I wanted to be and remain lucid, enduring everything that came.

The work in the laboratory had dwindled to a minimum. Straightening up was really all there was to do. I washed out the medicine chest.

I sterilized the syringes, I cleaned the bottles, though this was actually March's job. But today it was good to pass the time while waiting for the "either/or." I also found a package of solid morphine in the form of morphine hydrochloride crystals. This was more tempting than the whiskey. To avoid, to escape the pain of Y.F., the retching, the vomiting, the terrible headache! I felt a great temptation. I happened to notice a dead experimental animal, a rat, I believe, which must have given its life for experiments that required its blood. I left the morphine where it was and took the rat carcass downstairs to have it destroyed, as we did methodically with all animal carcasses once we had no further use for them.

VII

The night after I had received my mosquito bite, I was again unable to sleep soundly. Although I sank into a profound slumber when my head hit the pillow, I started up, covered with cold sweat, even before March had really gone to bed. In the uncertain light I saw him fingering something bright and shiny. It was a rosary that the chaplain, he of the "Amen" tattoo on his throat, had given him. So March too had joined the devout. For me, for my salvation?

I did not want to accept his consolation. Nor was I capable of giving him any. I envied him his faith. How fortunate someone must be, in all his wretchedness, if he was still able to believe in God. Perhaps March was now thanking the Almighty for protecting him from being infected by the mosquito? No, probably not.

He had sacrificed himself for me, and of course he was lucky that heaven had not yet taken him up on his offer and given him Y.F. But now he looked after me, as a kind and foolish mother looks after her only child. He expected everything of me. He yearned. A kiss, an awkward, loutish embrace with eyes closed, expressions of tenderness with which the unnatural love of homosexuals, not directed toward procreation, is satisfied often enough. I submitted to it uncomplainingly. But I never returned it. My face was cold. I did not want it. I was incapable of it.

Why deny it, I clung to him anyway. But only emotionally. Not physically.

He, and not Walter, who was my intellectual equal, was my friend. He had become my friend without my noticing.

I even thought now that if I had had someone like March by my side in recent years, things would not have gone with me as they had. But when he told me the same thing? When he expressed his affection in the silliest, but for that very reason the most touching way, "on the knees of his heart"? Had I not noticed the instinctive, fluttery movement to brush away the first mosquito that landed on my arm that evening? And had I not seen his face glowing with delight when Walter, carrying the second dangerous insect, had slipped on a carelessly discarded banana peel? March was normally tidy. Could I believe that he had deliberately left the banana peel there? It was just as plausibly an accident. I was the eternal unbeliever, despairing of everyone as a matter of logic, but I wanted to have proof of his love. *I wanted to believe*! Why *bother*? What was the point? A man with whom there was no way to talk about what we were doing, or about myself – what did he mean to me? But even this I wanted! Since that morning on the dock in sight of the steamer *Mimosa* as it lay offshore, I had felt the urge to confess. Just as he had. But only he had succeeded in easing his heart. Not I. How do people talk? How do people translate their innermost feelings into prattle and trivial endearments? This was beyond me. I asked him now to put off going to sleep for a little while. I wanted to get up again, go to the convent garden. The night was starry and relatively cool. I asked him to come with me. I was depressed. I was miserable. I had a foreboding that the disease would take its gloves off with me. It was only a foreboding, for from the standpoint of the knowledgeable physician, it was grotesque to imagine that the first symptoms of Y.F. would already be appearing three or four hours after I had been infected by a bite from a mosquito. But does anyone always think logically and behave consistently? Thus I accepted March's help in getting dressed. He pulled on my socks, clasping my ankles as tenderly as my mother had once done in earliest childhood. I still remember feeling her breath on my bare ankles as it puffed out the then-fashionable close-fitting, embroidered veil she wore (she was about to go out), and her hair, somewhat loose underneath her velvet hat, tickling my naked skin. I was a thin, wiry, headstrong, very quiet youngster, two and a half or three years old at the time. Not wild about inordinate tendernesses, nor spoiled by them. My mother had had her children in rapid succession; for all her loving kindness, she was unable to devote herself entirely to any of us. My father's thriftiness and his high standards of luxury meant that it was not an easy household to run. My mother never relaxed. When the youngest child, my sister, was a year old, my mother died. She seemed to be in a hurry even then. She took to her bed, we went to her for five or ten minutes, and she was never seen again. I am not generally one to reminisce, the reader of these lines will perhaps have noticed that it is not in my nature to draw useless and bitter comparisons between the present and the past. This evening was otherwise.

Apart from our underclothing, both of us were wearing only our lab coats, which billowed in the evening breeze. We went softly through the corridors, on our feet the woven straw sandals that are worn here. The Y.F. patients clamored, moaned, retched, and raved behind their doors. The half-grown youth who had provided us with his blood lay dying, or was already gone. We listened as we passed his door. The room was literally silent as the grave. And the door was locked. The foolish, curious, and, as must be admitted, extraordinarily fearless March could not refrain from laughingly rattling the door. He liked to laugh too much. He laughed at any opportunity. Nothing answered him. I pulled him away. A chlorine smell came from the room, much dissipated, but strong enough to irritate my always sensitive nasal mucosa and make me sneeze. The naïve March came out with a loud, laughing "Bless you!" on the hospital stairs, no doubt unaware that in the Middle Ages sneezing was thought to be the first symptom of the plague, and that for that reason the superstitious always responded with the pious exclamation "Bless you!" or "Gesundheit!"

Superstition or not, the die was cast and would soon determine what was to become of us.

We went out into the hospital's service yard, passing the stable of the mules and the decrepit nag that had survived the injection we had given it, as it had survived all the bitternesses of its hardworking life, the life of an animal proletarian. It pawed the ground in its stall and rubbed its muzzle on the walls. It even whinnied softly. Perhaps it had cocked its ears, had heard us, and had thought it was time to go to work.

We went into the garden. The flowerbeds at the gate were full of bouquet-like arrangements of bright, luxuriant blooms, gleaming in the radiant starlight. There was no moon. Insects flitted around the white blossoms, mostly moths but also mosquitoes, which we kept at bay with the cigars that we were smoking. Phosphorescent honey mushrooms on the ground glowed with a greenish-silvery light. The air was filled with a balmy fragrance that overpowered the smell of the cigars. Vanilla vines hung down from high branches like lianas. Other climbing plants, gold-green, strewn with cornflower blue and saffron yellow flowers, swayed in the night breeze; their tender, succulent, moist, light-green runners brushed our uncovered heads. Just a while ago, I thought, March had stroked my feet, and now the leaves of fragrant lianas were touching my brow. I wondered (all these thoughts that I never had ordinarily – was this already the beginning of the disease?) whether this might be my last day experiencing the natural world, by the side of someone who cared for me, whether I ought to say good-bye. How could I count on another such night? Should I wind things up? Should I dictate a will? A very last will, since I had already made one half a year earlier while I was in prison. On that occasion I had made my brother my sole heir. Should I now make dear March my heir in case, as a reward for his fearlessness, for bravely enduring the inoculation and the risk of Y.F., he was pardoned and returned home? He was not a real criminal, the big child with the cigar in his little mouth. But I might receive a pardon too. Walter had spoken of it. What I had taken upon myself today was certainly greater than the official punishment! We kept circling the trees. There were not many of them, but they were very tall. The soft green lights of the sickrooms shone up above, the moaning of the ill came indistinctly down to us. The footsteps of the patrols could be heard, regular and unhurried, with a metallic ringing when the guards marched over one of the iron plates set into the floors of the corridors. We said nothing. I laid my arm on March's bare neck. I remembered the kiss that my dead darling had not given me. I shrugged my shoulders, I shook my head. March, faithful March, did not ask. Above us a jungle tree, a jacaranda, stretched into the purple, fathomless night sky teeming with stars. Beneath it, on the ground, were fallen violet leaves, an entire carpet of them, but there were others still growing and giving off fragrance on the countless branches of the tree that whispered softly in the night breeze. Just above us was the glow of a celestial object I had often seen on my father's star chart, never dreaming that one day I would be deported to C. and see the real thing in the garden of a Y.F. hospital there. A tangle of silvery spheres, a kind of magical, soulful, cohesive Milky Way called the Magellanic Cloud, a distant galaxy with as much internal structure as a house, truly supernal, carefully wrought from soft light and serene radiance. March sighed. I had to smile: Georg Letham the younger, starstruck. Was it fever already? Was it still my optimism? It had to be good to be alive. I smiled. I smiled with such force, such delight, that my smile became a laugh. March, who always liked to laugh, joined in. Thus on the day of the inoculation we went home laughing. I was in a daze, but happier than I had been in all this time.

VIII

Despite the consolations of this sublimely beautiful night, I did not sleep in the hours following our stroll, perhaps because I was trying desperately to, so as to have all my strength for what was coming.

The next day, Tuesday, I took my temperature two or three times, but I found nothing remarkable either then or on any of the first four days.

Walter was uneasy too. The first series of experiments had been done, without successful outcome so far. Had it all come to nothing once again? I could not believe it. I spoke encouragingly to Walter. We could not give up. Five failed experiments or fifty, still we would have to try again.

"But will it be possible?" he asked me, turning his large, serious gray eyes away.

"Why not," I responded. "It will have to be."

He was silent for a long time, pacing unsteadily back and forth in the room, and oddly enough – whether it was the influence of alcohol (he smelled subtly but unmistakably of whiskey) or the mood of the moment – he began to melt, and told me of his cares and his worries about his "loving hearts," with which I was already more familiar than he knew. Later he also spoke of his fears for my future. He very much wanted to do something. Whether he believed I had been sentenced *unjustly*, this he did not say.

"So far the penal administration hasn't asked for you or your March. Your father's arm is long. If he becomes minister, he'll be practically omnipotent, but he isn't yet, and it might take too long for an SOS to reach him if it came to that. Don't let too much time go by. Ask him! Get hold of him! They know of C. only by hearsay. Write to him. Better yet, give me a letter for him. Give it to me unsealed . . . but if you're the man I think you are, I won't read it. Why shouldn't an appeal for clemency have some chance of success? At least as good a chance as our experiments here. I'll add a few words of my own, if you want. That might do a lot. And if fate wills it that I do as my family wishes and go back to Europe in the foreseeable future, maybe I'll take your letter personally."

"What are you thinking?" I asked in horror. "To Europe? You? Do as your family wishes? Now?! Do you think it's possible that we're mistaken? That everything we're trying to do here is futile?"

"What I *think* is possible or impossible won't change the facts," he said resignedly. He looked tired, old, exhausted. He reminded me of my father, and yet he was younger than I was. He said, focusing his thoughts with effort:

"Fourteen days ago we began our experiments with bites from infected mosquitoes. So far we're all fine and in the best of health, to the extent that this hellish climate allows." He was going to say something else, but March had come up, and he broke off.

I would have liked to hear what else he had to say (evidently it concerned his ruined finances, and perhaps he was thinking about some communication with my father, a very rich man and minister-to-be), but suddenly I was unable to keep my eyes open, although it was only noon. I blamed this peculiar, very severe fatigue on the fact that in the last few nights I had hardly gotten a wink of sleep. But as I lay on my bed, fully dressed and with my shoes on, a practice that was always very much frowned upon, I still found no rest.

March soon came down, saw me there, and took my shoes off, or rather he tried to, for I was seized by an abnormal irritability and abruptly pushed him away. He cried out in a high, soft voice. This foolish little-girl screech enraged me. I sat up and glared at him angrily. Then a pathological desire to laugh came over me and I burst out laughing, as though I were vomiting, with open mouth, trembling hands, starting eyes. I was frightened now. Even as I was laughing, I ordered him to go get my thermometer upstairs.

I always checked my temperature after I had washed and had breakfast, normally upstairs in the laboratory. He quickly ran up and very soon brought me the thermometer and my chart. This too, the fact that he had brought my chart without being asked, angered me. I wanted to shout at him, but controlled myself and silently put the thermometer in my mouth. I usually took my temperature this way after thoroughly cleansing the thermometer with alcohol. The dark room smelled of oil, vinegar, dust, and – rats. The thermometer's column of mercury was difficult to make out. March lit a pocket lighter. I flinched from the harsh light. He stroked my forehead with his big, cool, dry hand as gently as he could. He still hurt me! He burst out laughing. I could have struck him for that!

My temperature was normal.

IX

On the morning of the fifth day, Friday, I already felt so wretched that I would have preferred not to get up. March, with all his doggish love, looked at me doubtfully. This I could not bear, and, even though my feet would hardly support me, I got up and tried to do what little there still was for me to do in the laboratory at that time.

I did not take my temperature, for fear that it would be elevated. At noon I sat down to lunch with March. The old nurse who normally served us brought us our food. Nice, light, good food! But I was unable to force myself, even though I had no wish to worry March before I really had to.

It was an oppressively hot, humid day, but filled from morning till night with almost constant storms and cloudbursts of unimaginable ferocity. Water was pouring through one of the high basement windows into the oil storeroom that we lived in, and I asked March to go up and try to see from the courtyard whether it was open or whether a pane might even be broken. While he was investigating, I got up and tossed my food into a half-empty tub of soft soap. I still remember the gagging disgust I felt as the food sank with an unappetizing squelching sound into the slimy, alkaline-smelling mass. When March returned and laughingly reported that the hospital courtyard was knee-deep in water, I wiped my mouth with a napkin as though I had finished eating and then dragged myself upstairs to see for myself. March had exaggerated, the water was no more than ankle-deep. A cloudburst had just subsided. The sun was pouring out again between poisonous, glittering, lilac-colored clouds, and it felt good to put my hands into the runoff still streaming down from the eaves and splash some cool rainwater onto my forehead, behind which there was beginning to be a terrible uproar.

I did not go back to March. An unfamiliar restlessness had come over me, but it was combined with a painful lassitude. I thought about writing to my father. It had been so long. I did not have the peace of mind for it. It was impossible. I wanted to wait until everything was settled – meaning what? "Settled"?

The small of my back was hurting, as though someone had kicked me hard. I could hardly stand up. But I wanted to stay on my feet until the last moment. More tottering than really walking, holding on to the cool, rain-damp walls, I wandered among some of the buildings of the hospital complex. The guards leaned on their bayonets (well trained to busily kill time like so many civil servants – devoted to the appearance of order, not order itself) and watched me smirkingly, brownish stumps of cigarettes dangling from the corners of their mouths. One of them called out something I did not catch and imitated my shaky shuffle along the wall as a grotesque gag. He soon tired of this and stretched out for a nap next to his comrades and let me go on. If I had tried to leave the hospital, the guards would not have stopped me.

Did they realize how things were with me? I still did not realize it myself.

I went into some of the large empty sickrooms, still smelling of disinfectant. Huge areas, the ceilings supported by freshly whitewashed wooden posts, rows of fifty beds side by side along each of the two long walls, the bare rectangular rooms empty, clean, unused, just as though sick people, people who had suffered and died – people who had gotten better – had never been there. The facilities dated from the great epidemic periods and, thanks to the able matron's sense of order, had been maintained so that every square inch could be occupied immediately if the Y.F. should suddenly flare up again.

I heard March's voice in the courtyard, as though from a distance. Georg! Georg! Something seemed to be wrong with my hearing. My head pounded, I saw red. The posts in the room seemed to be flecked with blood. I crawled onto one of the hard beds (thanks to the efforts of March and Carolus, my bed in the oil storeroom was as soft as a doll's – March had just a few old blankets on the floor!). I put my fingers in my ears, actually my thumbs, while my other fingers lay over my eyes to shield them from the weak light that came in through the closed lids. Outside another violent cloudburst had begun. Lightning flashed from one horizon to the other. Thunder rolled. The racket was tremendous.

The onslaught of the storm shook the building to its foundations. From the underground corridor containing what remained of our animal material came the shrilling and screeching of the monkeys, the howling and yipping of the dogs. An entire concert of creatures kept in darkness under lock and key, giving vent to their feelings about nature unbound.

I would have given anything to be able to sleep soundly. But it was impossible. The voice of the only too faithful March kept waking me from a restless slumber. I was careful not to move, for any movement made the terrible lumbar pain – termed *coup de barre* by specialists –

more excruciating. I felt best lying quietly on my back and even tried to hold my breath as much as possible.

March finally stopped calling. Evidently he had gone back to the laboratory. I had to put in an appearance there too if I did not want to arouse suspicion. Suspicion? Oh, no! Joy and triumph for the others!

Rarely in my life has walking cost me as much effort as those few steps to the laboratory.

My strength of will had not yet suffered significantly. I was able to pull myself together enough that neither Carolus nor Walter noticed my abnormal condition. Fortunately my three collaborators, Carolus, Walter, and March, were busy with a new staining method that had to be tested very carefully, though, of course, in and of itself it could not deliver any results worth talking about. The uselessness of their feverish efforts angered me. What could be the point of all the huddled consultation? If there's nothing to find, even the best staining method won't find it. But they were entirely absorbed in their work, like children with a dish of soapy water and a nice straw. When March, sitting in a dark corner, threw me a worried glance from time to time, I did my best to give him a cheery grin.

Despite the awful feeling of bottomless misery, I was still in control of myself. Thus the stormy afternoon passed. I counted the minutes. At last the time came when, as was usual at the close of our work, the chaplain appeared and led Walter and Carolus away for their dinner together, which was generally followed by a game of chess (with three players – Walter and the chaplain against Carolus, who played a very strong game) or a game of puff-puff, a few glasses of whiskey, two or three phonograph records, and a little argument. This was their mental life outside of their work. Anyone familiar with conditions in tropical lands will marvel that Carolus and Walter found any mental energy at all for anything other than card games and whiskey.

I usually had my evening meal alone in my room. March had to take care of the animals. I no longer had the strength to toss my food away.

I threw myself down on my doll's bed in the oil-and-vinegar storeroom, pulled the blanket over my face, and pretended to be asleep. March came in whistling, but he fell silent and quietly approached my bed.

I heard him take the thermometer out of its metal sheath (this always made a faint clicking sound).

I was supposed to take my temperature twice a day, like all the other experimental subjects. But he did not want to wake me.

Now and then I had a chill, a shudder that usually began on my left cheek and ran across my forehead, neck, and spine like a sharp, wintry gust of wind and then faded in my leaden lumbar region. My teeth wanted to chatter. But I did not want them to. I clenched them and was as quiet as a mouse. March was fooled and went to bed. Soon I heard him breathing deeply. He snored a little. He was asleep.

To be able to believe in God! To love someone from the bottom of your heart and be able to wish him all the luck in the world! And to be able to sleep deeply! Enviable man, that March!

X

For a few moments I dozed off too, but I was soon awakened by the violent chattering of my teeth.

I sat up. I had icy chills all over. Waves of heat and cold, very much alike, passed over me in rapid succession. I put my hand through my shirt and felt my chest, my heart. It was thumping briskly, at a rate of 110 to 115 beats per minute in my professional estimation. The lumbago had worsened, if that was possible. My ears buzzed. I had a piercing pain behind my forehead. Without a doubt I was severely ill. Chills, elevated pulse, certainly elevated temperature too, lumbago, a sensation of terrible pressure in my head; anything missing? My throat hurt too, my tongue burned as though I had swallowed paprika.

The building was deathly still. March had stopped snoring. He lay quietly on his pile of rags on the floor. What should I do? Wake him up? How could he help me? What I needed was to try to gain some clarity.

What I had was not necessarily Y.F. True, all the symptoms were there. But the onset of paludism (malaria) is quite similar. I had gone for a walk with March in the hospital garden five days earlier. There had been mosquitoes there too, we had not been able to drive all of them off with cigar smoke. If I was lucky and it was only malaria, a couple of quinine powders would take care of it. And our Axiom I? I will confess frankly that, suffering as greatly as I now was, I was thinking only about saving my life. One would have to have gone through it to understand how a man feels on the brink of such an illness.

But was it not your own free will, Georg Letham? You did nobly put yourself at the disposal of science, did you not? You did *hope* that the experiment would be successful? Was it not a matter of the greatest importance?! The lives of countless people depended on it – the decontamination, the cleaning up of entire tracts of land.

Keep calm! Stay rational! Those are the thoughts of a person who is well. A sick, wretched, agonized fellow does not think.

I might have been able to think all sorts of great thoughts about the betterment of mankind and the blessing of moral self-sacrifice, but my teeth were chattering. I clenched them, groaning with pain. Making a great effort to climb out of bed quietly so as not to awaken my March, I put one leg over the edge despite the lumbar pain. The calf muscle seized up in an abominably painful cramp, just so I wouldn't get too cocky. My bed creaked.

It was a wonder that March slept so well, so heavily. Even now he didn't wake up! Or was it that he didn't *want* to wake up, because he understood that I didn't want him to, for I wanted no witnesses, I had to be alone? I gathered the last of my strength. If one needs it, one has it.

I stood up, went one step at a time, holding on to the cool walls, through the corridor to the laboratory, turned on the light, and, before I did anything else, sat down, croaking with anguish, in the comfortable armchair that Carolus, keen on luxury in any situation, had had placed in front of the microscope. I closed my eyes. I could not bear the light. Yet I needed light to do the first test.

The first test to see whether I had Y.F.? On the contrary, to see whether I did *not* have Y.F. When I took the microscope out of its wooden case, it was not my intention to search for the unknown Y.F. microorganism, but rather for the long-known pathogen of ordinary tropical malaria.

Such is man. He sets himself a goal. He builds himself an altar. When it comes to praying, he prays. But as soon as it costs blood, he wants to be on his way. Why lie? What I write here would not have the least value for me, never mind for other people, if I consciously lied. Everyone does enough unconscious lying as it is.

With a blood lancet I pricked myself valiantly in the pad of my left little finger. I dipped the edge of a paper-thin glass slide into the glistening ruby red drop. With trembling hands that knocked together like a jumping jack's, I smeared the drop of blood on a second, thicker slide. I had to dry it over a flame, so I passed it through a Bunsen burner and – burned my hand, so clumsy had I become. I saw the staining solutions neatly lined up on a shelf. But how to get them down? Stand up *again*? Impossible. Should I call March? Even more impossible. One wants to be undisturbed at such a moment. I desperately twisted my face into a grin. What better way to deal with any situation than with humor? I shook my head at my lethargy and gave myself an order, as though I were another person. Fortunately the brigadier general in his untidiness had left a small dish of the new staining compound on a corner of a little table that was easily reached from my armchair.

Could this be anything but a sign from fate? I had become superstitious. For the second time I was taking some silly little thing as an omen. And for the second time fate betrayed me. The first time with my beloved, the second time with myself.

At last I had stained the slide, rinsed it in water and alcohol, dried it, put it under the microscope. In a case of malaria, an investigator with some experience will see the familiar plasmodia characteristic of paludism on any well-stained slide of a blood smear. So I was eager to try. The micrometer screw, which raises and lowers the microscope's objective by a hundredth of a millimeter and thus establishes the precise distance from the slide, would not obey my twitching fingers. I pressed down with a bit too much force, and the slide of my blood cracked. What else could it do? It was not equal to the clumsy movements of a man trembling for his poor life.

I would be lucky if the expensive primary lens had not been permanently damaged too. Now I sat there, covered with sweat, half paralyzed, and still did not know what was going on.

At this point a man turns to his fellow and calls him brother, bosom friend, and physician!

I began calling to March. But my voice was no longer strong enough. It did not carry. Time went by. I heard the bells ringing in the hospital's tower and continued to lie prostrate in the armchair, teeth chattering, before me the broken slide and the wrecked microscope.

But I held out. I took a second slide and in stages, making one movement at a time and then resting and recovering thoroughly, I repeated the blood drawing, the smearing in a thin even layer, the fixing in the flame of the Bunsen burner, the staining, the rinsing and drying. After about an hour I was ready to put it under the microscope. I was ready. "I," I say, for I was still alone, I did not, could not, count on anyone but myself. This time I worked the micrometer screw with the utmost care. Luckily the primary lens was not damaged. The second slide was well stained, the round red corpuscles could be seen as little carmine disks, the white corpuscles with contrast staining were cornflower blue, and the nuclei of the leukocytes were splendidly granular, lobular, an ethereal sapphire green.

A wonderful slide – but no trace of malaria plasmodia. Everything "normal." For Y.F. causes no change in blood microscopy.

Gasping, teeth chattering, I sat before the instrument. It was only with the greatest effort that I kept my eyes open, eyes whose conjunctivae were already inflamed, as befits Y.F. Good heavens, man, son of your father, what more do you want? Yet I still did not want to believe! Is it so hard to believe when what must be believed is something grim and awful? Is it so difficult to look existence in the eye, to see its true face? Is it so difficult to read the newspaper instead of the Gospel? Will the conjunctivae always become inflamed? My father! Will one always become photophobic? Will one, painful throat or not, always call for one's bosom friend so loudly that he will *have* to hear no matter how soundly he is sleeping? And will one then, still trembling, take him by the shoulder and pull his head down to the eyepiece of the microscope: "March, look at this! Do you see anything?" Of course he saw something. He wasn't blind. But how would he, an untrained little official, a new boy in the bacteriology classroom – a boy who was grown up and already a little gray-haired, in fact, and who had gone to jail because of his excessive love for his cadet – how would he recognize malaria plasmodia? He had not been looking for "plasmodia" from childhood like mushrooms in the woods. He saw them or not, depending on what he thought I wanted to hear. Abruptly I collapsed. A blessed moment of unconsciousness. But it could only have lasted a second. When I came to my senses, I saw March running about the laboratory half-crazed and heard him shouting for doctors! But there were simply none there, though downstairs in the basement corridor the sleeping animals awoke and began to add their voices to the caterwauling of the loving and beloved March. And over the old hospital on the tree-covered hill above the city of C., a terrible storm erupted, booming and roaring with thunder and lightning.

XI

I still remember March's dumbfounded, almost deranged air. His features were so contorted that his face, usually quite pleasant if somewhat vacant, was hardly recognizable. The "fierce" expression that I had seen on it just once before was there again.

He was shaking. I was shaking. He with agitation. I with a temperature of thirty-eight and a half degrees centigrade and the associated chills. My mind was no clearer than his. That goes without saying. And yet somewhere within me there was still a spark of unclouded consciousness, observing from its sheltered spot the ruckus on every side. With the predominant part of my self, the G. L. that was running a temperature of thirty-eight and a half, I felt the fear of the disease, I had in me the dread that such a fearsome condition must arouse. But with the part of G. L. that had remained lucid, I was astonished that he, March, and Walter, who had just come in, completely soaked from the rain, were so appalled by my condition. Why *appalled*? Was our experiment not to be regarded as a *success*, as far as could be judged? I was forced to the realization that none of them, least of all Carolus (the last to appear, in his crushed, baggy old pajamas, a nightcap on his bald head, worn-out slippers on his feet, and his horn-rimmed glasses on his bony nose), had believed that our experiments would succeed.

I was more dead than alive, someone suffering greatly, one who now (falsely) believed that he was already at the limit of his capacity for suffering. Yet there was something in me that rejoiced. I had been right after all. My simple theory, based on pharmacist von F.'s long experience and the laws of logic, which were the same in C. as they were back home, had apparently proven itself. As far as could be judged? Apparently? I let Walter perform a clinical examination. I thought the riddle would be solved if he found that I actually had Y.F. But this too was a fallacious conclusion. Y.F. would pose many more riddles.

Walter stared at me vacantly for a long time. His hands as they probed about did not have the firm, unbudgeable, yet gentle touch of the great physician. I saw that Walter was not at his best this evening. His hands were trembling, and not with fever like mine, nor with human feeling like poor March's, but – from the effects of whiskey. He was fully clothed, just one little sartorial error was identifiable. Identifiable by me, over whom he was leaning and whose powers of observation were intact even now. Had Walter been wandering the empty streets of C. during the night? Had he been at the shore, his heart going out to his wife across the sea? Almost. He had been in the bar owner's docklands dive (in spite of the quarantine; that is, surreptitiously), where he had solaced himself with whiskey – I knew that whiskey of comparable quality was not easy to scare up elsewhere in C. Walter's beautiful gray eyes were somewhat glassy and he was belching the carbon dioxide from his whiskey-and-sodas. Could have been worse. His head cleared from one second to the next when he saw what I had. "We've taken a great step forward," he said – and belched, taking a great step away from me. He whispered with Carolus, and I saw on the faces of my collaborators – not exactly glee and exultation, but a very peculiar companionable joyfulness. They were rejoicing that experiment number thus and such had been successful. Why not rejoice? Yet for the first time since the beginning of our experiments, a bitterness rose in me.

March had laid me on the large table in the laboratory. The light over the examination table that Walter had turned on for the purposes of a careful examination was blinding even for a healthy person, never mind for me, whose conjunctivae were already inflamed. So I turned my head to one side and saw March standing by the table, breathing heavily. March was not happy. He cared nothing about science. Only about me. He wanted to take me away, put me to bed, nurse me to health! That boy! The doctors did not allow it. Another blood test! The result was inevitably the same as I had seen with my own eyes. No trace of malaria plasmodia. I wanted to explain it to the gentlemen. But there was a bit of a difference between wanting to speak and being able to, because the mucosa of the fauces and pharynx were inflamed and swollen and because my oversized tongue lay like a caterpillar in my mouth. And when at last, gripped by a new chill, I laboriously choked a few words out of my craw, the two doctors did not deign to look at me, but sat at the microscope, Walter at the left eyepiece, Carolus at the right, to examine my blood again with professional thoroughness, although there was nothing to see, in my opinion. But I (what was left in me of the levelheaded and serene Georg Letham of old) recalled the working plan that I had established in advance for the eventuality that I was the first to fall ill. They were only following what I had specified orally and in writing as the only proper procedure for the experiment. So I had to submit.

In my life I have hungered many a time: for food, drink, money, honor, women, freedom. For faith and for God. Sometimes voluntarily, sometimes because I was compelled to. But I believe I have never hungered for anything with all my body and soul as I now did for peace, quiet, darkness, and solitude, for a mattress under me and a good light blanket over me, for a cool pillow in a clean pillowcase under my heavy, dreadfully pounding head.

Instead I was lying like a corpse on the hard operating or examination table and waiting to see what would be done with me. They did not let March near me, though he was trying to help me, insofar as his agitated state of mind permitted. They needed him for all sorts of jobs, as befitted the laboratory assistant that he in fact was. What had he expected? He had not been taken out of the bagnio to have fun.

Sour and bilious vomiting had, to my horror, begun. What had *I* expected? Burning thirst tormented me. My tongue seemed to be covered with paprika. But why go through all this? Just one more tiny detail from the first hours of my illness. I mention only in passing that from now on, for a period of four weeks, I believed at every moment that it could get no worse. I had already suffered enough. Enough! Enough! This became the only idea I had. People who are feverish are always somewhat lacking in ideas. The few superficial ones they do have spin madly in their overheated and weakened brains. I just groaned "enough" all the time. Or at least I produced the *f*. To pronounce the *f*, one of course does not need the pressure of the tongue against the teeth, nor much wind. An *f* comes straight from the lips. The protesting tongue can relax in the anterior trough of the oral cavity. But one whistles out an *f*. The toneless, inarticulate utterance of the animal as it does not *want* to be, but *is*. But the gentlemen who were gathered around me and studying me were not interested in this "enough" or the *f* that was as much as I could manage, but in obtaining a bodily secretion of great importance for scientific study. The reader will know what I mean. But, God knows why, I could not produce it now. I struggled. My head roared with the effort, my belly strained, my hands shook so much that I dropped the empty cup, which broke. But that nectar did not come from my body, any more than hosannas from my mouth. A small misery, certainly! But, amid the hellish wretchedness of the raging fever, it was very distressing to be exposed by Walter and Carolus in front of little March so that they could remove what they needed with a catheter.

XII

When this comical and yet, for me, abominable procedure – I had always performed it on others but had never gone through it myself –

was over, I was going to be placed on the usual stretcher and carried to one of the sickrooms. I did not want to be. I rebelled. Even in my first days in this accursed building, I had shuddered at the sight of the old-fashioned, brown-spotted stretcher. I would be brave, like a knight of old, and walk upstairs to the sickroom. I had overestimated my strength. Even the faithful March's help was not enough. Two nurses had to be summoned with the stretcher, for me as for any other patient. I was moved from the laboratory table to the stretcher. We negotiated the familiar staircases and corridors to the sickroom. There nurses carried me to the bed and quickly but gently undressed me, which was very easy, as I was wearing almost nothing underneath my lab coat. I had done the stretcher an injustice, by the way. The canvas upon which the patients lay was removed after each use and sterilized in a boiling soda solution. It was always somewhat damp. The spots never came out, every wash only seared them in and made them tougher. It would have been unreasonable to require a brand new canvas for each new entry in the casebook (I was number 328 – the worthy stretcher had borne that many patients so far that year).

But what did it matter now? I would learn that beyond a certain degree of physical suffering, reached unfortunately all too quickly, the soul deflates; it gasps for air and then abandons itself to a numb, completely bottomless despair, of which the physically healthy can have no conception.

Thus it was that I too did not resist the chaplain's attempts to administer the last rites come hell or high water, as he would for any patient. There was no way to resist it. I was fully occupied with meeting my quota of suffering. I passively submitted to his talk and quotations from Scripture and the ceremony. What belief or unbelief did I have left in me now, with every part of my body burning hot and in unspeakable torment? What did the afterlife mean to me? I didn't grasp these ideas properly, I was hanging on to *this* world with grim desperation. I held frantically to the chaplain's hand, and when he drew it away for the ritual laying on of hands, I clutched at his flimsy cassock, to which more than one patient suffering "unspeakably" in his hellfire must already have clung. The chaplain understood something of what was happening in me, or rather to me. He was the best psychologist around, he had a feeling for people. And an invincible liking for this wretched product of the sloppy experiments of fate. He had demonstrated this to me before at the passing of dear little M.

How very indifferent to everything I had become may be shown by the following. My bed might have been the very same one in which the sweet body of the young Portuguese girl had rested, or had not rested, a few days previously. Or was I in the adjoining room that had served as a refuge for the unemployed but vigorous dockworker? I didn't know. It didn't interest me. It didn't matter at all. A bed was a bed. Portuguese girl, my father, March, Walter – it was all light-years away from me. In my baggage, which the good March had swiftly brought, the chaplain had discovered the two little books that I had rescued from the ruin of my old life: the Gospel and *Hamlet*. He assumed that I would still take an interest in the Gospel now, on the threshold of death. I only wanted to sleep. I only wanted the pain to go away. I wanted to get up. Be able to leave. I yearned for home, because there I had always been healthy!

I couldn't speak. I couldn't lie down. I couldn't stand. I couldn't drink. I couldn't even whimper. Only suffer. And yet this was just the beginning, this was the easiest period of the disease. It was only the first day.

The good man made his nice, energetic sign of the cross over me and left. March looked in on me for a moment. He could not stay. The gentlemen needed him. New experiments were being prepared. And following whose plan? What method? Why, mine, the one I myself had drawn up in case I should be bedridden and the others be carrying on the work we had begun. He was needed first as an assistant in the laboratory and then as a subject in a second series of experiments, for which he was going to be used as planned. As No. I-B. We had designated the first victims with Arabic numerals; thus I was No. 5. Now Roman letters were being added to keep the series straight. This was the way we had set it all up.

I was gradually losing my normal sense of time. When a healthy person wakes up during the night, he has a feeling for approximately how much of it has gone by. At least I had had such a feeling before, even when it was dark and I couldn't see the clock on the night table. But someone with a fever of thirty-nine and a half loses his ability to estimate time. Thus it was in my case. I was living through different hours and seconds now. They passed one by one, no skipping allowed.

The old matron honored me with a visit. As when she had paid her visit to the poor little one, she took a particular interest in cleanliness. She glanced into the corners, ran her hand over the rail of the bed to see whether it had been dusted, she lifted the bedclothes to see if my feet were clean. Luckily they were. Even in the worst of times I had always set great store by hygiene. Even in recent days, when I had been feeling so wretched that bathing, washing, and shaving were difficult for me.

Now, as though to reward me, this old soldier of Y.F. planted herself by my bed and told me in her droll accent that I would not go back to the camps if Dr. Walter had anything to say about it, I would be spared the penal colony. Did this mean she was expecting my speedy demise? I laughed feverishly and did not understand. Other than that *f*, still the only sound I could get out without great pain to my tongue, oral cavity, and pharynx, I was unable to speak to her. And what would we have talked about, anyway? She assumed I had understood her and laughed back gamely, showing a row of fine teeth and splendidly rosy red gums. As with many persons of an ecclesiastical calling, her laugh was somewhat unnatural. But it was a laugh, and it made her feel good. Mine made me feel bad and I did not repeat it for the time being. My gums were so swollen that they stood out over my teeth like a coxcomb. My skin, from my forehead down to about my waist, was as though sunburned, stretched tight. When, in my agonized restlessness, I touched myself, it was like touching a boiling or roasting body that belonged to someone else. But this was only one of the horrors of the first day. Very soon I had a second attack of chills. And off into night and darkness and killing frost! I must have fallen out of bed when the nurse was out of the room, for March, who came in with a sheet of paper in his hand, found me on the floor. At that moment I must have taken leave of my senses. I tore the paper out of his hand and started chewing on it. But I must suddenly have understood, perhaps when he had taken me back to bed, the natural home, the cradle and casket of man, that it was a letter. A letter at last! News from home! I lifted my chin, I pursed my lips, I looked at him imploringly with my inflamed eyes, I formed an *r*, I made a snarling sound, meaning that March was to read to me – I myself was unable to read because of the conjunctivitis that was making my eyes burn. But how could my dear friend read me anything if I wouldn't let the precious letter out of my hand! Great dumb show, understood, too – but no good! What was left of my idiotic energy went toward not letting go of something I had taken hold of. Let go! he cried. Read! I snarled and whispered. We did not come to an understanding. I kept the paper in my hand, I tore it apart with twitching movements, I didn't know what I was doing. Why had he given it to me? He had carefully hidden the enclosure, the money. Why not the letter too? He just had no notion what I was going through. He overestimated me. Now he was urgently called away by Walter. I must have gone on making my *f* of lamentation and my *r* of supplication for a long time yet. I was still making them when he appeared again in the late afternoon.

What could he do? He saw a little book on the night table amid the dishes of fruit, ice chips, and the other items helpfully provided by a helpless medical science. He did what I would have done in his place. With his back to me he opened the little book, quietly tore out a much-read page, page forty-three of the British Bible Society's small octavo edition: the Sermon on the Mount. I will not quote the words of Scripture that have had such an impact on world history. The interested reader can look them up at the place I have mentioned. He wanted me to think he was reading me the letter. His eyes scanned the page. He read it out loud.

XIII

The third day of my illness was a Sunday. In my feverish fantasies I kept hearing voices: "Dr. Georg Letham is dead." "The younger?" "Both." Then back to the beginning: "Dr. Georg Letham is dead."

On the Lord's day, March had a bit more freedom. He came to visit me, and once more I held his soft, seemingly boneless hands, on whose account I had given him the nickname Gummi Bear, in my own. The silly "voices" stopped then. I have completely forgotten the rest of what happened that day. I awoke on Monday evening at a somewhat lighter moment. I must have been vomiting a great deal all this time; there was a bilious taste in my mouth, the bitterest taste you could imagine. A kind of gutta-percha bib had been tied around my neck and my upper chest so that I would not unconsciously make a mess of myself. No sooner had I touched the unpleasantly smooth and cold material than my innards rebelled violently once more. I gave in. I had no choice. And the faithful March clasped my brow and held my head. Meanwhile the old nurse who had the difficult job of caring for me was cleaning the room with broom, dustpan, and cloth.

In March's good-natured, mournful, haunted face there was a flicker, a flash of something. He probably wanted to bring me an important piece of news, had perhaps spoken it directly into my ear ten or twenty times without my understanding it. Now he let go of my head, levered my arm to clamp a thermometer in my armpit (he could not put it in my mouth because of the terrible pain in my mouth and pharynx), and took my temperature. I glanced at it out of the corner of my eye. Even in my current, how shall I say, barely human condition, the clinical course of my illness interested me. My temperature must have been above the critical mark (forty). When he looked at the thermometer, he turned away, awkwardly shrugging his shoulders, and I heard him, as though from afar, as though through two doors, emitting a kind of wooden sob. He was just as brave as the rest of us. He came back, coughed, and put on a desperately jolly face. I wasn't able to thank him. The moment he had dried my face with a fresh, snowy napkin, the nausea and retching began again, and as I groaned and tears flowed from my eyes, the sluices opened all over his soft hand. But that was the easiest test his friendship and love had to undergo that day, or rather that evening. The facts posed greater challenges, purely impersonal ones. Without regard to who was involved.

In a short while Carolus and Walter came in, their hands full of jars containing fresh young *Stegomyias* whirring about. At first I did not understand what they might want from me in this room, which really was not a pleasant or stimulating place to be anymore. Oh, nothing, just a drop of my precious, peerless essence. Blood, I mean.

They wasted little time making sure it was all right with me if they went on carrying out my working plan to the letter. They examined me no further, but simply set to work. First they had March let a good amount of light into the room, which until then had deliberately been kept dim. They needed light for their delicate work. I would have preferred darkness. I could not even tolerate the weak light that I saw with my eyes closed.

And did I at least close my eyes, as would have been the thing to do? Unfortunately not. Someone like G. L. *had* to see what was going on around him. I had to make use of that brief illuminated moment amid the incalculably wide, vast desert of my fever to take note of my situation and everything that was going on around me. It was just not in my nature to turn a blind eye. Thus I stared with frantic interest at the blackish, white-barred, six-legged, tiny-headed insect that Walter had placed on my bared upper arm and that was using its hair-fine proboscis to pick out a good place to bite and feed. It was running restlessly about on my arm, held captive by the test tube as though in a cage, unable to fly away.

I saw the veins on Carolus's age-weary hand, underneath the skin with its satiny sheen, the old-man's skin that had been thinned by the years. I saw the long, badly warped, horny nails, with bluish dirt underneath them. Finally I flinched. During the past few days I had been almost unconscious. I was conscious *now*. I felt the bite of the tiny *Stegomyia* as though I had been stabbed.

A comparatively small pain added to all the great pain I was suffering. But I would very much have liked to avoid this one. I groaned loudly, thinking it would get through to Carolus and March and Walter that this bite had been enough and that I was asking to be left alone. March noticed. The others might have noticed too, but they paid no attention.

They conferred: Walter said he had sent two wires. The first to the Department of Health . . . As his voice dropped to an inaudible whisper, he quickly but gently moved the mosquito from my arm to a test tube, which was then placed in a wooden rack and labeled with grease pencil. Then came a second mosquito. The nurse, whom neither of the gentlemen had deigned to look at, left the room to eat her evening meal or have a little break.

I stayed. I stayed in bed. My sufferings went on. And why wouldn't they? March took the bilious mucus I gagged up from my swollen lips and gazed at me ingenuously, full of sympathy. When I was inspired to lurch upward, as anyone might to toss his schnapps, Walter forcefully pushed me back. Not out of concern for the salubrious "horizontal position," but only so as not to disturb the biting and feeding insect. On his serious features, furrowed, lately somewhat puffy, decaying from within, could now be seen a tense expression of ardent commitment to the experiment, of joy in his work. His hands no longer shook as they had on the first evening. No doubt he had sworn off drinking again. If only he would go away! Off with him! Leave me be! Dear God! To hell with everyone! Enough of the horror! *That* was the fervent prayer I choked out, that was what my heart and my insides yearned for. That I hated Carolus, to whom I had had an unspoken aversion even on the *Mimosa*, was understandable. But now I had a much greater hatred for Walter, who, when the second mosquito had bitten amply, licked his narrow, beard-fringed lips with the lewd pleasure of the experimenter.

There were perhaps five mosquitoes together in the jar. One or another of them might fly away as they were being taken out. For this reason the window had been shut tight. The heat and the stench of my humble self had become still more unbearable. But at least the experimenters and their precious, hard-to-replace little beasts were protected. So patience, I told myself. Pull yourself together, Georg Letham the younger, be a man, stick it out. Stick it out, get hold of yourself, one mosquito bite more or less won't kill you. Fine. I gritted my teeth and got hold of myself.

The shiny little test tube that Carolus held in his hand, pressing its open end against my upper arm, glittered cruelly under the electric lights. I lifted my eyes to the glinting test tube, its rounded end. I was anxious to see the last of the insects and waited with terrible impatience for them to bite or not bite. Finally it was over.

They goose-stepped off, Carolus, Walter, March. The nurse appeared, freshly washed and brushed, with a clean headdress over her hair, smelling of soap. She opened the window, turned off all the lights but one, a very dim one at the head of my bed, she plumped the pillows, she gave me some ice chips, she cleaned my gutta-percha bib, she straightened the bedsheets at my feet, and she nodded mysteriously to March, who had just come in carrying a fat letter in my father's writing. She seemed rather serious, whereas the old boy was merry. I saw and did not see. Unexpectedly I slipped into a shallow sleep. I had been almost entirely without sleep for so many days and nights. Truly I had become as avid of sleep as only someone dogged by fever can be. When March first came in, before the mosquitoes had been placed on me, it must have been six o'clock. Now it might have been eight. I stretched thoroughly. I noticed that my breathing was becoming slower and that everything in me, from head to toe, was drifting off, dying down. It was a good, peaceful dying down, a gradual, completely inescapable, yet absolutely voluntary and lovely sinking. It was like what happens when you shut down the iris diaphragm of a microscope using the condenser knob. The light coming through the eyepiece gradually becomes weaker and weaker, but things emerge with a new sharpness, a serenity and an inevitability they did not have before. Now I heard myself sleeping deeply.

XIV

I was in my hometown. In my house. I was returning late after a walk to visit a patient, an older lady. I had had dinner in town and assumed that my wife, exhausted from her journey, would have long since gone to bed. In such cases I sometimes spent the night on a comfortable leather sofa-bed in my study, so as not to disturb her light sleep. I too was extraordinarily tired. The barometer was unusually low for this time of year, mid-August. The air abnormally pillowy, suffocatingly close. Humid, but with no tendency toward rain. Before going to bed, I took the little glass vial of Toxin Y out of my pocket and put it aside, on the mirrored top of my cabinet. But I could not sleep. Suddenly I heard my wife walking back and forth in her room directly above my study. She was awake now, or had not yet gone to bed. She was talking in a loud voice. To herself? I had gone quietly into the bathroom. The footsteps in my wife's room had stopped. As had the sound of her voice. I was just about to settle down when she appeared on the landing, wrapped in a sumptuous salmon-colored nightgown heavily embroidered with glass beads, her fine jewelry still on her throat, on her ears, wrists, and fingers. In her eyes was an expression that in the most unfathomable fashion always both attracted and repelled me. A doglike tenderness, a lust to be beaten. I drew my shoulders together. I bowed my head. I let her know that all I wanted was to be left alone. Turning on the lights in the study, she noticed the glint of the glass vial that held the toxin. She thought it was medicine. Morphine. She asked me to give her an injection, from which she expected a favorable effect. I felt the deadly irony of fate so strongly that I could not help smiling too. This put her in a better mood immediately. Conquered once more by her voluptuous urges, she embraced me with her short, rosily powdered little arms, she dragged me upstairs to our bedroom. She drew the curtains and enfolded me. She sank down at my feet and I felt the wet warmth of her tears on my lower legs, which she was clasping firmly. I bent down to her, gripped by a feeling of sympathy normally foreign to me. She seized the opportunity, reached up next to me with her right arm and switched off the little lamp on the night table. As she made this movement, the catch of her expensive jeweled bracelet bit hard into my right upper arm and not only tore the sleeve of my shirt almost up to the shoulder, but also scratched my skin so deeply at one spot that I flinched with pain. A few drops of blood flowed from the little wound.

I merely smiled a superior smile, and it was she who was distressed, I who calmed her; I was already calm. I comforted her, and she, her eyes fastened on me imploringly, clung to me until weariness overcame her and she sank into a deep sleep. I did not bend. My little wound had stopped bleeding. A scratch, no more. Her valuable bracelet lay glittering on the Persian carpet, in the middle of an ornament representing a flower or a dragon. At this point the dream became unclear. I saw myself with her head in my lap for a long time, playing distractedly with her emerald bracelet.

I gave a start. "Please keep still," Walter said.

He was still standing to my right, Carolus to my left. The light was still burning. There were no nurses to be seen. On the rack in front of me were exactly two test tubes containing mosquitoes whirring about. The third insect sat on my upper arm, hunching as they do, jiggling its last pair of legs, and was just then preparing to bite. I flinched. I did not want to go through with this. I had to.

When the insect had done its job, Walter carried it in its test tube to the wooden rack, and the fourth insect was placed on me. I groaned. Everything I have just described at length had happened in the space of a few seconds. Is time just a dream too?

March came in with another load of hungry mosquitoes. He took the engorged ones back to the laboratory. Walter seemed to continue with something he had been saying: "Secondly, I've wired my wife to tell her we're making progress now and ask for a little patience." Carolus, to whom these words were addressed, made no reply. He only shook his sage head thoughtfully and then nodded. Yes or no? Best not to choose.

Carolus assisted as dexterously and handily as was possible for him.

His thoughts were not with me. I looked at him. Not vice versa. Lord only knows on what difficult chapter of medical statistics they lingered.

I was very distressed. I was not permitted to move and had to keep still even when I was vomiting. The transfusion of my blood to twenty-five or thirty thirsty mosquitoes took until almost midnight. This was part of our experimental program.

But there was no provision in our program for the kind of dream I have just recounted.

XV

Walter had chosen the right moment to have the mosquitoes designated for new experiments feed on my blood: the morning after the scene I have described, my temperature had dropped considerably. I felt like a new man – bright yellow all over, but free of the dreadful pressure in my head, the vomiting, the epigastric pain, and all the rest of it.

I knew this was only a deceptive window. I knew these hours of relatively lucid awareness were numbered. Nevertheless something like hope awakened in me. I thought back on my life. I thought about little M., whom I had loved and whom I still loved. Why had it been she that I loved? Just because she was there. This is beyond reason.

This love had not changed me outwardly. Everything I went through had necessarily followed strict laws. And even if this late feeling had transformed the old Georg Letham the younger into an entirely different being, this "entirely different being" would have to go on living under the same name, with the same responsibilities, in the same world, and with the same past.

But what lay ahead was open. If my feeling for the little Portuguese girl who had died so young was genuine, I might one day be able to leave this hospital room as one changed within. I began to hope. I began to rejoice. I delighted in the great gift of these hours of freedom from fever and pain. For the first time it dawned on me that I might be *more fortunate* by far in my suffering than most people were in their normal lives.

My Y.F. had meaning. For the first time since this terrible illness had begun afflicting and killing people, it had meaning. The experiment was a necessary one, whose result would be that things would change. It had great significance. Though I lay powerless in the grip of this awful disease, my mind and my will made me superior to it.

I told myself that if I pulled through the second, more terrible period – I could not imagine it and did not want to, was only too happy to savor these few good hours – but if I stood the test of the second period, better days would dawn for many people, and for me.

The people around me had happier faces too. Carolus reported to me what the matron had already suggested: if I recovered, we, March and I, would not go back to the camps. I and all those designated for lifelong exile who had been experimental subjects would be recommended for clemency by the governor, in return for having voluntarily permitted the use of their bodies. This improvement in our fortunes could only have been due to Walter.

The inoculations continued. My case had been the only one so far with an unambiguously positive outcome. But when I asked after March, who had not appeared at my sickbed for some time, Carolus's leathery features twisted into what he intended to be a zany grin. But he made no reply, as though he had an especially nice surprise for me, the leathery bald rogue!

The solution was not long in appearing. My brief period of illusory well-being was already over when I heard the footsteps of nurses carrying a patient past my door on a stretcher. Was there a new case from the town? Hardly! It was March who had fallen ill. He was being accommodated in the adjoining room. His bed, against the left wall of his room, and my bed, against the right wall of mine, had only that wall between them.

I was heading for difficult days again. The good ones were past. My condition rapidly became very serious, even more agonizing than before. And then my new neighbor! The poor boy's muffled moaning and groaning might have made me despair. I would not have withstood all this had the new G. L. not been in possession of something unknown to the old G. L., the hope necessary for any new life. As long as my rapidly climbing fever left me conscious at all, I hoped for deliverance, and I hoped just as much for his, for the success of the experiment, for freedom.

But I must very soon have lost consciousness. The last thing I remember was a hollow, monotonous, but rhythmic knocking on the fairly substantial wall between us. There were only a few bricks separating us; on one side was his feverishly burning head, on the other my own, horizontal as much as possible, the better to cope with the dreadful gag reflexes. Anyone who saw us might have thought we were like the caged experimental animals in the basement that also tried to put their heads together during their time of suffering.

Sick as he was, March was trying to stay in communication with me by rapping, as prisoners commonly do on radiators or walls or toilet drainpipes. But whether he was sending me love letters in his Morse code, or complaining about the cruelty of the experiments, or making fun of it (he was capable of anything), or telegraphing me further chapters of his life story, soon I heard nothing more. No more than a corpse hears the clumps of earth pelting down on the top of its casket, those handfuls thrown down in threes, one group of three by each of the "loving hearts."

The nurses, who knew how to treat severe cases like mine, spared no effort. I was cared for as though I were His Excellency the Governor himself. The good nuns and the resident, who had somewhat less experience, did not stint on adrenaline to stop the hemorrhaging from the mouth, stomach, and gut, the ice bag did not leave my tormented brow, I was given mustard plasters for the small of my back and the lumbar area to ease the hellish pain (who invented pain – God, or the devil?), I was fed spoonfuls of milk, jelly, meat juice, fruit juice, nor was there any limit on expensive champagne (Walter paid for it!) – I found out for myself that champagne may be fine for the tongue of an epicure, but not for a tongue with no papillary layer. No doubt I ranted and thrashed about furiously every bit as much as most people who are seriously ill. When I suddenly returned to somewhat lucid consciousness one night, the nurse and the priest were next to me, and I found bits of plaster in my hair and in my wild beard. But I had no time to reflect at length, I had to vomit, and that is what I did. Nothing is sacred to someone suffering so much. Never mind the other eruptions.

I may have brought things up, but nothing could bring me down. I wanted to live more than ever. If someone who is seriously ill has anything on his mind, if his thoughts manage to focus on anything whatever, it is simple self-preservation. Survival at any cost!

No amount of suffering could make me, the person I now was, stop wanting to survive. I did not want to die. I did not want to go under. In my delirium, when the nurse had turned her back for a moment to remove the bedpan, I pulled down my "chart," as it is called, on which the course of my illness had been neatly graphed by the excellent Carolus. And despite my temperature of forty-one, I recognized the death omen, the blue and red lines for pulse and temperature going up and the black line for detoxication, urine output, going down. During the last twelve hours, I had produced not a drop of urine. That was the reliable symptom of a speedy exitus.

The nurse came back, her hands washed, the same gentle smile, the same expression of motherly reassurance on her face, and asked me to pass water. I was unable to produce a drop. Tears flowed, but not urine. What can the human will do? It cannot force nature to its knees.

She catheterized me. She did it without shyness and I permitted it without shame. I, who had never even shown myself unclothed to my wife!

One suffering so much is not a man. Yes, I say he is no longer a person in the usual sense.

The sufferer is no longer entirely of this world. He needs more love than a human being can otherwise expect. More than he deserves. Much more.

The nurse was only doing her job. Nothing bothered her, neither my terrible carrion smell nor anything else on earth. She was not experimenting. She was doing what was necessary. She brought relief. Unexpectedly she removed three hundred grams of bilious brownish green urine, and the way she held the jar up to the light told me that she herself, in her unshakable faith, regarded this relatively small amount as a good omen.

March's room was as quiet as the grave. Tears came to my eyes, I shivered, and I fell asleep.

XVI

An image of the sick March pursued me into my sleep. All the stories he had told me in earlier days, along with memories of young M. (who had his face in my dream), passed confusedly through my thoughts – nonsensically, but with such verisimilitude, such surreal brightness and clarity, that when I awoke with a somewhat lower fever my mind was thronged with them. And March was going to perish for my sake? Not seeing the poor fellow for the last few days had strengthened my devotion and gratitude. Suddenly I didn't know how I was going to live without him.

Even when I was ill I had always limited my utterances of pain and delight to those even the strongest will could not suppress, but I cried out softly, and for joy, when I suddenly heard the rhythmic knocking on the wall between our rooms. I have forgotten what message he was sending me. Probably it was not really Morse code, for his condition still did not permit the full use of his intellectual faculties. But he was alive! He was not out of danger, he was at the beginning of the second of the more serious stages of the disease, while I was at the end of it. But his case had been milder than mine, his temperature had stayed below thirty-eight, and the nurse hoped he would pull through.

Carolus and Walter came to see me. I expected reports of the experiments then in progress, but both maintained a dogged silence.

Walter looked enervated. But it was not the enervation of a man consumed by internal conflict, a man killing himself with narcotics. It was only the fatigue of a scientist at the top of his game.

Walter's silence about the experiments did not mean he mistrusted me. On the contrary, more than ever he saw in me someone not to be given up on, and despite his reserve, both inborn and acquired, he confided in me much that concerned his personal situation. I have already reported what he had wired to his wife, who was supposed to be relaxing with the children on an epidemic-free island a few days away. He seemed to regret it. In a whisper, perhaps because he did not want a loud answer, he told me she had wired back, congratulating him, but saying that now he could let it go at last, he could not go on tempting Providence, challenging fate. She had mentioned the five children by name and then – two exclamation points. This was really just her ordinary way of speaking, despite the fact that each word of this gas (and the punctuation, too) cost a pretty penny and took up space that might have been used for more important news. For at the end of this expensive dispatch regrettably not written in telegram style, she said that she was unable to say more because she lacked the funds.

This in itself insignificant message had the toil-worn, anxious doctor-gentleman very much on pins and needles. How was the pregnancy going? How was his wife doing, how were things with his children? Not a syllable about any of that! He had forebodings of some disaster and would have averted it only too gladly. There was only one path for him to take – the one we had all chosen for him. But he feared for those to whom his heart cleaved. Why have one, I might have asked once. Now I held my tongue. I looked at the polished ring on his finger and said not a word.

Was it conceivable that he told me this and many other details about his marriage, whose principals may have loved each other but never understood each other, merely so that, if his experiment on himself went wrong, *I* would offer his family a protective wing? It was possible. He hesitated, looked around the room, picked up my chart, sent the nurse out. His words became fewer, and yet he did not want to leave me. No doubt he realized that on my first day without fever I was still as weak as a kitten and that every word cost me a great deal of effort no matter how softly I whispered it. I struggled to keep my eyes open, and between his laconic words I listened for my friend's knocking and scratching.

Oddly enough, my hearing had become much sharper now. My ears were more sensitive than they had ever been. I had noticed this in other patients after they passed the crisis, though the phenomenon had been less marked than it was in my case.

Finally the old nurse must have given Dr. Walter a sign that I needed rest. No sooner had he gone than March started in behind the wall, monotonously giving the same signal until he too was quieted.

My sense of time was not yet functioning. I spent the days following the crisis in rapidly alternating periods of sleep and waking. I didn't know what day it was and often woke up in the morning thinking it was still the evening of the previous day.

I found myself in an indescribable state of physical weakness. My hand would fall as it brought the spoon to my mouth, I spilled any liquid I was given. But I wanted to be my old self as quickly as possible, get up, work, move around, and live.

I had become fond of life.

I was living, perhaps for the first time, without a feeling of guilt.

I had passed through a great deal. Whatever I had done, I had paid for it. I could face the future better now.

I had been burdened (unconsciously?) by a heavy feeling of guilt – I can say this now – from earliest childhood, long before I actually became guilty of anything. With his story of his expedition and the rats, my father had revealed to me the imperfection, the senselessness, and the cruelty of the world and the human heart, not just once but a thousand times over. But, pious as he was, no, worse than that, pietistic, as life had made him, he had tried to teach me religion and patriotism – a belief in something of unattainable goodness, perfection, and power standing above us – as a corrective to what we know of the world. God in heaven, the fatherland on earth. I could not make this God of absolute goodness responsible for the obviously senseless suffering of the world down below. When I heard about some catastrophe, the sort that the newspapers are full of day after day, when my eyes were opened to these things too soon – who was I supposed to blame? If not myself? I could only blame myself and my kind. God was just. The human creature was guilty. Man was sinful and stupid from the beginning. He inherited the sins of his fathers together with their stupidity and bequeathed the lot to his children. All were guilty. God the Almighty was not.

I had this vague guilty feeling as far back as I can remember. I had it as a young man when I saw the suffering of vivisected animals. I had it at the bedside of my patients. I had it when, searching for a way out of my predicament, I took my wife's life into my own hands. As mortal terror might make someone shoot himself in the head, my guilty feeling made me feel guilty. Whether the jury acquitted me or not, it could not relieve me of my feeling of guilt. I was my own judge. The jury could dictate a punishment for me. That was part of the record, like the criminal charges. But *inner* vindication through *outer* suffering, this rehabilitation was not in its power to bring about.

Long before I understood I was guilty, I had felt that I was very much complicit in the grotesque ghastliness of the world. Everything I saw, at first with my father's eyes and then through my own observations, only made this guilt heavier. Then, on the island of C., it swelled, this guilty feeling of original sin. Not immediately. Not all at once. The loss of the little Portuguese girl was just the beginning. My truly frightful sufferings as a Y.F. patient – you would have to have gone through something of the kind to have any sense of them – were only the second step. Not the last, not by far.

I do not say: my love for the Portuguese girl (a paternal, a physicianly love, a hopeless, a foolish, senseless one, but still mine, the only love I still had in me) – I do not say that my love for the unfortunate child changed me morally. I do not say I was cleansed by the atrocious physical suffering, the vomiting for all I was worth and the loss of the last of my wind, the living putrefaction and the carrion stench, the sorriest thing that ever happened to my miserable body. That would take a lot more, including a good deal that one might find surprising in an inner transformation.

Happiness was needed too – a feeling of recovery and joy in being alive, and a hope that nothing could destroy.

XVII

My recovery was very slow. March had a much easier time of it. I didn't begrudge him his good fortune. What I had gone through was something I wouldn't have wished on my worst enemy, never mind my only friend.

When I took my first steps in the sickroom, I shuffled like an eighty-year-old stroke victim. Any movement produced wild heart palpitations accompanied by shortness of breath, forcing me to stop and rest. March, inoculated by one of the mosquitoes with my Y.F. blood, had fallen ill after I had, but he was already back on his feet and steady on them, though his eyes were sunken in deep hollows and his hair had fallen out in clumps. I suspected that this had very much wounded his male vanity. March, bald – the handsome blond youth with a dome, from above his weary eyes to the nape of his neck! As strange as it may sound, I felt drawn to March as he was, depleted by severe illness; I had more of a liking for him than ever. A liking? What am I saying? It was pure joy when he came into my room holding the nurse's hand (the nun towered over him by more than a head) and literally threw himself on my neck! His bald head, which looked like a billiard ball and felt like one, smooth and regular, bobbed on my throat, in which my pulse pounded madly at the least excitement, and his tears flowed under my hospital gown, down to my lower chest. What a reunion! I joked. We had both risen from the dead and could thank the heavens.

I did, in my way. He in his. He reported to the chaplain for confession and Communion, since he believed that the confession he had made and the Communion he had received in the hospital at the beginning of his illness (like all new patients) were insufficient.

That day he practically had to be taken by force out of my room. My energies were hardly worthy of the name, they were only sufficient for staying alive. I only wanted to sleep. I ate very little, afraid the terrible vomiting might return, and what that meant can be judged only by someone who has gagged and vomited himself nearly to death as I had. I could barely speak. "Barely" was the word for everything I did. I could barely even think.

March, a person of almost inexhaustible energies, did not understand this. Six or seven days after my defervescence, he was sitting by my bed as happy as a clam and feeding me in his awkward way. I bridled at his overbrisk ministration. But I didn't want to hurt him. Nevertheless it became too much for me. My stomach, whose lesioned walls were only lightly healed, could not accommodate much food at one time, even if it was as delicious as the black cook in the hospital kitchen was able to make it for convalescent patients. But when the good March sat by me and rejoiced at every morsel I forced down, who would have had the heart to tell him: go away and quit tormenting me with your love! It makes me want to th . . .

So I submitted to him. Then I collapsed on the pillows. A gnawing pain began in my stomach and climbed up my throat to my mouth. I belched – always an ominous sign with me, who never belched when I was healthy – though I did my best to suppress it in order not to worry March. I made myself lie still and hold down everything that wanted to come up.

The good fellow was now standing at the window. He closed the blinds, but then held two slats apart for a last swooning look at the evening landscape. The hospital was on a hill. On clear days the view was enchanting, the islands, dark, craggy, but partly ringed by lush vegetation at the shore, could be seen gleaming in all the colors of the rainbow in the light of the setting sun, the sea reflecting its blazing brilliance and the copper and sapphire tints of the clouds. The massy, towering structures of the clouds were motionless. Also motionless were the rocky islands in the becalmed sea. Between the two was the suspended blaze of the gradually subsiding evening sun. It was a strange feeling to hear my friend's oohs and ahs at the sight of these empyrean natural wonders while the pain inside me was eating me up. He sat on my bed. Dusk was falling rapidly. He caressed me with his fine, stupid eyes and ran his fingers over his skull to see if he could feel his hair growing back, and asked me half seriously, half jokingly, if I thought there was anything there.

Anything there! Why not say what was really on his mind? His future and mine were a thousand times more important. He had learned, in fact earlier than I had (at that time I was suffering the initial attacks of fever), of Walter's humanitarian plan to officially recommend clemency for every convict who had volunteered for life-threatening experiments. Now it was of great concern to me (and not without reason) what this freedom would really mean. Was it only the freedom to move about freely on C. and in all probability perish here from the hardships of unemployment and poverty and the climate, especially if, as would be the case for the two of us, we could not count on support from munificent family members? Or was it the true freedom to be allowed to live again, as one wished to do?

As I said, my hearing had become extraordinarily keen as a result of my illness. Although I was in the grip of a new wave of fever, my ears could detect the slightest sound. I must also note that I was much more attentive now to the things around me. I was struck by much about people and things that I would never have thought worthy of notice before. Thus my eyes were opened to innumerable character traits in people, ones that were both ridiculous and affecting, repellent and poignant. I understood people better. I found their behavior natural and not always internally inconsistent.

I could never have engaged with March and Walter this way before. With my keen ears, I could hear something dejected, weighed down, in March's regular breathing. Possibly someone with gloomy thoughts allows a tiny bit of phlegm to rattle in his windpipe as he breathes, whereas a happy, carefree person will just hawk it up. The way he clears his throat, the way he hawks . . . March did not clear his throat, he rattled. His eyes hung on mine with an anxious expression. He must have been worrying about the same thing as I was. He wanted to be considerate, he didn't want to agitate me, he had tact, and the ears of his soul had always been rather keen by nature, more so than mine, I fear. But what was the good of that if there was still no way for him to help me? So he may have suspected the state I was in, but, with horrible anxiety, I felt the nausea coming and I only wanted to spare him the sight of his friend being sick again. I was silent and put on an annoyed expression, I didn't want him around now. Not because I was not fond of him, no, precisely because I was. Was he so reluctant to understand that? Was it impossible for him?

Why was it that the nurse who was just coming in did understand it? In less than three seconds he had been hustled out the door, I was lying horizontal, the pillows were on the floor, the ice bag was on my stomach (where the detestable pain was appearing in all its fearsomeness), the gutta-percha bib was flapping around my neck. The light was turned out, perhaps so that I would not see what I vomited, the dreaded coffee substitute-like matter. And the orders: breathe deeply, breathe deeply, lie still, lie flat! No movement. Nothing. No *r* (read), no *f* (enough)! Breathe. Be silent.

Perhaps it was my last day. In any event it was a relapse and the more serious in that I had no reserves of strength. The nurse stroked my brow. There was nothing else she could do at the moment. Then she sat down in a corner, and I heard her rattling her rosary beads rhythmically as waves of gagging rose from my wasted but distended and drum-tight belly. I thought about my past and future life. I turned my spirit away from the pain and the retching. I did not pity myself. Instead, amid raging, heart-wrenching pain, I reviewed a broadly conceived agenda for the shape of my future life, provided fate saved me now. Did I have hope? Only hope of hope! The relapses were too perilous. But I wasn't going to die just yet. The retching finally stopped.

They kept March away from me until I was completely out of danger. Walter and Carolus came often.

XVIII

Walter intentionally kept March far away. By way of compensation he gave me as much as he could of his own scant free time. If only I had been able to repay his interest in some way!

My good days were beginning. His were over, for he was in frightful shape. He didn't know what was happening to him. And although the various attempts to induce infection with bites from mosquitoes had failed completely in his case, his appearance was not much better than mine. I am not just saying this in hindsight. Even then, three months after our experiments began, I saw in his features a dissolution, a shadow of something that had already passed the point of no return.

An observer as levelheaded and as determined to be precise as I was could see, every day, every morning when I greeted him and accompanied him to the laboratory (where I just watched, still much too weak to work), how he was wasting away.

What the grueling twelve-hour workdays, made that much deadlier by the fiendish climate, could not do, worrying about his family could. Since that fragmentary telegram, particularly excruciating in its mysteriousness, he had received no news. He waited. Nothing arrived other than scientific journals and medical books. He reproached himself the most bitterly not for having embarked on the experiments, but for having failed to give up his life with his family at the outset and send them to relatives in London long ago, irrespective of what happened to him.

When the sea was rough, he had visions of his family blundering into a typhoon, of the kind not infrequent in the environs of the Pearl Gulf at this time of year, on their way here. When he was paid at the end of the month, he was unsure whether to send them the money or wait until he found out what they planned to do.

Carolus wrapped himself in the reserve of a high official. March stayed at a certain distance, consumed by furious jealousy of Walter, yet always full of respect for his rank and his gentlemanly qualities. March then vented his agitation on me, and had I not been so very fond of him in my way (while never entertaining any carnal feeling), I would have become impatient and told him to go hang. But my self-mastery was necessary as never before. Four weeks after the last relapse, I was still in a condition of extraordinary weakness. Or should it be called peace? In any event it was an inactive hiatus. I felt I would never again be able to summon the determined energy for work that had always been my companion.

During this hiatus an unexpected figure suddenly appeared, one whose impact would be momentous in more ways than one – the ardently longed-for, the loving and beloved wife, Frau Walter.

I have already said that her husband's efforts to infect himself with a mosquito bite had been without success thus far. As things stood, I had suffered a very severe, March a mild but typical case of Y.F.; Carolus had shown quite mild fever symptoms that might have had some other cause; the chaplain we had thus far regarded as a reserve and had not yet inoculated; von F. the pharmacist had been ruled out, he no longer came, and that was nice of him. Walter remained the puzzle in our experiments, designated with question marks. He had been bitten five times by mosquitoes carrying *my* Y.F. blood, and even more times by other mosquitoes that had fed on the blood of patients who had been even sicker and had since died. All had been in vain. Let us say he was lucky. We did not envy him, and I thought highly of him and felt sorry for him.

Now it is known in bacteriology that experimental animals such as guinea pigs may be robustly resistant to a given infection, able to withstand it just as long as they are well fed and have normal blood volume. They remain frisky and healthy despite being infected. But if they are artificially run down, an infection that was harmless before is now immediately fatal. There are strains of bacteria whose effects are disastrous only in winter, not in summer, when the animals enjoy greater vitality.

This old rule, though not so clear and irrefutable in every case, would unfortunately be borne out in our Walter's. And I, who for the first time in my life was beginning to overcome my antipathy to the "loving hearts," would see – but why jump ahead, let us again allow the facts of the experiment to speak for themselves.

I said earlier that Frau W. eventually appeared. The strident voice we knew from the telephone might have brought to mind a tall, thin woman with a military bearing. But, quite unexpectedly, the person who appeared, naïvely violating the restrictions against entering the hospital, was a petite little thing, graceful despite her advanced pregnancy, who, with her pretty, lively, pale oval face, much more resembled a girl in her late twenties than a woman in her forties who had given birth to five children and was expecting a sixth. A magnificently shaped head, wonderful naturally curly auburn hair with a few brighter strands (bleached by the sun on C., or turned gray by worry?). A Spanish shawl with a long deep green fringe that she had thrown about her fit closely on her still tautly modeled bust, more loosely on her protuberant abdomen, perhaps to hide the disfigurement of pregnancy. Thus she entered the examination room, her high heels clicking on the tiles, and looked around her. Without taking off her light-colored gloves, she extended her hand to her husband, who was pale as a corpse and speechless with astonishment; she nodded somewhat loftily to the rest of us. Only on me did her gaze linger a moment. How had she come back? A small motor vessel that plied the coastal waters was blowing its whistle in the harbor even now, and an automobile sounded its horn in front of the building, though there was surely no reason to honk in the insignificant traffic of this desolate convent area on the hill. The car belonged to the insurance subagent of whom I have spoken. He was no doubt giving the lady a prearranged signal to hurry. Had she thought her husband could simply be led away, as though he were a dog being sent off to be boarded in a good home?

She pulled her husband into a corner near the telephone booth, on her full, tight cheeks a fleeting blush of the kind common in pregnant women. She took both his pale hands in her gloved ones as though to hold him fast and lowered her overly loud voice so that we did not have to be in on the conversation. Nor did we wish to be. They could have talked just as well or better in his room. But the wife seemed to be extremely tense and edgy, she did not want to waste a second. She talked madly at him. In the heat of the conversation she let go of his hands and waved hers about. The fringe of her shawl fluttered, and her massively protruding belly was suddenly revealed. Walter was visibly shaken. His wife, back without his knowledge and against his oft-expressed wishes! And here! Inside the cordon! Invading the laboratory, in violation of the rule that affected every resident of the city up to the highest officials (even if most of them abided by it only because it was in their interest to do so)! But how could such arguments move a passionate, death-defying woman who shrank from nothing? And now more than ever. We could not understand her words. But we heard her occasionally let loose with a raucous laugh and then, remembering her breeding, vainly attempt to cover it up with a fit of coughing. This spoke clearly enough. Walter, deathly pale, lost his composure. This man whom I had never seen discomposed, whom I would never have thought capable of a failure of nerve, suddenly had tears on his face behind his spectacles!

His wife brushed them away with her gloves. She gazed at us all as though she were superior to us. Was she? Even now she did not take her gloves off. And as poor Walter, crimson with shame, tried to break free, she dragged him along. We looked away. Carolus left the room. When Walter managed to tear himself away, she ran after him impetuously, tripping over the drooping shawl. He vainly tried to free himself as his wife pulled him out of the laboratory. But no woman, however virile, was this man's equal. Carefully yet forcefully, he disengaged himself. He came back to us and bent over his microscope. He did not see his wife standing next to him, he did not hear her shout into his ear. He was at his microscope. It was merely a gesture, for at that moment there was no slide on the stage of the instrument. But what did the impassioned wife care about that? She wanted her husband back. And then she wanted to take him by the hand and leave, with the children on her lap and the fetus in her belly, leave the satanic, epidemic-plagued island for London. Back, back! And when he resisted, she slapped him in the face with her gloved hands, once, twice. His spectacles clattered to the floor. He said nothing, merely ran his hands down his cheeks, which, ashen though he was, had an unnaturally flushed, bright brick red color. We were as though paralyzed. The woman left the laboratory unhindered. March, who had just come in, was thunderstruck. Walter had to ask him twice to bring a particular jar of mosquitoes.

I was the first to collect myself, and for the first time since my convalescence I assisted my comrades in our experiments. And the experiment on Walter was successful. A mosquito fastened itself to Dr. Walter, and four days *post infectionem* he became ill.

XIX

The doctor was strangely agitated even the day before the onset of fever. He worked with a haste that can only be called feverish, though his body temperature was at that time still precisely normal. He had not been the same since the scene with his wife. But his desperate composure and the strenuous effort he was making could not disguise the fact that something in him had broken. In contrast to the irascibility he had lately often shown with March and Carolus and the chaplain (though not with me when I was convalescing), he was very gentle. When we had finished our work in the evening (an occasional helping hand from me now being permitted once more), he insisted on thanking us before we separated. It was as though he were clinging to us, his comrades. He had heard nothing more from his wife. The coastal steamer was again under way; whether it was taking his wife and children away from C. once more he did not know.

But he heard from the intrusive subagent, who may have been animated by true devotion too, who knows? I almost had that impression. Walter did not admit him. He would have nothing to do with him. When the subagent pushed himself forward nonetheless, Walter ignored him completely, closed his ears to what he said. Never have I seen someone cut so very dead. Yet this was not haughtiness. The only one of us who knew class distinctions was not the gentleman-physician Walter, nor the mysterious chaplain, a mute and impassive man of unknown origins, nor yet that honored high official of medicine Carolus, but March, who came from humble circumstances. I did not understand this trait of his. I was astonished by his patronizing manner toward all blacks, the self-sacrificing nurses as well as the prosperous subagent. But he made a point of it. Later I would see that my knowledge of human nature had often let me down in judging March's character.

Now I was preoccupied with Walter on the one hand, with March on the other. On the one hand the man from my own sphere of interests, the intellectual hub of the commission, my old school fellow, the man I looked up to. On the other the young, indefatigable, passionate March, flourishing once more, who mastered his sensual impulses as I never would have thought possible in such an uninhibited person, but who instead gave himself to me with all his heart and whose assistance (and good humor) I believed I could count on if I had any sort of problem, day or night. He was a great help to me here on C. I gave thanks to my Creator (if this phrase is allowed) often and thought that only death could end this first "true" friendship of mine.

Even though he was working very hard, Walter was unable to sleep at night during this period, whether because the disease was already smoldering in him or because he was wrought up to such a degree that even at night he was unable to compose himself, calm down, relax.

One night I awoke, as I often did. There was such a nice cool breeze blowing through one of the basement windows of our airless, rat-filled bedroom, a rarity in the washhouse steaminess of this sultry climate, that I slipped out as quietly as I could. I thought I would walk around outside a little until my sweat-soaked underwear had dried on my body and then go back to bed. I was no longer required to be the first one in the laboratory in the morning; as a convalescent I had the freedom to come and go as I pleased. Thus if I made use of the nighttime hours for a stroll, I could sleep for as long as I wanted afterward.

My steps echoed hollowly in the silence as I headed toward the main entrance. In the corridor I encountered, leaning on the ledge of an open window and gazing down on the dim lights of the city and the church and the sea, Walter. He was still dressed for the lab. Evidently he had never gone to bed. When he noticed me, he raised his heavy, swollen eyelids and looked glassily at me for a long time without a word. Then he joined me and we wandered in silence through the deserted hallways and empty rooms of the hospital. It was equipped for patients in much greater numbers than the four or five that currently happened to be there, all of them on the road to recovery. But just as many had lately perished of Y.F., whose mortality rate was now fifty to fifty-five percent. Abruptly he took my arm and linked elbows with me, as a father might do with his grown son. Still not a word. Only the night before, he had been telling highly amusing stories about his not very lengthy but eventful service as an army doctor. But this had been illusory. As I leaned against him I felt a half-empty liter bottle in the pocket of his lab coat. It must have been half empty, because it made a hollow gurgling sound. But when the poor man turned to me, opened his mouth wide, and laboriously brought out words as halting as his steps, I noticed that his breath did not really smell of whiskey. It was much more strongly perfumed by something else, by something bizarre and abominable. The reader will have guessed what it was.

I gave a start and stopped in my tracks. The poor fellow noticed nothing. He was thinking about his wife, who had gotten the better of him, not about Y.F. He was no longer afraid of the disease, now that he had tried and failed umpteen times to infect himself in experiments. He did not know or had forgotten that a person who is weakened, who is broken in spirit, no longer has the same resistance to the Y.F. microorganism as an unbroken constitution. The blows he had received from his wife had affected him so deeply that he had become a lesser man. Thus the wife had aided our experiments. Unwittingly she had laid her husband open to the poison of Y.F.

The poison of alcohol he could deal with. He confided in me that he was driven to drink more than ever, that he felt terribly restless, he had to walk around, he had to have the whiskey on him, he even had to take a whiff of it every so often, but he had sworn "on the lives of his wife and children" that he wouldn't touch another drop of alcohol as long as he was on C. "That would be the beginning of the end," he said. Then came long discussions of the progress of our experiments. Should we move quickly to make public what we now knew, the experiments we had done on ourselves and what we had learned? Would the two clear cases, March's and mine, and the one unclear case, Carolus's, suffice to demonstrate the momentous fact of yellow fever's way of propagating from person to person and surprise the scientific world – or were control experiments necessary too?

He agreed with me or came to agree with me that we had to wait. But in any event we would put everything to date in writing and deposit this documentation with the city notary in order to guarantee our priority. "My children," he said with a vestige of his old radiant smile, "will benefit from what their father did for this part of the world." He again went to a window and leaned far out. The guards, two of them as always, were just then passing on their morning patrol, unarmed and shoeless. A wave of fragrant air rose from the harbor below and from the trees on the small area of raised ground near an old church that dated from Spanish times. The stars, no longer at the height of their luminosity because of the approach of daybreak, stood in great profusion above the still hospital and the old trees of its garden. A very slight shudder went through Walter's greatly emaciated body – I felt it through the thin dress jacket that he always wore in the lab. It was like what happens when one casually brushes one of the bottom keys of a piano. There is a thrumming, a purring, but it subsides immediately. So too here.

As always the night was incomparably cooler than the day, but not so much so that a fully clothed man would have shivered. He understood this too, grasped his right carpus with his left hand to take his pulse, but then lost interest, laughed, and said, "I almost thought . . ." He left the sentence unfinished, pursuing a different train of thought entirely, and I knew that this was what had been on his mind, not the idea that he might be ill: "When women are expecting, you can't argue with them. It's a crisis. They're all pathological. When one of them is going through as much as my wife is, you turn the other cheek – you just have to make sure she isn't hurting herself and the baby." Right! That was my response, of course, but I must admit that I hated the woman's guts, even if I did understand her in a way. Later I was too angry to sleep.

XX

The next evening the doctor suddenly fell ill with chills. His noble, manly face swelled. The puffy cheeks, the pout, the piercing glitter of his eyes in their hollows gave him some resemblance to a drunk. But no one's mind could have been clearer. As though he were standing by someone else's bed, he dictated his own case report to my friend March. "C., date, year, and so forth, Dr. Walter, forty-two years old, army medical officer, medium build, malaria tropica four years ago, otherwise always healthy. Inoculated by *Stegomyia fasciata* B3 four days ago, sudden onset of illness with chill, temperature 39.9°C, pulse 120, very strong – heart sounds?" He had had his autostethoscope brought from his room. This is a listening device placed on the heart (or rather the chest wall, etc.) and connected to the ears by two rubber tubes, allowing one to listen to one's own heart and breath sounds as though they were someone else's. But who wants to eavesdrop on himself, except when he has to?

Walter listened to his heart beating, his lungs breathing, his bowels protesting. Then he placed the autostethoscope on his aching brow. He smiled; a forced smile, but still. Then, his teeth chattering feverishly and his limbs twitching like a galvanized frog's, he took the earpieces out of his ears and gave the stethoscope back to me. "The heart sounds are still very strong. If that changes, keep on top of it. Give me digitalis beginning tomorrow and try to get the heart rate down to ninety from 120. I know my heart, it's been through worse."

He trusted in his constitution and in me, whom he regarded as his physician. We wanted to move him out of the laboratory where he had been overcome by chills and take him to a sickroom right away. He refused, insisting that we do another blood test first. He had had tropical malaria in the army years before, and he wanted to rule out that possibility. But was he still *hoping*? Was it that he did not *want* to know? We did not ask. He did not say.

Carolus did this test. He had been schooled by Walter for months now and had become so accomplished that he was entrusted with the relatively simple blood test for malaria plasmodia.

As expected, the results were negative.

We arranged everything as quickly as possible. Walter deteriorated visibly as we were tending him, his consciousness faded, and March, who had remained largely unprofessionalized and must have conceived a kind of liking for Frau Walter (!), urged us to put off the tests and notify the patient's wife down in C. as quickly as possible. What we wanted at the moment was to bring our work as far along as we could. If at all possible we still wanted to keep the public out of it for the time being. A woman who could physically attack a man like Walter was obviously capable of doing all sorts of imprudent things. Not to mention that I wanted to do what I could to spare Walter's wife – she was about to give birth, after all. It was very likely, though not yet a hundred percent certain, that our last experiment (Walter) was a success. Perhaps we could spare her the excitement. To cut a long story short, Carolus, the chaplain, and I were opposed to informing her, the three of us against March.

Walter was the head man and it was his decision. He nodded mechanically in response to all questions. Should we notify his spouse? He nodded. Or should we wait? Again he nodded. Might it be better to spare your wife, in view of her condition? As so often in laboratory experiments, nothing is certain yet, and even if it were, your case may be no worse than those of March and Carolus, it might be and let's hope will be a brief (!) episode that won't necessarily go beyond the second stage (!!). To this too he nodded, adding in a hoarse, failing voice, seemingly already much pained by every word, "Yes, that's the best thing."

We, Carolus, March, and I, carried him to his room on the aforementioned stretcher, on which March and I and countless others had lain, then tiptoed out as the chaplain came in bringing him the sacrament. The doctor, no longer lucid, received it. The chills, which had gone on for an hour in March's case and for a bit more than four in mine, lasted for eight solid hours with him, poor fellow. This was an ominous sign.

I did not give March an order, but I gave him permission to alert the doctor's wife at about noon the next day. I have forgotten what prevented her from appearing immediately. Relatives were normally strictly forbidden to enter the epidemic-ridden hospital, but the director of the hospital made an exception in her case as a tribute to her husband's heroism and permitted her to come at once at her own risk. But she did not come until two days later, in the late afternoon, unfortunately just when we were setting about having two dozen mosquitoes feed on Dr. Walter's blood for new experiments.

It was necessary. We wanted to find out whether the blood was still infectious after seventy hours, reckoned from the onset of Y.F. Thus we needed mosquitoes engorged with infected blood for more experiments. Who in our place would have called a halt at this point? I ask this in all confidence. I am quite sure of the answer. The experiment was unavoidable. We had to do *everything* to find out, or all our efforts would have been wasted. The doctor took no notice of the bites. He was no longer himself. He was thrashing about unconsciously. It took great effort to hold him down, but he did not feel the mosquito bites.

He lay there with a temperature of forty-one and a half degrees centigrade and cold extremities. We had covered him with a camel-hair blanket that had accompanied him on all his campaigns in the army and all his travels. I felt his thin limbs trembling under the napped, already somewhat worn material that smelled of leather and tobacco.

I had by no means regained my strength and I sighed heavily; holding him down as he kept trying to lurch upward was very tiring.

He felt nothing, I repeat. And even if he did feel it, I also repeat, it had to be.

But how was his wife, storming in half mad with her aggrieved love and boundless despair, going to understand that! On top of everything else (pregnant women often seem to be out of their minds) she had brought along the little dog that Walter had taken her. Picture it, a distraught, heavily pregnant woman and an idiotically barking dog with hostile intentions toward all of us in the hot, cramped, cell-like sickroom.

The woman held her nose silently in horrified self-defense. The smell of the disease was indeed awful. She had a markedly swollen neck, as is frequent in mothers-to-be. A kind of goiter had formed, which heaved tempestuously. Even the dog was unhinged. The beast jumped on the sick man's stomach, out of joy or out of hatred going back to painful experiments done in the past or for some other reason – and this was the epigastric region, which seemed to be hurting the poor fellow the most just then. But dog and wife cared not a whit. She elbowed her way through and hurled herself on top of him, she wept and sobbed, bewailed his lot and hers. She "whispered" to him, so loudly that we all heard it, that she was worried about the pending delivery. The baby was in the wrong position, it was like a stone, it would surely kill her, he would come to regret his callousness, he should bethink himself, get up, chase us away, and come with her.

She pushed us, along with our mosquitoes and our test tubes, all the technically sophisticated paraphernalia we had laboriously contrived for a difficult experiment, away from her husband, or rather she tried to. The job of stopping her from interfering with our plan could only fall to me. I was the least involved elsewhere. Carolus was keeping the mosquitoes held down on the doctor's skin so that they would bite. March was helping him. If anyone was free, it was me. Off with the lady. For the good of the enterprise and her own.

She had to yield. Firmly but gently I drew her away. I challenged her: for the sake of her unborn child she should go easy on herself and avoid any excitement. She looked at me furiously – and suddenly fell silent. What could she do? She gave in.

The experiment could continue as it had to. Carolus did his job well.

But that ornery March, that sentimental fool, what did he do but suddenly draw himself up and resign his post. Was he going to run after the lady? From behind the door that we had quickly locked, she was again keening into our already tormented ears (I was hypersensitive) and souls (I was only human, after all). I controlled myself. No harsh words. No violence. I waved him away and took on his job in addition to my own. He shoved off. I heard him behind the door calming the lady at last and then leaving with her.

Our work took a long time. I have already described how the patient had to put up with the nuisance of the experimental mosquito bites over a period of hours. In itself this is nothing. During this long period Walter did have lucid moments of a kind more than once: "Where am I? Who are you?" he would wheeze hoarsely. "Water! Thirsty! Ice!"

The nurses, of course, hurried to get what he wanted. But before they could return to his bed, before they could bring the spoon to his inflamed mouth, he was deeply unconscious again. His beautiful, strong, sinewy hands had slowly begun to "floccillate," plucking threads from the camel-hair blanket. (Later, when I was back within the four walls of my basement room, I found the little tufts on my lab coat and removed them with a peculiar feeling that is better left undescribed.)

Finally the last insect seemed to be about to bite. The silvery little spots were visible on its dark abdomen as it sat hunched on Walter's skin.

The doctor groaned heartrendingly and pointed to his head with his free left hand. The ice bag seemed to be too heavy for him, and Carolus, forgetting that you can only do one thing at a time, took it off. As he did so he unfortunately let the mouth of the test tube come away from the skin. The rascally mosquito, already greatly engorged, escaped and could not be recaptured. It was evidently hiding in a dark corner.

The doctor was again murmuring all sorts of things. Apparently he was writing to his wife in his thoughts. He drew letters on the blanket and read the words out as he went along, putting them together with effort: "Be glad, dearest" (there seemed to be a benign smile on his face, an expression it seldom wore), "our achievement will be the greatest . . ." What our achievement would be never became known. He merely wheezed, gagged, coughed, breathed deeply, suddenly opened his eyes, looked at us each in turn, for a particularly long time at March, who was just then coming through the door. He faced him directly and asked, articulating the words laboriously: "Do you have good news from my wife? I'm a bit sick just now. She should stay where she is. Rio de Janeiro, Montebello Hotel. Tell her I'm sorry! The baby will be in the right position, because all her deliveries have been easy, thank God! And you must know, that's been my prayer for twenty years . . . But please take the ice bag off my head!" (There was no ice bag.) "Hark, there go the twenty-four buglers in concert, all sounding 'Taps' for the old year." Again the sense of these words was not clear. Much as we loved him, how little we knew him!

"What are you trying to tell us, my dear Dr. Walter?" I asked, for I saw that his hours were numbered.

"You? Nothing. But do you know," he said, turning again to March, weeping like a child, "I'm leaving my wife and children so little . . . If you knew how little. But it's all for the best. Ice, please, some ice! I'm thirsty."

We gave him ice and left the room to put the mosquitoes in darkness.

XXI

Twenty-four hours later we were again gathered around Walter's bed. His temperature had fallen, so much so that it was below normal, 35.8°C; we could leave the thermometer as long as we wanted, Walter's temperature would never get up to the normal 36.9. Dr. Walter lay quietly in bed. His skin was the color of a faded beech leaf.

His gaze was lucid. He was conscious. The illness was in its deceptive remission period, but his eyes did not light up when we expressed our joy over his improvement. When I tried to take his pulse, he made a clearly perceptible effort to pull his ice-cold, already saffron yellow hand away. He was suffering greatly. Psychologically perhaps more than physically. He knew he was lost. His strength had dwindled away in the last four days. It could only be a matter of hours.

We spared him any tiring examinations.

Before leaving to speak to the governor by telephone, Carolus shook his hand. As he did so, he prudently felt for the artery that runs under the skin at the wrist. But he found no pulse. He bit his lip. He stayed. The significant look he gave me told me to repeat this little maneuver. I felt the familiar slightly meandering blood vessel, as fat as a knitting needle, but I too was unable to feel a true pulse.

And yet our friend was still alive, he knew what was happening. But his deathly weakness did not permit him either to sit up properly or to utter a clearly articulated word.

His features showed disquiet. It was easy to guess that he wanted to see his wife once more. Under these circumstances I asked March to go at once to advise her of the state of things.

For the last few hours she had been in a guest room where a prior of the order sometimes stayed (despite the quarantine!). She had just gone to bed after a sleepless night and a hectic day. But there was nothing for it, she had to be awakened and brought to her husband's deathbed.

Should we leave the two of them alone? Carolus was in favor, I against. "Not yet!" I whispered. Why should we bring into the dying moments of a great man (and he was one) any more agitation and anguish than was necessary?

As I was waiting for March to return with her, the dying man's restless, harrowed gaze fell on me. Was he expecting final spiritual consolation? The chaplain appeared as though by chance. Not the expected wife. My impatience had become extreme. This time she could not delay. Fully dressed or not – there was no time to lose if she wanted to see her husband again while he was still alive. Walter's searching eyes moved from me to the night table, where there was an already disinfected Pravaz syringe of the digitalis solution, which was capable of spurring his heart, debilitated by the Y.F. toxins, to one last burst of strength. I realized what the doctor was trying to tell me with his eyes. He wanted to live a while longer so that he could say good-bye to his wife. And so that she would not be shocked!

Next to the digitalis solution was a practically identical syringe of morphine. Should I switch the two drugs?

Poor Walter was suffering atrociously. He was in control of himself, a gentleman in death as in life.

It took a connoisseur of human nature to see the muscles around his mouth working, the agony and anguish behind the friendly, polite expression on his face, to notice the nose wrinkling slightly, the poor man's fingers involuntarily tightening with pain. His breathing became deep, slow, heavy, then stertorous. His throat inflated like the throat of a songbird. And still he did not have enough air. He was suffocating and he knew it.

The respiratory center must have rapidly become completely paralyzed, just as cardiac function had already stopped being effective enough to fill the peripheral arteries.

Nevertheless I did as he had asked me at the first onset of his illness four days before.

I did not make his excruciating death easier. It was neither my right nor my duty to do so. Reluctantly I left him to the (there is no other way to put it) inconsiderate outcries of his wife, who, in her current condition now twice as unrestrained, covered the distance from the door to the bed in a single bound, then shriekingly threw herself on him, on his still extremely tender hypogastrium, with the weight of her heavily pregnant body, squeezing out of the poor man what little wind he had left! I tried in vain to pull her off the dying man, I strove to calm her, to console her, to get her to go away again so that her husband could die in peace. As though he had ever been able to live in peace during the difficult years of his marriage!

But her love asserted its prerogative, or the world's notion of what love's prerogative is. She bombarded him with voluptuous caresses as though he were her bridegroom, she talked and wept and howled and laughed hysterically all at once as he became increasingly still and wan. The pallor normally seen in people in their death agony was in his case obscured by his jaundice, but anyone seeing his eyes, already glassy and bright, in their yellow sockets, unmistakably touched by the finger of death, would not have begrudged him the last calm moment of his life. The chaplain stood by helplessly and tried in vain to administer the final consolations of faith. Walter only lifted his eyes to him and the crucifix in silence and (being left-handed) made a weak gesture with his left arm, a sort of sign of the cross.

I stood at the foot of Walter's bed. But not for long. His wife still did not understand the situation and sniffed at a little bottle of cologne. She wanted to be alone with Walter, wanted me to leave, but I did not. The dying Walter threw me glances, he was trying to tell me something – he formed words with his lips, without speaking them, a *p* for insurance policy or premium, perhaps. I couldn't leave him alone. She hissed furious words at me, things like "convict," "murderer," which may have corresponded to the facts but would have been better left unsaid under the circumstances. Or should I have thrown the word "murderess" back at her? For if she had stayed where she was on the distant island or in Rio de Janeiro, Walter would have been able to withstand all the infection experiments. What was the point of the theatrics? The pain may have been real, but what good did it do?

She was astonished that Walter made no effort to move or speak despite the absence of fever. She clutched at his wasted body. And she blessed and cursed her beloved husband in the same breath, whipping herself up into a new fury at his polite, composed silence, then set upon his torso until there were damp blotches on the shawl over her breasts. She didn't know what she was doing, had forgotten where she was. Tears streamed down the still pretty cheeks into the gaping, shrieking mouth, and the little room reverberated with her lamentations like a lunatic's cell. We knew her harsh, screeching voice from the telephone booth, but now it was shrilling directly into our ears and his. March had come back with her, but, as kind and gentle as he tried to be, he too could not get her to exercise a self-control that simply was not in her nature. And she still had not even understood the true state of things.

Thus it was that I never found out what my great friend wanted to tell me in his last hour. Was it something to do with the experiments? Was it something to do with his property, his provision for his wife and children, his payment of his insurance premium, his protection for his children – could one of these have been the word beginning with *p* that he seemed to be trying to form? I do not know, will never know.

Before I report on Walter's final breaths, I must make mention of a detail that will perhaps be difficult to understand. Be that as it may, I do not wish to make a secret of it, nor is it permitted for me to do so.

As the distraught wife was bending her bare neck over her husband, I saw on the right side of the nape, near where the hair began, half covered by freshly arranged (that was what had kept her!), glossy, auburn, now somewhat loosened hair, an insect. It was a mosquito of the genus *Culex*, one of ours, a typical *Stegomyia*. It squatted there, hunkered down. Jiggled its long hind legs. The silvery, lyre-shaped marking on the insect body sharply segmented by the constricted waist was clearly distinguishable. The abdomen gleamed with a ruby red color. Engorged with blood? Human blood? Perhaps so. Perhaps not. I almost believe it was the same *Stegomyia* that had gotten away from us twenty-four hours before, after its ample meal of Walter's blood during the last experiment, having presumably lurked in a dark corner since then.

In my excitement I drew March's attention to it with a silent gesture. If only I had not done that! I thought he was me and I was him. But this decision, like so many before and after it, was one I could only make on my own. I could not share responsibility for the results with anyone else. What I wanted to do required responsibility. I was the one who bore it. Not him. I didn't want to chase the insect away. I didn't want to crush it. I wanted to let it bite. I wanted one more useful experiment. Yes, she was the wife, or soon to be the widow, of my esteemed friend. The reader has not often seen the word "esteemed" together with "friend" in these lines. I am writing it here. She was the mother of five young children. She was a pregnant woman near her time. But if I had known respect of person, if I had allowed a distinction to be made between one experimental subject and another, we would never have achieved what we had to achieve. That's the way it is.

March turned deathly pale. He trembled so much that the woman became aware of him. This was *not* what he wanted. For the first time he did not want what *I* wanted. But I dominated him. I looked at him. He chewed his lips, so uncontrollably that a drop of blood appeared. But he let me do as I wished. He had to. The poor doctor was breathing stertorously. His eyelids gradually sank, without entirely obscuring the glassy glint of his beautiful gray eyes surrounded by the yellow conjunctivae. I took out an ampule of camphor and filled the syringe, for it is considered a rule of medicine that no one should be allowed to die of cardiac and respiratory paralysis without an injection of camphor as a last attempt to juice him up. But this was only a formality.

He had been given his digitalis and had to have his camphor. Neither could do any good.

But when the wife of the man now breathing his last gave a start and grabbed at her neck with her lovely, plump, pale hand and found the crushed insect engorged with her blood (all done unconsciously, for her mind was on her husband), I knew I would be able to add a new experimental subject to our protocols. If the infection experiment was successful, we would also see whether Y.F. in pregnant women was transmitted to the unborn child.

Walter's last moments had come. The woman saw this. "Save him! Help! Help! He's not breathing! Oh God, oh God, he's passing out!" And in her distress she mindlessly shook her cologne into his face, into the half-closed yellow eyes. But he was beyond noticing. I went out, leaving the last camphor injection to the resident, who was practiced in such things. Along with Carolus (he had put off his talk with the governor), I left the room that smelled of cologne and the rot of yellow fever. I wanted to take March, who was staring as though galvanized at Frau Walter as she wailed and flung herself about. I took his hand in mine. But he struck at it and stayed with her.

Was I so odious?

SEVEN

I

We were now deep into the most important phase of our experiments, and without a leader. I am unable to describe the despair in which the passing of this man Walter left us. All of us, March no less than Carolus, the hospital director as well as the chaplain, were in shock. Our team sat in the hush of the laboratory, heads sunken on breasts. The only sounds were the muffled stirrings of the animals in the basement and the patients in their rooms over our heads. He was dead, and there was nothing to be done about it.

Our friend lay downstairs in the small, electrically lit autopsy room. We found his instructions in his desk drawer. One of us was to go to the body and pin his war medals to his chest. No one dared to. His gold-rimmed spectacles (broken) were also found in the laboratory. They had been with him for so many years of his life – should he not have them to take along, too?

Finally we voted by matchstick again (it was March who thought of it), but the result meant quite a different thing this time. A match with its head snapped off was placed in a preserving bottle along with three intact matches. Whoever drew the broken match would carry out the mission that no one would volunteer for.

It was not the same thing, of course. I, who thought logically even under these circumstances – because I couldn't help it – realized that it would be easy to tell which match was the broken one, even with eyes covered. You would only need to finger the matches one by one. But no one else thought of it.

The task fell finally to the chaplain, who not only honored the dead man but also took that opportunity to lay a silver crucifix on Walter's chest, the same one that Walter himself had taken from the chest of the waterworks director at his autopsy a few months earlier. We decided that it should be given to the doctor to take to his final resting place instead of being pressed into further service. We refrained from examining the body. No one would have been able to wield the autopsy knife.

The findings were clear in any case. The lab report that I now drafted with Carolus, to be deposited with the notary or the governor as agreed, described Dr. Walter's experiment along with our other experiments as successful and conclusive beyond all doubt.

I had assumed that I would be permitted to be one of the pallbearers at my late friend's funeral. We had been promised freedom, after all. But I had failed to take into consideration the legendary ponderousness of official process. Besides, our fate was still entirely uncertain. Walter had been the animating force behind the magnanimous administrative decision. He was no more.

The next day, late in the afternoon, the sisters carried the body from the hospital's chapel to the public hearse in a lovely hardwood casket (the work of convicts). The coachmen (more freed convicts) and the marines provided as an escort were not permitted to come into contact, however fleeting, with any of the occupants of the Y.F. hospital.

Why was this? Nothing would have happened to the twenty-four splendid lads who served as sentries at the shore batteries even if they had shaken the corpse's bile yellow hands. It was not contact that spread the disease, but mosquitoes. It made no difference whether the body was interred between layers of quicklime or in plain soil. It was for *this* idea that Walter had died. This axiom was what he had suffered for – suffered more, that soft, sentimental, chaste man, than we could ever know.

But that did not matter. As far as the world was concerned, the old wisdom held true, and neither I nor Carolus nor the dead man's unfortunate wife was permitted to join her husband on his final journey.

From our window we watched the twenty-four marines form up in full regalia. The evening sun glinted on their weapons and their musical instruments – not only the "bugles" that poor Walter had raved about but also trombones, cornets, and so on, along with the percussion that is usual in military bands. I thought of the military band at the dock.

The top men in the colonial administration, the director of the prison camps, and so forth, strode on ahead. The music started up, the baleful funeral march from the familiar Chopin sonata. Thus they bore our teacher and master away to the lime pit, feet first, as in the old song.

I kept at my work, which had to be taken care of sooner or later. It did not have my full attention, as will be readily understood. I did not relax at the microscope. The lugubrious crashing of the march music had no sooner faded than Frau Walter's distraught wailing and shouting resounded from the room above us, where she was being held by force. The hospital matron was attending to her, Carolus offered his services, even March came forward – hearing the shrill cries of the poor woman, he had become deathly pale, shooting me one dark look after another from his handsome, foolish boy's eyes. But all the carrying on was becoming actual fits of madness, she was screaming like a lunatic now, stamping, tromping on the floorboards. All attempts to soothe her, all well-intended words of sympathy, all helpful suggestions were in vain. She had acquired superhuman strength. No one dared to give her a tranquilizing injection for fear of harming the baby. Three nurses, the chaplain, and the entire physician staff were there, trying to subdue the frantic woman through friendly persuasion or gentle force. Meanwhile new patients were being admitted. Some of them were already at the dangerous stage, needed the doctors, the nurses, the chaplain; it was not clear what to do with Walter's widow, this now very inconvenient guest.

Finally, against my better judgment, I let March drag me up to see her.

I have already reported that I had the ability (possibly inherited from my father) to exert a calming influence on children, the insane, animals, and the ill.

I now calmly went to the raving woman. There were fat, distended violet veins in her neck area. At that moment she was on the point of throwing herself out the window, shrieking intolerably in her harsh peacocklike voice. She was unable to do this, of course, because her enormously protruding belly was too big for the relatively narrow opening. I made no effort to stop her. I asked the others to leave the room. They all seemed to be glad to, with the exception of March, who did as I asked with reluctance, devouring me and the poor woman with his eyes. I had not seen this expression on his face for a long time. But it was too deliberate, this look could not be completely genuine. When everyone was gone, I approached her, took her as gently as I could by the sleeve of her dark dress without touching her, and carefully drew her away from the window. She cried out as she followed me but did not offer much resistance. I pushed her down onto the convalescent's reclining chair that stood in a corner, here as in every sickroom, and whispered to her a few meaningless words, accentuating the syllables as sharply as possible. Sometimes one must whisper with extreme clarity if one wants to make oneself understood to the hard of hearing. Not shout. She had not yet stopped her drawn-out, deafening cries when she noticed my mouth moving. She looked into my eyes, I into hers. Now she fell silent and read the simple words on my lips. "Your husband wanted me to tell you . . ." She opened her eyes wide and looked at me mutely. At this moment of complete silence came the thunderous shots of the marine honor guard rendering a final salute for her husband at his fresh grave. She heard three blasts spreading over the city's hilly terrain, amplified by the echo. Her face turned dark-red and white in alternation, the contorted features relaxed. And tears rolled down the unmoving face in total silence.

II

I must in all honesty confess that, watching her tears start and stop as the shots came and went, I did not have an entirely clean conscience toward Walter's wife, Alix, her name was. She had let her pretty, somewhat mannish head sink into the crook of an elbow, and the place where the mosquito had punctured her skin was still visible below the hair on the nape of her neck. It was encrusted with the tiny blackish remnants of the insect's body. Evidently, in her mad anguish, she had not properly washed or brushed her hair since her husband's demise.

Must one not feel sympathy for a person reduced to such misery? But unfortunately there was more than just sympathy. The inner voice was there, the war was going on within me. One part of me was in revolt against another, and already I knew that good times were not on the way. But the poor creature had just lost her best, indeed her only friend. Was she not a thousand times worse off?

The woman was now complaining of spasmodic lower abdominal pain. Putting the matter as delicately as I could, I asked her if this could be the first labor pains, but she said no, and I presumed that she had enough experience from her previous deliveries to know what her condition was.

My only concern was that she leave the Y.F. hospital as quickly as possible. If she should suddenly give birth here, who would provide the necessary assistance? I did have some obstetric expertise, acquired at the request of my late wife before I opened my private clinic. But I had had enough of risky experiments. This will be readily understood by anyone.

The only one who did not understand it was the very person I had most looked to until then, March. "I guess you want to get rid of her, you don't want to take responsibility for your rottenness?" he hissed at me when I asked him to use his influence over our late friend's widow to get her to return to her lodgings in the city (in the hospitable sub-agent's house).

"Rottenness?" I repeated the word quietly and held March's gaze until he looked down. I still dominated him, and he knew it. Something else would have to happen to tear us apart.

But he too could compose himself. He answered me, falteringly, but with irrefutable logic. In this regard he had been schooled by me, just as Carolus had been schooled by Walter in regard of medical and bacteriologic technique. "Don't you see, Louis" (this was the first time he had confused my name with that of his deceased friend, the "cadet"), "don't you understand, Georg, that the woman can't leave this building now? She absolutely can't go back to her children, we can't put them in danger too."

I thanked him silently for that "we," thrown in so casually. I drew closer to him and asked him never to judge me before he had spoken to me. He promised, just like that. This did not make the problem go away.

I would have been only too glad to be deceived, I trusted him as I had never trusted anyone apart from my father and my brother. It was unfair, for human nature cannot tolerate unconditional trust, absolute surrender of the soul. One must deal with facts only.

Fortunately the delivery did not seem to be imminent. We, Carolus and I, worked out the month of the pregnancy and came to the conclusion that there were at least four more weeks to go. Somewhat reassured, we parted.

As soon as I was alone, I heard the voice of my conscience once again. Was March right? Was it "rottenness"? When I had allowed the mosquito to bite the woman's neck, I had not only been without "respect of person," as I called it a moment ago. Up to that limit, everything would indeed have been permitted. But it was not permitted, and, even to me now that I was able to think about it more calmly, it was unjustifiable to intentionally enlist, against her will, a woman so sorely tried by fate in an experiment that, as the example of her husband showed, could very easily end in death. And what then? The vain and superficial subagent was still letting the five children stay with him, out of a kind of sympathy, but this could not continue in the event of a longer illness. And what would happen to the poor tots then? The pension to which the widow was entitled was small. But the amounts allowed for orphans were even smaller. And even if they had had millions, who would take the place of their mother? I knew from my own experience what it was to lose one's mother early.

I understood now why poor Walter had suffered so much. He had felt regret. He should never have brought his wife, still less his children, into this hellish climate. On his own account he might make sacrifice after sacrifice as long as there was breath left in his body. But that did not entitle him to expect such sacrifices of his family too. When I had allowed myself to be bitten by the *Stegomyia* and thereby knowingly, with eyes wide open, taken upon myself the entire ordeal, I had made a sacrifice less easily asked of a person of my cold-blooded nature than of someone else. But I was my own master. I had no right to impose that degree of suffering on another person. If the woman now actually became critically ill following the incubation period, then I had intentionally inflicted a severe physical injury. March had not been wrong when he knocked my hand away.

But if she died and made the poor little ones orphans, I would have a second true murder on my conscience, in addition to the murder of my wife, the crime for which I had been deported. Granted, I had not committed this second murder for selfish reasons. But did that give the victim her life back? Did I have to have a conscience? Unfortunately I had one just as I had eyes in my head and fingers on my hand.

My bit of peace and inner equilibrium (all ethics is equilibrium of inner moral forces), it was all gone. I did not love myself. I cut myself loose and was thus entirely isolated. The night that now awaited me was no less harrowing than the nights of suffering with Y.F. during which I had lain in despair and cursed my life.

March was not sleeping now, either. In former times I had often reached over the edge of my bed and gently tugged on my March's tousled hair as he slept on the floor beside me. If he was awake, he would answer me with his silly but pleasant laugh, and we would spend part of the night talking. But if he was asleep, this gentle touch would not disturb him. I did this now. My hand reached for his head, with its luxuriant new growth of downy hair, like that of a young animal, a week-old lamb, perhaps. But he, awake now, or awake all along, jerked his head away. He did not reply to my whispering. And I would have heard what he said no matter how softly he said it, for my ears had become so sensitive since my recovery that they picked up the scurrying of the rats in the cellar, the marching of the guards in the corridors there and on the ground floor, the light footsteps of the nurses on the upper stories, indeed even the lamentations of the patients in their rooms all over the building, the ticking of March's watch (a present from Walter), I heard everything in turns, one sound confusedly giving way to another.

I now saw in my mind's eye, with a clarity impossible in the light of day, what the ill-fated mother and wife was going through and would go through.

I did not want to see it, I did not want to imagine it. I stood up and paced in the cramped basement room as dawn began to break. I ignored

March and tossed my boots at the rats, accurately enough to make them squeak but not accurately enough to bring one down. Even this silly hunt could not take my mind off Walter's widow. Would I repeat my last crime if I now had the opportunity before me, instead of the accomplished fact behind me? The question tormented me, I could not shake it off. Fixed on this one obsessive idea wrenched entirely out of its context, I threw myself back onto the creaking bed and fell into a restless and sweaty sleep over this problem that was not a problem, dreamed about it. I could not make up my mind either way.

It would perhaps do me credit if now I had at least been able to repent my crime properly and done everything to make amends. But I did not have what it takes for that.

When I awoke late in the morning, I was a wreck, more tired than when I had gone to sleep and more despondent than ever before. March had long since gone to the laboratory. He had not touched my clothes, though he generally cleaned them punctiliously and enthusiastically. All my things were in the same disorder, had not moved from where I had thrown them in my despair toward daybreak. One sleeve of my lab coat had fallen into the tub of soft soap, and I cleaned everything with difficulty.

In the meantime shrill cries had begun to echo throughout the building: Walter's wife, Alix, was howling with pain, wailing as I had never heard a living creature wail. Was the world nothing but a hell?

III

I immediately suspected that the woman would want me there. In vain did I try to get myself off the hook by telling the matron, who had come for me, that I was not a specialist in obstetrics and had not delivered a baby in ages. In vain did I advise bringing in one of the doctors from the city of C. No sooner was this suggestion out of my mouth than I myself realized its absurdity. We were under quarantine. No doctor from the city could officially come here if he did not want to run the risk of spreading the Y.F. microorganism among his patients. (In reality the prohibition was often circumvented; von F., for example, had come on many occasions. But in view of Walter's death, it had to be formally complied with.) The matron saw this almost as quickly as I did and said that I should go to the bed of Walter's widow merely to "quiet her mind." The woman's mental state had become unsettled as a result of the recent upset, she said; I, whom she trusted, had it within my power to get her to take heart. In the matron's view, which followed that of the old hospital director, labor had begun somewhat prematurely but still normally; the vocal expressions of pain, currently a renewed nerve-racking screeching, were surely much exaggerated. Carolus came in, put his (never entirely clean) hand on my shoulder, something very unlike him, and he too reasoned with me. To win a temporary reprieve, I promised to come if the pain did not ease within an hour. During that hour the woman's bladder and bowel were to be evacuated and she was to be placed in a bath of thirty-six to thirty-eight degrees centigrade – an analgesic method that had often proven itself at the clinic.

I huddled in a corner of the laboratory, lost in thought. March circled me, looking daggers at me, but he did not speak, nor did I speak to him. The hour passed quickly. At most fifteen minutes seemed to have gone by when, as though on cue, the unfortunate woman's piercing shrieks came once again from the sickroom above the laboratory. Was the sound different – I do not know, I knew only that it was time. It was serious. I understood that I had to go. I had to meet my fate.

I dashed past the dumbfounded March, then went back, grabbed his hand, and dragged him down to our room. I laid out clean clothes for myself, including a white coat that had not yet been used and that I should have worn the day the governor visited our laboratory. March would sprinkle sterile water on it and then iron it with a very hot flat-iron. This will sterilize a piece of linen to all intents and purposes. I did not know whether there would be enough disinfected surgical linen in the building. If necessary, our little disinfecting chamber could be used to sterilize gowns, drapes, and some bandaging material. Improvisation has always interested me, and March was clever enough to grasp my hasty instructions and carry them out to the letter. While he heated the disinfection apparatus, I bathed.

Finally we were ready. Carolus and the young resident had knocked on the bathroom door more than once. I had not opened it. It would not have been responsible to appear unwashed at the bedside of a woman in labor. All the laws of morality may not always have been holy to me. But the laws of asepsis were.

I opened the chamber containing the disinfected articles. The gowns and drapes were still hot and steaming. I put on a fresh white coat (not the ironed one) and directed March to disinfect a second white coat and more bandaging material.

Anyone watching me ready myself would have believed that I was confident and self-assured to the point of imperturbability and that I knew exactly what I was doing and what I was going to do. Unfortunately this was not the case. I did things that did not matter, neglected what did. I was racked by doubts: I was simply the creature of my surgical training with all its arrogance and ingrained ways of doing things, of the old school through which I had gone. Just how gladly I would have avoided this task may be seen in the fact that now, at the last minute, outside Frau Walter's room, I proposed to the young resident that *he* perform the delivery, that he take charge. He looked at me in surprise, but he accepted. When I asked him if he had ever performed a delivery on his own, he shrugged his shoulders and smiled faintly. There was nothing for it. I had to go, I had to step in, I had to do the experiment, although nothing could have been of less interest to me than doing a second experiment on this incessantly, heartrendingly wailing woman. It was an irony of fate that she was asking for *me*, that she had beseeched the heavens for *me* to come, and that she expected a miracle from me. And she knew who I was. Murderer, convict. She knew my past as well as she did my face. But she had faith, and her faith yearned for me!

I composed myself as best I could. First of all I needed assistants. March would have been a good one. A good one? What am I saying? He would have been the *best* assistant. But could I trust him now? Had he not become half an enemy – twice as dangerous as an unambiguous one? Aside from March, there was only the matron. An old, very sanctimonious, but competent, practical, always firm female who had never seen a delivery in this yellow-fever hospital, let alone assisted at one, but who had nerves of steel and who, buttressed by her rock-solid Catholic faith, was able to face any situation with courage and submission to the will of God.

I wanted to have her by my side, to look to her, not to March, and least of all to Carolus. Carolus's goodwill was not in doubt, but he had fallen back into all his uncleanly habits since the decease of our great friend. It took no more than a glance at his neglected hands to see that he was not the proper assistant. It would have been irresponsible to let him participate. Nor did he push himself forward. And he, the brigadier general, gave me, the criminal sentenced without possibility of appeal to exile on the island of deportees C., free rein, even where the widow of his friend and collaborator Walter was concerned.

In my heart of hearts I still nourished the hope that the diagnostic findings would be normal and there would be no need for me to perform an intervention of any kind. It was her sixth delivery, after all, and the earlier ones (I remembered what Walter had said before his death) had gone normally without exception.

When I went to her bedside, I was met by a joyful expression in her tearstained eyes.

Joy, in someone who must have gone through truly frightful things in the past forty-eight hours!

A to-the-point (external) examination was enough to convince me that her complaints and fears were only too justified. Her uneasy feeling, expressed at her husband's bedside, that the baby was "in the wrong position" had a cogent basis. Unfortunately this was not the hysterical moaning and squawking of a querulous female. It was the sound of someone reduced by pain to the level of an animal.

I will try to suggest the medical facts, although I do not know how comprehensible they will be to the lay reader. The baby was in the wrong position. The normal position is cephalic, whereby the head of the baby, the largest and heaviest part of it, is oriented so as to occupy the lowest area of the uterus. The baby was very far from this normal cephalic lie. It was in the wrong position, its lie was transverse.

An analogy, to make this clear. A plum pit that can slip lengthwise through the narrow neck of a bottle and out again will have a great deal of trouble getting out of the bottle in a crosswise orientation. And here there was just as little hope that the baby's body, lying transversely with its legs by its head, one bulky, shapeless mass, could safely pass through the natural birth canal. Never. Rather, it would tear the poor mother's viscera to pieces, and even now the screams, the almost continuous hypertonic contractions without any time for recovery, were only too understandable. For the baby's head, much too far to one side, was pulling at and grinding against the tender internal organs. It was causing contusions, internal wounds, hemorrhages. Even the woman's most bloodcurdling screams would make sense to someone who knew what was going on inside her. A warm bath may work wonders for a nervous, oversensitive lady whose baby is in the proper position, but here it was as useless as a shot of morphine. Unless all one wanted to do was to give the two of them a painless end, both mother and child. That I could not do. No doctor could.

The conservative school of obstetrics cherished in the bosom of our university faculty for a century had always recommended as the first recourse that the baby's body be shifted with the greatest care from the transverse lie to the correct one, the longitudinal lie, bringing the head away from the side and downward, if possible without surgical intervention. I, an experimental bacteriologist, attempted this now. I would work only on the outside, on the abdominal wall, where I saw streaky horizontal striae attesting to earlier pregnancies; if at all possible, my hand would not even touch the exposed internal organs. If this was successful, the delivery could take its course in a normal fashion, with the head first.

Then the mother would not be infected by my bacteriologist's hands; but only then.

IV

Turning the baby's body from its transverse lie onto its head in the mother's womb was without a doubt the simplest and gentlest intervention *if* it could be done by simple dislocation, from outside. Usually the baby's head lies somewhat closer to the mother's pelvic inlet, that is, somewhat farther down, than the baby's bottom. The mother must therefore be positioned so as to be resting on the same side as the baby's head in order for the delivery to take its natural course.

I asked the matron and a young but competent nurse, her factotum, to give me a hand. We put two beds together on their long sides with a crossbrace and then tried to reposition the mother. Though I was not the strongest person in the world since my illness, I undertook to lift the woman from her single bed. I carried her in my arms to the double bed and established the desired position. Her cries of pain had not stopped. As her blotchy, sweaty face lay on my chest, I felt her frantic, hissing gasps on my throat. She was doing her best to keep from screaming.

Finally she was in the position we wanted. She was immobile. But not relaxed. She should not, could not relax, she had to help. Much as we might have liked to, we could not administer a narcotic that would have anesthetized, sedated, paralyzed her, she had to help us with the delivery by bearing down with all her strength.

Even in normal births it is not easy to get a mother-to-be to deliberately increase her own pain by bearing down to contract the abdominal muscles and squeeze the baby's head deeper through the sore, tender lower abdomen. And how much more difficult it was in this case! But I had so much power over this woman who was almost unconscious with brute suffering that she did her best. I helped the process along methodically with my hand on the outside of her belly.

The baby does not lie directly beneath the skin and the muscular sheath; it is surrounded by amniotic fluid within the womb. Often, when one thinks one has grasped the head, it slips away again like a fish in water, and the stronger the contractions become, the denser and tighter the muscular wall of the uterus becomes and the more difficult it is for a hand to correct the baby's wrong lie by pushing vigorously from the outside. The things I tried! The maneuvers I attempted, the torment I caused! At last we seemed to have succeeded. The woman was on her side on the bed, holding on to a support with both hands; her beautiful reddish hair shone, spread out on the damp pillows. Every so often she reached out for me, but then she controlled herself to keep from annoying me, making an effort to stifle her screams.

When everything was taken care of, I put her cold hand back where it belonged, squeezed it, and at the same time counted her pulse on the radial artery. It was somewhat elevated but fortunately gave no cause for concern. Then I checked the baby's heart sounds by placing my late friend's stethoscope on the outside of his widow's abdominal wall. The unborn baby's heart was clearly perceptible, pounding like a kettledrum. I counted 140 to 142 beats per minute. The young resident (he was wearing his old, no longer entirely clean white coat and his presence here was not to my liking, but what could I do) was very concerned about this high rate, the pulse rate of healthy adults being no more than sixty-eight or seventy per minute. I had to inform him that an unborn child's pulse rate is twice that. His polite but incredulous smile told me what a good thing it was that I had not entrusted the delivery to him. For he was as innocent as a Capuchin monk.

A slight improvement in the woman's condition seemed to be at hand. Her haggard cheeks were losing their blotchy flush, her breath was not so spasmodic, and her screams were dwindling to deep, prolonged groans. The muscles in her meager arms were tense: she held on and held out.

I am unable to describe how very happy this slight seeming improvement made me. The woman wanted to say something, she gestured, and when I bent down, she asked me – to send word to her five children in the city? No, Georg Letham, you poor excuse for a psychologist – she asked me to look after the little dog that was shut up in the guest room she had been occupying and was surely suffering from hunger and thirst and loneliness.

All my life I have been vulnerable, ultimately, to sentimental impulses. And I succumbed to them now. First I searched for the woman's bag, finding it under her clothes on the reclining chair, and opened the clasp to look for the key to her room.

A strange feeling came over me as I found, along with small bills, a tortoiseshell comb, coins, handkerchiefs, lipstick, compacts, the key, and other odds and ends, my friend's passport and the telegrams to whose composition and dispatch I myself had been a witness not long before. I put everything back, smiled confidently at the woman, took the key, and went out into the corridor. March was waiting for me, feverish with worry and impatience. "She's doing better, bosom buddy, much better!" I called out to him. I hurried as quickly as I could through the rambling building to the wing where the guest room was located. I could already hear the little dog's melancholy whine like a repeated question.

But at the same time my ears, so inordinately keen since my illness, picked up unmistakable sounds of distress from the woman once more: not the feral shrieking of the first hypertonic contractions, but twice as dreadful to me in the subdued, weakened form signifying surrender to despair.

I threw the room key at the feet of a young assistant nurse who appeared in the corridor just then, shouted a few incoherent words at her. It hardly mattered whether she understood them or not. I had to go back.

On the way I reproached myself most bitterly for having left the sickroom. But had it been so inexcusable? I, who had always wanted, who had needed, to take upon myself what was most difficult, had felt the desire to be part of something lighter, more human for once. To go to an animal that had been left by itself, that was half dead from hunger and thirst, to show it all the acts of kindness that an animal lover can (I had begun to love animals, and did I ever!) – was that such a crime? It seemed so.

In that brief interval, the woman's condition had worsened a great deal. She no longer lay compliantly on her side, but on her back, her legs propped on the bar that we had provided. She was moaning and crying out, feebly, but so heart-wrenchingly that no ear could have borne it, even one much less keen than mine.

The matron too was white as a sheet, and the good-natured resident shook like a leaf when the woman in her anguish suddenly lurched upward, sat up on the shuddering bed, got to her feet, hammered with both fists on her spherical belly, and then let herself fall face-first back onto the bed with all her weight, as though to destroy the child inside her with the force of her fall – and herself, too. Only with the greatest effort was it possible to bring her to reason, at least for a short time – and this effort consisted chiefly of a potent injection of morphine and atropine. Dangerous or not. It had to be. Her pupils dilated immediately from the effect of the atropine, which was stronger than the pupil-constricting effect of the morphine.

Now she gradually stopped screaming, but pointed to her belly with both hands. I examined it very gently. The uterus was visibly contracted beneath the thin, brownish, striated skin, with no sign of wanting to relax completely.

Suddenly a greenish liquid poured out of her, the amniotic fluid began to be expelled. The amnion, the amniotic sac, had ruptured. What to do? Act fast? Yes, but how? Was there any way to help? There had to be. The delivery could not proceed naturally. Do nothing, just put my hands in my lap? In hers? Bring in the chaplain, who was knocking on the door, impatiently now, and demanding to baptize the child in the womb with an injection of holy water? The matron was in favor of this. The hospital director, an excellent administrator but an extremely mediocre and unresponsive physician, also arrived, to make matters worse. All of them assailed me loudly with advice, worries, senseless talk. Were they sorry they had put a convict in charge of the delivery? It was too late for that. They were shouting so confusedly that the woman herself was inaudible now.

I do not know how I found the strength to get them out of the room, all but the matron and the young assistant nurse who had followed me with the key from the corridor. Her face, in its chaste, unspoiled austerity, gave me a certain confidence in her moral steadfastness (which proved itself). The air was stifling. We tore open the window. One had to be able to breathe before making grave decisions affecting the life and death of two people.

A colossal cloudburst was now hammering down on the city. The air, with a smell of burning sulfur, was a lead weight in the lungs.

There was a rumbling like the bottom notes of an organ in the branches of a tall jacaranda. Some of the ubiquitous vulture-like nocturnal birds, startled, rose from it, their dripping wings stretched out horizontally.

Back to the bed, which was soiled by the greenish, disagreeable-looking, but odorless, fluid. I placed the stethoscope on the rock-hard, yellowish abdomen, pointing upward like a gently shining dome.

The baby's heart sounds? They were subdued. The pulse rate was decreasing. It had fallen from 140 to 110.

A bad sign. A terrible danger signal. We had to make haste, or all would be lost.

V

The air that evening was so humid that our shirts and coats stuck to us as though they had just been pulled out of water. The heat took our breath away. It was like wearing a helmet made of lead, a diving helmet. But this was no time to be thinking about personal discomforts.

All that mattered was the prepping for the unavoidable intervention.

Luckily the room had running water. And outside the windows, water was pouring down as though the sluices of heaven had opened.

The first preparatory procedure consisted of the disinfection of my hands and arms up to the elbows and the equally careful and meticulous aseptic prepping of the woman now half conscious and writhing in contractions. This disinfection could be entrusted to the trained matron and her very skillful, intelligent assistant.

The second preparatory procedure was the induction of deep anesthesia. If I wanted to turn the baby in the womb, the uterus and abdominal musculature had to be as relaxed as possible. The mother could not suffer any more pain. She simply could not take any more. Human feeling and medical duty were one.

This anesthesia I would in good conscience much rather have entrusted to my friend March – who had spent many hours anesthetizing monkeys and dogs down in the laboratory and possessed a natural, inborn gift for this difficult task – than to anyone else, than to Carolus, say, who soon withdrew. He could not watch such things. Thus I called to March, telling him to scrub thoroughly as I was doing and then begin the anesthesia. While I scrubbed, the assistant nurse went down to the hospital pharmacy for an anesthesia mask and the necessary quantity of anesthetic, a mixture of chloroform and ether in alcohol.

The storm had abated momentarily. It was quiet outside after the rumbling of the hurricane-like thunderstorm. Now there was more trouble. The electric light was beginning to flicker ominously. There had been similar disruptions every so often since the death of the Swedish power-plant director. What could we do? There was no time to think. The mother, who was only whimpering now, was looking more critical every minute. She was deteriorating. She was slipping away. I had to operate, even if darkness reigned as before the creation of the world, when all was a black chaos.

I barked at March. Why hadn't he begun the anesthesia? "Get going! Mask on! Administer the mixture one drop at a time, faster or slower as needed. Grab the lower jaw with your left hand and pull it forward! Then the tongue will come along and won't lie on top of the laryngeal inlet, so respiration will be free; monitor her breathing, breath by breath! Keep your left index finger on her pulse and count off the breaths till I say stop. Wait! Have you checked for false teeth?" March had forgotten this, and why would he have thought of it? Dogs and monkeys do not have dentures to slip down their throats in deep anesthesia and choke them. "False teeth! Oh, come off it!" objected March, normally so clever and quick on the uptake. "Get that stupid look off your face, you idiot!" I cried. "Open her mouth, and do it right! Like that, yes, and have a look!" "Stop shouting," March responded resentfully, but he obeyed. (Her teeth were real.)

In my agitation I ignored his defiance. It was enough that he cooperated. My thoughts were elsewhere. When I had almost finished disinfecting my arms, I ran through my plan of action again in my mind.

The young nurse to my left. The old matron to my right. Each would hold one of the mother's knees. A sterilized drape over her lower abdomen.

One of my hands working inside the mother, the other hand on the drape helping from outside.

Both hands always working together. Neither by itself.

Turning the baby from its transverse lie onto its rump by these manipulations would be a last attempt to bring about a normal longitudinal lie.

If it failed, the woman was lost.

But I was sure of my business. I still had the self-confidence to trust in my ability to perform this intervention, which in its rudiments was very simple and which I had executed at the clinic more than once.

Which hand should I use to turn the baby, that is, which hand should I use to go inside the mother's womb, the right or the left? Which should help from outside? My best hand was my right. My late friend Walter's best hand had been his left. In my place he would have preferred his left, just as I favored my right. But this makes no difference in operative obstetrics. One always turns the baby using the hand corresponding to the side of the mother where the baby's feet are. In the case of the left occipital transverse lie (the baby's feet on the right, rump on the left), using the right hand. This position, the left occipital transverse lie, was what my late friend's widow presented with, and thus I had to go in using my right hand.

Without drying my dripping hands, in order to keep them sterile, I moved to the bed.

The woman, with fresh drapes underneath her, was already breathing under the anesthesia. Good. March counted her respirations carefully – they were regular, if somewhat rapid. I put my ear over the mother's belly, taking care not to touch it. I wanted to know what the baby's heart sounds were like before I began. My hearing was keen and I imagined I could pick them up without direct contact.

But I had not counted on the thunderous drumming of another heavy squall beating down on the hill and the hospital, shaking the entire building to its foundations, even the posts of the bed on which the woman lay.

No matter. The turning had to be done, the normal lie had to be produced.

On with it, no more hesitation.

Calm, self-control, logical thinking, precise movements, the utmost gentleness and care even with the most intense effort. Heads up! Stay calm! Not a single abrupt movement. Not a single unconsidered maneuver.

The drapes were finally all in place, the two assistants stood by me, doing what they should. The woman was breathing deeply and regularly.

March had counted to nearly a hundred – he thought he had to enumerate every breath.

I let him be. This was not the time to be giving him a long lesson. Besides, the counting gave me a yardstick for elapsed time during the intervention, which had to be kept to an absolute minimum.

I took a good deep breath and drew my head up from between my shoulders, where it had hunched due to the great strain of determination that many operating physicians feel before any major intervention. But as I extended my right hand and let my left hand slide over the smooth, cool, damp drape on the woman's abdomen, the last of my abnormal excitation left me. I was as lucid as I had ever been.

I nestled the four fingers of my right hand together as much as I could and pressed the thumb into my palm, so that my hand would take up as little space as possible. Then I carefully slid my fingertips forward, the soft, warm flesh again clinging tightly to my hand, and reached the inside of the womb, that is, the transitional zone separating the external sexual organs from the internal ones. In a sudden contraction, the uterus snapped at me like a fish snapping at a lure. Then the tension relaxed. At this point, to my relief, I already felt what I had expected to feel: a broad, smooth surface with a faceted ridge in the middle, no doubt the baby's back and spine.

The light above my deeply bowed head was flickering, going out momentarily. This did not disturb me.

Completing an operation of which one is technical master affords a feeling of happiness like that of an athlete who has set a record. It is a turbulent, but very intense happiness.

But now I became uncertain, and I paused. I became alarmed. The numbers that the faithful March had been counting off were coming more and more slowly and hesitantly, and he suddenly screeched: "She's dying! She's dying!" In a flash I removed my hand and ran around the two beds placed side by side to where the woman's head was, used my left hand to tear off the anesthesia mask, which was coated with saliva and chloroform mixture, and saw what the trouble was.

The woman was not dying. On the contrary, she was regaining consciousness. Hence the apnea, the tachycardia. Suddenly she raised her swollen, velvety eyelids, and the large, bloodshot eyes that rested on me held an expression of returning consciousness. "Go on! Go on! Keep it up!" I cried softly but very urgently to March. Stay calm! Stay calm! I hurried back to where I had been. "Give her a few more minutes! And we'll have it! Go!"

VI

It took perhaps half a minute until the anesthesia was deep enough for the operation to continue. But this half minute of waiting made me very impatient. Even before the intervention, the baby's heart sounds had not been the best. For this was a vulnerable preterm baby, at least a month premature. Things must be wound up as quickly as possible in such a case. But I had to wait. No anesthesia, no intervention. So I stood and waited. My hands were tired. My right hand in particular was sagging, as though paralyzed, from working inside the contracted womb.

Very inappropriately, I thought of this child's departed father. I saw Walter on his deathbed. I saw him saying good-bye to his wife. I saw him making the sign of the cross with his left hand in his last lucid moments. I thought now that the anesthesia was deep enough for me to resume the intervention that I had had to break off so abruptly. There was no time for another careful disinfection. The process takes ten to fifteen minutes. But if I spent that much time disinfecting myself, the baby would have long since suffocated and the woman have bled to death. However, I had kept the hand I needed, the "inside" hand, clean.

This time I did not set to work with the same joy and courage. Taking great care not to inflict an internal injury, I slipped my left hand inside while my outside hand, the right one, on top of the drape, supported the maneuvers of the operating left hand. Something was holding me up. I felt as though I had rushed out of the house forgetting the most important thing, had wanted to turn around at the bottom of the stairs and go back but had not been able to, and was now going farther and farther in the wrong direction on the street, putting my patient at even greater risk. But what I had forgotten did not come to me! It simply was not there.

The drape slipped suddenly and my right hand was lying directly on the woman's damp, cool, velvety-smooth abdomen.

At last my left hand, folded up to be as small and narrow as I could make it, had reached the inside of the uterus. A sudden contraction, beginning at the top and intensifying as it moved down, clutched at my hand. It is an indescribable feeling to be surrounded by the bleeding, quivering, grasping, vibrating flesh of another body. It is paralyzing. One fights it, one wants to act, to move, to find and seize the baby's foot once and for all. Wait! Stay calm! Be patient!

The anesthesia took its normal course. The breaths that March continued to count off, functioning as a clock for me, had long since passed three hundred and were approaching four hundred; the intervention had thus been going on for well over ten minutes. But my left hand remained as though paralyzed, even when the grip of the clenched uterus had loosened and I should have made haste to finish my work. I didn't know my way around in this hot cavity. Everything was strange to me here. I knew nothing. Except that the blood was draining from my head. I felt about uncertainly in the strange interior, as someone in a dark room where he has never been before might stumble, fall, bump into sharp corners. But the place was not strange to me – how could it be! I had explored the terrain no more than five minutes before and found it normal; the baby's back in the expected place, head and rump where they were supposed to be. Could everything have shifted so much in that short time that it now seemed strange and incomprehensible? Where was the back? Where the tips of my index and middle fingers had felt the subtle but clearly perceptible faceted prominence of the baby's spine, now I found a soft body surface with no longitudinal bone. Tiny little bones ran transversely, evidently the rib cage, or was it a soft, unresisting mass, the baby's belly? Where I had felt the foot earlier, now I found the fine, articulated bones and fleshy forms of a hand. Where was I? Had the world shifted on its axis? I stopped. A new contraction was beginning. I had to break off. Rooting about in the dark was senseless and life-threatening. I stood silently. My heart was pounding in my throat, behind my eyes.

March had been watching all my movements and my face with his hostile expression. Suddenly he burst out with the puzzling words, "Which hand?" I stared at him. How did he know that all I had found was the baby's hand, not the foot that I needed? I didn't understand him. He smiled with defiant derision. I looked at him dumbfoundedly, and when the woman suddenly groaned under the anesthesia, I groaned too. I said earlier that I sometimes imitated the emotions of others in moments of despair. And I had reason enough for despair. My groans were now really and truly from the heart.

Now I understood March's question. All was lost! The second time I had not, as would have been proper, gone in with my right hand, which could have finished the job without difficulty and which I had prudently kept sterile by taking care not to use it to touch the anesthesia mask and so forth. Instead I had used my left hand, the unclean, unsuitable, wrong hand, to go inside the woman entrusted to my care, the hand that was not capable of doing the job, or only with the greatest effort, the hand that was contaminated with countless microorganisms.

That was how it was. Those were the facts. I will not and cannot describe what went through my mind. Nor can I reconstruct the logic that finally brought me to a decision. The decision had to be made: Quit? Go on? And if "go on," should I take the wrong hand out again and insert the correct hand, my right? But now my right hand had been on the skin of the woman's abdomen and had not been sterile for a good while. There was even less time for disinfection now than there had been before. It was a matter of seconds, not minutes. One question after another. Thinking instead of acting!

I was not a doctor now! My medical certificate had been revoked, almost a year back! I was a convict on the island of C. Tolerated. The recipient of unearned confidence, a fraud, nothing more. Nothing more. A wife murderer. No, much more, something very serious, and *that* was the significance of the resentful and contemptuous expression on the face of my friend March! I had abused my friend Walter's poor wife once already, abused this woman who had truly been battered by fate by experimenting on her without her knowledge, against her will, and now I was doing it again! Never had a conscience been so belatedly heard from. Why? Why? And an infectious, clumsy, half-paralyzed hand in an exposed pelvic region!

What's done is done. In all my life I had never felt so shattered. Incapable of doing anything, deciding anything. I closed my eyes.

But then I rallied myself. I had to meet my fate. Things had to be done. No one was going to act for me, so I would act as best I could.

The baby's body moved under my hands. A shudder ran through it. Was the tiny creature trying to take its first breath? It would never be able to while it was inside. With this premature breath the baby would inhale the surrounding amniotic fluid and inevitably choke.

A baby's first breaths are not restricted to the rib cage, the windpipe, and so on. The entire little body tenses up, mobilizes all its strength in its urge to live, to act. No, that's not the way! Not like that! Not like that!

I changed hands. Better to save *one* life if both, mother and child, were at risk. I would save the child. For the child it was irrelevant what microorganisms my hand was covered with. Anything was better than doing nothing and knowingly, despairingly, losing both mother and child. *I* had never really known my mother. I had never had to lose children of my own. Fate had ordained that this mother and this child be placed in my care. At this truly frightful moment I did not think of myself. I forced myself not to feel the terrible burden of my conscience.

My fingertips would do the thinking, I would be guided by my exquisite sense of touch alone. No past. No dickering with the fate that had given me such rotten treatment. No shifting the blame onto my father, who was on my mind at that moment as the one among my betters who had always overcome all difficulties for as long as I had known him.

Thus I proceeded. In with my right hand! Again, and even more gently and cautiously than the first time.

Immediately I had the baby's back and spine before me again. Good! I slid farther down, now to the side, now at an angle and upward, and took hold of a piece of the thigh just below the baby's bottom.

Now my right hand, effectively supported by the left, outside hand, could slide down the meager leg. To the ankle. This I grasped with great gentleness so that my hand took up as little space as possible, the foot clamped between my index finger on the dorsum and my middle finger on the anklebone.

The tip of my thumb was barely touching the sole of the foot. And now back! Out! Quickly but without haste, forcefully but cautiously, despairingly yet certain of success! The hand holding the foot between two extended fingers of course took up much more room than the same hand had going in. Thus I had to maneuver with particular cleverness, artfulness, and caution, with bated breath, I might say, in going back the same way and pulling the foot down and outside.

As the foot moved down, pulled down steadily by my hand, with my other hand I pushed against the abdominal wall to move the baby's head upward. It readily did as I wished.

Now my hand, full of blood and greenish mucus, appeared at the opening of the birth canal, and between my fingers was the tiny foot, as though made of yellow ivory beneath its layer of filth.

I waited a moment to see whether the head would follow on its own or whether additional assistance was required. It was the latter. By gentle pushing and pulling, I first freed the baby's leg up to the knee. The hollow of the knee was directed outward, turned toward me, and so too was the baby's back: the presentation was normal, thank goodness. Thus I was able to carry the delivery through immediately by extraction.

This was easy up to the arms. The baby was not full-term; everything was smaller and thinner than normal. Now I more or less wiggled the left shoulder out by taking hold of the baby's leg and moving the shriveled, meager body up and down, all the while using every trick to take advantage of the least drag. The baby was luckily not breathing yet, but almost. A convulsive shudder ran through the slender limbs for a second time. Then quiet again. So not yet.

Not a second to lose, go! Keep it up! But no force, no wrenching, no, wait a bit, a little to the right, a little to the left, the hand supporting from below, release the "engagement" with fingertip pressure, not too much muscle. "No more anesthesia," I cried to March, who was glad to put the chloroform bottle aside. Lucky March! He could stretch, wipe his forehead, take a deep breath! *He* had no responsibility!

The other arm came now, and already the pulsating, bluish red, convoluted umbilical cord too. Now the main thing, the head. Holding the baby's body tightly between the palms of my hands, I had quickly rotated it clockwise; the gentlest possible leverage exerted by a finger introduced between the baby and the mother's body freed the occipital area so that it could emerge, first with difficulty, but then easily, with the greatest of ease. It was coming, it was coming. Keep going! Good! At last the entire head was outside. I turned the baby around, so that it could see me. It was a boy.

"You have a healthy boy, Frau Walter," I cried to the woman. Perhaps she heard me? I took a deep breath, looked at the baby I was carrying in my arms, which were covered with blood and trembling from exertion. The boy's nose was flat, the face as though pushed in, bent out of shape, shriveled. No resemblance to Walter. He had not yet breathed, though it seemed he would decide to any second. A good sign!

March had abandoned his duty, deserted his post as anesthetist and pulse monitor at the head of the mother's bed. He was looking at me. He shouted at me maliciously:

"Mother dead – baby dead – doctor saved!"

I let him talk. I knew better. As I quickly clamped the umbilical cord, ligated it with sterile thread, and scissored it, the little boy's bluish red body convulsed in a prodigious effort.

But the first breath was like the whispering of a spring breeze in the tiny chest that was so thin you could count the ribs. The nurses, smiling with astonishment, took the baby from my arms. They washed off the blood and residue of greenish muck, weighed the baby in their hands, gazed at it steadily, made kissing noises with their lips, and looked at the baby's head as though they had never laid eyes on a newborn. But perhaps, spending their lives here in the Y.F. hospital, they had never seen how a human being is born.

VII

Would these two maidenly creatures also have to look on as, after terrible suffering, a mother paid for the existence of her baby with her life, a life that was now irreplaceable for her children?

As I walked away from the bed and went to the washstand to wash my hands and my bespattered face, I must say I was approaching a despair I had not thought possible since my recovery from Y.F. and the disappearance of my inner guilt.

My friend's spiteful words – which I now took to be veracious, although the prophesy of doom was belied at least by the loud crying and mewling and struggling of the small but well-formed baby – pierced me to the heart. I could not understand how March, he of all people, for whom I had lately begun to feel a tender affection, could have stabbed me in the back. But I pulled myself together, and I believe my face betrayed nothing of what was going on in me.

I went back to the mother, made sure she was properly positioned for expulsion of the placenta. She was regaining consciousness. As the aftereffects of the anesthesia were asserting themselves in gagging and vomiting, she opened her eyes. Whispering with weakness, she told me she was still having contraction-like pains. But when I asked her if she thought she could bear this without sedation until she had been completely delivered, and showed her the baby that the nurses had swaddled very lovingly and very inexpertly, so tightly that the poor little creature was almost suffocating, she, Walter's widow, brought her pale, moist lips, from which came a strong chloroform smell, toward my hand, and, in her foolishness, tried to kiss it. What could I do? Only one thing, jump back, so that I nearly slipped on the damp, dirty floor. March, who was still present, gave a theatrical, derisive guffaw. But I was soon steady on my feet. I was ashamed of the unfortunate woman's gratitude, and my only thought was to spare her as much as was humanly possible.

I sat down on the edge of her bed, took her trembling hands in mine to calm her, and waited for the conclusion of the delivery, the normal expulsion of the placenta. This was another critical moment. The release of the placenta is only too often followed by life-threatening hemorrhages, and the woman's condition was such that she could not afford to lose another drop of blood. Fortunately this moment passed off well. With a heavy but truly unburdening sigh, she sat up, bore down, and quickly forced the placenta out. There was hardly a trickle of blood afterward. We put fresh drapes underneath her, gave her a little cold tea (as cold as was possible in the great heat), placed the baby in a basket normally used by the matron for household purposes (for no one had remembered to obtain a cradle), and turned out the light, leaving only a small oil lamp burning on the night table.

The others had already tiptoed out. The room filled with the regular breathing of the mother as she drifted off, joined by the much softer and more rapid breathing of the sleeping child.

The delicate smell of the iris powder the nurse had sprinkled on the baby mingled with the sweetish odor of the milk already seeping from the sleeping mother's breasts. I covered them with a light layer of sterile absorbent cotton and before leaving felt the woman's forehead. The fever that I so dreaded (yellow fever or puerperal fever?) had not begun. Her sleep was not deep. As my hand passed over her face, she opened her eyes and her long lashes brushed my palm. She wanted to tell me something, and, making an effort to lower her normally loud, harsh voice, she started a sentence a few times, but I did not want to listen, could not listen, I just pressed my hand gently to her lips and told her that she needed to rest. For the risk of postoperative hemorrhage is great in any operative delivery.

The assistant nurse came in once more to sit up with the woman overnight. With any luck, no special assistance would be needed. My only instruction was that every two hours the nurse should take the woman's pulse and temperature and lift the quilt to satisfy herself that there was no hemorrhaging: it has happened more than once after such difficult deliveries that women have quietly bled to death in their beds without a soul noticing. I begged fate to spare this woman.

As I was giving the nurse my instructions, it struck me that her eyes were focused on me with an expression of recalcitrance. I was unable to explain this to myself. Perhaps the thin, flickering, pale gold light of the tiny oil lamp was to blame, I thought.

I returned to my bedroom. I was exhausted and hoped, as I had after the death of the dear little Portuguese girl, to escape my self-tormenting thoughts in deep, dreamless, unharried sleep. But to my astonishment my bed was occupied. March, dressed and with his shoes on, had thrown himself on it as if to proclaim his dominion. He was not sleeping, but stared up at me challengingly. I bit my lip, but undressed silently and lay down on the floor where he had made his bed until now. The one on which March now luxuriated was no French courtesan's four-poster. How would such a thing have gotten down into the Y.F. hospital's oil storeroom? Nevertheless it was princely compared to the thin bed of rags with which March had been happy until now. Except that it was mine. But what could I do? Should I mourn the loss of this great child's love? If I had only known why I had lost it. Or did I know everything and just not want to understand?

I put my left elbow under my head to raise it a little and tried to sleep. Fruitless effort. I was still too wrought up. I could only pretend to sleep. March was as restless as I. He got up, undressed, got himself a cigar (it came from the stock of the brigadier general, who smoked very good, strong cigars that were almost unobtainable here), and began puffing away. I saw the tip glow dull red, heard March jam the cigar in his mouth and draw on it with a smacking of lips, heard it with all the terrible hyperacuity that one who has not experienced its torment could never imagine. All I wanted was some peace and quiet! But he did it as though to spite me! What got on my nerves most of all was his way of taking the cigar out of his mouth with a slight disgusting pop. He knocked the ash off on the edge of the bed, letting it fall on my knee, uncovered because of the frightful sultry heat. Fine, let him do that. I controlled myself. I had much greater problems on my mind.

With the eye of a bacteriologist, I saw the bacilli entering the tissue tears caused by childbirth; I saw the microorganisms proliferate unchecked, saw them vigorously infiltrate the bloodstream of Walter's widow. Pyemia, fever, sickness, death . . . And no one more helpless than the physician who had caused it. Without meaning to. But not without having to. Should I offer fate another deal? Let Frau Walter live, take back the infection caused by my left hand, take back the infection caused by the *Stegomyia* at Walter's deathbed, let both experiments turn out well – and I would pay the price. What did I have to pay with? What could I give up? What else could I do without? Nothing? Wrong! Wrong! In recent weeks, when I had recovered from my Y.F. and our experiments were advancing as planned, I had felt a kind of happiness, a great, often almost glorious vitality, such as any constructive activity that is making progress will lend the spirit. I could let that go. But how? Only by finishing with myself. I could give *myself* up. I could commit suicide. It was a radical solution, but only by putting an end to my existence could I put an end to my experiments. The fact was that I would keep trying to finish this job for as long as I lived.

Should I do it? Or not? Should I once and for all "sacrifice" myself, to speak this portentous word at last?

A dribble of lukewarm liquid smacked onto my left hand, which was stretched out, palm upward. March had hit me with some cigar spit. I could no longer contain myself and said only one threatening word: "March!" But that was what he had been waiting for.

"'March, March!'" he repeated, enraged. "Who is your March? What am I doing with a murderer?" he hissed. "Let me sleep and don't touch me."

He fell silent, waiting for a response. But he could wait until the sun came up in the morning. I lay awake and did not answer him. Perhaps I should have kept that "March" to myself too. But I was only human.

VIII

How much I would have liked to crawl into the deepest hole on earth! How happy I would have been not to go on living! But I could not put a violent end to my life now. I had to face the facts and resolutely go on with the task I had set myself as far as my feeble energies would permit. Everything would have been easier after a restful night. But there was no question of sleeping in, the work in the laboratory had to be done, and above all I had the truly bitter task of going to Walter's widow, whose excessive and much-too-heartfelt gratitude of the previous evening was still making my cheeks burn with shame.

But if I was afraid that I would be showered with more exorbitant and undeserved thanks, fate had a pleasant surprise in store for me. I was in luck. Why the irony? The facts were perfectly serious. There was trouble even before I got into the room. Bobby, the little dog belonging to Walter's widow, lay in the sun at the door; a strong wind had come up and the morning was bright and pleasant. Bobby's silky coat shone. His breathing was calm. He was asleep. Or he was pretending to be, for he could not help pricking up his ears and swishing his bushy tail a little at my approach. When I tried to slip past the handsome dog by carefully stepping over him, over his back with its bluish and golden markings, he became fully awake and glared at me vindictively. He was frightened. Like all alarmed creatures, he was at once vicious and fearful, and I had not yet gotten my left leg clear when he bit down firmly, not with the full strength of his sharp little teeth, but hard enough to draw blood. And the little creature raised his voice, he howled as though he had been stepped on, as though *he* had been bitten. He panted, whined endlessly as though I were tormenting him the way the now dead and buried Walter must once have tormented him in his scientific experiments. I remembered this, and the dog, who had two names, M-S-33 in the lab report but Bobby to his friends, remembered it too.

Where did these memories get me? Nowhere! Keep going! The room I was on the point of entering was the same one in which that most unfortunate of all creatures, that most enchanting, dearest child, the little Portuguese girl, had lain, and now Walter's widow was sleeping here with her tiny infant brought too soon into this hard world.

Was the woman febrile? Was she on the road to recovery? Or to the grave? Through my doing? I did not venture forward. I waited.

Regrettably I was still not entirely my own master after my sleepless night. I was thinking about things that were long past and could not be changed, yet I needed to focus on what was all too glaringly present, what was taking from me the confidence I needed that morning more than ever.

Some of these inopportunely remembered details had to do with the little dog that stood at the door snarling and panting relentlessly and would not let me pass. I had had an encounter with him many weeks back. Walter had needed the animal for an experiment. March normally performed services of this kind but had been busy with other matters, and I had been obliged to go get the experimental animal out of his pen in the basement corridor, to put him on an old leash that was used only for this purpose and smelled of blood and chemicals, and take him to the laboratory. I still remember how he willingly followed me at first. But the closer we came to the laboratory and the muffled sounds of distress and pain emanating from it, the sounds of one of his fellows suffering on the operating table, the more reluctant he became. He dug in with all four feet, his fur bristling like quills (to use that painfully accurate expression), in his handsome golden brown eyes an expression of panicky terror – an almost human terror. I felt I had never experienced anything of the kind. "Let's go," I exhorted myself, "Move," and yet I hesitated, not daring to cross the threshold. But what was the use? I had to do what was necessary. The animal had then suffered a great deal. There were no scars. Everything had healed. But he had not forgotten. Suffering had made him vicious. For he may have resisted us, Walter and me, who put him on the table, and Carolus, who did not take part actively but looked on, but he did not resist with teeth bared as he was doing now.

So did the creature's bitter suffering not elevate him? Or is betterment through suffering peculiar to man, who is more highly developed? I don't know. What awaited me now as I chased the animal away and entered the sickroom through the slightly open door gave me no evidence either way.

The woman lay in bed. The room, brightly illuminated by the morning sun, looked peaceful and very tidy. A small, old-fashioned zinc washbasin stood on a chair. Clean, damp diapers had been hung to dry in pairs over the backs of chairs and on lines. There was a smell of milk and chamomile tea. A makeshift vase, a water carafe, held some magnificent flowers, orchids, if I remember correctly. The woman was pale, but her eyes were clear. Still no fever. Her eyes as they looked at me were clear and malignant, filled with hate. The woman had spread her husband's old camel-hair blanket over the bed and pulled it up to her chin. The child lay sleeping, its mouth half open, in a basket to her left.

I was uncertain. Should I go first to the mother, despite her blazing eyes? Should I take care of the child first?

Happily, it was plain that Y.F. had been unable to lay a hand on the tiny creature, no matter how the experiment on the mother turned out.

Had I been my old self, I would have gone to the mother first. Perhaps, thanks to the power I had always had over people, I could have become master of the situation. But I turned and bent over the child, as an involuntary but for that very reason all the more furious flush (what a rare occurrence with me!) spread over my face, to the roots of my hair. I had already taken hold of the slight little body from underneath to lift the baby out of the cradle, had begun to take comfort in the moist warmth that a baby's body gives out, when the mother, however weak she may have been, abruptly sat up in bed, bent down for the baby with a sudden movement of her upper body, and violently knocked my hand away, hurling these words in my face:

"Keep your hands off my baby! I know everything!"

But this passionate outburst was all she could manage. She was unable to hold on to the baby. Her days and nights of terrible suffering had left her with only a fraction of her strength and she had to let go of the child. A good thing the young nurse who followed me in and had planted herself in front of me was able to tear her furious eyes away from my face in time to attend to the infant, which was beginning to mewl softly. She hastily took it from the mother and soothed it in her arms with one hymn after another (as though that was all she knew).

"Oh, just go, would you, please," she hissed at me, interrupting her singing briefly. Her broad, flowing white hood rippling, she nodded angrily toward Walter's widow, who now tossed like a madwoman in her creaking, squeaking bed, threw the camel-hair blanket to the floor, groaned, tore her hair, and in her jarring voice cursed me and herself and her husband all in the same breath.

"I know everything?" I reflected. She and the nurse could have learned the truth only from March. But if only she had vented her rage and despair on me, instead of on herself, I could have left the sickroom with a lighter heart, I must say.

I looked at her. Her lips were pale, contorted with feeling. Unconsciously she pressed her heavy breasts together with both hands. She mastered herself, evidently because of the child – turned her face away from me and toward the wall and got herself under control just as suddenly as she had been overcome by her fit of rage. Suffering had helped her grow as a person, at least.

I understood that I had brought about an irreparable change in this woman's existence. She had trusted in me; in her delusions about life, which she refused to recognize for what it inescapably is, she had grasped at *me*, a vision, a phantom. She had seen in me a misunderstood humanitarian, a benevolent and knowledgeable physician unjustly condemned and deported, had invoked the testimony of her late husband in my favor. Perhaps she had even seen in me her future sustainer, for she knew of a bequest that Walter had made to me. She may have been thinking of letters we had drafted together, she knew of our last conversations. And she thought that if there was anyone to whom she owed her life and that of her child, it was me.

The child was going to be baptízed at noon that day, as I learned from Chaplain Amen, and she had wanted to christen it both "Walter" and "Georg" in the holy sacrament of Old Catholic baptism!

She *had* wanted to do that. No longer. For it was I, Georg Letham, who had tried to infect her with the same terrible disease that had killed her dear husband. Y.F. How can one explain this?

One cannot explain it.

One tiptoes away from the scene of one's crimes, eyes averted. Quietly closes the door behind one after gingerly letting the little dog in to comfort the woman as best it can. The little dog barks joyfully and dances about the room. The nurse glowers, the child mewls, the dog barks – and does the poor woman laugh? How I wish she would. If only she is saved!

IX

Perhaps Frau Walter, in her boundless desolation, had begun to love me, and this unnatural, ill-founded, pathological love had then turned into an equally unnatural and pathological hatred. But neither her hatred nor the animosity, now constantly on furious display, of the once faithful March could bedevil me more than my conscience did. Yes, Georg Letham the younger – with a conscience! And yet so it was! I wanted to maintain a humorous, ironic attitude as I bore everything that came along in this atrocious and farcical world. But who can make himself be calm, act superior and amused, when, through his own doing, a flourishing human life is about to be brought down?

Fortunately it turned out otherwise. In one case out of a hundred, a woman will withstand without ill effect an infection during delivery as grave as this one had been. And this was that one case!

I am unable to put into words the truly wild happiness I felt and my beatific sense of relief when the first week passed without fever and I saw that everything was going to be fine. No puerperal fever! And, what is more, the perilous four and a half days' last respite that most of the subjects of our experiments had had between being bitten by a Y.F.-infected *Stegomyia* mosquito and coming down with Y.F. passed in Frau Walter's case without the appearance of fever symptoms. So neither childbed fever nor Y.F.! What a stroke of luck, I say again. These were hard days for me. A great deal of work, as March no longer did anything without a direct order from Carolus, and Carolus, temperamentally phlegmatic as always, let others make the decisions unless he absolutely had to. He practically had to be forced at gunpoint to sign his name to anything. But in a really urgent situation, a critical moment, he showed what he was made of, and the hellish climate had not sapped his strength of will. Even if his intentions and objectives were not always the same as mine, we got along, and I had a mainstay in him despite the great disparity in our natures.

March's antagonism may have affected me deeply, but it had no power to truly injure me once I had adapted to it. For the time being he was letting the matter rest with his first and most consequential rottenness, his disclosure to Frau Walter of my *Stegomyia* experiment on the evening of her husband's demise.

When he saw what he had caused, he backed off. He was not happy about it. Until that time he had presented a comparatively good appearance. But from then on he began to decline. He couldn't live with me and he couldn't live without me. It was like knives cutting him up inside. No one could have helped him. I least of all.

I had to be content with moving our experiments forward to some degree. The external difficulties mounted from day to day. But fate's interventions on my behalf – Frau Walter's continued good health and the unexpected success of what had been a desperately difficult delivery (I could not imagine what would have become of me if she or little Walter had died) – gave me new courage.

Walter's widow remained one of the chief difficulties. In her hatred for me, she went so far as to slander me with elaborate, ingenious accusations, like a lunatic with persecution mania. In addition to the serious but unprovable crimes of the attempted murder of her and her unborn child, I was also alleged to have committed a theft. She maintained that when I had looked through her purse I had tucked away some of the loose banknotes, a not insignificant sum all told. Now in former times I had often been without resistance to the allure of money. But if there was any respect in which I had changed, it was this one. I had taken out the key and that was all. Was it March who wanted to pin on me this small but for that reason all the filthier crime? Our things had been searched while I was away from our basement room, and some banknotes had been found among my possessions. But it turned out that they had been enclosed with the letter I had received from my family when I had been severely ill with Y.F. March was my witness. It was he who had removed the money before giving me the pages of the letter. Through this clever shift, he had kept the money from being ripped to shreds, the fate met by the letter, whose contents and even whose author remained unknown, to my sorrow. March himself was forced to clear me. He did it grudgingly, but he did it. I was able to point out that Dr. Walter had on repeated occasions entrusted large sums of money to me (this was a violation of the regulation prohibiting the possession of money, but it had been relaxed in our case) and that I had never abused his trust. And what could I have done with the relatively insignificant amount in my situation, and what would I have done given the plans I had? But some of this stuck, and the sidelong looks from the hospital staff were not always easy to bear. Were they meant for the man who had perpetrated the attempted murder of Frau Walter, if passively standing by while the mosquito bit could be called that, or for the alleged petty thief?

The woman's hatred was evident not only in such grave charges but in little things too. I have not yet reported the fact that in addition to wood and leather, clothes and linens soon begin to rot in this sultry climate, because they never dry out, literally falling to shreds in the hands of the washerwomen. Now Carolus (who was particularly open and generous as long as it was other people's property that was involved) had had a small bequest from Walter's estate in mind for me, namely, an assortment of his surgical gowns, his linens, his tropical suits, of which he had several dozen and which were made of a very robust material, silk, I believe, blended with linen, or a similar blend of fabrics. After the doctor's illness these articles had gone into the disinfection chambers to be sterilized in jets of pressurized steam at a hundred degrees centigrade, as a result of which they had lost none of their durability but a good deal of their beauty and glamour. If I would not be reaping the benefit of them, though I had been blowing my nose with nothing but filter paper for weeks, they could also be used as dishcloths. And this was the purpose for which Walter's widow had intended them. All the persuasion of the good Carolus was to no avail.

I had other things on my mind, and I had no trouble getting over the loss of these items, to which I had no claim.

Diapers could have been fashioned from these things too, of course. But no one thought of that. Instead the necessary articles, very expensive and of very poor quality, were purchased down in the city. Was the old stuff going to be dragged all over the world as a memento of Dr. Walter? I said nothing on this point.

But another point was more critical. I reported earlier that Walter had had to take out and sign a new policy with the insurance company's subagent under which any liability on the part of the company was excluded in one precisely circumscribed case, namely, that in which the holder of the policy, Walter, departed this life by suicide or by "self-inflicted accident." Here the subagent, whom the wife had set against the husband, was of course thinking of Walter's experiments on his own person.

Now Walter had clearly perished as a result of his heroic experiment (and his inner conflicts, to which no one of his sort is equal). Once this was established, the widow would not get a penny. The family of six children, four boys, two girls, was so poor that public assistance and the like would have been needed even to raise the money for the return trip. For how far would the widows' and orphans' benefit go? It would hardly even cover the most pressing debts! But if the death of that great hero without a weapon, Walter, was found to be "natural," the widow would immediately come into possession of a relatively large sum of money, the interest on which would give her and her children the means for a modest but adequate life in simple circumstances, say, in a country town in England.

So now what? Carolus, who was entirely on the side of Walter's widow (if only out of fear that she might go to him with new demands for money in the event her claim fell through), locked himself in with Frau Alix for hours on end. The woman held her baby, which was thin but agreeable and cried only rarely, in her arms, nursed it, put on its diapers or took them off, or else she played with the little dog. She sniffed at her eau de cologne or shredded the lovely flowers she had received from the subagent. And she discussed with her husband's friend how her financial problems were going to be solved. My evidence, albeit only that of a criminal sentenced without possibility of appeal, was not unimportant. I had been the right hand of the deceased at the end, after all, and he had entrusted his last writings to me. I was ordered in, not offered a seat, and regarded in baleful silence, but

Carolus whispered to her and convinced her to reconcile with me. He himself did not have such a tragic view of the inappropriate experiment on her. In his opinion she ought to be able to get over it with a little effort. But she bared her pretty teeth instead of smiling. She pursued me remorselessly with a hatred that I believed I did not deserve in this form, any more than I deserved the hatred of my former friend, who was quietly doing me as much damage as he could. But the woman lived and gradually began to flourish again, became more beautiful than ever, while poor March in his self-destructive fervor gradually became "a shadow of his former self," as the saying goes.

X

With his treachery, March had hurt me a great deal – our enterprise even more. We had to break off for the moment. How could I have been so wrong about him? I had taken him for a "man in full." Or, if not that, then at least a "frog." Never a "rat." But he was both. I realized that my father's excellent teachings were wonderfully applicable after the fact, but of no use while life is actually being lived.

March had told the woman not only that I had exposed her to infection by a disease-bearing mosquito when she had been bending over her dying husband, but also, to twist the knife, that I had said she had false teeth. I had never made that allegation. The woman's teeth did not have the smooth bluish sheen of fired porcelain dentures. It had been simple medical conscientiousness when I had had him check her mouth for dental prosthetics, something I would have done for anyone, no matter who it was, before administering anesthesia. March understood that as well as I did. He was a person of extraordinary intelligence. Otherwise he could not have learned the skills necessary for our work as quickly as he had. It was not until I no longer had him by me for anything and everything that I noticed how necessary he was to me and to our work.

I did not allow it to come to a confrontation. And this was the worst punishment. I was silent.

I did not want to punish him with silence. But I had no choice.

I cared about him, I cared like nobody's business, as people say. I was thankful to him for the many fine services of the heart that he had done me on the ship and here in the hospital. He was almost a substitute for all human company. He had become, and this is no figure of speech, like a brother to me.

I no longer hated my real brother, I understood him. My father had a lot of money, my brother needed it. Not for himself, for his family. Was the solution to the puzzle so difficult?

But I could have spent my entire life on a lonely island with no one but March for company and perhaps never have needed anyone else. And yet I was unable to pluck up my courage, collar him, and lay before him what was in my heart, my misgivings, my hopes, my sufferings, my joys.

We remained distant. Time went by. The woman had long since risen from her bed of pain, the child, delicate but healthy, was carried outside in a woven basket, which, tightly netted from top to bottom against mosquitoes, was set down in a shady spot in the rampantly flourishing, stupefyingly fragrant hospital garden.

For some days I had had my bed back. One night I returned to our basement room later than usual and found March sound asleep in his old place on the floor. My clothes and other personal items had been cleaned and straightened up, as though nothing had ever happened between us. And one day the foolish youth – one never knew what he might do, yet he was only too understandable, in his way – surprised me by quietly smuggling into my things a half dozen monogrammed handkerchiefs that had been among Walter's possessions. He had wheedled these articles out of Walter's widow. She would not have given *me* so much as a rag. Toward March she was all sympathy, gratitude, comradeship, and friendliness. And yet neither he nor she was happy. She never stopped trying to turn the hospital director, the resident, the matron against me and imputing to me all sorts of crimes and warning everyone she talked to against the devil in human form, the wife murderer, the Mephistopheles brazenly wearing physician's garb that I was as far as she was concerned. She also threatened to do what she could to prevent any other human being from falling victim to my diabolical experiments.

By that time all her threats and fulminations were harmless to us. They were much more dangerous for her. For the poor dissatisfied woman was ruled day and night by hatred of me. It had become an idée fixe with her, overshadowing even her grief over her late husband and her worry about her five children, who had in the meantime been taken in by the family of one of her husband's comrades from the shore batteries.

She should long since have been capable of leaving our building ("our building," I call this dreadful Y.F. hospital, as though it had actually become my home!), should have been made to go. Anything but that. She did not want to leave here, or leave me. What she wanted to do was sweep past me (an unbelievably chilly expression on her face), with her silk Spanish shawl wrapped about her and showing off her once again slender figure, she wanted to cast poisonous glances my way and try to make me persona non grata with Carolus and the chaplain. But for Carolus I was a sine qua non.

As long as all this affected only me, an individual of no consequence, I did not regard it as anything serious. But now that sunshiny, sweltering weather had begun, the hospital was filling up with patients. She and her delicate infant no longer belonged in this dangerous place of contagious illness. Not only were there *Stegomyias* in test tubes here, but there were also free mosquitoes flitting about (not to mention a thousand different kinds of nocturnal creatures) and laying their eggs in any discarded jam jar that had a few drops of stagnant rainwater in it.

We all wanted Alix gone, March not excepted.

Her husband had died as a result of the experiments. An avoidable death, as I saw it, and was it grounds for continual bitterness against us? Yes, and against the dead man too. She hated me. But it was possible she hated him just as much – as though he had intentionally left her in the lurch!

Carolus became the savior of our plans. I had given him too little credit at the beginning, on the *Mimosa*. He was neither a lummox nor a dry-as-dust pedant, nor yet a mere ambitious grind. But why sing a hymn of praise to him, which would have to be quickly followed by the qualification that must apply to all of us frail mortals. The facts showed how fortunate it was that our little team boasted not only an extraordinarily noble and in my view perhaps even great man like Walter, but also someone like Carolus. He was very far from mediocre, though it had taken me some time to realize that.

He grasped the situation before I did. He reproached me, in the languid tone that would once have exasperated me, for my imprudent experiment on Frau Walter, and he did this upon examining our experimental records, in which I had not yet entered the infection of the woman at Walter's deathbed. I had not been afraid to do the experiment (fortunately without repercussion), but I was afraid to record it. He, great statistician and by-the-book type that he was, could not tolerate this lacuna. We therefore worked together to draft a simple statement of the facts, and only as an aside did he take me to task to my face for having breached, on my own authority and very much to the detriment of all, the law of solidarity that we had unanimously and of our own free will imposed upon ourselves at the beginning of the enterprise.

I had to concede the point. Thereupon he merely shook his long, sallow, withered, hairless head, which I had once likened to a thin, jaundiced baby's bottom, and returned to business as usual.

We discussed how we could induce Frau Walter to leave the island. She had to go. Our experiments were imperiled as long as she was here, and the climate was certain to be her and her children's undoing in the long run. And it had been our late friend's last wish that she return to her family in England. Now there was still the *nervus rerum* of money, that is, the life insurance, and this was the salient point. Carolus conducted this part of the negotiations with Frau Walter and the chaplain and me as a group, or at least he planned it that way. It was not easy to overcome the woman's practically savage hatred for me. Nearly four weeks after the attempt on her life by mosquito, though no harm had been done, she could still hardly look at me. She chewed her lips, turned red and white in alternation. Once she stepped on her little dog, then took him onto her lap and stroked the flat, densely furred head of the worried, golden-eyed, dumb brute, who didn't know what was happening to him. But we had to achieve some result with her, and since the new experiments had to begin soon or not at all, we had to achieve it quickly.

XI

One might have assumed that the poor widow would have welcomed nothing so much as the prospect of getting away from this epidemic-ridden island, with which she could associate only the unhappiest memories. Not so. The fancy the unfortunate woman had taken to me, currently expressed only in hatred and suppressed outbursts of fury, drove her to put one obstacle after another in the way of our plan to send her and the children away from the island as quickly as possible.

We were at pains to explain how the insurance matter was to be settled. She leaned in, cupping her ear as though unable to make out what we were saying. As she did so she brushed my cheek with her slightly wavy, rustily lustrous hair, in which there were already a few quite pale, colorless strands. I reared back as though stung by a tarantula. Anyone else would have noticed this abrupt, unexpected, I might say explosive, flinch of mine, and, as hard of hearing as the woman pretended to be or actually was, her eyes were good, and she must have seen it. But she acted as though nothing had happened and continued with her objections, which were based on the idea that the tightfisted insurance company would not pay her anything but instead initiate a major court action; for this she would have to prepare, and to prepare she would have to stay. We disagreed and said why, and the discussion went on. A corner of her pink raw-silk housedress, which was tailored for pregnant women and now hung much too loosely on her once again slender figure, fell on my left ankle. I pulled my foot back but could not prevent the wide, Japanese-styled sleeve of her dress from touching my hand as it hung by my side. "Why do you want to get rid of me?" she said, apparently referring to the business negotiations. "I'm not hurting anyone." What clumsy maneuvering by a woman who could not have been much for tender caresses, a woman more masculine than maidenly!

Then she suddenly took a new tack. "Who's going to tend my darling's grave?" We said nothing. "What? Eh? What?" she screeched in her strident voice, looking at me with eyes blazing. I said nothing. Carolus was admirably calm, taking another stack of papers out of his briefcase, a barely perceptible smile on his thin lips in response to this inappropriate outburst. I got up and stood behind Frau Walter. Now there were neither meaningful looks nor the old "What? Eh?" and suddenly she heard every word. But to reveal to me what had been no secret for a long time, she rocked back and forth on her chair, showed off her still firm, lovely, heavy bosom, and tossed her head, perhaps in order to "accidentally" brush me with her hair again. Decent women are often the very ones who are coarse and tactless in their demonstrations of love. I saw the place on her neck where the insect had bitten her. She must have guessed my thoughts. She felt her neck with her narrow white hand, on which she was wearing her wedding ring and Walter's, but said nothing to me, simply stopped rocking.

The woman was intelligent and now understood the situation completely. She let everything pass and we were soon agreed. That is, she and Carolus were agreed. The chaplain's aid had been enlisted too; he was passive and forbearing as always and stayed neutral. But it was not easy for me to concur. They were quite right, the huge pile of insurance money had to be secured, and that could not happen by the direct route. Her husband had too knowingly taken part in life-endangering experiments. His spirit of sacrifice might entitle him to a bronze memorial in front of the hospital or back home, he might be entitled to an entry in the encyclopedia, perhaps even the Nobel, but for all that his heirs were not entitled to the insurance money.

Cash was needed. What to do? The global insurance company that was worth millions had to be lied to and defrauded for the good of the financially weaker but morally stronger party.

The full insured amount had to be claimed through the subagent. The claim would run as follows. Dr. Walter had indeed been researching Y.F., as was his duty and official job. But he had never conducted life-endangering experiments on himself, and his highly regrettable death had been caused by an infection whose route was still unknown. An occupational hazard of which the insurance company had taken full cognizance, both in the first policy and in the addendum.

This Carolus, the chaplain, and (mainly) the resident, who had taken formal responsibility for the expert opinion and was putty in our hands, had to put in writing. They had to sign their names to it. In the likely event of a lawsuit, they would even have to swear to it. Ill-gotten gains. Do they profit nothing? Everyone was for it, everyone but me.

I was going to declare our work null and void? Pretend to? A written, sworn declaration is not pretending. It had been the last wish of the deceased that the results of our work, which we had obtained not in an ivory tower but in epidemic-ridden sickrooms and laboratories, be deposited with a notary.

Thus I expressed my opinion candidly, and it was *No*. The widow turned to me, enveloped me, unseen by the others, in an imploring, beseeching, distraught look, in which all her fervent love and hate were intermingled, and then she said to me with the sweetest, with the gentlest, the tenderest, the most girlish, the most caressing sound her raucous voice could produce: "I'll forgive you for that word!" Unexpectedly, abruptly, with touching awkwardness, she began to smile, whispered to me that I was a good doctor, perhaps *too* good, she was not ungrateful, she knew how much I had done! I flushed, but she displayed her full complement of beautiful teeth, and remarked, with a mischievous smile like a seventeen-year-old girl's, that she really didn't have false teeth. This? Now? Such coquettishness at a moment like this! And out of the mouth of the wife of someone like Walter! She exhibited her open mouth, the dazzling rows of teeth revealed by the two moist, pink lips, as though she were offering herself to me. I backed off, forced a polite grimace, murmured something about pressing work that couldn't wait, and withdrew in great distress.

It never makes me happy to be loved. But the other part of it, the great, overpowering feeling of loving, was not something I had a gift for, either. If I loved anything now, it was not human beings, at least none that were still attainable in my life, but something else. In its entirety it resided in my work.

XII

Further very great effort was required in order to finally induce Frau Walter to leave the Y.F. hospital.

I will not go on about the pathetic woman's various attempts, either the ones that failed or the one that eventually succeeded, to come together with me in some fashion and "have it out" where there was nothing to have out. She loved. I did not. I saw in her simply a sick person whose illness expressed itself not in the body that had been blessed with such tremendous robustness and splendid will to health, but in her mind. It was not within *my* power to cure her mind. I had no choice but to punish her with silence, because every word I said to her would have encouraged unrealizable hopes, to her certain undoing. The woman had other things to take care of. The future of her unprovided-for children had to be more important to her than any phantasm that happened to appear to her. For it was only a phantasm.

Eventually we would all have the pleasure of seeing her leave the Y.F. hospital. The valediction took a week.

I spent most of my time hiding in the laboratory, and we put it about that entering the area was more dangerous than ever. In this way I protected myself from her last good-bye. Sometimes I thought back on the truly frightful physical and mental suffering she had gone through, I might almost say in my hands. But there was no trace of it left in her face, which, framed by the beautiful wavy, reddish brown hair, she occasionally, and most desperately on the last day, pressed against the glass door that connected the laboratory with the corridor. And her mind?

I pitied her from the bottom of my heart. Let no one doubt this brief statement.

At last she was sitting in the subagent's automobile, which the subagent had gallantly sent up the hill to the convent hospital. The young assistant nurse was going along to look after the infant during the coming days and help the widow with the eventual move. Everyone overlooked the quarantine. It had to be done.

The little dog too kept his rendezvous with disinfection. To his horror he was shaven smooth, brushed down with sublimate solution, and sprinkled with phenol, and now he was huddled in the automobile, barely recognizable and hoarse from hours of barking. He was looking forward to better times.

I was not spared the task of putting my name to the aforementioned document concerning the cause of death in the case of the heavily insured medical officer Walter. I had to do it, against my better judgment, as Carolus did against his. It was with a peculiar feeling that I traced my signature, for the first time in a long while. I thought of the day when, my hand guided by my father's, I had first scrawled it in an exercise book using his otherwise jealously guarded gold fountain pen. Now, after the name Georg Letham, I wrote: Gr. 3. Convict, third grade. In my youth I had also written: Georg Letham, Third Grade. Gone. On! Thus do all things return in this short life. On all the more!

In C., as in his former posts, Walter had always enjoyed the greatest respect and love. The insurance company, which often had to rely on the goodwill of the administrative authorities, knew this and forbore from making further difficulties for his heirs in a legal challenge. More detailed investigations were also dropped. And it was better that way. The resident's medical opinion was admitted, although it did not deserve to be. But we were all firmly resolved to make ten perjured statements in favor of the widow rather than deliver her almost destitute to a cruel fate.

After five years of unbroken service on C., the governor was no longer in the best of health.

A short vacation in Europe or some other Y.F.-free country was out of the question, for the simple reason that an absence for any length of time would have caused him to lose his immunity to Y.F., which he had survived shortly after his arrival here five years before. He was not staying here unwillingly and was socking away a lot of money and lived like a prince. Where did that get him? His liver could not cope with C. any longer, and he had to leave.

Thus, as a convenient consequence of His Excellency's weakened health, a relatively large, comfortably appointed ship intended to accommodate the governor was also able to take Walter's widow and her children to Europe. It was already lying at anchor.

As we stood at our windows watching the great two-funnel steamer (not the little *Mimosa*) getting fired up and the government launch speed from shore and back again, the telephone, whose harsh jangle had so often startled our late friend from his work, rang once more. Carolus picked it up, listened briefly, then called me over and handed me the receiver with a strange smile, baring his long yellow fangs. I will say nothing about the substance of the conversation. It was the last adieu of the widow, who had been unable to bring herself to leave without saying something. She had tried and "succeeded at last." The discussion did not drag on. It cannot have lasted more than two or three minutes, and I myself hardly got a word in edgewise.

More or less as a service in kind, Carolus, who had lately been treating me as someone in his league, had a favor to ask of me. But it was impossible.

I was grateful to him. I could only be, had to be grateful to him. And yet I could not comply with his request, his first and only one (which he had expressed on the *Mimosa*, to no effect then too). What he wanted was no more and no less than that I remember my duty as a son and brother and get in touch with my family at home. I could not. That life, I felt, was dead, I had it behind me. I could as little take it up again as nourish myself on shit. Not even for the sake of our enterprise. No. Other, greater men, heroic types who are able to rise above the fray, they could have. Here I will cite only that brilliant discoverer of the syphilis spirochete, Schaudinn, who experimented on himself using human excrement. Humanity was already in his debt for a tremendous, epochal, seminal discovery, but he perished in the prime of life a few years ago as a result of this abominable experiment, "as the law he set himself commanded."

I could not conquer myself that way. My father was the land of my birth. The land of my birth lay behind me. I had been deported. I had been deported inwardly. I wanted to regard my former "loving hearts" as dead. I wanted to be dead to them too. I wanted to wish for nothing from them and have nothing to fear from them. Is this understandable?

He did not understand it. I only shook my head in silence at his request, no matter how earnestly he put it in his awkward, grating way. I appreciated old Carolus's good advice.

That evening, after we had watched the government boat vanish among the craggy black islands in the wine-dark sea, trailing a golden banner of smoke, March, my former friend, approached me again for the first time. He did not have glad tidings for me. He was seeking consolation from me, and I – I tried to give it to him, determined as I was to wipe the slate clean of everything that had passed between us. He wanted to leave here. Our experiments were over at last, weren't they? He yearned for home! And for me! And number three on his list was the "loving hearts" he had left behind, his morphine- and cocaine-addicted father, who, as the son had learned from his mother's letters, had run afoul of the law for perpetrating the most devilishly clever frauds and scams, always at the expense of the poorest, out of whom he had wormed everything they had. Thus it might conceivably come to pass in this most farcical and most atrocious of all worlds that the degenerate old druggist would turn up here among the deportees in a puce uniform, a black number on his chest, perhaps on the very day that his son, pardoned for his heroism, left this accursed deportation island.

I did what I could to calm him. I dodged the questions about the experiments and the ones about my feelings. But I strove to paint the prodigal father's conviction as unlikely, even though I thought it very possible. I preferred to believe that the morally debased old man belonged here much more than the son, whom I still did not want to see for what he was. I did not want to know what he was. I laid all the blame for the way things were on the clumsy or malicious hand of fate. And that very night I would see to my sorrow that I was still not equal to the world as it really was, what was it I said, to its mindless earnestness, "beyond improvement" in the best, the most hopeful, or in the worst sense. Was there no way to improve it, to change it? Did one have to regard it and oneself as the butts of a cruel, inhuman, cynical joke? Could I laugh, could I smile, if that was what everyone had to do?

XIII

That night I awoke suddenly. Even as I gave a start I knew that something much earlier had been the cause of this abrupt awakening. I turned the gradually fading dream over in my mind, listened to the rustling and nibbling of the rats that dashed about in great numbers among the many crates and kegs in the cellar and sometimes scurried under our bed, too. Our bed? I was now becoming wide awake and noticed that March's place on the basement floor at my feet was empty. I waited a moment, imagining that he was answering the call of nature, for we had come to an understanding between us that there would be no relieving oneself in this bedroom. Sissy that he was, March had been in the habit of doing this from boyhood. It had required a fair amount of effort to break him of the practice of employing for this purpose a familiar article of indispensable utility to children and the infirm. But what was keeping him now? I became concerned, got up, and went looking for him. I hurried through the familiar corridors and up and down stairs. I knocked on the door of the room in question. Everywhere silent as the grave.

How odd! I had something like a feeling of home as I walked through the Y.F. hospital. I felt, as I looked for March, something of what I had felt as a child the times I had gone looking for my – my only too dearly beloved father in our big, often very bleak house.

To make sure I had looked everywhere, I rushed back through the labyrinthine architecture of the rambling building, which had been completely ruined by numerous additions over the many years of its existence, and ran finally toward the laboratory.

I ran, I walked, I slowed and stopped. I did not want to go on. I told myself that March and I must have missed each other and he was surely long since back in his bed. It was only out of a kind of dutiful opposition to my own inclinations that I conquered my misgivings and forced myself to go into the laboratory.

It was horribly hot and I was dripping with sweat underneath my tattered pajamas.

At last I was at the laboratory, not at the entrance with the glass door, but at the other end, in front of a solid door, and to my happy surprise saw a chink of golden light. I told myself how foolish it would have been for me to have trusted my feeling and gone back to our bedroom.

I opened the door softly and to my great horror saw, in his familiar red-and-white-striped pajamas – my dead friend Walter, bending over a little table by a corner window and doing something with mosquitoes in jars. "Walter!" I cried involuntarily. He straightened – and what I saw staring at me was not Walter's unforgettable, gaunt, serious face, but March's handsome mug. March was whey pale and no less aghast than I. One of Walter's colorful pairs of pajamas had come his way through Walter's widow and he was wearing them tonight for the first time. "March?!" I whispered in consternation. "What are you doing here?"

March stammered a few incomprehensible words, and, a hot flush spreading over his features, he made himself laugh, a laugh that was croaky, unnatural, and yet came from deep in his chest, a laugh that continued almost nonstop throughout the ensuing brief conversation. I had gone up to him quickly and I saw that he had two jars in front of him. The smaller, empty jar was labeled "M. (St.) G. II Y.F. 5/9 II" in blue grease pencil. This meant second-generation mosquitoes (*Stegomyia*) fed on the ninth day with yellow-fever blood from a patient who had fallen ill after five days of incubation. In the other, larger jar, numerous mosquitoes startled by the light were flitting confusedly and occasionally clambering about on the walls; it was labeled simply "M. (St.) II III o." This was thus the large cache of insects, all in their second and third generations, that had so far not fed on human blood and were being kept in reserve for further experiments. It takes fifteen to twenty-three days for a larva to develop from egg to adult insect, and the mosquito is fecund two to three weeks after emerging from the pupa.

"What's going on? What is this? What are you doing here? Where are the mosquitoes?" I asked. March's foolish convulsive laughter prevented him from answering. His eyes flooded with tears and he hung on to the laboratory table with both hands, so that the two jars knocked together and rattled violently. The smaller one had lost its gauze top. There was not a single mosquito in it. Or so it seemed at any rate. For after a long moment had gone by and I was still gazing at March in perplexity, unable to find any plausible explanation for all this, a young, unusually small mosquito emerged bashfully and perched on the rim of the jar, sitting hunched over as these insects do and jiggling its long hind legs, the white markings visible on its dark abdomen; in two seconds it had spread its elongate wings, and, the white lyre-shaped marking clearly visible against the lip of the jar under the light, pushed off. After a few zigzags it found its way to the ceiling and the lamp, where a fair number of its kind were already performing their familiar jerky dance. There was mosquito netting over the windows, so the dozen *Stegomyias* up there, knocking about in choppy corkscrews and steep parabolas, could only be the previous occupants of the jar.

Who had let them out? March. Why?

I had no time for calm consideration. Immediately my blood was stirred, as the saying goes, I felt my temper get the better of me, and, face terrible, fists clenched, I advanced toward him. He was laughing, white as a ghost. He backed off, still laughing idiotically, and whispered between fits of laughter: "Go on, hit me! Cut me down! Riddle me with bullets!" He reached into a pocket of his pajamas. "Stop that laughing," I whispered. Extremely silly of me, for (as I realized at once) he was not laughing of his own free will at all, but out of compulsion. "Stop that foolish laughter now and help me catch them. Get a ladder!" Still laughing, he brought a ladder on his shoulders. The late doctor's nice pajamas were soaked with his sweat. "Hold the legs," I said, "and when I get up there, hand me the bottle and the cotton wool." I gave him a piece of cotton wool and a bottle of chloroform, the same one he had used to anesthetize Walter's widow. "Spread the stuff one drop at a time, not too much, not too little," I said, or rather I shouted. But this time he did not dare to retort, "Stop shouting!" His laughter was broken, it was threatening to become compulsive weeping. He was trembling all over. The swaying ladder, rotting and weakened like anything made of soft wood in the tropics, picked up the trembling, and I felt the vibration. That we did not need. I had in mind to stupefy the freed *Stegomyias* with the not overly concentrated chloroform-alcohol mixture, which was evaporating quickly in the heat, so that I could catch the highly infectious beasts dead or alive.

But that was easier said than done. The wad of cotton wool was too wet or too dry, I held it too high or not high enough, I could not jump while I was perched on the clumsy, unsound, half-rotten ladder, but the nimble creatures up there in their element could. Finally we had recaptured seven of the eleven fugitives. The others we had to leave for the time being. They swerved so cleverly as they flitted about on the ceiling that they got away from me despite all my tricks and stratagems. March and I were more dead than alive ourselves from the fumes of the chloroform mixture, from the effort, from fatigue, from the heat and the excitement. We checked the mosquito screens on the windows once more to make sure the dangerous creatures could not find their way outside, locked the doors carefully, and retired. Or at least we tried to. It was about two in the morning. I was as though drunk from the enormous amount of chloroform I had used. Incapable of thinking clearly or acting with any sort of decisiveness.

XIV

The true brother of a man like me is not the one nature gave him. March had come to mean more to me than my brother had. That night I realized this more clearly than ever. And yet I had no choice but to separate from March.

The question was, should I keep my reasons from him or explain them. Or rather my reason, the reason I could never trust him again after what had happened. People can live together without love, if necessary, but not without trust. He could get personal with me, abuse me, if that was the way it had to be; that was fine. It was understandable that he did not want to be merely a "means to an end" for me. I understood why he had lost faith in me over the experiment on Walter's wife that was of such fundamental importance to the progress of our research. It certainly had nothing to do with love for her. March's abnormal orientation meant that she had no power over him. No, it was only jealousy of me, and especially of the research that had gradually consumed me body and soul, that had made him stop being consumed by me body and soul. What did he care about all the world's women and widows? What did he care about the unborn child?

Ungovernable as he was, he wanted to possess *me*. He wanted, if a physical union was impossible, to play the most important, more than that, the only, role in my *emotional* life. He wanted to be on top – and be a man. To assert his dominance, he had installed himself in the bed on high and shown me my place in the pit of hell, cheek by jowl with the rat pack. I had gradually understood him and had forgiven him. Without a word. One need not speak. Without reproach. One need not square the accounts. But now I understood him even better, for on this last night he had made me see the unbridgeable chasm between us. I could no longer ignore it. How little we know of what we do! *Tout comprendre, c'est tout pardonner*. Fine, with pleasure, March, dear boy, life companion, as long as it was only me. But if he turned against my work and tried to destroy it? Never. My final word? Without the slightest hesitation my final word.

The next morning I saw the signs of desolation in the face that had once been so pleasant, had become a fat and happy face here, but was now nothing but skin and cheekbones. Again he hung on me with his fine blue-gray dog's eyes, expecting some reproach, a fit of temper, some "human" emotion from me. It was hard for me to do what I had to do.

I went to see Carolus up in the room that he had been sharing with the young resident since Walter's death. Carolus was brushing his long yellow teeth. And the way he did it! He dipped an old, discolored, sparsely bristled toothbrush, repeatedly and without rinsing, into a glass with three fingers of mouthwash in it. Economy! Economy! He stinted, even here. And the drops ran down his nightshirt.

I interrupted him while he was thus unappetizingly employed, asked him to hurry, and went to wait outside the door.

March skulked by, head on breast, once, twice. Like an animal without the power of speech, he nudged me with his elbows. The way a dog bumps his master behind the knees to elicit from him a response of some kind, to ask for a walk, a treat, or simply, in his naïve brute way, to remind him of his, the dog's, existence. March, don't worry, I thought to myself, without acknowledging him, I won't hurt you. But, March, you know as well as I do that it's hopeless, we have to part, and you can't go into the laboratory anymore.

Carolus had the best relations with the acting governor and his staff. His influence and his general's rank could accomplish a great deal.

Through his mediation I wanted to make sure that the overly devoted, overly emotional March suffered no consequences, but instead received a comfortable post in the administration of C., which was within his capabilities thanks to his innate intelligence and his willingness to work. Then too there was the prospect of special amnesty, under Walter's plan, for those deportees who had volunteered for life-threatening experiments and had in fact become ill, as March had.

Carolus came out of his bedroom, washed and tidied up with as much attention to detail as he could manage, and we went to the laboratory. Much to his astonishment, I shut the door in March's face. March had been slinking gloomily behind us.

Carolus had an indestructible trust in me. And I, now I realized it, had the same in him.

Without mincing words I explained the situation to him, touching on the personal side of the matter as little as possible. Our first order of business was to get the missing mosquitoes out of the dark nooks and crannies where they had hidden, as these creatures do during the daytime. Little by little we collected quite a few.

Eventually we had even more than were missing. Mosquitoes were relatively uncommon on the rise where the Y.F. hospital was built, but some of these must have slipped in from outside. And how could we distinguish, while the creatures were still alive, those that had fed on human blood from those that had not? Unfortunately we had no choice but to put all of them together in the now inaccurately labeled jar and kill them all with chloroform.

Carolus had confided to me some days previously that the simple soldiers of the shore batteries had not been unmoved by the noble examples of Walter et al. We were going to have the opportunity to work with these splendid young men. And now they were here, but the infected mosquitoes were not! What to do? We had to get fresh ones from the insectarium and, toiling side by side for many hours, get them to consummate the act of feeding on severely ill and dying Y.F. patients. And then wait. For ten to twelve days, optimally. What might not happen in that time?

My face was grim and I vouchsafed March not a word. My suggestion that a place be found for him in the office of the chief of public health for C. had met with the approval of Carolus, who was now beginning to rely on me unquestioningly for many things. But we know how slowly the wheels of bureaucracy grind. Thus it happened that March, unemployed, languished in quiet despair, and then, after dark, in loud despair, and finally, wordlessly but also unceasingly, tried to appeal to my sympathies.

I kept him hanging, until, on the eve of his new employment, I told him. Clearly, succinctly, and as gently as possible. He blanched and grabbed me by the neck in a frenzy. But then, in an abrupt transformation, the expression on his face changed, his menacing gestures turned into an awkward but for that very reason all the more touching caress; his trembling fingers had sought my chest. No more harsh words, he no longer appealed for my forgiveness; he merely asked me, in an artificially firm voice, whether I did not stand in awe before my godlike self.

Godlike? I was only doing what I had to do, and I did not respond to the mute and tender supplication in his eyes. I stroked his hair, which had begun to grow on his head like the downy plumage of a young bird. Perhaps he prayed to me, as people pray to God, unbidden by Him.

And if I did not want his doglike submissiveness, I did not want what he did that night, either. He had sneaked into the laboratory, his paradise lost, for the last time, had mixed up a terrible intoxicant out of the pure alcohol on hand there in bottles (he was his father's son, as I was mine), and, toward morning, after God knows what kind of awful night (I had no inkling, I swear it! I was asleep!), had tried to shoot himself in the heart with Walter's army revolver, his hand made unsteady by alcohol and fear of death. But his hand must have dropped at the crucial moment. He hit himself. But he hit himself in the epigastric region, the area below the left costal arch, not in the heart.

XV

I had never toyed with the young man who now, unconscious and white as a sheet, breathing shallowly from the upper chest like a woman, his abdominal muscles rigid, lay before me on the laboratory tiles. I had never toyed with him, I swear it by the holiest things there can be for a man like me, I swear it by my self, that I had never experimented on him. Rather he had experimented on me: he had tested *me* to see how much he was worth to me. Could he really have thought he could make my life and my work easier through his suicide? He had wanted to be my god, as I was his. But I was only a human being like too many others.

His experiment having failed, he had lost interest in life and tried to exit. I gazed at him a moment with tear-dimmed eyes (as the phrase goes). Then I did what was necessary.

The pulse was thready, very rapid, between ninety and a hundred, but still perceptible, and it remained so. The face displayed that rapt, unnatural expression that is seen in the field often enough in cases of severe abdominal injury and that physicians call *facies abdominalis*, "abdominal face." It was not his heart that was killing him, but his abdomen. Irony is far from me now. The facts are what they are. I cut his clothes off his body with great caution. He did not have much on. He groaned heavily, seemed suddenly deeply unconscious. The entry and exit wounds caused by the small-caliber bullet were about the same size. The entry wound was contaminated with powder residue and shreds of clothing, the shot had apparently been fired at close range. So he had been serious.

Both I and the stunned Carolus, who had lately become almost as fond of the good lad as I was, were just as serious about trying to save him, whatever it took. Carolus, with his unduly high opinion of me as a surgeon (he did not know the circumstances of the difficult delivery), advised me to attempt a lifesaving operation at once. In all probability the intestinal walls had been pierced by the bullet; a blood vessel in the abdomen might also have been hit. I considered, and shook my head. There was no way I could risk an operation here. I had no competent assistants. I no longer had any. A difficult delivery might possibly be improvised by a daring physician with luck on his side; a technically complex operation like opening the abdominal cavity, never. I said so to the brigadier general.

He did not want to see it my way. Perhaps he was afraid it would come out that the convict entrusted to his custody had not been supervised, or not closely enough to prevent him from obtaining the deadly weapon. My fate hung in the balance too. Would I continue to be left unwatched now that there had been a killing (suicide is killing, too) using the gun? Had March and I deserved our "freedom" here?

But for me there was no conflict. The situation was clear. I drew the consequences and aseptically bandaged poor March, who was just then awakening with a groan, gave him one injection of camphor after another, and asked Carolus to telephone the main hospital of the penal administration. A passably modern operating room and an X-ray department had been added there only a few years earlier. (This was after an inquiring, courageous, and high-minded journalist had exposed to a horrified public, in grisly but brilliant reportage, the dreadful conditions prevailing on the island in general and characterizing the medical care provided to the deportees in particular.)

Carolus was happy to have someone give orders and pedantically carried them out to the letter. All that remained was for me to administer an analgesic injection, as the unfortunate youth had regained consciousness. It might be the last favor I could do him in this life.

The effect seemed to be markedly slow in coming and weak when it came. Had the poor devil become habituated to morphine? A review of our stores of drugs confirmed this suspicion. Not just alcohol, but narcotics too! Here again young March was his father's son. He had long ago fled from his seemingly insoluble difficulties into morphine. And I had seen nothing! It had all escaped the attention of the observer, the friend. He had long since given up. But why play the sober, objective physician and primly draw the veil over his fate? Was *I* blameless? It affected me as I thought nothing could since the death of my beloved little Portuguese girl. I bent over him. I thought he was finally under the soporific influence of the morphine. But he was still lucid.

He knew what he was doing when he hooked his thin, feeble arm around my neck and drew my head down. I did not resist his lips. I will not conceal it. It was the first kiss I had given anyone since the death of my poor wife. But he – did he take this first kiss for what it was? I don't know. It seemed to be making him gag. He pressed his lips together tightly. Did I understand him correctly? Was it his body, or was it his mind that made him seem to be spewing my kiss back out? Gummi Bear! Which is it now, you or me?

Had he spewed me out? And that most justly, in the words of Scripture. For this is just what will befall those who are not warm and not cold. But could I be any other way?

He bore his pain bravely and did not ask for another injection. His face sagged, and he began belching continuously. Not a good sign. It was a wonder that he was still alive and his heart was working. He refused the third injection I tried to give him. My medical objective was not only to provide an analgesic, but also to shut down the autonomous movements of the injured viscera and delay the spread of infectious microorganisms as long as possible.

To spare him any unnecessary jostling, we had made him a bed on the laboratory table as best we could. Now he held tightly to my hand. I thought of the time I had first held this almost abnormally soft, seemingly boneless hand in mine, that moment so long ago when I had awakened aboard the *Mimosa*, close to him, under his protection. All his sufferings and passions were there to be read in his handsome, clay-colored face. I thought of my prognosis when I had first encountered him. He has suffered, he is suffering, he will suffer. But how senselessly he was suffering! My wife had died quickly.

At last, after more than three hours, the car came for him. The trip over the marshy log road from the catchment hospital had not been as easy as I had assumed. But that was not the only problem. Another was fear of entering the pestilential Y.F. hospital and – what did the public-health department and the administration of the great catchment hospital, accommodating some hundreds of convicts, care about the life of any particular one, still less one who wanted, as this March did, to leave this best of all possible worlds? I waved to him, I waved him good-bye.

As I saw him being carried out of the building by trained bearers on the stretcher that had been taken from the vehicle, I did not know if I should be happy to be spared the sight of his death. Should I hope for him to be saved by a miracle from heaven? (Are there miracles? Is there a heaven?) Should I grieve? No, I did not ask that. I cast myself down, racked by abnormal dry-eyed trembling, in my basement room, from now on and forever and eternally my room, which he would never again share. I did not weep. Nature did not want to give me that consolation, that relief. That valve does not open for me. I thought – just one thought.

I still had in my pocket the nickel case containing the syringe.

Never in all my life, even in the worst of times, not in the remand prison observation unit, not during the first nights on the *Mimosa*, had I felt the hunger, indeed the almost invincible lust for stupefaction that I felt now.

But in the other pocket of my white coat I was also still carrying the precisely made gun that Walter had owned. The magazine held six cartridges. One was missing, five were there.

I told myself: If you can't go on living, fine! Die! But don't drug yourself. Destroy yourself, but don't escape!

A person wants to live. Even if, like March, he takes his life, deep down he wants to live. Just in a different way. He tries to blackmail fate. He experiments with his last stake, and no matter how the experiment turns out, *he still perishes* . . . I didn't want to do it. My suffering and my death would have proven nothing. Changed nothing. I was not deceiving myself. This consolation too was beyond the reach of my father's son.

XVI

If anything kept me going during this period (I do not say difficult, I will not call it terrible, hellish, these words do not express it) – if something kept me going during the period after March was taken away, it was the demeanor of the brigadier general. He was accepting of me in a way I did not deserve. Indeed I myself had not allowed "humaneness," as it is called, to influence my actions. In my hardness, which was not cruel but only logically consistent, as the business required, I had perhaps, who knows, gone too far with poor March. I had sought to pluck out the eye that offended me, in the words of Scripture. Could I moan? I was all the more surprised by the comportment of Carolus, this man who was bourgeois, narrow-minded, and pedantic in all his endeavors but who had become absorbed in our enterprise and for its sake eventually sacrificed what was most difficult for him to part with, his money. But of that more later.

During the first few days, he spared no effort in doing everything he could do from his remove to help March, who was in critical condition. He was persistent on the telephone just as Walter's wife had been. Two or three times every day, he did not rest until he had obtained precise information on the condition of the would-be suicide. Surgery had been ruled out. I do not know what state the unfortunate lad had wound up in, whether he was looking so grand or was so clearly at death's door that the gentlemen in the catchment hospital did not want to attempt an intervention. They must either have believed in miraculous spontaneous healing or have regarded him as a goner for whom nothing could be done, providing him with painkillers and otherwise leaving him alone.

Fate (call it God or the devil or nature – it comes to the same thing) proved kind to me. Fate had dismissed the little Portuguese girl from this delightful earth she had barely trod. Fate had silenced the great Walter just as he was beginning his most brilliant work. (I had studied the notebooks he had left. In them he had sketched out scientific and medical ideas of incalculable value, whose realization had been kept waiting due to the pressure of family worries and was foreclosed by his early death.) But fate had saved the son of a bitch Suleiman on the ship, had given the dockworker who was a burden on the entire world the gift of convalescence from Y.F. here in the hospital, it had left Walter's widow and his posthumous son alive (his mother then had him christened Walter Posthumous). And now the mortally wounded March, so it seemed, was on the road to recovery! He had gotten lucky, had probably only nicked his spleen, and would soon mend.

I am unable to describe my feelings as I received the news, every day less pessimistic, from his sickbed. Finally he passed – what a prosaic conclusion to his act of passion! – his first normal bowel movement. The young man was thus out of danger. About two weeks later Carolus arranged for March himself to come to the hospital telephone. Carolus spoke to him. March's voice was apparently weak, and Carolus, whose hearing was not what it was, could not always understand him right away, and thus I heard his dreary but very soothing voice repeat those ritual words: "What? Eh? What?" But March was not only on the road to recovery, he had even regained his gallows humor, and though I could not hear what he was saying to Carolus, I saw a very reassuring smile on the old man's leathery features. Then Carolus noticed me listening in. He was annoyed. His face darkened. He waved at me – was he waving me over? No! He was waving me back to my work. He exchanged a few more words with the convalescent, apparently ones of great importance. "What?!" he asked then, his voiced raised. "Why not? Are you serious?"

He came out of the booth and closed the door gently and carefully. He did not look at me and did not speak to me further. The next day I waited in vain for the telephone to ring. Carolus was not waiting for it. Slowly I understood what the final conversation had been about. Carolus had asked the recovered March whether he wanted to come back to us, whether he wanted to see me again. March must have answered "No" or "I don't know." He did not want to come back.

I tried to bear it with humor. To take it philosophically. Perhaps humor is no different from philosophy and philosophy at bottom nothing but humor. But true philosophy and true humor are rare. Enough of that. Now I come to the change in Carolus's attitude that I hinted at earlier, the change that loosened his purse strings.

When, for the first time since I had known him, old Carolus spoke of contributing his considerable financial resources, it seemed he was doing all he could to stimulate what remained of my spirit.

At this point we had to continue our experiments on a larger scale. The Y.F. hospital, now beginning to fill up with patients who were not "true" Y.F. patients, was not the right place for this. Our experiments would have a disruptive effect on the normal operations of the hospital, and, conversely, normal operations in the hospital would take up the space needed for our experimental patients. This was crystal clear.

But why not say: "Enough experiments! Enough horrors! Enough deaths!"

Why not take poor March's lot as a warning from fate that it had been tested enough? Why not content ourselves with simply caring for those human beings who had contracted Y.F. by the natural route? Pointless questions. We still knew far too little.

The chaplain had dropped out too; his professional activity had become extraordinarily intense. So our team was down to the two of us, Carolus and me. We complemented each other. We had each other's number. We put up with each other. We were in agreement as to our ultimate objective. Our answer to those questions was "Because," or better yet we studiously did not pose them. We wanted to go on. From etiology to treatment, or, in lay terms, from knowledge to action. From the microscope to medicine.

We received word that the "American" commission, which actually included a highly gifted Japanese, had not been unsuccessful. Regardless of the substance of this success, our work would either refute or confirm the results of the American commission.

We could not rest satisfied with what we had achieved. We had to strive to approximate the truth as closely as we could.

Before long I would once more be bringing to bear my old energies and joy in my work (it was a true, wholehearted joy, and it remained my only one); Carolus had yet to turn to account his very considerable financial means and his name, his standing, his military rank, his impeccable past. He did so now without hesitation.

One might have thought the government would have done all it could to support our endeavor. No. The post of governor was still vacant. No one would say yes, no one would say no. The penal administration had its own public-health officers. The men in the bureaucratic back rooms held mysterious conclaves, the top public-health director in the penal administration produced a report on the most recent wave of the Y.F. epidemic, including statistics worthy of old Carolus. But this man pridefully took no notice of us. He had lived and worked here for twenty years and had found nothing to speak of. So what did we think we were trying to do?

Without the old rivalry between the colonial administration (Ministry of the Interior) and the penal administration (Department of Justice), and had Carolus not played them against each other, they would have put paid to our work. We would have been not only not encouraged, but stymied. But when Carolus put his considerable financial means into the hat on top of everything else and certainly used part of them for "diplomatic purposes," that is to say, for a kind of bribery, the way became clear once more.

Without wasting time we began – to act? No, to think in earnest. We drafted a comprehensive new work plan that would enable us to achieve definitive results that could not be disputed by any objective person. Good.

XVII

I will give as brief an account as possible of our next experiments, with which we intended to bring our research to a provisional close. These experiments were in part novel ones, in part replications of the old "controls," as they are called.

The difficulties are not easy to describe simply. Anything that can be found *without* difficulty today, now that science has already discovered all the easy things, is usually wrong. One must therefore keep a sharp eye on oneself, check everything down to the last detail, be suspicious to the point of pathology, and yet retain the ability to believe as one perseveres.

There was a bit of a delay at the beginning: the money that Carolus wanted to use had to be transferred from home. This was done by wire, but still took some days.

Meanwhile we located the site for the experiments. It was a place between two warehouses. A plot of land that had been cleared by the convicts over a period of years, treeless, covered only by the brambly scrub that grows in these regions, with no water source nearby. That is to say, as far away as possible from the habitat of the insects known as *Stegomyia fasciata*. It had a small tent camp on it, consisting of five tents, plus two little cottages. We could be cut off from the rest of the world, almost as isolated as my father and his companions had been on the polar sea; it was not easy to think of everything we would need to study the transmission of Y.F. there.

The administration let us have the property free (no great sacrifice!), and also provided gratis the barbed wire that is available in great quantities in a penal colony. So the administration and the government were occasionally good for something after all! Still more important was money. We needed money to buy test subjects, in the form of people. People cost money.

But there are also people who will, that word again, sacrifice themselves for nothing in a cause they believe to be important. The best case – no cost. And among them were some marines from the shore batteries whom Walter had known when he was an army doctor. Carolus offered them a sum of money that was comparatively large by their standards. But to our surprise, they responded: “Herr Brigadier General, our only condition is that we receive no compensation whatever for our voluntary service.” Carolus blushed, a phenomenon I had never before observed in the leathery old medical statistician. He wasted little time in thanking them for this generous gesture. He accepted it and treated the youths as the gentlemen they were.

One of the fine marks of our time is that generosity has become an untranslatable foreign word, I said once. Obviously I was wrong again!

Just the fact that people of this uncommon type existed in our mean old world at all lightened the load I had to bear, which was frequently not easy to do now without my friend March. But why speak of myself? My personal fate was now bound up with the success or failure of our experiments. This is all I want to report on in the end. Incidentally, two criminals also came forward, lured as much by the hard cash as by the chance of an early parole, and they were newcomers to C. like us: they had been on the transport that had brought me. One of them was Suleiman, who had been so lamentably worked over on the *Mimosa*, whose face still bore highly disfiguring scars from his wound, and who wept day and night; that is to say, the torn nasolacrimal duct continually discharged aqueous matter with the chemical properties of tears. He recognized me immediately, even though he was half blind, asked, laughing an uncouth, teary laugh, after "precious March," and furtively proposed to share the promised payment with me if I would set up the experiments "mercifully."

I said no. He understood yes.

He, Suleiman, could not believe that venality had limits. Thus he awaited the experiments with great equanimity, convinced in his heart that I would exempt him from actual infection so as not to pass up my thirty pieces of silver. And he was deeply determined to cheat me out of the money he had promised me. He took me for one of his own, and with one of his own he thought all was permitted. But I was a different kind of criminal. I had killed. But not trafficked in human flesh as he had. He wanted to swindle the swindler, but it did not come to that.

This time we began the experiments at the "negative end." To be demonstrated was Axiom I, that Y.F. can be transmitted *only* by mosquitoes.

Only transmissible by *Stegomyia fasciata* means *not* transmissible any other way.

Does this help? At that time it was still widely believed that Y.F. was communicable by contact with a sufferer's clothes, bedding, and other articles. Or the culprit was even thought to be bad air ("mal-aria"), or rainwater and cistern water used for drinking.

We were going to investigate and solve the problem in the two cottages. Each was four meters long, six wide. One entered through a double door set up in such a way as to keep mosquitoes out. The cottages had two south windows, on the same side as the doors, to eliminate drafts. Then a small wood-burning stove was installed, which ensured that the temperature never fell below twenty-one degrees centigrade, even now, in the cooler season, or at night. Water tanks kept the air as suffocatingly humid as in the rainy season in the midst of the jungle, in the heart of the primeval equatorial forest. Into this cottage two volunteer assistants from the shore batteries (whose heroism was sorely tested by having to watch the first experiments) brought some tightly sealed crates. Then the two convicts, Suleiman and his crony, were taken into their nasty accommodations with the bad air. In their presence the pillows, blankets, and sheets were taken out of the crates, soiled with . . . But why spell this out? The two convicts were prevailed upon to undress, put on the dirty pajamas, lie down on the stained sheets. You'll stay here now! Eat here! Sleep here – and die here? Could we mean it? Suleiman threw me appalled glances. I made no comment on these preparations. During the days that followed we had nothing else to do but keep watch like veritable Cerberuses on these men in their horribly hot, evil-smelling cell.

None of the familiar awful symptoms of Y.F. appeared. You should have seen the faces of the two criminals. They rejoiced no less than we. Their steady temperatures, their ascending weight curves, and their thriving appearances announced the disconfirmation of the false hypothesis – hence the confirmation of Axiom I.

After three weeks (which were a torment only in their tedium), this experiment could be regarded as finished.

Next we considered the following question: Was the experiment really absolutely probative? True, neither of the guests in Huts A and B had gotten Y.F. But how could we know if they were susceptible to Y.F. at all? The chaplain in the Y.F. hospital had not been susceptible, it appeared, and very likely Carolus had not been either. Therefore we had to do the counterexperiment whether we wanted to or not, and we did it. Suleiman the weeper had thought himself saved. He was now hoping for release. Not that he had been wasting his time here. He remained the most revolting voluptuary, every bit as filthy in his soul as the Y.F. pajamas that he wore. His comrade was to be pitied.

In the worst case, namely, that in which Suleiman was set at liberty but had to stay on the island, I believe he was going to go halves with the docklands gin-mill proprietor and join with him, another blood-sucking insect, in bleeding the convicts dry. But for that he would have to stay. Behind the barbed wire. Here with us. He had promised, he had accepted a lot of money, we took him at his word. He did not understand much, but he suspected something. The whole thing was giving him the creeps, but the hard cash, the fat silver coins in little bags, a hundred in each one, that Carolus jingled before his ears, were too tempting. He nodded to the brigadier general. He winked at me. He meant I should not forget our pact. I had not made one.

Using our old methods, Carolus and I placed on one of the two men, namely, Suleiman, mosquitoes that (through the offices of the young resident) had been amply fed on the blood of the sick and dying in the Y.F. hospital. The other man we injected with the infectious blood of a patient in the Y.F. hospital, directly under his skin.

In keeping with the axiom, both became ill, promptly and severely. Suleiman died even before he reached the apyretic period. In his ravings he cursed me and himself and the world. Even a vile human being's suffering could be very touching. I felt sorry for him. But that changed nothing.

The sailors carried him to his grave, hastily getting him under the ground at the edge of Camp Walter. The other man's case was serious, but fate was kind to him and he made it through. Later he received not only his own honorarium but also the money that had been intended for Suleiman, and I suppose he took his place with the gin-mill proprietor too. He still lives here and is healthy and wants to have his family come, if the administration permits it.

We still had to demonstrate the inverse – and attempt to find a cure. To do this we experimented on the sailors who, carefree, idealistic youths that they were, had been generous enough to put themselves at our service.

By then we, Carolus, the sailors, and I, were living together as a sort of family. The boredom was deadly, but nobody died of it. Carolus told us of his deeds and adventures, or rather those of his children and grandchildren, among which loomed large the droll utterances of the little granddaughter who, with her nanny, had come to the dock to see him off on the *Mimosa*. I neither saw nor heard anything of March. Both Carolus and I were preoccupied with the prospects for our discovery. These were happy thoughts. We pictured a grand future but did not talk about it for fear of tempting Providence, instead just grinning at each other a lot.

XVIII

We had named our camp Camp Walter, and Walter was in our thoughts, though we did not speak about him. The next experiment used the two sailors, who had been joined by a third, one of their comrades. Two of them were housed in Hut A, which was divided in half by a fine wire mesh. The third was in Hut B by himself. Both cottages had been remodeled. We had had a door made in the north wall, so that each building had two doors. Fresh air could now blow through freely; the two doors were closed only by mosquito-proof netting. The experiment was designed in such a way that Sailor X, freshly bathed, as healthy as the climate permitted, wearing a thoroughly disinfected nightshirt, took up residence at twelve noon in his cell, if I may call it that. A jar containing fifteen female mosquitoes fed on infectious blood had been opened in that area of the cell five minutes earlier.

During the first quarter hour, X received a bite from one of the female mosquitoes. The others had holed up in dark corners. They got busy as soon as the sun went down, and by nine o'clock that night, fifteen to seventeen bites could be counted. His neighbor to the left, Sailor Y (the control), was in equally perfect health, also wore a disinfected nightshirt, came from his bath just as clean, but the fine wire mesh meant that the female mosquitoes could not gain entry to his cell. Sailor Z was housed by himself in Hut B. He moved in at the same time as the others, but was left unmolested for some days.

For this experiment we had selected the pluckiest and most morally steadfast of the three, a man who never lost his sense of humor. We wanted to hold off from infecting him until Y.F. had appeared in Sailor X. That is, five days after the preliminaries just described.

Z meanwhile remained fit as a fiddle, but had unfortunately lost interest in this tedious bivouac (he was still entirely isolated), suddenly considered it all futile, bloodthirsty tomfoolery, wearied us with complaints and grievances, and demanded to be sent back to the shore batteries. We had been wrong about his character. He was a gentleman, a grand fellow, very funny and witty, knew the best card tricks, and spoke three languages, but we could not discipline him to the most important thing, patience, and in any case we were unable to do as he wished. He thought he deserved special consideration for his generosity in putting his health and his life at our disposal. But this man's past and his present, all the ins and outs of him, were of no interest to us. It was all neither here nor there as far as we were concerned as long as the experiment had not been completed. He, Z, had to submit.

The authorities of the convict camp had furnished us with guards, just as they had assigned us construction workers and other tradesmen. We also needed a large staff, for there was not a drop of water in our camp. The healthy test subjects had to have food, their clothes had to be washed, their meals had to be brought to them, their personal hygiene had to be scrupulously maintained. The sick test subjects had to be cared for, and their care could not be one iota worse in our primitive cottage lacking all medical facilities than it would have been up in the well-appointed convent hospital above the city of C. The truly incalculable labor that Carolus and I had taken on may be imagined when I say that the two of us had to get by on five hours of sleep, and even that was interrupted often enough by the medical care required by the sick men. Carolus had never come down with Y.F. But when the old man, afflicted by rheumatism, constipation, and the circulatory complaints of his years, voluntarily exposed himself to such strain, when he declined before my eyes and lost the little bit of color he had gained in the interval between the experiments – then I had to ask his pardon for all the derogatory things I had said about him. You were wrong, I had to tell myself. Forget what you know, Georg Letham, and change your ways in your later years.

During these critical days I began to see a father in him. He saw in me a son, he began to call me by my first name, and he spontaneously changed his unappetizing habits, much to my delight, for we lived together in one tent. If I had been able to get him used to handling his cigarette by the business end instead of the other one, to holding his teacup by the handle, taking the spoon out, washing his hands a bit more often, and brushing his beard, then everything would have been joy and glory. But if only that had been all I had to worry about!

Let us not talk about me now, but about the test subjects. X became severely ill, but passed the crisis after almost three solid weeks of terrible fever and recovered.

But now the most important thing. To infect a man, but use serum to protect him from becoming ill.

For this experiment we had to use the recalcitrant man Z. He had watched the terrible suffering of his comrades. He had seen for himself that the mosquito-proof walls between him and the bloodsucking insects had been the only thing preventing him from getting the disease. And there we were with the same insects, expecting him to hold out his upper arm. Carolus doubled his bonus. This man Z, though capable of noble impulses at bottom, irately rejected Carolus's proposal. But this experiment was as essential as the rest of them. They were all fundamental.

I, the social outcast, did my best to efface myself as usual. But when I saw Carolus, who was now dear to me, going away with a literally long face, I resolved on a step that may appear strange to some. I sat down with the unruly, exceedingly rancorous young man, told him candidly who I was, explained to him what we wanted, and promised him that he would absolutely not become ill. And this man Z did not ask whether I would be able to keep this promise even if I wanted to. He trusted me, like so many before him (and fortunately after him).

Trust is the foundation of the world, is it not? He spat furiously, jabbed me with his knees, and called me a cunning criminal and a brutal slave driver; but all the while he was putting out his upper arm and holding on to it with the other hand to keep it from jerking and getting in the way of the experiment. And when the first mosquito had bitten (we had three, to be on the safe side), he began to laugh, and from that moment he was his old self. He calmly let himself be injected with the blood of X, who was pale as a corpse and almost wailing with enervation – and remained healthy.

Toxin against toxin makes antitoxin. Hosanna! This was the best thing that could happen.

During this period Carolus received many letters and telegrams from his family. They had expected him to be gone for three months, but it was more than twice that now, with no end in sight. He was an old man, sixty-seven. He was attached to his daughter, to his son-in-law, to his only grandchild. He was attached to his beautiful big house, to his friends back home, to his chess game and his bank account, to his cactus collection, to his honor and dignity. Every day here – but why speak of it, when he himself never did? We were completely taken up with our XYZ. But one day he violated our unwritten compact to keep anything of a personal nature to ourselves and told me, so happy that his head bobbed like a hen's, that we had been pardoned. We, meaning March and I, Suleiman (†), and the fourth man. As a reward for our spirit of sacrifice (and thanks to the efforts of my influential father?), we were being pardoned. March, whose crime had been one of passion, could return home; I, who had committed a worse offense, would remain in exile, as would the fourth man. But I was exempted from forced labor, and steps were being taken to make it possible for me to practice my profession in C. I did not ask about March. – "Don't you want to thank your father? Won't you" (Carolus amended) "write to him?" "My dear Carolus," I said, "what can I do? I've forgotten what my father looks like."

XIX

During this period there were two pieces of news. One came as no surprise to us. The old pharmacist von F. lay dying. What he had prophesied four months earlier had come to pass almost to the day. He had preferred a death in his comfortable bed to one on the lab table. Could he be faulted for that?

He left no great riches. The city was impoverished. The environs were almost entirely depopulated, apart from the masses of deportees.

The city was so down-at-heels that no doctor could prosper there even if he devoted himself to the well-being of the populace for almost fifty years, as the old pharmacist had. The brigadier general hinted that *I* might take over that post. I shrugged my shoulders and said nothing. I had no interest in a job like that. And yet it would soon emerge that fate had nothing better in store for me. The second piece of news was more important. It concerned the commission mentioned earlier, the one that had been studying Y.F. in Havana. One day Carolus appeared, pale with shock, and murmured that he had something of grave import to tell me.

I thought of March, who had still not left the soil of C., though his commutation allowed him to and he was fully restored to health (an indestructible man!). Carolus, in a gallant gesture, had given him some money to permit him to travel home on a small packet steamer. March had taken the money but had been seen not long before in the old part of the city. I did not want to believe it, but he had been drunk and in the company of some clapped-out old thieves and vagrants whom earthly justice had given up all its efforts to reform. I did not exist for March. He would have had plenty of opportunities to approach me, if only just to pay me a visit at Camp Walter, which was now deserted – but he did no such thing. And I could hardly have needed him more. I considered our problem solved. There had been a time when this outcome would have made me proud, vain. I would have announced the results at a medical congress and would have accepted the congratulations, the honors, the appointments to professorships of pathological anatomy and experimental bacteriology as a fairly earned reward, too skimpy if anything. Now, here, it was something else again. My personal life meant nothing to me now unless I had work, this kind of work. For me work was truly forced labor, though not as most people understand that. And now I would soon find my work completed and my existence futile, superfluous, and absurd.

But it was nothing of the kind. This was only the slump experienced by every working person at the end of a working day, soon vigorously overcome and gone without a trace. And I soon had to put my strength of will to the test. This was made necessary by the second piece of news that Carolus whispered so discreetly into my ear.

The commission had been successful in its work in Havana. My face lit up. Carolus did not understand. "Don't you see, they didn't find what we found."

"Impossible," I said calmly. "They found the pathogen – and we didn't," he said. "So much the better," I responded, "we're now far enough along that we can pool our results, and the best thing that can happen to us is to have the opportunity to compare our results with those of the American commission." "Whatever you think," he said worriedly. "You'll see, we'll have them here today or tomorrow." "The sooner the better," I said. We sat all night in Hut B, which, well disinfected and thoroughly aired out, was quite tolerable now. We formulated our experiences as is done in scientific reports. As old Carolus was leafing through our records, he was strangely overcome. He cried like a child. A crying child is poignant to see, but that is something natural. Tears being shed by a man successful in life and (ultimately) in science, rich, well regarded, general, grandfather, recipient of high honors – is this not a grotesque sight, one that might provoke laughter as much as pity? But I had understood what this only outwardly ossified man was. I stroked the smooth, velvety skin on the top of his bald head (he did not notice this). He instinctively put his thin arm around me and with his somewhat unclean fingers gestured at our dead friend's chart. But I quickly drew his head away so that his tears (and the ash from his big cigar) would not dirty Log W. and smear the writing and the diagrams. The old boy soon got a grip on himself. We sat together until morning by the light of a petroleum lamp.

Camp would be struck before long. Where would we live then? Should we go back to the Y.F. hospital? What was there for us to do there? The epidemic was on the rise again in C., and there was little room for us up in the hospital. Where should I go? The new governor was still awaited. No one wanted to take any steps without him. Everything was still entirely up in the air when the aforementioned commission arrived.

We, Carolus and I, were compelled to take up quarters in the Y.F. hospital, and the next day we were visited there by three gentlemen from the commission. They drew blood from a severely febrile patient and were able to show us the Y.F. pathogen in dark field. Not immediately. We sat at the microscopes from morning until night. Finally a specimen of *Leptospira* (its scientific name) was gracious enough to show itself to us. And even this one *Leptospira* was a fluke. The tiny thing was that much of a rarity. I recognized it. I had seen it before the Japanese who discovered it. But this is a frequent occurrence in the history of discoveries and inventions.

The gentlemen had brought some excellent slides, and we were able to examine the pathogen closely. It is an extremely delicate, supple entity about 4 to 9 microns long and 0.2 microns wide. In dark field it is active, exhibiting lashing lateral movements as well as rotational and very rapid retrograde motion, the latter clearly produced by the propeller-like torsional action of the ends, the "whips." The international

("American") commission was also able to culture the microorganism, which stains with difficulty and is found only very sporadically in the blood of the sufferer, playing hard to get, but all the more dangerous for that. The artificial culture, the bacillus patch, was invisible to the naked eye. A misty opacity was all there was to see on the culture medium, even when growth was the most abundant. But the microorganisms were there. They were infectious to guinea pigs. It was possible to use them to infect guinea pigs artificially and follow the phases of the infection in animal experiments. Walter's experiments at the Institute however many years ago were thus confirmed in their entirety. This did not surprise me.

What the commission showed us was impeccable and we happily recognized the correctness of the research that we had failed in (that I had failed in, thanks to my mistake, as I have related). Their discovery and ours complemented each other ideally, like the two halves of a letter torn in the middle. They had the pathogen; we had the means of transmission and the prophylaxis, the method of epidemic control. The only problem was that the commission (headed by a man with whom I had had a scientific feud – this had been years before but was still vivid in my mind) regarded *our* results with the greatest skepticism. It was unwilling to believe us.

We had just come from the funeral of our colleague von F. "Why are you bothering with his old theory? That was rigorously disproven decades ago." They would not acknowledge the *Stegomyia*. So were we supposed to start the experiments all over again? We could never have convinced these men. They held their ground: breathing the air or (or!) drinking infected water was the cause of Y.F. One member of the commission favored the air. Another member the water. A third left the question open. Three heads. They could not agree. Meanwhile everything was going on as before, and the patients were getting to know element number three, the cold, cold ground.

They were dropping like flies.

But I was a criminal sentenced without possibility of appeal and a former convict, and the gentlemen did not think me worthy of another glance. They looked down on old Carolus, and Walter's death wrung from them no more than a regretful shrug. It was not *their* theory that his passing had corroborated.

We collapsed when they left.

Carolus had completely lost his equilibrium. He cried on my shoulder. Good.

XX

After the setback delivered by the American commission, there had to be a windfall, and it came from the least likely quarter, the new governor. He was none other than my father's one-time assistant at the Ministry, La Forest, some of whose career I have recounted earlier in this report. I do not maintain that he was more benevolent than his predecessor toward me, the son of his former mortal enemy, possibly out of some antagonism toward my father, who had turned his back on me. The motives are irrelevant. The facts speak for themselves.

It happened that we presented ourselves immediately after the high official's arrival and laid our results on the table.

Ten men, ten reports, ten experiments.

We all expressed ourselves freely. Now I must report something that will be difficult to understand. It may have been exhaustion due to the excessive strain of our work, or it may have been the effects of the Y.F.

that I had passed through and had still not properly recovered from – I don't know why, but *I* was now filled with doubts about our Axiom I. I doubted myself, I doubted everyone.

When our report was lying for review on the official's desk, I returned to our accommodations, uncommunicative and trembling as though with chills. I was now living with Carolus in the apartment of the late municipal medical officer, von F. the pharmacist, whose position I was going to assume. But was I up to the job? I didn't know. I saw none of our dearly won results as certain. I was filled with regrets. I had lost faith in my godlikeness. Walter's fate, March's, that of Walter's widow, the children, even Suleiman's death, weighed heavily upon me. Would I have done it all over again? Perhaps so! I would have done it again – and regretted it again!

And even if everything accorded with the truth, how was it possible to credit Axiom I? Were our experiments convincing? Perhaps we had done too few after all! How often investigators have deceived themselves! If the commission had refused to believe us, would it be possible to convince a governor? I think not even Carolus was free from doubt. It is very difficult to be a judge in one's own cause.

Even without speaking we understood each other very well, and soon I was able to master myself sufficiently that the next morning I ventured a small jest. A silly thing, hardly worth mentioning. Carolus used a rather worn-out old shaving brush to lather himself. He neglected to rinse his face properly after he shaved and there were bristles from the brush stuck in the creases on his cheeks. I pointed out with a laugh that he had become young and blond again. He replied equally gaily that I had become old and gray. It was as though he had responded to my innermost being and not to the silly thing I had said.

But how were things with him really? Only one who knew how to read his face could see the dreadful unease in it.

It was also in the words he whispered into my ear before we visited La Forest for the second time: "Whatever you do, Georg, keep calm! *I'm* not giving up on our cause, even if it costs me the last years of my life and the last coins in my pocket." Nevertheless we came out onto the street in a very somber mood, and this state of mind did not become more cheerful when I ran into March on a street corner, again in the company of some completely wild riffraff. And he was no different, he was every bit as seedy looking, I might almost say every bit as brutalized, as those pitiable creatures that the colonial administration was allowing neither to live nor to die here. Shall I describe him and them, shall I repeat their snatches of cynical talk? Why should I? He looked past me, his eyes glittering abnormally. The pupils were tiny. He was evidently under the influence of alcohol and morphine. How he could have fallen so far, what had stopped him from finding his way home as anyone else in his place (except me, probably) would have done with boundless joy, what had become of the money that the generous Carolus had given him – of these matters I will not speak. They are of personal significance only.

Now the *enterprise* was front and center. And if anything could console me for the loss, the seemingly inexorable decline and fall of my friend, it was the discussion that we began with La Forest that afternoon and that stretched into the night, with short breaks. It was mostly between Carolus and La Forest. Since my experience with the commission, I had felt it was best not to push myself forward. I, the pardoned convict G. L., could serve our cause in no better way than to efface myself entirely. In all the scientific publications that would soon appear presenting our work, I am cited only as "Case 4." The honors that attached to these events in the course of the year accrued to Carolus and to Walter's memory. My name was not mentioned. Here in this report I have also concealed my real name.

The most important thing was that La Forest stood as resolutely with us as the American commission did against us. Neither had verified Axiom I. Such terrible experiments could not be simply and mechanically replicated, nor were they. But the governor, a practical administrator, showed us another way to validate them. He let the truth prove itself in practice. He devised a two-year program (later extended). He was going to wipe out the mosquito *Stegomyia*, genus *Culex*. Then (if our theory was correct – and it was, it was as sure as death) Y.F. would be wiped out too. In one of the camps, which bore the number 54, a fresh Y.F epidemic was just then breaking out (the first among the deportees in a long time). He drove out to the camp with us. First we reached an agreement with the director of the penal colony. We put together a new team; it was not the last. La Forest had not studied at my father's knee for nothing. He knew the art of handling people, he could strike a chord in everyone, play a tune anyone could dance to. For the first time in the history of the colony, all sorts of different departments worked together harmoniously. Success came. Quickly. Regularly. Unimpeachably. The statistician's heart in Carolus was gladdened. Mortality, which had attained monstrous dimensions, declined with every passing month. My old friend soared! He became young. He was in the pink for the three years that he held out before turning home.

The administrative district gradually became free of Y.F. Coupled with this were measures to combat malaria. We found that the two closely related insect genera did not have at all the same habitat. The genus *Culex* prefers to lay its eggs, standing on end in the shape of an artful little boat, in artificial reservoirs of water, rain barrels, cisterns. But *Anopheles*, which causes malaria (actually it is the vector of the disease), places them in natural but small pools of water. The eggs are loosely arrayed, perpendicular to the surface of the water, so that any gust of wind will disperse them. Uncontrolled rivers and streams overflow almost everywhere in the tropics at certain times of year; puddles and stagnant pools are left behind when the waters retreat. This is where the mosquitoes live. This is where the public-health people must go to work. Free-running water does not harbor mosquitoes.

In the initial public measures, high-flow trenches, frequently cleaned, were used to drain bodies of standing water, or else they were filled in. We built. We had cheap human material in vast quantities; the work was beneficial, it was possible to substantially improve the circumstances of thousands of people who had been merely existing, their lives more wretched than those of animals. To combat the mosquitoes, we used asphyxiants, agents known from long experience in malaria regions, which work by sealing the surface of the water off from the air. The mosquito larvae die because they have to keep coming to the surface to breathe through their tracheae or respiratory tubes. We used disinfection and mosquito-proof doors and windows to inhibit the transmission of Y.F. We had an unbelievable amount of work, but an even greater amount of success.

We gradually cleaned up an area larger than Europe. We brought mortality down to a fraction of what it had been. We stamped out Y.F. here. Others followed us. The battle to eradicate the mosquitoes and develop the fertile region was a fascinating one that lasted for years and turned out well.

The territory flourished.

This is where I leave the scene.

I disappeared into the crowd, and that is for the best.